The Scarlet Landscape

'I've been trying to get through to you all day, but the switchboard's been jammed this end. I haven't got long, darling. Just a minute or two – just long enough to say goodbye.'

She couldn't marshal her thoughts. 'Why goodbye? It isn't anything to do with – ?' She was about to say 'anything to do with Russia', then remembered the ever-vigilant operator and altered it to 'the events of today'?

'No connection. There's been a flap on all week but I didn't think I was part of it. Now it appears I am. We move out tonight. I'm allowed one letter which I'll post to you from the docks if I get the chance.'

Her ears filled with a great rushing sound which almost drowned his voice. She grabbed at the table as she felt the floor tremble beneath her feet. 'The docks! Leo, you don't mean you're being sent overseas . . . Leo . . .'

'No careless talk, please.'

She screamed, 'Don't cut us off. Oh please – please – don't cut us off . . .' But all was silence.

Elizabeth Tettmar has written numerous short stories for women's magazines, children's books and romances for Mills and Boon. *The Scarlet Landscape* is the third in her Thornmere series. She lives in Harwich.

*Also by Elizabeth Tettmar
and available in Mandarin*

House of Birds
The Years Between

ELIZABETH TETTMAR

The Scarlet Landscape

Mandarin

A Mandarin Paperback
THE SCARLET LANDSCAPE

First published in Great Britain 1995
by William Heinemann Ltd
and Mandarin Paperbacks
imprints of Reed Consumer Books Ltd
Michelin House, 81 Fulham Road, London SW3 6RB
and Auckland, Melbourne, Singapore and Toronto

Copyright © Elizabeth Tettmar 1995
The author has asserted her moral rights

A CIP catalogue record for this title
is available from the British Library
ISBN 0 7493 1942 9

Printed and bound in Great Britain
by Cox & Wyman Ltd, Reading

This book is sold subject to the condition
that it shall not, by way of trade or otherwise,
be lent, resold, hired out, or otherwise circulated
without the publisher's prior consent in any form
of binding or cover other than that in which
it is published and without a similar condition
including this condition being imposed
on the subsequent purchaser.

For Peter
best of pals

Prologue

Out of a pit of darkness and suffering the girl surfaced into a world of light and brightness and a feeling of weightlessness. As memories came flooding back she struggled to sit up but the painful drag on her stitches stopped her. She lapsed back on the pillows, biting her lip.

She was alone, that was the first thing she established. There was only one bed in that neat and sterile room, but someone had placed a bowl of roses on the mantel-shelf and at the kindly thought behind that action her eyes welled.

'Oh Joe,' she faltered, 'how am I going to carry on? . . . What have I got to live for now?'

For months she had been told that she mustn't cry for the baby's sake. A weeping mother makes for a fretful child. She heard that said over and over again, and for that reason she had stemmed her tears when she needed them most. Now that need had gone, and she could cry as much as she liked but only a few, hot, unheeded tears trickled down her colourless cheeks. Had the long agonising hours of her labour drained her of all emotion, she wondered, but she thought not. The anaesthetic might have numbed her body but not her feelings.

She lay in a state of weary tearlessness waiting for someone to come to her, someone to give her news of her daughter. That it was a daughter she had no doubt though nobody had told her so. Her recollection of what had happened after she had been given chloroform was hazy. The pain that blotted out time and sense and dignity – and afterwards the darkness and void. Had she dreamt that someone had shaken her, saying, 'Wake up dear, you have a little daughter'? Imagination or wishful thinking? 'Are you real, Jennifer Anne? Are you really here?' she whispered aloud.

Her first visitor of the day was the Red Cross nurse who had booked her in at Bardney Place. When? Two – three days ago? – or only yesterday? for continuous pain had no timetable. She was a plump, fair-complexioned young woman with a sturdy self-confidence which the girl in the bed envied. I've never been sure of anything in my life, she thought.

'And how are we now, mother? Feeling better?'

'I want to see my baby.'

The nurse's heartiness faded. 'Sleep first. You need a lot of rest. A high forceps delivery is nothing to sneeze at, but you don't remember anything about that, do you?'

She had been doped up to her eyebrows but she remembered – images rather than happenings. The hovering nurses, the whispering voices, finally the obstetrician and local doctor bringing with them merciful oblivion. Then the dreams had started. Mostly of Joe of course, with his smiling, brilliant blue eyes and the crisp black curls she had delighted in running her fingers through. Other, no less memorable images. Her first visit to Bardney Place in June when the rhododendrons in the park where alight with crimson or purple blossoms. Of being shown over that wing of the house that had been converted, for the duration, into a maternity home; the contribution that Brigadier and Mrs Abbott had made towards the war effort. Her private interview with Mrs Abbott later in the grey and green morning room. Feeling sick in her stomach at the thought of the pending interrogation, and taking her hostess at first sight for an elderly member of the Women's Land Army.

The nurse coughed. 'You weren't listening, mother. I just asked you what you would like for breakfast. You've had a very bad time. You've got to build up your strength, you know.'

'All I want is my baby. I don't even know if everything's all right or not . . .'

'She's perfect – a lovely, bonny little girl . . . Now will you tell me . . .'

'*Bring me my baby*,' the girl shouted.

'I'll come and see you again when you're in a better mood,' the nurse said, and closed the door firmly behind her.

The day wore on, broken up not by meals because she still refused to eat, but by visits from the nursing staff. Red Cross nurses until the morning duties were finished with, and then the two midwives, one following close on the other. Sister Martin, buxom and kind; Sister Harvey, younger and prettier, rather brusque compared with Sister Martin; a third, Sister Biddy, whom she knew hardly at all; and finally, Matron. To all she made the same plea: 'Please, let me see my baby. . . . Please let me hold her . . . just for a minute or two.'

It was Matron who said, 'It would be less cruel for you not to see her. Mrs Abbott decided that, and I agree with her. Your baby is doing well; that is all you need to know for now.' Each word came out of her prim little mouth as if it had a stamp of approval on it.

'It would have been less cruel still to let me die,' the girl screamed after her.

When the door opened again late in the afternoon, it was to admit not someone in uniform but Mrs Timms, the occupier for a short time of the second bed in the labour ward where she had spent such a long and pitiless night. Mrs Timms was now clothed in a bright blue kimono heavily embroidered with dragons which had obviously seen better days and was fastened at the front with a large safety pin.

'I've been wanting to come and see you all day,' Mrs Timms said, carefully glancing behind her before she closed the door. 'But I had to pick my moment. We're not supposed to be up until the eighth day. If I were home I'd be doing my washing by now.' Gingerly, she eased herself down on the edge of the bed, wincing a little. 'Gosh, I'm sore, I wasn't like this with the other two. Both big boys too.'

When she smiled, which she did quite often, she revealed strong white teeth and a lot of gum. She said, 'I thought I would come and keep you company until they chucked me out. I think shutting you away like this on your own is dreadful. This is the room they keep for mothers with stillborn babies – ' She stopped and coloured up. 'There I go, putting my great flat foot in it. Sorry dear. By the way, the mums in my ward send their love.'

The girl lowered her eyes, hiding them beneath long,

dark lashes. 'I suppose they all know about me?' she said quietly.

'They only know that your fiancé is out in Burma. That you've had a rotten time of it and that a specialist had to be sent for. They think that's why you've been put in a room on your own so that you can rest – there's not much rest to be had in the main ward, I can tell you. That's all Mrs Abbott intends them to know. But you can't keep secrets long in this place – it's a hotbed of gossip. Nearly as bad as the village I come from. Thornmere. D'you know it?'

A look of pain flickered in and out of the girl's brooding eyes. She hesitated. 'I don't actually know the village, but I do know some people who live about two miles further out. But you don't sound Norfolk to me. Were you born in Thornmere?'

The woman laughed. 'With this accent! No, I'm a Londoner but I married a Norfolk man. He was teaching until war was declared and then because he was in the Terriers, he was called up. Otherwise he would have been exempt because of his age. He's a sergeant in the Education Corps and not likely to be sent overseas, thank goodness. Though when I found myself pregnant again I could have wished him in Timbuktu. I suppose you could say I'm an evacuee – moved in with my mother-in-law when we got bombed out at Wanstead. She keeps the post office stores at Thornmere and I used to help in the shop until I was too big to get behind the counter.' She paused for breath. 'But here I am, nattering on about nothing when I really came along to tell you that I popped into the nursery and had a peek at your little girl. She's really beautiful. Just like a little doll . . .'

Colour rushed into the girl's face and her eyes shone

feverishly. This time, with effort, she raised herself on to her elbows. 'Oh, please – please, could you smuggle her in to me?'

'Ducky, I wish I could. Perhaps it wasn't such a good idea to tell you. It's upset you.' Mrs Timms reached over and took the girl into her arms. 'Don't cry love, don't get worked up. I could kick myself.'

The girl clung to her. 'Thank God you did. Everybody else is going around acting as if my baby were dead. She is all right, isn't she? You'd tell me if there was anything the matter with her?'

'All right! I should say she is. She's the liveliest one in the nursery. All the others were fast asleep, but her eyes were open and all over the place. I'm sure they focused on me. She's as bloomy as a peach, and has the loveliest blue eyes you ever saw. All babies have blue eyes, I know, but hers are bluer than most. Who does she take after? . . . Not you, your eyes are grey.'

'Her father. He had bluer eyes than most, too.'

Her last visitor of the day was Mrs Abbott, not dressed in breeches and headscarf and boots as when the girl had last seen her but in a satin evening gown that clung, wraith-like, to her angular figure. Her scanty, iron-grey hair was held in place by a Spanish comb inset with diamonds, and her rings seemed too weighty for her long thin fingers. The girl stared at her with dry, despairing eyes.

What chance have I against such wealth and position? she asked herself. Here we are in the fourth year of war living among shortages and austerity, yet the people here still cling to the trappings of peacetime; changing for dinner, waited on by footmen. A cook, housemaids, butler. It was such a different world from the one she had been born to that it was like living on another planet. Then because she was someone who could see just as clearly from another person's point of view, her censure withered. They were good people really, who at their time of life had every right to take things easy but instead they had taken on extra duties and given up their privacy and their home to an invasion of strangers. Pregnant strangers, and all that that entailed.

'What is this nonsense about you not eating?' said Mrs Abbott, her friendly tone belying the apparent severity of her words.

The girl looked at her beseechingly. 'Please, would you let me break my promise? I want to keep my baby. I desperately need my baby – I – I had no idea, when I agreed to the adoption, just what I was doing. I was in a state of mind then, not really knowing who to turn to, and having the baby adopted seemed the best thing to do in the circumstances.'

'It was, and still is,' said Mrs Abbott quietly. She had seated herself beside the bed and was leaning slightly forwards, her expression tense.

'For the people who are adopting my baby perhaps, but not for me . . . certainly not for me.'

'You told me you wanted to do what was best for your child. Have you changed your mind about that? Can you provide for her? Give her a home – education – a stable life and a respectable name?'

'I'm not ashamed of my name,' said the girl spiritedly, 'and I'm not entirely without means.'

'My dear, you misunderstand me. I was thinking of the stigma – the disgrace. It isn't easy, you know, for an illegitimate child, even in these enlightened times, especially for a girl.'

She had all the right answers, Mrs Abbott. In that quiet and reasonable voice she demolished every protest and plea the young mother put forward. She went at last, leaving the girl exhausted but resigned and with one small, compensating promise.

'I have already named her,' she said. 'I always believed I would have a girl, and right from the beginning I thought of her as Jennifer... Jennifer Anne. By something you let drop once, I believe you know the people who are going adopt her. Is it too much to expect them to keep that name? Please, could you use your influence with them. Ask them – beg them. It would be easier to bear if I knew that Jennifer Anne – *my* Jennifer Anne was out there somewhere.'

Mrs Abbott surprised the girl then by lightly brushing her cheeks with lips as dry as tissue paper. 'I will do what I can,' she promised.

The day of the girl's leave-taking was a day of high, white, scudding clouds, blue skies, and trees bending to the wind. During her two weeks lying-in the cornfields had been harvested, and now a spreading swath of blowing poppies was turning the stubble into a scarlet landscape.

She had lain in her lonely room looking out of the window at the wide Norfolk skies and thinking constantly of Joe because keeping her mind on Joe kept her from thinking of that other part of Joe that she had given away to another woman.

'I was meant to be a concert pianist,' Joe had told her once, during a reminiscent mood. 'My godfather paid for me to study music but I chucked it up to become a fighter pilot, much to his disgust.'

'But why a fighter pilot?' she had asked, feeling even then a trickle of fear like an icy finger sliding down her spine.

'Because the thought of being up there in all that space and silence appealed to me. I never had enough space or silence when I was a child,' he added in one of his rare moments of gravity, then quickly laughed. 'Actually, the silence is all in the mind. I buzz around like a bluebottle...'

And like a bluebottle he had been swatted down, she thought, out of a sky as clear as this.

The friends she had made during her stay at Bardney Place gave her parting gifts. A few sweets from their precious hoard; a bar of scented soap, even more difficult to come by. Flowers, tomatoes, and fruit from the greenhouse. Even Matron unbent so far as to give her some advice.

'I usually tell my mothers to treat their babies as they would like to be treated themselves. To you I say – treat yourself as you would like your child to be treated.'

She turned round to have one last look out of the rear window of the car that had been put at her disposal. At the tall brick chimneys of the ancient house; of the stately elms, home for generations of cawing rooks, then back to the vista of scarlet poppies.

And she knew that for the rest of her life the sight of a field of poppies would bring back the memory of this suffocating sense of heartbreak and loss.

One

War came dramatically and somewhat ridiculously to Philippa Byrd one lunchtime in late August 1940 in the female locker room at Brundle's Bank. Though she saw nothing funny about it at the time, later when recounting the story to her father she was overtaken by a fit of laughter.

'You see, Mr Barley is such a pompous and correct little man, and never raises his voice. When he suddenly burst in upon us and shouted what we thought was "good morning", we all chorused "good morning" back. He looked so surprised. What he had actually said was "Warning!". It wasn't his fault really. What a place for an air-raid shelter – leading straight off our locker room.'

War, of course, had been going on since the previous September, boringly so for the first seven months, then getting bloodier and bloodier as neutral countries fell victim in turn to Hitler's ruthless plan to redraw the map of Europe. Twice a week, sometimes on her own when Leo was on call, Philippa would visit the cinema in order to keep up to date with the latest news.

Her stomach churned as she watched the straggling lines of refugees being 'strafed' at intervals by the Luftwaffe, knowing that if Hitler's boast of invasion came true Britain could be the next victim.

'What will happen to us if Hitler invades?' she asked Leo once as they walked along Oxford Street after an evening performance at the Odeon in Leicester Square. There was no moon but the cross-hatching of searchlights against the night sky gave them enough light to walk by.

'To the country as a whole or just to you and me?'

She thought carefully before replying. 'You and me, say?'

He had no doubts. 'You'll be given to some German officer as his fancy bit, and I'll likely end up in a labour camp.'

'Doesn't it worry you?'

'Of course it worries me, but what worries me more at the moment is that if we don't get a move on you'll miss the last train back to Woodside.'

Philippa had spotted an open milk bar across the street. 'Haven't we time even for a coffee?'

'Do you want to walk all the way back to Woodside?'

'Of course not.'

'Come along then.'

Not everybody took the same view as Leo who like his Celtic mother was inclined to pessimism. Travelling to the City by bus the following morning, Philippa saw in Aldgate a notice in white paint written on the window of a jellied-eel shop: 'In the event of an invasion we will stay closed for half an hour.' She felt uplifted. Atta boy, that's the spirit! Her father deplored the way in which she had picked up American slang from the cinema, but how neatly it expressed one's feelings.

The bus dropped her off at Fenchurch Street and from there it was only a ten-minute walk to Brundle's Bank. Like many other City workers hurrying to their places of employment, Philippa's gas-mask case slung over one shoulder made a useful container for her lunch and makeup bag. Complacency had set in with the phoney war and many people no longer bothered carrying gas-masks. They were not compulsory wear except for those in uniform.

Philippa had been working at Brundle's for three years now, and much to her joy was gradually working her way up the holiday roster. During her first year, 1937, when she was nearly eighteen, the only weeks on offer to her were the first two in February or the last two in October. She plumped for October and went with her father to St Ives, spending most of her time staring out of the hotel windows at the rain.

This year she had been offered the two middle weeks in September; a lovely time of year for a honeymoon, she thought, often with sunny and mellow days rich with early autumn colours. She had still not given up hope that her holiday would double up as a honeymoon even though Leo still thought it best to postpone their marriage until after the war. It was the one cause of friction between them.

She thought back to the previous September – 1939 – when Leo had taken his finals. They had planned to marry if he passed, which he did, but Hitler marching into Poland had put paid to any thought of a wedding. She had waited so long to become Leo's wife; all through his student years – agonising with him when he was taking exams and agonising even more while awaiting results. Planning their future, dreaming of their wedding

– dreaming with a quickening of her heart of the honeymoon. She had a rough idea of what went on then but was ignorant of the finer details.

When appealed to, Great-Aunt Dot who had never been married tried her best. 'I was told,' she said, 'that the wedding day belongs to the bride and the wedding night to the groom. Is that any help?'

Not a lot, but on the whole Philippa was quite satisfied with the answer.

They spent what little time they had together, she and Leo, during that long hot summer before peace ended, planning their future: a country practice or junior house job in a teaching hospital with an eye to specialising? Philippa didn't mind what Leo decided as long as it ended in marriage.

She had started her bottom drawer when she was fifteen, a few months after their first meeting at a Boy Scouts dance. They had danced (or at least Leo's version of dancing which was to overtake every other couple on the floor) to a then popular song, 'I'm dancing with tears in my eyes because the girl in my arms isn't you'. Philippa thought it inappropriate for if there was anything in her eyes at all it was stars, and in Leo's the light of battle, for there were other ex-Scouts waiting all too ready to take his place.

Leo's love was no less deep than hers, she reflected now, biting into an egg and Marmite sandwich, it was just that he didn't show it. Or rather he showed it in a restrained and gentlemanly fashion like the way he made love.

The fact that they had not yet slept together rested on two influential factors. One, that Philippa wanted a white wedding and according to her upbringing non-virgins could not or should not wear white. She was superstitious enough to think that if she broke that rule she might be struck dead by a vengeful God. Secondly, and even more importantly, if Leo got her into trouble he would more than likely be struck dead not by his Heavenly Father, but by his father on earth.

Leo relied on his father for his keep, his clothes, his medical books, his college fees, and a very basic personal allowance, and though he had a great respect for his father, he also had a deep-rooted fear which sprang from the time when at the age of four he had bitten through every one of a row of unripe tomatoes. Recalling the consequences could even now, twenty years later, bring him out in a cold sweat. Never, Philippa realised, would Leo go against his father's wishes.

He could never quite understand or cease to envy, Philippa suspected, the easy relationship she had with her own father. 'It's because, since Mother died, we've only had each other. Besides Great-Aunt Dot I mean. I'm not like you with loads of relations,' she added.

'One unmarried sister and three married brothers does not constitute loads,' said Leo with a thoughtful expression. He was mindful of his siblings, the youngest of whom was six years older than he. They, like his father, had a lot to say about the way he conducted himself which did not include, during his student years, having a girlfriend. They knew about Philippa of course, but as long as she stayed in the background and posed no threat to his studies, she could conveniently be overlooked. Philippa dreaded the day she would be introduced to the Brooke household. None of Leo's sisters-in-law wore makeup or high heels or went dancing. They were all the sensible, low-heeled kind of women. His sister was more unconventional, using a powerful motor bike to take her backwards and forwards to the school where she taught domestic science. Her brothers all thought her quite mad but admired her grit.

Philippa knew she would never measure up to what the Brookes considered a suitable wife for their most promising son, but she consoled herself with the thought that once Leo was independent, none of that would matter.

And Leo had been independent for a year now, working first as a house officer in a voluntary hospital for £120 a year plus free board, lodging and laundry, and then for another six months in an LCC hospital where his stipend was increased to £250 a year. Immediately he took up this appointment wedding bells began to ring in Philippa's ears, but when he reminded her that his calling-up papers could arrive any minute and he didn't think they should rush into anything in the circumstances, the bells jangled to a sudden stop.

'*Rush into anything*! Gracious, we've known each other for six years – I don't call that rushing. Your father's got at you, hasn't he?' Philippa regretted that as soon as she saw Leo's face. That wasn't the way to get round him. But rushing into marriage, and they weren't even officially engaged yet! When she got home she poured out her woes to her father.

'You and Mother got married in wartime,' she said. 'You didn't regret it, did you?'

'The only thing I regretted, my dear, was that I hadn't done it sooner.' Even now, sixteen years after his wife's death, Jonathan's voice saddened as it did whenever he spoke of her. 'But you see, I came through unscathed. Many weren't so lucky. There were a lot of young widows left with children to bring up, often without any means of support. I expect Leo is thinking of that.'

More than likely, with his sense of prudence, Philippa thought, but it didn't help her disappointment. It wasn't that Leo didn't want her, his recent lack of restraint made her aware how much he did, and if it weren't for the idea drilled into her by Aunt Dot that once you allowed a man to have his way with you you'd lose his respect, she would willingly have given in to him. She might just be able to live without Leo's love, she told herself, but not without his respect, for that would include the gallantry he bestowed upon her, raising his hat whenever they met, walking on the outside of the pavement, helping her down from trams and buses, holding doors open for her, draping his jacket across her shoulders when the night air brought out goose pimples on her bare arms. He made her feel precious and she would miss that terribly.

She accepted without resentment that she had many rivals. His rugger team, his rowing club – just two of the many outdoor pursuits he followed assiduously. She was pleased to think he was a man's man rather than a ladies' man even if it did mean she had to spend Saturday afternoons on her own. He had footballer's knees and rower's muscles and when in high spirits would sometimes grab her and swing her round and round or hold her upside down by her ankles with no more effort than if she were a sack of feathers. Boasting of Leo's strength to her father one day, she was surprised by the look he gave her and his odd remark that she should advise Leo to take more cold baths.

Nobody could accuse her father of being the sporty type. Reading and listening to music were more in his line. He did enjoy walking, however, and she would join him in long leisurely strolls through Epping Forest, where he would point out to her a wild flower or a particular bird. When they got home he would quiz her on what she had seen and if she had missed something which he had not he would mutter impatiently, 'Eyes and no eyes; eyes and no eyes'. Leo enjoyed walking too, but with him it was more like taking part in a cross-country race.

She finished her sandwich and took out an apple which she polished on her sleeve before taking a strong bite. She had good teeth, white and even.

'You're just like your mother when she was your age. Good teeth, beautiful grey eyes, but not her figure. Still, you'll do.' That, from her father, was a compliment. Her memories of her mother were patchy; not memories as much as sudden startling images: her mother in a black hat with a red rose fixed to its wide brim; her mother dancing her round the room to the music from a record; her mother in her father's arms and both of them weeping quietly. And lastly, the one image that would never fade: her mother propped up in a hospital bed and holding out her arms to her.

It was Christmas; the side-room was festooned with paper chains and tinsel, and there were cards on the windowsill, and her father was laden with a huge bunch of flowers and a basket of fruit and Christmas packages bulging his pockets. Her own present she had made for her mother at Sunday school. A teapot stand, made of raffia that she had wound and weaved around a cardboard disc. It wasn't quite round and some of the ends of the raffia stuck out untidily, but her mother loved it. She said so with her eyes, for by then she could hardly speak.

Philippa was not allowed to go to the funeral. She

stayed at home with Aunt Dot who had left the comfort of her charming cliff-top house in Leigh-on-Sea to come to Woodside to keep house for her nephew.

'Why did Mummy die?' Philippa asked her. She could rely on Aunt Dot to tell her the truth and not fob her off with 'because the angels wanted her,' which was what the daily help had told her.

'She had an enlarged heart.' Then Aunt Dot had added something rather frightening. 'She was all heart – that was her trouble... All heart and no stamina.'

All heart. The idea haunted Philippa for days. She imagined a heart growing bigger and bigger until it finally burst through the wall of her chest. It might happen to her too for was not her father always telling her she was her mother's daughter. She took her worries to Aunt Dot for she knew by instinct that this was not the time to put such a query to her father.

Aunt Dot adjusted her spectacles. 'So you think you've got an enlarged heart, do you? Well, let me put your mind at rest, young miss. Anyone who could cut all the buttons off her great-aunt's new coat has very little heart at all.'

'I was only three then,' Philippa protested, 'an' you're always telling me about it.' Aunt Dot laughed and kissed her good night.

'Now go to sleep and don't have any more bad dreams about dying. You're going to live to a ripe old age for as sure as the moon is made of green cheese Old Nick takes care of his own.'

Philippa found her aunt as puzzling now as she was then, but always, in her own peculiar way, very comforting.

Dear Aunt Dot, she thought now, taking another bite

of her apple. A legend in her own lifetime. As enduring as the Albert Hall – and nearly as big. Her eye caught the eye of Miss Jolly opposite, another lady of considerable bulk, and an inclination to laugh came over her. Her sense of humour would be her undoing one of these days, she thought, as she hastily swallowed a subdued guffaw. Being the youngest of the small circle that took their lunch in the locker room she knew the importance of keeping her place in the hierarchy of the banking staff.

There was a perfectly good canteen provided by the bank where a three-course meal was available. Philippa could afford the shilling it cost but not the time to eat it. A whole hour spent over lunch – what a waste! She preferred to be out and exploring, mostly in the direction of Queen Victoria Street where she could feast her eyes on the engagement rings in the windows of Mappin and Webb's.

Miss Jolly and her close friend and colleague Miss Watson were two of the longest serving members of the female staff who had joined the bank during the Great War when Brundle's, for the first time in its history, recruited female workers. To Philippa the two ladies seemed part of the bank's institutions – immovable and unchangeable as the fittings, and she wondered at first why they preferred the informality of the locker room to the more congenial surroundings of the canteen where, if nothing else, they would be waited upon.

She soon learnt, however, that in the intimacy of the locker room they were better able to indulge in what they liked doing best, reminiscing. This, Philippa informed her father, consisted of chit-chat about the 'good old days' before the noisy and unreliable ledger machines banished forever the leather-bound accounts so accurately kept in copperplate writing.

She would listen open-mouthed to the peccadilloes committed by the now heads of departments in their salad days. She found it hard to believe that the manager, a godlike figure rarely seen outside his office, had, when a junior, been caught dancing the cancan on one of the desktops. 'I must say, it's reassuring to know that bank managers are actually human,' her father said.

But Philippa did not think Mr Duncan at all human. She had only crossed his path once (one time too many in her opinion) when he had caught her without her overall and sent her back to the locker room to put it on.

The bank had strict rules about the apparel worn by their employees. The men on weekdays were soberly dressed in dark suits but on Saturday mornings were allowed to indulge in more casual wear such as tweed jackets or blazers with flannels. The women had no such privileges. They wore their navy-blue overalls summer and winter alike because, so Philippa was told, sleeveless dresses or bright colours might offend the customers.

Actually the overalls were extremely smart and tailor-made, and cost the bank the incredible sum of two guineas each, the equivalent to Philippa's weekly earnings. They were made of gaberdine, warm in winter but insufferable in hot weather. It was on one very hot Saturday morning when she had only been at the bank for a few months, that Philippa decided to leave it off. Mr Duncan's cold, clear eyes spotted her as she crossed the banking hall. He beckoned her over.

'Is there anything wrong with your overall, Miss Byrd?' Even in her dilemma she could not but admire the ability of this formidable man to memorise the name of everybody on his staff.

'No,' she replied in a small voice.

'Then why are you not wearing it?'

'I was hot.'

'May I suggest that you leave off something underneath instead.'

With reddened cheeks she had bolted back to the locker room, but she took Mr Duncan at his word. She removed her dress and went back to the ledger room wearing her overall over her camiknickers.

She watched now as Miss Watson spooned out pickle on to her plate. The bosom friends (very bosomy in Miss Jolly's case) made quite a meal of their lunch, laying their end of the table with a white cloth and heating up soup over the gas-ring in winter. Not for them sandwiches from the sandwich bar across the way, but plates of cold meat and salads which they brought to the office in airtight containers. Philippa, like everybody else in the bank, liked Miss Jolly who lived up to her name and bore with good humour the atrocious puns ('Miss Jelly' being the worst) fired in her direction. A good humour not shared by Miss Watson.

It was at this point that their lunch was interrupted by the sudden eruption of Mr Barley from Foreign Exchange shouting his warning and barging through on his way to the shelter. Open-mouthed, they stared after him.

Miss Watson bristled.

' "Good morning"! Doesn't the man realise it's nearly two o'clock! And coming in without as much as knocking – one of us might have been changing.'

Miss Jolly, shaking with silent laughter, was struggling to get to her feet. It took two of the younger ones to get her off the sofa. 'He didn't say good morning, dear, he said warning. He's gone off to the vault to sound the alarm. There it goes. Come along – you know the rules. We must set an example to the young ones.'

'I'm going to finish my peach first,' said Miss Watson stubbornly.

Air-raid practice had been brought to perfection in the months leading up to the war. When the alarm sounded, everybody stopped what they were doing and made for the nearest shelter. There were four of these, converted from vaults and stocked with tins of food and blankets and first-aid equipment in case of a lengthy siege.

Sitting in one of the shelters now, between two gently perspiring girls from Mailing, Philippa thought back to the dummy runs of 1939. It had been fun then, she recalled, sheltering in a kind of Aladdin's cave instead of working, though that had to be made up for later. Now it was a nuisance because everybody was anxious to get out of London as soon as possible; besides which, the knowledge of the punishing raids other areas had experienced in the past few weeks had given them a foretaste of what to expect. As always when in trouble, Philippa took refuge in silent prayer. Please dear God, she pleaded, please don't let anything happen. Please don't make me late tonight, not tonight, it's too important.

Forty minutes later her prayer was answered. The All Clear sounded. Chafing inwardly at their slowness, Philippa joined the orderly procession of bank staff making their way up the basement stairs.

Back on the department she found her wire tray piled high with banking slips. Every one of those had to be posted into the ledger machine and balanced before she could leave. She switched on the current and set to work, anxious to make up for lost time. The other machines on the department were just as busy. Trays were emptied and filled again. Another of her urgent prayers went winging upwards.

She had arranged to meet Leo outside the bank at six o'clock. At last he had managed to book seats to see *Gone with the Wind*. The film was the talk of the town, upstaging even the lastest war news, and most girls of her age were wearing the snoods that Scarlett O'Hara had made so popular. Her own she had crocheted from black chenille wool and if they were still in fashion in September she had dreams of wearing a white one threaded with silver instead of the customary veil.

Her work completed and balanced; her makeup repaired; her honey-blond hair beneath her hat bobbing on her shoulders, she was tripping on high heels towards the revolving doors when the alert sounded again. She was within inches of freedom, her fingertips actually touching the outer door, when it began to revolve admitting the substantial figure of Mrs Fuller, the caretaker's wife.

The Fullers occupied the flat on the top floor and Philippa had on some occasions shared the lift with Mrs Fuller when she was going out or coming in with her shopping basket.

'I was in Leadenhall Market when the siren went,' she volunteered breathlessly. 'Quite a trot home for me, it was. Are you going down to the shelter, miss? I'll come with you, if you don't mind.' There was nothing Philippa could do but comply.

The raid lasted an hour with intermittent gunfire rumbling like distant thunder. Philippa strained her ears to listen above Mrs Fuller's nervous chatter. Some place on the fringe of London was getting a battering. The docks, perhaps? Her stomach turned. Please dear God, let Leo be safe. Please God, I won't mind missing *Gone with the Wind* as long as you spare Leo.

To give up seeing *Gone with the Wind* was quite a sacrifice for she had convinced herself that something very important was going to happen that evening. She had had a tingling in her right palm which was a signal that something good was coming her way. She had hoped that sitting beside Leo in the small and cosy underground cinema watching the most romantic film of the year unfolding before their eyes, something of the poignancy of unfulfilled love might rub off on him.

Normally they didn't go to see love stories. *North-West Passage* starring Spencer Tracy or Arthur Askey in *Charley's Aunt* were more in Leo's line. Screen kisses embarrassed him, as did any show of sentiment, but she didn't think there would be a lot of either in *Gone with the Wind*, for the press reviews had made much of Scarlett slapping not one but four different faces.

Her mind, running out of control along a one-way track, envisaged an evening of heightened expectations, and how better to cap such an evening than to name the day for their wedding. A woman's prerogative normally, but she would gladly cede that to Leo if he would only make up his mind. Tonight's the night, she told herself, and when her right palm began to itch again she mentally hugged herself in blissful anticipation.

Leo wasn't outside the bank at six o'clock. He didn't arrive until nearly seven, flushed from hurrying, and with one lock of his wavy fair hair flopping over his right eyebrow. It had pleased her immensely when he had started going without a hat, for bareheaded he looked his age. Hats, especially a trilby, put years on him. She had made an effort to look her best this evening, and was wearing a new hat with a flattering little eye-veil. For once she hoped Leo would pay her a compliment but he wasn't one to notice what she was wearing, and even if he did it wouldn't occur to him to remark on it.

He was out of breath. 'Sorry I'm late,' he said, giving her a perfunctory and rather moist kiss which just missed her mouth. 'Mac held me up.' Mac was Mr Mackay, the senior surgeon, Leo's chief and also his god. 'He wanted to discuss anaesthetics with me – thinks I have the making of a good anaesthetist. Something to consider specialising in, he says, when peace comes.'

Philippa experienced a moment's outrage. All those prayers and misplaced sympathy. 'I thought you had been caught in a raid.'

'You would have heard it if we had. We're not so far away as a plane flies. Croydon Airfield copped it – I don't know how seriously. Hope to God it wasn't another Biggin Hill.' The Luftwaffe had switched their tactics from attacking shipping in the Channel to bombing airfields and radio installations. Day by day the number of enemy planes shot down by British fighters was on the increase. Leo switched his thoughts from the triumphs of the RAF to the silent girl beside him. 'You're not disappointed I'm still in one piece, are you?' he asked whimsically.

She didn't reply. How could he jest at a time like this – in such poor taste too. She sensed a suppressed exhilaration about him. His high colour wasn't only due to exertion, and his eyes, which he described as hazel on official forms but which to her were a fascinating mixture of green and gold, held a subtle gleam of satisfaction.

Something had aroused his excitement and she wondered if the talk with his chief had put ideas in his head, for Mr Mackay she knew was a happily married man with five children. Her hopes began to rise.

There were many jewellers between his hospital and her bank, she recalled, especially along the Whitechapel Road. Had he stopped to gaze in their windows? Had he, on the spur of the moment, gone into one and bought a ring! It was hard to imagine Leo doing anything on the spur of the moment, but his adrenalin (she had learnt a lot of medical terms since he commenced his training) was doubtless flowing after his interview with Mr Mackay, and now the ring in its little square box might well be reposing in his pocket.

When he said, 'I've got a bit of a surprise for you, but I'll keep it till later,' her own adrenalin began to flow.

He jogtrotted her along Gracechurch Street, Old Broad Street and into Liverpool Street were they caught the Central Line to Holborn and then changed for Leicester Square.

Leo looked around him as they emerged into the open. 'Wonder where we can go for a quick snack? A milk bar? There's sure to be one around, somewhere.'

She pointed out a coffee stall in a side-street. 'What about over there. I've always wanted to eat at a coffee stall.'

He was amazed at her suggestion. 'You never see ladies using coffee stalls! They're for down-and-outs and late-night revellers.'

She laughed with the joy that was bubbling away inside her. 'We're early night revellers, aren't we? And anyway, I feel like doing something really daring.'

Her high spirits were infectious. 'All right then, but don't tell your father I took you to a coffee stall.'

'Dad wouldn't mind – he'd be amused.'

'Don't tell your Aunt Dorothy, then.'

Philippa pouted. 'Chance would be a fine thing. The beastly Ministry of Defence won't let me visit her, even.'

As soon as Philippa grew out of her teens Aunt Dorothy had decided she had fulfilled her duty to her great-niece and there was nothing now to prevent her returning to Leigh, but she was hardly installed in her old home before war was declared. War made little difference to her life at first, but since the fall of France, followed swiftly by the threat of invasion, the coastal areas of the east and south had become heavily guarded defensive zones. Anyone living outside those zones needed a visiting permit. Aunt Dot was highly pleased about it. She wrote to say how peaceful Leigh was this summer without the usual influx of holidaymakers and day trippers. At last the residents could have the place to themselves.

'I'm sorry for any Nazi who gets in her way,' said her nephew after reading this.

The coffee at the stall was good and the ham sandwich freshly made. They downed them quickly for already a queue was forming outside the Ritz.

'You have the tickets, I hope,' said Philippa anxiously.

Leo patted his breast pocket. She wondered in which pocket the ring was secreted. Hardly aware that she did so she took his hand and held it against her cheek. Self-consciously, he pulled it away, for he deplored that sort of intimacy in public.

Later, when they emerged from the cinema into the warmth of the summer night, the moon had risen and now bleached the blacked-out streets with its pallid light.

Moonlight also brought bombers but, weighing the threat of that against tripping down kerbs and walking head-on into strangers or knocking herself out against a brick wall, Philippa preferred the less dangerous option.

Not that her mind was on the moon at present. She was still lost in the arms of Rhett Butler, except that in her imagination Rhett Butler did not have Clark Gable's face but Leo's, and Vivien Leigh's ethereal beauty was replaced by her own more homely brand. The scene where Rhett had snatched Scarlett into his arms and sprinted up the grand staircase two steps at a time sent a tremor of expectation through her veins every time she thought of it. If that meant a fate worse than death it was a fate worth having, she decided, and she wondered whether she would ever be able to goad Leo into such an action. He had the strength, but had he the inclination? She sighed regretfully. Alas, no... He was far too much of a gentleman.

His voice cut in on her speculation. 'We're not going to get anything to eat around here. Everything looks shut up.'

She wished he could get his mind off food, but he was incapable of thinking of more than one thing at a time and at present his thoughts were concentrated on the inner man.

'Did you enjoy the film?'

'Up to a point.'

'Which point?'

He was silent, thinking it over. 'That scene in the church – the men dying. The amputations without anaesthetics – that concentrated the mind very acutely.'

That was the part where she had sat with her eyes closed. In any case she didn't want to get back to the subject of anaesthetics. 'But didn't you think it was all very romantic?'

'Actually, I don't see war as a romantic subject.' He took her arm. 'Look, over there – a milk bar. Nothing else seems open. Willing to risk it?'

The milk bar was packed and airless. On such a hot night with the windows closed and the black-outs up and the atmosphere thick with cigarette smoke, the smell of humanity was overwhelming. After the magic of the cinema it was a sad coming-down-to-earth. There was nowhere to sit and they had to squeeze into a spot at the counter.

'There's coffee but no milk and only corned-beef sandwiches,' said the counterhand not bothering to conceal a yawn.

'I'm sorry, sweet,' said Leo when he had given his order. 'I should have booked a table at some restaurant, I just didn't think. I was hoping to find somewhere quiet and intimate because there's something I want to say to you.'

'Not here!' she cried in a panic. Even the Koh-i-noor diamond would look second-rate in a place such as this. 'You're coming home tonight with me, aren't you? Wait until then.' Ideally, on the chesterfield in the drawing room after her father had gone to bed.

'I'll see you home to Woodside, of course, then I'll have to get back to the hospital. I'm on call this weekend.'

They ate their dry and curling sandwiches and drank the tepid coffee, then made their escape into the fresher air outside.

'Whew, it must have been eighty degrees in that place.' Leo wiped his hands on his handkerchief. 'Let's walk down to the river. It'll be cooler there.'

Victoria Embankment in the moonlight with the black waters of the Thames lapping softly against the retaining walls seemed to her at that moment the epitome of all that was romantic. She purposely stopped at Cleopatra's Needle for if she were to become engaged tonight where better than by this ancient landmark. In years to come she would be able to bring her grandchildren to see the spot where on a momentous occasion their grandfather placed the ring upon her finger.

There was a moment of silence between them. They seemed to have this particular part of the Embankment to themselves. A bus lumbered past, its lights so efficiently dimmed it was difficult to tell whether it carried passengers or not. Occasionally, a searchlight swept the sky and each time it did so it captured in its beam one or more of the fish-like shapes of the barrage balloons. Silent guardians of London skies, thought Philippa, and was so pleased with that phrase she memorised it to put down in her diary, later.

Leo took his arm from around her waist and felt in his inside pocket. Philippa tensed, but all he produced was a letter.

'I received this this morning,' he said.

Her mouth went dry. 'What is it?'

'My calling-up papers.'

She didn't instantly panic. Her first thought was, 'Now perhaps we will get married,' – then the full realisation of what this meant swept over her. She swallowed and tried to speak but her voice defeated her. 'When?' she managed finally in a whisper.

'The seventh of September, a Saturday. I'm to report to the Royal Army Medical Corps at Aldershot.'

The seventh of September was the start of her holiday.

Leo, unaware of her silent screams for help was amazed that she had taken his news so calmly. He was vastly relieved. Philippa was not one for hysterics, but she could cry copiously at times. He took advantage of the moment to bring up a subject that had been on his mind.

'Isn't it time you came to meet my folks. It seems silly to keep your distance when they live so near, especially as they know I'm always over at your place. I know they've hurt your feelings in the past, but that was when I was a student and they didn't think it right for me to have a girlfriend. Things are different now. I'm going away soon and I'd feel much happier about it if I knew you were all friends. Please dear...'

'But you are happy, aren't you – about going away?' she said dully.

She was thinking of the day he tried to join the RAF. He had been qualified a week, no longer a student – more of an unemployed doctor. War had started. Those on the reserves had been called up straight away, so too had the Territorials. The rest, eager to do their bit for their country, discovered that unlike the first war, this one was a difficult war to get into. Leo found this out when he applied at the recruiting office in Buckhurst Hill. He told Philippa about it later. 'What they said in so many words was – "Don't call us, we'll call you." '

'Bally cheek! I thought they'd snap you up.'

'A month-old doctor? I've got to get some experience first.'

Now he said, 'What do you mean – I'm happy about going away?'

'You're pleased about getting into this war at last, aren't you?' Again that accusing note in her voice – she couldn't stop herself.

'We're all in the war this time, sweet, but yes I am, though pleased is too strong a word for the way I feel. Relief actually – I couldn't make any plans with this hanging over my head.'

'What plans?' she said quickly. 'I can never tie you down to making plans – that's just the trouble. Now that you'll be going into the army does that you mean you want to get married? Oh Leo, if I could only make you understand what being married to you would mean to me. I've had this dream for years ... I thought it was coming true last year, but now ... Don't you want to marry me?'

He swung her round to face him. His eyes glittered in the moonlight.

'I've had a dream too,' he said quietly. 'For years, I've had this dream of standing at the altar and watching you coming down the aisle to me. My bride. Mine – the woman I waited for. The woman I worked for, made a home for. Our own home with our own possessions in it – things that we had both planned for. That isn't possible in wartime, and in your heart you must know that. I don't want to join the assembly line for a registry office wedding like the one we saw in the newsreel. I don't want furnished rooms because we can't afford a house or because mortgages are not available in wartime. What about when the war is over? I won't have a job to come back to. And supposing I wanted to specialise which would mean becoming more or less a student again? What would we live on? Darling, please be sensible. I don't want us to make do with second best. I'd rather wait.'

'Supposing I said I wouldn't wait ...'

He stepped away, into the shadow. She heard him sigh.
'I'd have to risk that, wouldn't I.'

'You know there's no risk,' she answered disconsolately. 'That's the root of the trouble . . . you've always been so sure of me.'

Two

On Saturday, 7 September, the day she had fondly hoped would see her married at last, Philippa was having her first permanent wave.

She had worn a page-boy bob for the past two years because it suited her and was easy to manage. It also suited her type of hair which was fine and silky. Now she felt in desperate need of making some form of statement, for since Leo had left for Aldershot without further discussion of their future, she had been in a continuous state of rebellion. Changing her hair-style was one way of giving vent to her feelings for she knew that would get Leo's back up. She had never forgotten his reaction when she had once worn a fringe. Lucky for her that the salon was able to slot her in at such short notice, but they weren't so busy since the raids had started.

Leo had set off early for Hampshire the day before, following a week or more of interviews, medicals and a fitting at a military tailors. It was too soon yet to receive a letter from him, but she hoped he'd find time to call her on the phone. A perm could take anything up to four hours. It would be just her luck if he tried to get her when she was not at home.

The worst of the process was over; the tedious winding and unwinding of metal curlers, and the heating and stretching of hair. Now shampooed, she was sitting with her hair wet, awaiting the attention of the stylist, when the alert sounded.

In the past few weeks the raids had become heavier and more frequent. So far, air-fields in the south and east had been the main targets, but now the bombers were turning their attention to London. Nobody who had seen on the newsreels the damage that the Luftwaffe had inflicted on Rotterdam had any doubt as to what was in store for the towns and cities of Britain.

Hardly had the last warbling note faded before Philippa found herself with the other customers being shepherded to the door. Staff and clientele together made for the nearest public air-raid shelter. It was crowded. Philippa sat opposite an elderly lady who gave her an encouraging smile.

'See that old dear over there,' a woman next to Philippa whispered. 'She was here last night. Sat for hours with a back as straight as a ramrod – didn't move once – didn't sleep either. Never complained. Game old bird.'

The All Clear sounded three hours later. The shelterers streamed out into the open, looking about them for damage, and were relieved to find there was none. Yet there was an eerie and undefinable feeling that something was not quite as it should be. There was no dawdling, everybody was bent on getting home as quickly as possible. Philippa, returning to the hairdressers hoping it wasn't too late to have her hair set, found it closed.

The sky to the east glowed with an astonishing sunset,

the most glorious she had ever seen. She stood still to admire it, wishing that her father or Leo were with her to share the amazing spectacle. The windows of the houses opposite had turned a brilliant red. Everywhere she looked was bathed in light. She wondered why the few other pedestrians about didn't stop to comment on it. But they hardly gave the sky a glance. They hurried, heads down, with only one thought in mind: to get home.

Then realisation hit her, and a cold trickle of fear ran down her spine. *The sun set in the west.* This was no sunset – this was fire. London was on fire! She broke into a run, anxious like everyone else to be home.

Her father had gone to the works as usual that day and hadn't returned before she left for the hairdressers. Normally he did not go in on a Saturday, but two of the compositors had received their calling-up papers, and extra help, even unskilled such as his, was always welcome.

Byrd and Son, a small and élite publishing and printing house, had been established by Philippa's great-great-grandfather in the early part of the nineteenth century. The story went that Jonathan Byrd, newly married and hopelessly infatuated with his lovely young bride, had written down his feelings in a collection of love poems which to his chagrin nobody wanted to publish.

Determined to see his work in print he set up his own publishing house on the site of an obsolete brewery in Stratford, the brewery which had originally made the Byrd family fortunes. But works of poetry, and fine art, and *belles-lettres*, unlike the strong brew that had previously emerged from that site, did not sell in such large quantities, and the firm would have foundered if it were not for the second Jonathan who had more in common with the financial world than with the literati. By wisely investing the narrow profits made by the family business, he ensured that future generations of Byrds, though they would never be extremely wealthy, would never go in want either.

Why this should go through Philippa's mind now, she didn't know, except that the vivid spread of sky, redder than ever now that dusk had fallen, seemed to her fearful eyes to be hovering exactly over Stratford.

'Dad,' she yelled, as she charged through the front door. 'You home?'

No answer.

She bounded up the stairs two at a time. Through her bedroom window she could see the part of the forest that adjoined their land, and the small footpath which her father used as a short cut when travelling by bus which he had been doing since petrol was rationed. One of the forest ponds, just beyond their boundary, shimmered in the half-light like a pool of liquid amber. Even in the midst of her anxiety the beauty of it got through to her.

The glow in the sky was spreading like a living thing, quivering and shooting up a shower of stars each time something combustible exploded. Thank God, she thought, that Leo was out of danger. By her reckoning his hospital would have been one of the first casualties.

She was hailed from below. It was her father who had reached the garden unnoticed. 'Don't you think you had better close the window and draw the black-out curtains,' he suggested mildly.

'The light isn't on.'

'I can see the light from the landing behind you.'

She hastily drew the curtains in her bedroom and in the other upstairs rooms including the bathroom and lavatory. Dealing with the black-out was the first priority as soon as daylight began to fade. Tonight when it was more than ever essential she had forgotten.

She jumped the last few stairs to the hall and into her father's arms. 'Dad – what's going on!'

He held her at arm's length and stared at her appalled. 'What on earth have you done to your hair. It looks like candy floss!'

'Oh, never mind about my hair now. I want to know what's happened to Stratford. Is it still there?'

'As far as I know. Why should it not be?' He turned her round and studied her from all angles. 'I don't like it. I don't like it one bit. I liked you better with your page-boy bob, it made you look demure. Now you look as if you've been electrocuted.'

'I don't know how you can joke at a time like this,' she said, almost in tears. 'I got caught in the raid and my hair dried before it could be set. Oh Dad, it looks as if the whole East End is on fire.'

'It is on fire,' her father said, solemn now. 'The Jerries have lit a flare path with their incendiary bombs and they'll be back with the heavy stuff as soon as it's dark.'

'You don't really believe that?'

'I'm afraid I do, Pippa.' And even as he spoke the warning sounded.

Philippa eased her aching bones, stretched and turned once more on to her other side. If we're going to make a habit of this, she thought, we'd better do something about these mattresses. Three inches of straw-filled palliasse was no protection against the hardness of the cellar floor.

As a shelter the cellar could not to be bettered. As

somewhere to sleep it left a lot to be desired. Her father had given up trying. He was sitting up and reading by the light of a Tilly lamp. There was an electric light hanging from the ceiling but too far away to read by. The Tilly lamp was bright, but hissed and spluttered though not loud enough to mask that other more menacing sound – the drone of enemy planes and the distant thud of bombs.

'What's the time, Dad?'

'Half past three.'

'We've been down here nearly eight hours. Is that possible?'

'I'm afraid so, and likely to become a habit.' He looked with distaste at their surroundings. 'We'd better do something about making this place more comfortable. We've had a year thinking about it, and so far done nothing. Shame on us.' He sounded tired. 'Fancy a cup of tea, Pip?'

'You're not going to risk going upstairs?'

'I certainly am. I want to stretch my legs. Tea or coffee?'

'Tea please, and if there's anything to eat... I'm starving.'

He was back in less than twenty minutes with a flask of tea and a plate of luncheon-meat sandwiches. He had changed into flannels and a sweater.

'There's a marvellous display outside,' he said, as he poured tea. 'Searchlights, tracer bullets, flashes of fire when the guns go off, and great flares. If I weren't concerned for your safety Pip, I'd send you up to take a look.'

'I'm quite happy to go without a look, thank you.'

'Show a little imagination, girl. You're living in history.'

'I could live without history, too,' she said morbidly, thinking that tonight, if things had been different, she would have been with Leo gazing up at the stars over the Isles of Scilly, not at tracer bullets over London.

They had chosen Scilly for their honeymoon, or rather Leo had, for he had spent many a school holiday with his relatives in Penzance and from there had often watched the *Scillionian* set off for the 'Fortunate Isles'. Now Scilly was part of the coastal defences out of bounds to visitors, and marriage, until the war was over, was out of the question anyway.

Her father, cup in one hand, saucer in the other, said, 'I've been thinking, Philippa, you've got two weeks' holiday in front of you. I'd like you to go off somewhere quiet . . . away from London.'

'I'm not leaving you . . . I'm not running off to some bolthole, waiting all on edge, for news of you.'

His answer was drowned in a sudden loud burst of gunfire, then a whine and a crump. 'That was too near for comfort,' he said in the lull that followed. Then, 'Be reasonable, Pip. What about me being all on edge, worrying about you? Go and stay with Aunt Dot. You'll be company for her. I don't suppose she's feeling too happy about us, either.'

'You know we can't get permission to visit defence areas. You tried.'

'Aunt Dot hasn't tried. An elderly lady, living on her own? Who's going to refuse her a permit?'

'I'm staying put until I've heard how Leo is getting on,' she answered stubbornly.

He gave up and turned back to his book. Philippa tried to compose herself for sleep. A distant whine she mistook for another bomb was, she realised a moment later, an early tram. It was reassuring to know that life was going on as usual. She fell asleep as the All Clear sounded.

She woke suddenly. She lay in complete darkness trying to orientate herself. Then it all came back. She groped for her torch and beamed it on her watchface. Eight o'clock! Next she beamed it on her father. He was fast asleep, still wearing his glasses, his book open facedown on his chest. She slipped it from under his hand; it was a slim, calf-bound, much-fingered copy of the *Rubáiyát of Omar Khayyám*. A present from his wife on their wedding day.

She heard the telephone ringing above her. She grabbed her slippers and dressing-gown and belted up the cellar steps fearful that it might stop before she reached it.

'Oh Leo, darling, I was praying it was you.'

He was all concern for her, for his parents, for his friends at the hospital. He had phoned the hospital first, in dread, and was relieved to hear it had only suffered minor damage. His ex-colleagues had worked throughout the night, patching up casualties. A fleet of temporary ambulances was standing by to ferry the wounded to safety.

'You're on holiday,' he said. 'Why don't you take the opportunity to find somewhere more quiet – away from London . . .' Almost exactly her father's words. Had there been collusion?

'I could always come and join you in Aldershot.'

He took her seriously. 'That's not what I meant. You couldn't come here, it's a military zone. I can't help worrying about you. Don't take any risks. Do take care of yourself.'

'You too,' she said. She replaced the receiver, disappointed that the call had been short and uninformative, with no endearments. Oddly, Leo never addressed her by her name but he was generous with terms like darling and sweetheart. Possibly there was a queue behind him all anxious to speak to loved ones. But he had phoned the hospital before he phoned her and she was ashamed of herself for minding.

'Let's get out into the fresh air,' said her father when they had breakfasted. 'I feel I've been breathing in coal dust all night. You too?'

'We were going to do something about the cellar.'

'That can wait. Let's take advantage of this fine weather while it lasts.'

It was more like midsummer than September, warmer in fact, warm enough to go out in a short-sleeved blouse tucked into her navy-blue slacks. Her hair, having been flattened by her pillow, was not so fuzzy this morning and under a wide bandeau was hardly noticeable. Her father too was in casual wear. A pair of disreputable but spotless cords, his alpaca coat, a panama yellowed by countless summers, and his walking-stick which he used mostly to keep dogs at bay and to flick into the gutter any empty packets or cigarette ends, sweet wrappers or banana skins that lay in his path. He was a fastidious man and any sign of litter was an offence to him. A greater offence was what Aunt Dot called a dog's 'visiting card'. At the sight of one of these, his nostrils would quiver and his eyes flash.

'Who is responsible for this abomination?' he would cry at the top of his voice and Philippa would hurry ahead pretending she had no connection with him.

But litter or fouled pavements had no power to annoy him this morning. He walked preoccupied, reliving the events of the night. There was no visible sign of bomb damage, but more people seemed to be about than was usual on Sundays. The women had left their stoves in order to be with their husbands and children; perhaps, Philippa thought, after the events of the night families had a strong inclination to stay together.

'I have a feeling,' her father said, 'that the Moletrap will be very popular this morning. It's the sort of place people make for when they hope to run into someone they know.'

They followed the route that Jonathan Byrd usually took when out for his Sunday constitutional, leaving the main road and taking a bridle track through the forest. Epping Forest had been Philippa's stamping ground for as long as she could remember. Here, in the spring, she knew where to find the first violets, and in summer wild mushrooms, and later on blackberries and sloes. Here, Leo and she had done most of their courting, and on many a tree-trunk and ancient log Leo had carved their initials. PAB and LB, encircled in a heart.

'Change the name but not the letter, marry for worse and not for better,' Aunt Dot had quoted on more than one occasion. Philippa just laughed.

Her father was right. The Moletrap was crowded inside and out. Philippa found a vacant seat in the piece of rough grassland that served as a garden and promptly claimed it. Nothing could induce her to go inside on a day like this for the bar was thick with cigarette smoke. It was an attractive little inn with its original wide brick fireplace still intact and heavy oak beams supporting sagging ceilings. It had the reputation of giving shelter to Dick Turpin when he was wanted for horse stealing and highway robbery, but then many of the little public houses on the fringe of the forest made the same claim.

Over the squat and crooked doorway was nailed a notice, 'Duck or Grouse', which, on her first visit, had to be explained to her.

She was fifteen then and feeling very much an adult accompanying her father to a public house, something that was looked upon as unconventional and almost sinful in a girl of her age. But Jonathan had never been one to uphold convention and he made sure that Philippa had nothing stronger than lemonade or ginger-beer to drink. Sitting there in the garden, surrounded by the forest trees and feeling rather self-conscious as she sipped her drink, her eyes came to rest on a large water butt with a notice pinned above which said, 'Please do not disturb the water otter.'

'What is a *water* otter?' she asked, puzzled.

'Presumably an otter that likes water.'

'But all otters like water.'

'Perhaps this one prefers static water.'

'He's got to come up to breathe. I wish he would come up – I'd love to see him.'

'Well, give him a little nudge. There's a chain – pull it and see.'

'But it says not to disturb . . .'

There was a pause while Jonathan Byrd rolled and lit a cigarette. 'I didn't know I had such a law-abiding daughter,' he said. 'Go on, it won't bite you.'

She pulled up the chain and found tethered to its other end a rusty kettle.

'Ha ha – *very* funny,' she said, colouring up. Her anger was directed not so much towards her father who enjoyed his amusement quietly, but to a noisy group at the next table who were beside themselves with laughter. When you are fifteen years old and on your first adult excursion it comes hard to find yourself the butt of a childish joke. However, later that year she met Leo at the Scouts dance, and any free time in future was in hock to him.

There was no interest in the water otter this morning, not even among the children skipping expectantly around their parents waiting for the promised treats of lemonade and arrowroot biscuits. Philippa, sipping her port and lemon, a cocoction that made her father shudder, listened in to bits of broken conversation.

'Quite a show they put on last night, Bert...'

'Did you 'ear that last stick of bombs come down? One fell in the allotments behind us, put paid to Tom Reynolds's marrer... He was 'oping to get a First in the show next week.' Laughter.

'Blew my fox fur right off the hallstand and into the cellar...'

'Must have been a landmine. It shook the foundations.'

'Woodside got off lightly, I didn't see any damage, coming along, did you? Reckon the East End copped it as usual.'

'Surrey Docks, I heard...'

'You believe they'll come again tonight, then?'

'Stands to reason...'

There was no anger or fear or even resentment in the voices around her. Instead a subdued arousal and 'a Britain can take it' attitude. Another example of the stiff upper lip syndrome? she asked herself and believed it until she looked again at their faces. In the eyes of some of the women, especially those with children, she saw a dread that made mockery of their laughing voices.

She had been separated from her father. He was several yards away talking to a golfing friend, and in the space between them a group of three soldiers, young enough to be National Servicemen, were making eyes at her. She ignored them. Silly boys, she thought, though secretly flattered. Little more than schoolboys, still wet behind the ears, lacking the charm and glamour of the foreign soldiers who thronged the streets of the West End, yet their cheeky grins and bold stares reminded her that she was not unattractive to the opposite sex and that she could, any time she liked, make Leo jealous. But could she? It was that doubt which stopped her putting her theory to the test.

Just then she became aware that her attention was being sought by yet another soldier. An officer, in service dress, hailing her with his cane.

Philippa had one secret she managed to keep from everybody except her father, Leo, Aunt Dotty and her closest friends. She was extremely short-sighted. Her near sight was good, almost perfect, she had no need of glasses for reading, but an arm's length away she saw everything as through a mist which gave her grey eyes an enigmatic expression, and was the envy of other girls.

'Philippa has unusual eyes,' one said of her.

'Sexy, you mean,' countered another. 'Are her lashes her own, do you think?'

Philippa, squinting into the sun, saw her father turn and go across to the young officer and shake him warmly by the hand. The penny dropped. 'Leo!' she yelled, jumping up and waving.

She would have gone to him, pushed her way through the throng if necessary, but he was already working his way to her, wearing the self-conscious grin he usually wore when he had done something clever. The three young National Servicemen made way for him, then putting their heads together began to snigger.

'Didn't expect to see me again so soon, did you?' he said when he reached her side.

How attractive he looked in uniform. How it suited him. It was hard to stop herself flinging her arms round his neck, but that she knew would be breaking the rules of his code. Her eyes devoured him. 'Why didn't you tell me you were coming? You said nothing about it on the phone.'

'I didn't know myself until a couple of hours ago. I didn't have time to ring you then, I only had time to ring my parents. Ramsey was getting impatient. You remember Steve Ramsey? He was at school with me, then went up to Cambridge to study medicine. Got his calling-up papers the same week I did. He has this rather super car, an Alvis, and what's more, petrol to go with it. Not surprising as his father owns a string of garages. He didn't have to ask me twice if I wanted a lift home. His young lady lives at Loughton, and it's on his way. I knew this was one of your father's favourite haunts and so when I couldn't get an answer at your place, I came on here.'

'How long have you got – leave, I mean?' she said eagerly.

'We're not exactly on leave. We've just slipped away for a few hours. Steve is picking me up again at seven. Oh sweetie, don't take it like that. I'll be back again before long, on official leave next time, I hope.'

She swallowed her disappointment. 'I'll keep you to that. But you'll come back and have lunch with us?'

'I wish I could, but I'm expected back at Belle Vue Road, and – I hope you don't mind – you're expected there too, for tea.'

She was horrified. 'Oh, Leo . . . just like that, without any warning!'

'How much warning do you need? I've been pleading with you for months. Please, dear, say yes or we won't have any time together.' He broke off as Jonathan, who had been hanging back, joined them. 'I'm trying to persuade Philippa to come to my place for tea. Well, not so much tea but to meet my people. I don't think I'm going to have much luck.'

'You must go, Pippa,' her father said, and as she never went against him when he spoke in that tone of voice the matter was settled.

'Quid pro quo, my boy. Come home with us and share our lunch. We haven't a calf we could fatten but I'm sure we could rustle up a tin of bully beef.'

Leo never felt quite at home with his future father-in-law, never knowing if his leg was being pulled or not. Banter between the generations was something unheard of in his family. He made his apologies. Roast beef and two veg were awaiting him at Belle Vue Road, he said.

'You had it pretty bad last night? We could see the glow from the fire all the way from Aldershot. There's been an exodus from the barracks today, the men checking up on their families. I was dreading what I would find when I got here after what we saw coming through the East End. Comparatively speaking Woodside has been let off lightly.'

'Yes, we were lucky here – but some parts of London, where you used to be for instance . . .' There was a moment's silence fraught with unspoken misgivings, then Jonathan roused himself and slapped Leo on the back. 'If you can't stay for lunch, at least come back for a quickie.'

They started off three abreast, but Jonathan soon fell behind. Philippa drew closer to Leo.

'Am I allowed to hold hands with a man in uniform,' she said cheekily.

'Only when you're in danger of being attacked.'

'Any chance of my being attacked now?'

'Not with your father watching.'

They were taking the short cut through the forest. In places where the track was narrow they had to walk single file. There were signs of the approach of autumn – in the bracken, in the leaves of the silver birches and the oaks, all now turning bronze or yellow. Philippa took a deep breath. 'I love the forest in autumn,' she said.

'I remember you saying you loved it best in the spring.'

'I love it all the year round.'

'You love too easily, sweetheart.'

Behind them her father was slashing away at some intruding brambles. Leo did not know quite what to do with his cane. She felt it would not be long before he discarded it altogether.

When they turned into Forest Way he looked at his watch and decided not to stay for that quickie after all. 'By the time we've had tea and you've been taken around the garden,' he said, 'for my father is sure to want you to see his chrysanthemums, it will be time for me to think about leaving.'

She stood with her father at the gate of their house and watched Leo as he picked his way through the dust of the unadopted road. At the corner he turned and touched the peak of his cap with the cane by way of a salute. Philippa blew him a kiss. He was gone. 'There seems something not quite right about his harness,' she said.

'That, my dear, is a Sam Browne belt and yes, there is something not quite right with it. Something quite wrong, in fact. The strap should go from the right shoulder across the back and fasten at the left-hand side of his waist. He's wearing it straight down instead of diagonally.'

Her eyes widened indignantly. 'Is that why those three young idiots were sniggering!'

'I shouldn't be at all surprised. At that age they snigger at anything.'

'At Leo's expense. Oh, how beastly... If you knew what was wrong why didn't you tell him?'

'And make him feel foolish. Such a trivial thing to get upset about, Pippa.'

'But I *am* upset. Would you like somebody sniggering at you behind your back.' Her voice rose. 'And he travelled all the way from Aldershot with his belt like that, with people taking the mickey no doubt. Why didn't his friend warn him?'

'Perhaps because he didn't know any better. A couple of rookies, first time out in uniform. But they'll learn, and Leo pretty soon I should think from what you tell me about his father. He'll have no qualms about speaking his mind.'

'Oh Dad, don't rub it in – I've got to face him this afternoon. Two precious hours of Leo's time spent with his parents. How could Leo have let me in for such an ordeal? I'm dreading it.'

'The dread is all in your mind, girlie. I daresay the Brookes are no more looking forward to it than you are. Why don't you go upstairs and change into something pretty and do something about your hair. Preferably shave it off.'

He went off to the kitchen whistling, and presently Philippa could hear a clatter of pans. Her father was a better cook than she and concocting a meal for Sunday lunch was one of the things he was good at.

She trailed upstairs, dragging her feet. First impressions were important and she knew that any of the pretty dresses in her wardrobe couldn't cancel out the impact of her hair on a woman who thought that all artificial aids to beauty were a form of vanity. Unfortunately, Leo shared his mother's views to some extent. He hated Philippa wearing lipstick and once he accused her of using mascara too lavishly.

She was so incensed, she pulled one of her lashes out to show him. 'Look,' she said. 'Take that home and look at it under your microscope. You won't see any mascara on that. It's all my own work.'

'Nature's you mean.' Then he laughed, and hugged her. 'I adore it when you get your rag out – your pupils enlarge which makes your eyes look black. You're so easy to tease, sweetheart, but I wouldn't have you any other way.'

She wouldn't change him either. So stern and masterful one minute, like an overgrown schoolboy the next. She loved him so much it hurt.

There wasn't much to choose from in her wardrobe but the few things she had were good. The grey marocain with the white collar and cuffs was a leftover from her school-days, worn at the last speechday. Its simple style never dated, and it still fitted well. If anything, she was slimmer now than she was then. She would rather have worn her white voile with the red polka dots, which her father called her 'tart's dress' because of the way it clung to her figure, but she thought the grey marocain would go down better at Belle Vue Road.

When she had finished dressing she went downstairs for her father's approval. 'Very smart, very chic. From the neck down I can't fault you. Pity about the hair though.'

Leo arrived on the dot of three looking more like himself in his old school blazer and baggy flannels. He rarely made any comment on her appearance but today he was driven to it. 'Gordon Bennett! What have you done to your hair!'

'I made the mistake of having it permed during an air raid, but I wasn't to know that when I made the appointment. Don't worry, it will look better when I have it set – tomorrow, I hope.'

'You mean you're coming home with me looking like that?'

'I'm afraid so, unless we can find some obliging person willing to scalp me.' She was near tears.

Leo looked down in the mouth. 'I like it best the way it was.'

'So do I but I can't do anything about it now.'

Jonathan put in a timely word. 'I see you've changed into civvies, Leo. Find them more comfortable, eh?'

'Uniform has many pitfalls,' said Leo sheepishly, and with that admission the subject of the Sam Browne was laid to rest. Not so Philippa's unfortunate hair-do.

'You're ashamed of me,' she said when they got outside. 'You're wondering what your mother will think. I don't suppose she's ever had her hair permed.'

'She hasn't even had it cut, my father wouldn't allow it.'

They had been walking with daylight between them,

now Leo reached for and took her hand. 'It isn't just what my mother thinks, it's more that you don't look like yourself any more. Your hair always looked like silk. Now it looks like hay.'

'Thank you. That makes me feel a lot better.' But she wasn't as peeved as she sounded. Leo was not one for paying compliments – but hair like silk! It was the most romantic thing he had ever said to her.

He said apologetically, 'The trouble is we're both terribly on edge – what with me going into the army and you having such a disturbed night. Darling – I can't stop worrying about you. Why don't you take your father's advice and go and stay with your aunt for a while?'

'She's not on the phone. I'd feel so cut off from everybody. Besides, the threat of invasion still hangs over us and I'd hate to be down at Leigh-on-Sea, with my father here, and you goodness knows where if anything happened. I want us all to be together.'

'I think the threat of invasion is the least of our worries. When was it Hitler said he'd be marching down Whitehall? August the eighth? That was a month ago today, and before that the invasion was due sometime in July, I believe. I don't think we have much to worry about from that quarter. But these raids... they are a different matter. Please go and stay with your aunt. You could always persuade her to have the phone connected.'

It was a two-mile walk from her side of Woodside to Belle Vue Road, a distance that in the past, waiting for Leo to call, Philippa had thought too long by half. Today it seemed not long enough.

Woodside, now a sprawling conurbation had, a century ago, been four separate and independent rural communities. Woodside Green, Woodside Wells, Woodside Bridge and South Woodside, all now joined by new housing estates and major roads. Pride in their boundaries, however, kept each different part of Woodside as an individual entity, each with its own shopping centre, church and school. It wasn't surprising then that Philippa and Leo, living within walking distance of each other all their lives, had never met until that night of the Scouts dance at nearby Buckhurst Hill. As with Leo then so with his parents now – she didn't know them even by sight. His sister Phoebe she would recognise, but that wasn't surprising. A woman on a motor bike was not that common, even for Woodside.

Philippa had always been the envy of her friends for living not in a street, but in a forest clearing. Great-great-grandfather Byrd had built his house in a woodland glade at a time when Epping Forest was there for the taking. Whole swaths of the primeval forest were being enclosed or encroached upon by those powerful or wealthy enough to get away with it until a public outcry at the loss of commoners' rights forced the government to take action. Queen Victoria's visit to Chingford in 1882 (an event that Great-Aunt Dot remembered as one of the highlights of her life) was to mark the occasion when the Lord Mayor of London declared amid ceremony that the forest was 'open and dedicated to the delectation of the public for ever'.

By this time the two maples that Jonathan Byrd the First had planted in the front garden of his substantial residence had grown into mature and beautiful trees, but whether the family was called upon to pay recompense for his little bit of jiggery-pokery was never known. What was a fact, however, was that The Maples, as he had named his villa, having those words boldly painted in gold leaf on the fanlight above the front door, was never known by that name. Byrd's House it became, and Byrd's House, Forest Way, it still was and would continue to be, Philippa suspected, even when the last Byrd had flown the nest.

And the same with Belle Vue Road, her thoughts continued. The view had changed but not the name. The large bay windows now overlooked a widened highway where trams and buses and an ever increasing number of private cars had taken over from greensward and trees. Yet the houses still clung to their semi-rural roots and displayed names like Brackens and Everglades and Forest View. There were many instances of modernisation, not always successful, such as crazy paving replacing the Victorian tiles of the garden paths. Some of the houses had exchanged the original dark paint of the woodwork for two-tone shades of lighter colours, or in some instances grain and varnish which had become very fashionable in the early thirties. Not number 33, however. There were no modern touches about it, whatsoever. Thrift or sentiment? she wondered. Thrift, she suspected. The front garden was small and completely enclosed by a privet hedge. Partially closed Venetian blinds afforded privacy to anyone sitting in the bay. She felt herself under scrutiny as she followed Leo up the garden path.

'Well,' said her father. 'You look as if you survived. You came home all in one piece, anyway.'

'It wasn't quite the ordeal I expected,' she admitted.

'Nothing is ever as we anticipate. You'll realise that by the time you're my age.' He paused to make another cigarette. He preferred to roll his own, thin, weedy, delicate little things, hardly thicker than a matchstick and difficult to keep alight. 'What do you think of the improvements?'

The expected warning had already sounded and they were back in the cellar which, with the help of their nearest neighbour, a forest-keeper who lived even deeper in the forest than they did, Jonathan Byrd had transformed while Philippa was out visiting. The straw palliasses had given place to camp-beds, unearthed from the attic and belonging to his army days; army blankets too, khaki and grey. 'I hope you aired them,' said Philippa doubtfully.

The powerful spotlight on a long lead that belonged in the garage was now hanging over their beds, and Lloyd Loom chairs from the bedrooms added a homely touch of comfort. The cellar floor had been thoroughly swept and all trace of coal dust removed, and the heap of coal stored at the further end was covered over by a green tarpaulin.

'There's still a lot more to be done,' said her father, pausing again to relight his cigarette. 'But at least it's better than it was.'

'You must think these raids are going on for ever or you wouldn't have gone to all this trouble.'

'Not for ever, Pip. Just until Hitler gives up trying or makes a false move. Now tell me about your party.'

'Not exactly a party, Dad.'

The introductions had been rather formal. Mr Brooke had addressed her as Miss Byrd which momentarily floored her, but Mrs Brooke did not address her at all, just gave her a look that took in at one swift glance her hair and the varnish on her nails which she had forgotten to remove. When Leo pulled out a chair at the table and said, 'Sit here, dear', she heard a muttered '*Dear*, is it!'

which was Mrs Brooke's only spoken contribution at the tea table.

Mr Brooke wasn't much of a conversationalist either, not while there was still food on the table. Philippa was used to mealtimes as opportunities for light-hearted conversation, but for the Brookes it was a time for serious eating. Leo was fond of quoting his mother who said, 'Sauces are only used for covering up poor cooking' and 'Only lazy housewives serve meals out of tins,' and Philippa had gained the impression that Mrs Brooke was a superior cook. Now seeing the evidence on the table she began to feel she had been deceived.

Tinned pilchards and *tinned* fruit? Difficult to come by now unless one had a well-stocked store cupboard. Homemade jam, naturally. She had listened with awe to Leo telling her that his mother made seventy-five pounds of jam a year from fruit grown in the garden. The jam she had on her plate hadn't set. Either Mrs Brooke hadn't boiled it sufficiently or she had been too economical with the sugar. Philippa, trying to spoon some on to her bread, dropped a blob on the tablecloth. She felt herself go hot.

'Don't bother about that, Miss Byrd,' said Mr Brooke as she surreptitiously tried to mop it up with her napkin. 'That happens all the time with Mother's jam. It's a family joke that we don't know whether to spread it or drink it.'

Family jokes! Things were certainly looking up. She threw a reproachful glance across the table at Leo who was spooning up the runny jam quite happily. How could he have so misled her. Her reproach turned to indulgence. How could you blame a boy for thinking everything his mother did was wonderful? She hoped one day Leo's son would feel the same about her.

After tea came a tour of the garden. Philippa tried hard to enthuse, but how could one enthuse over a long rectangular plot given over to the exclusive cultivation of things to eat?

Not a tree in sight except fruit trees. No shrubs but plenty of fruit bushes. Rows of regimented vegetables, but no lawns or flowerbeds. No flowers either except chrysanthemums in the greenhouse with heads as big as cabbages. Growing chrysanthemums, Mr Brooke said, was his occupation since becoming retired. And growing food was a necessity with a large family, he added. If they all ate as he did she could see the point, but where did all the food go now that their daughter was evacuated with her school, and Leo was living away from home, and there was only he and his wife to cater for? Bottled and preserved she suspected, for she couldn't see anything going to waste in that thrifty household.

The rest of the afternoon went quickly. Every minute brought the parting with Leo closer. She wouldn't allow him to see her home though he was anxious to, as he had to change and be ready for Steve Ramsay by seven. As she was leaving, Mr Brooke presented her with a bunch of chrysanthemums.

She was so overwhelmed by this unexpected gesture she overdid her thanks to the point of sounding sycophantic. Mr Brooke beamed with gratification. He shook hands and told her she must call in any time she was passing and not wait until Leo brought her. Mrs Brooke mumbled something inaudible.

Leo was like a puppy with two tails as he walked her to the end of the road. 'He likes you, he was quite smitten with you. I've never known him give any of his chrysanthemums away before.'

They reached the corner. He took her hands in his, his eyes suddenly and suspiciously bright. 'I'll be home again as soon as I can,' he promised. 'In any case I'll ring you when I get back to camp. Take care of yourself, and don't do anything foolhardy like going out during a raid. And do think seriously about going to Leigh.'

His lips brushed her cheek. Only in the dark did he let himself go. On a fine Sunday evening with people about, as much as he wanted to, he couldn't.

She walked away and every time she looked back he was still there, watching her. A forlorn figure, he looked, as forlorn as she was feeling. Would partings always hurt like this, she wondered? Would the pain never cease? She tried not to think of that final, inevitable parting that an embarkation leave would bring. But the thought persisted like a maggot, nibbling away at her peace of mind.

Her father said, 'That was a very deep sigh you just gave. What's on your mind, Pip?'

'It's only that I hate partings . . .'

'We're not back to hair-styles, are we?'

'Please Dad, I'm not in the mood for jokes.'

He reached across and squeezed her hand.

'Are you in the mood to tell me about this afternoon? You must have made a good impression. I expected you home with a migraine, instead you came with chrysanthemums. Did you have Mr Brooke eating out of your hand?'

She smiled at that, not because of the absurdity of the suggestion, but because eating was such a suitable word in connection with Leo's father.

Jonathan was persistent. He wanted to know more about the tea party as he insisted on calling it. 'Tell me; is Mrs Brooke the superb cook Leo has led us to believe?'

'I think superb is hardly the word, but she makes the kind of fruit cake you prefer . . .'

'Remind me.'

'Sunk in the middle.'

'Sensible woman. Much better flavour – more moist. Something to do with the fat content, I believe . . .'

His words hung on the air, unheard and unanswered. They listened as a stick of bombs screamed down. A scream. A thud – another scream, another thud; nearer – nearer – nearer – then not so near. They breathed again.

'Would you like that cup of coffee now,' her father said, rising.

'Is there any left?'

'Enough for you.'

'What about you?'

'Personally, I prefer something stronger.' He went across to the cupboard where he had laid in a small stock of what he called, apologising for the pun, his spirit booster. He poured out a glass and toasted Philippa's future.

'It's bad luck to talk about a future with bombs dropping all around us,' she said.

'You have a future. Don't you remember the fortune-teller on Southend Pier telling you you would marry a professional man and have four sons?'

'Chance would be a fine thing,' she said sorrowfully.

In the Anderson shelter buried deep in the garden of number 33 Belle Vue Road, Mr and Mrs Brooke were preparing themselves for the long and noisy night ahead. Not for them sleeping rough in their clothes, they did it properly. Mr Brooke even wore a night-cap to protect his bald pate from the cold coming off the metal sides of the shelter. Mrs Brooke wore her hair in a scanty plait, a cardigan over her flannelette nightgown, and knitted bedsocks. As an extra precaution against the cold she had two hot-water bottles, one for her feet and one to cuddle. On the tea-chest between the two bunks was a lighted candle, a torch, a flask of tea, a packet of sandwiches and Samuel Brooke's top set of teeth in a tumbler of water.

'What did you think of the girl, Mother? Pretty little thing, wasn't she?' Lack of teeth had no effect on his lung power.

'Clever too.' Sniff. 'She knew when to say yes and no in the right places.'

Mr Brooke was surprised at the tone of his wife's voice. Normally it was flat and unemotional. 'You're not put out because I gave her a few chrysanthemums? They were only the ones not good enough for the show. I would have given them to you, but you always complain that they drop their petals on the floor.'

'So they do by the time I get them...'

'Look Em, if you're worried about that girl, forget it. It won't come to anything – it's just calf love.... She'll be no good as a wife to Leo. He needs someone who will nanny him – someone capable of taking charge. The chap's an idiot – didn't even know how to wear his Sam Browne until I showed him. Good grief, hasn't he got eyes in his head. There's been enough officers walking the streets for the past twelve months. You would have thought he'd notice how they wore their belts. I even had to look up the time of the train to Aldershot for him on Friday. He knows his anatomy book inside out, but he can't read a bally timetable.'

'Only because you've never let him try for himself.' His wife was quick in defence of her youngest child. 'And don't fool yourself about calf love – they'll be talking weddings next.'

'There's no question of a wedding. The boy can only just manage to keep himself, so how can he hope to support a wife? He hasn't got a bean behind him and I'm jiggered if he is going to get another penny from me. I've spent more on him than all the others put together. He'll just have to wait until he can afford to marry as I had to, and that won't be for years yet.'

'Things are different now. They get married first and worry about the expense later.'

Mr Brooke blew out the candle. It was an effective way of stopping any further conversation. Within minutes he was asleep and the walls of the shelter vibrated with the sound of his snores. Mrs Brooke gave up any hope of sleep herself. As she feared, it was going to be a long and noisy night.

Three

Philippa's previous visit to Leigh was during the cloudless days of May when the British Expeditionary Force was in full retreat before the advancing German Army. Not the sort of weather conducive to despair, yet despair blanketed the country then like a funeral pall. Now in September it was just as sunny and the skies as cloudless, but the pall had gone. The unthinkable had happened, France had fallen, but they were still jogging on, refusing to admit defeat.

She looked back from the station on a sea as calm as a lake. Hitler's weather, they called it. Sunshine all the way for him, she thought. Whatever happened to 'The sun shines on the righteous'? Put in cold storage for the duration?

A frightening rattle of equipment and a barked challenge startled her out of her wits. She froze, staring blankly at the armed sentry who had sprung into her path. Her mouth went dry, her heart thudded. She felt as foolish as the time she disturbed the water otter. She couldn't speak. Then she saw a flicker of laughter in the sentry's eyes and indignation swamped all other feelings. Two can play at this game, she thought, and waited.

He lowered his rifle. 'Where you off to then?' he said chattily.

'To visit my aunt. Her house is up there. I have a permit – do I have to show it?'

He stood aside. 'Pass, friend.'

No friend of yours, she muttered crossly but she passed, and further along passed also a newly erected blockhouse from which the faces of two further armed soldiers grinned out at her. She had hardly got over the threshold of Cliff Cottage before pouring out her grievances. 'It made me feel such an idiot.'

Aunt Dot chuckled. 'They wouldn't hurt you for the world. I expect they just get so bored waiting for fifth columnists and couldn't resist a little fun. I make them a pot of tea when I can spare it. My boys, I call them. One comes and does a bit of gardening for me when he's off duty. My dear, the place is full of soldiers – just like a garrison town. You'll find a few changes since you were here last.'

Changes? thought Philippa as she did her shopping in Leigh Broadway the following morning. Not so much a change as a complete metamorphosis. Aunt Dot was right. The once popular little seaside resort did now look like a garrison town. Civilians were in the minority, but those shops that still remained open were doing a brisk business and both cinemas, she noted, were advertising coming attractions.

She was out on some errands for Aunt Dot, and hopefully would find some cigarettes for Leo. He had mentioned a shortage at the camp during his brief visit on

Sunday. Only one packet per person allowed, she was told. The tobacconist's manner was grudging.

'Are they for yourself?'

'No, for my fiancé. He's in the army.'

At once another packet of twenty was produced from under the counter. 'Is that enough?'

'Plenty, thank you.' She didn't hold with under-the-counter transactions. She didn't hold with Leo smoking so much, either, as she was convinced it was bad for his health. It was something he had taken up as a student to help him keep awake during lectures, he said. He was no longer a student but he still couldn't do without his cigarettes.

Every officer she saw approaching made her hopes rise. She longed for Leo to surprise her as he had surprised her at the Moletrap. But from experience she knew that those sort of surprises rarely repeated themselves.

She saw a queue beginning to form outside a fishmonger's and crossed the road to join it. Such a stroke of luck to be in the right place at the right time and even luckier to get the last two pieces of smoked haddock on the almost empty slab. Two meals a day was becoming a problem and the haddock would do nicely for their supper. She wondered if Aunt Dot had enough butter to spare to go with it.

It had been a successful shopping venture on the whole. A savoury for supper, two packets of Goldflake for Leo, and she had been able to arrange for a phone to be installed at Cliff Cottage as soon as possible. Whether she would ever persuade Aunt Dot to use it was another matter.

She lingered on the pleasant walk back to the cliffs through leafy avenues and solid Edwardian houses. The day was warm and the sea looked inviting, but there would be no more swimming in these waters until the war was over. A seat overlooking the cliff gardens was unoccupied and she sat there for a while, not because she was tired, but because it seemed such a pity to be indoors on such a fine, and yes, she could safely add, peaceful day.

The atmosphere was so clear she could see the Kent coast quite distinctly and could, if she used her imagination, see the hills beyond. From this angle, the station on the lower road looked as if it were squatting on a breakwater. Nearer, and to her left, the roof of Cliff Cottage was visible through overhanging trees. The word cottage was rather a misnomer as it was quite a sizeable house, built by Aunt Dorothy's father as a weekend retreat when his family was young.

It was beginning to look its age now. Its timbers were rotting and it suffered from subsidence as did many of the other properties built on the side of the cliff. The garden had become a wilderness since the gardener, an ex-army man, had been recalled to duty, and it was a difficult garden to manage anyway, for it climbed almost perpendicularly from the back of the house to the upper road.

When she had visited Aunt Dot back in the spring she had sat on a deserted beach watching the gentle incoming sea and thinking of the men across the Channel queuing patiently for rescue on the beaches at Dunkirk. She could see that same beach where she had sat in the spring now barricaded behind barbed wire; the most popular beach on that part of the esplanade where visitors had gathered in peacetime to watch the concert party on summer evenings, and girls two or three abreast walked arm in arm in their summer dresses or beach pyjamas along what was known locally as the monkey parade, attracting admiring whistles or saucy winks from hopeful young bloods.

It was all so innocent then, she thought. Holiday flirtations that came to nothing. War clouds were already gathering but when you are young the sun seems forever shining. She was amused to find herself thinking like some middle-aged woman lamenting her lost youth. I'm not twenty-two yet, she thought. Her birthday was in November, Leo's in August. He had been twenty-five last birthday. She had given him a pair of gold cuff-links, spending more on him than she could really afford, and now what chance would he have to wear gold cuff-links in the army?

The tide was full and the open-air swimming pool that jutted out into the sea was practically submerged. 'The cleanest pool in Essex,' her father said of it. 'It gets washed twice a day.' If not the cleanest it was certainly the coldest and, at high tide, the deepest.

Philippa had learnt to swim in that pool during one of her visits to Leigh, for every summer Aunt Dot opened her house and they spent the school holidays there with her father joining them for weekends. He kept a small sailing dinghy on a running mooring near the pool, and on fine summer evenings he would take her sailing.

They would sometimes sail over to Canvey Point, to a sandy beach where Philippa would paddle and her father smoke one of his limp cigarettes and the gulls would scream abuse at them for invading their territory. Returning from one of these trips one evening a sudden summer squall blew up, drenching them within minutes. The only other craft in sight was a dinghy similar to theirs but larger, with orange sails and a helmsman in oilskins the same colour. At least he had some protection from the weather. Her father had on a linen coat and she her school blazer, both now so sodden they looked the same colour.

The storm fascinated her. She loved nature in all its moods, even when as frightening as it was then. There was something awesome about its savagery as lightning split the low black clouds and rain slashed against them horizontally. Their boat bobbed up and down like a cork. She sheltered under the transom as best she could and prayed. Her father mouthed, 'Feeling all right?' and she nodded.

The bigger boat made its way towards them and as it got nearer they recognised the man at the helm as Dr Campbell, Aunt Dot's GP and also a keen sailor. He manoeuvred alongside, got a hold on their gunwale, and bobbed up and down in company.

'You wouldn't have such a thing as a match, would you,' he said. 'My pipe's gone out.'

Jonathan felt in his jacket pocket and brought out a sodden box of matches. 'I don't think they'll be much use.'

'Aw weel, I'll just have to do wi'out. You're managing?'

'Fine . . . everything's fine. . . .'

'And the lassie. How are you, Philippa?'

'A bit wet.'

Dr Campbell chuckled. The rain dripped off the tip of his nose. 'Tell Miss Byrd I'll call on her tomorrow, just to see if ye're none the worse. It's at a time like this we could do with a wee engine,' he added.

'It's at a time like this I could do with a wee dram,' Jonathan countered.

Dr Campbell agreed. 'You'll have to wait until tomorrow night – at the yacht club. My treat.' The last two words were brought to them on the wind as he shouted them over his shoulder. They watched him sail away until he was just a blurred orange blob lost in the rain.

'Fancy worrying about a smoke at a time like this,' Philippa said impatiently.

'I think he was worrying more about us. The match was just a ruse to see if we needed help.'

'And we don't?'

'I think we can manage, don't you?'

'You're enjoying this aren't you, Daddy?'

'Let's just say I've been in worse situations.'

And where are all those little boats now, she thought, scanning the empty moorings, the yachts, the cruisers, the launches and dinghies. The little boats of Leigh that had done their part in the evacuation from Dunkirk. Stored away, those that had survived, until the war was over?

She rose reluctantly to her feet. Aunt Dot would be wondering what was keeping her. Standing up she had a better view along the estuary. As far as the eye could see the beaches were closed to the public, safeguarded by rolls of barbed wire, and nobody in their right mind would force an entry on to the sands, fearing them to be mined. The promenade was still open to the public, but many of the large houses and hotels and even the pier had been requisitioned by the army. Wouldn't it be wonderful if Leo could be posted here, she thought. But things didn't work out like that in real life.

On the second day of her visit she went shopping (or rather, scouting for that was what shopping was like these days, scouting for things before they disappeared) in the opposite direction, along the London Road towards Southend through a part of the town that had suffered most by the exodus of its former occupants. Shop after shop had its shutters up or blinds down. One or two sported notices that read, 'Business as usual' but was it usual? Butchers had meat for sale, but on ration cards only. Fishmongers' slabs were empty and greengrocers had only homegrown produce on offer.

Milliners and dress shops were still well stocked, and Philippa dawdled to admire the latest in autumn fashions. Since she had changed her hair-style none of her present hats suited her, but she was reluctant to spend out on replacing them. Should Leo have a change of heart and decide on a last-minute wedding she'd need what savings she had to augment her trousseau.

She came upon a woman staring wistfully into the windows of a small furniture store. Intrigued, she stopped to see what was on offer. Her mouth dropped when she saw the prices. She had been pricing furniture since Leo passed his finals, but she had never seen anything to equal these. One and six for a table-lamp! Twenty-five shillings for a hall chair! Giveaway prices. A leather upholstered footstool caught her eye. Five shillings! Ideal for a Christmas present for Aunt Dot. She tried the door.

'It's locked,' said the woman in a resigned voice. She was poorly dressed and had the downtrodden look of someone who constantly has to make ends meet. 'I've been coming here every day since the place closed down hoping someone might open up. They haven't yet. They just went off and left everything behind. Shame, in't it? See that divan bed? I've had my eye on that for weeks. I've been wanting a new bed for years and couldn't afford one, now when I can there's no one to sell it to me. Shame, in't it?'

Philippa walked on sickened by a sudden sense of hopelessness. What sort of people would slash their stock to rock-bottom prices, then run off leaving it all behind. Desperate people? Escaping from who knows what? Most of Aunt Dot's neighbours had gone. Most of the big houses along the front were empty. The invasion hadn't taken place but the threat still hovered. She sighed. Pity about the footstool, though. Aunt Dot would have loved it.

A letter from Leo arrived in the second post, her father having forwarded it on. It had taken five days to reach her. Good going, she thought, considering the disruption caused by the nightly bombardment of London. 'My first from Aldershot,' she cried, waving it at Aunt Dot.

The letter was mostly about his army life. Sharing a batman with three other MOs. Drill, lectures, physical training, poker in the mess; the opportunity to play in a football match, officers v. sergeants ('You should see the size of the opposition. Most of them are physical training instructors, some even ex-professional footballers, but never fear we'll go down with colours flying'). He called the insignia of the RAMC a snake up a gum-tree. His tone grew more serious when enquiring after her welfare. He hoped she had taken his advice and gone to stay with her aunt and while at Leigh could she find out the state of the cigarette situation as it was pretty dire in the camp. (I'm way ahead of you there, darling, she thought smugly.) The letter was signed as usual – 'Yours ever, Leo'.

Aunt Dot, sitting opposite, busy with knitting needles, smiled indulgently. 'Happy news, dear?'

'Do I look happy?'

'Very. What has Leo to say?'

Philippa held out the letter. 'Read it for yourself. Parts of it are quite interesting.'

A look of bewilderment crossed Aunt Dot's broad face. 'In my young day,' she said reprovingly, 'love letters were supposed to be private, not interesting.'

Philippa laughed. 'There's nothing private about Leo's letters.'

'No lovey-dovey bits?'

'No lovey-dovey bits.'

'Never?'

'Never.'

Aunt Dot lowered her knitting. 'My dear, do you really think you two are suited? I mean, all these years and not a single love letter. Are you sure Leo really loves you? Has he ever told you so?'

Philippa racked her brains. 'Not in so many words.'

But in his student days he had sung to her as they had walked hand in hand through the forest. He had sung 'Pale Hands I Love', her favourite, but more often ballads which he had learnt by heart from listening to records on his father's gramophone, 'Parted', and 'Leanin'', and 'Dearest, our day is over', which she looked upon as a form of love song. He had a good baritone voice but stretched it often to sing arias from the opera. Every time he sang 'Vesti la giubba' she came out in goose pimples knowing what it would lead up to. Leo had told her the story of *I Pagliacci* and had promised to take her to see it at Covent Garden as soon as he could afford to. That was a treat still to come.

Aunt Dorothy concentrated on turning the heel of a sock before speaking again. When war started she had laid in a stock of khaki wool and ever since a stream of Balaclava helmets, mittens, scarves and socks had been coming loosely and shapelessly from her needles. Everything she produced was large enough to fit a regiment of Grenadier guardsmen but that didn't worry her. She was doing her part as she had done in the first world war, not knitting then but driving a milk float behind a tired old horse who knew his job better than she did, and stopped at all the right places.

'What worries me,' she said, 'is that when you and Leo first met you were little more than children. You haven't given yourselves a chance to meet anybody else. Are you sure that what you two mistake for love is not just, well, little more than a habit?'

'Oh, Aunt Dot – we made up our minds about each other *yonks* ago.'

'What is to stop you marrying then?'

'The war – the beastly war. Leo says it's too much of a risk.'

'Marriage is always a risk . . .'

Philippa thought that was rich coming from someone who had never tried it. Not something she could say, however. Aunt Dot had no such qualms about speaking out.

'Anyone frightened of taking a risk should not even consider marriage,' she declared.

Philippa's colour rose. 'Leo is not frightened on his own account. He's frightened of me being left as a young widow with perhaps a child. He's thinking of me, of my future and I admire him for it.' She knew she didn't sound very convincing, but then how could she expect to convince Aunt Dot when she couldn't convince herself.

'I think you're deceiving yourself.' Aunt Dot spoke not

unkindly for she had detected a certain note in her niece's voice that told its own story. She leant forward, her busy hands at rest. 'My dear, from what I've learnt in my long life, a lot of men are frightened of marriage. It isn't that they don't want to get married – it's the thought of the responsibility. They have to be pushed or cajoled. According to my married friends cajoling is more successful. Using one's feminine wiles.'

'Feminine wiles?'

'Coquetry – or flirting as you would call it. Bewitching a man until you have him eating out of your hand. I understand fluttering one's eyelashes is helpful. Your eyelashes would flutter beautifully.'

Philippa's spontaneous laughter echoed throughout the house. 'Oh Aunt Dot, you funny, old-fashioned thing – I could eat you.' She wiped her eyes. 'Your trouble is, you've been reading too many Victorian novels. And you call *me* romantic. Do you know what would happen to me if I were to flutter my eyelashes at Leo? He'd think I had something in my eye and before I knew where I was I'd find my eyelid everted.'

'I don't know what that means, my dear, but it sounds rather alarming.'

'It *is* alarming – it's horrible. Leo was always doing it to me when he was a student. He would take my eyelid by the lashes and *turn it inside out*! I was always frightened he wouldn't be able to turn it right side in again.'

'Why on earth should Leo do a thing like that?'

'He was practising. That's the way doctors remove foreign bodies from the eye.'

'Then all I can say, dear, is that it is rather fortunate that you didn't fall in love with a dental student.'

The night of Saturday, 10 May 1941, Philippa was on her own as her father was fire-watching at the works. She had gone to bed early with *Gone with the Wind* which she had borrowed from the library, and had just got herself nicely settled when the sirens sounded.

At first she wasn't unduly worried. There had been two very nasty all-night raids during April but since then comparative peace. Not that the enemy was idle. The sort of punishment they had meted out in November that all but demolished Coventry was now being meted out to other provincial cities, Birmingham, Sheffield, Manchester and Glasgow. And even those nights when there were no fixed targets, bombs were still falling on Random. Nearly every news bulletin gave a mention of bombs being dropped at random. 'What's poor Random done to deserve it?' was a much-quoted joke. It's not random this time, it's poor old London again, thought Philippa as the nearest guns opened fire. She put down her book, and though it was not necessary, dowsed the light. For some reason, she felt safer in the dark.

She couldn't keep her thoughts from her father fire-watching on the flimsy roof of the publishing house. Or Aunt Dot alone in that creaky old house, though she knew her aunt was comparatively safe at Leigh. She thought of Leo now stationed in the north-east in the midst of heavy industry. Her stomach churned at the thought of all those she loved in danger.

Sleep was impossible. Every crump of bomb and splatter of shrapnel and crack of gunfire seemed to vibrate against the cellar walls. She had never suffered from any form of phobia but now she felt she would have hysterics if she couldn't get away from the claustrophobic effect of this temporary shelter. She had an urge to jump out of bed and run through the garden and into the forest. It was an urge that didn't take much resisting, it would mean getting dressed first. She did get up, however, but only to take two aspirins. Then she lay down again, waiting for them to work.

She slept late the next morning. It was Sunday – a day of rest for her; for others a day of hard work in the aftermath of the raid. Her father returned home about midday looking tired out, too tired to talk or to eat. He went straight to his room and when she looked in later he was on his back on the bed still fully clothed, his face grimed by dust and sweat, dead to the world.

Later that day, when the newspaper finally arrived, she read with despair the damage the raid had inflicted. The House of Commons had been reduced to rubble; the roof of the twelfth-century Westminster Hall had been set ablaze and the tower of Westminster Abbey had collapsed.

Part of the country's heritage had been' destroyed. Some of the historic buildings that had survived the first fire of London in 1665 were now charred remains – what an irony she thought. And what about the thousands of little homes also reduced to rubble, she wondered? What about the City? What would she find when she got there on the morrow – and how would she get there? The paper spoke of four of the capital's main railway stations out of action. Of roads blocked, telephones out of order, thousands of homes without gas, electricity or water.

They were fortunate here in this part of Woodside. Apart from the phone, the other facilities were working. She tried the line several times but it was dead. Aunt Dot would be wondering about them. Leo too. She sat down and wrote a long letter to him, not knowing how long it would take to reach him. That it would eventually she had no doubt. She had great faith in the perseverance of the GPO.

Her father promised to get her to work the next morning, at least most of the way. He still had a little petrol put aside for emergencies. He tried to persuade her not to go in at first.

'What's the point?' he said. 'There won't be "business as usual" today – there's too much clearing up to be done. Have you thought, Pip, that Brundle's might not be there.'

'That's why I have to go. I have to see for myself.'

He recognised in her the same stubbornness of purpose which had kept him on the go all Saturday night, fighting fires with a stirrup pump. He didn't argue.

'It least I'll try to get you to the nearest Underground,' he promised.

Since the Underground stations had been taken over as air-raid shelters Philippa had avoided them whenever possible. It wasn't so much the smell that gripped her throat as she descended the escalator, it was dread of falling on the line now that only a narrow space was reserved for passengers. She had always been nervous of being sucked under a train as it rumbled into a station and for that reason stood well back from the edge of the platform. That was no longer possible for a chalk line behind which was shelterers' territory prevented her.

They made a slow and tortuous journey as far as Bethnal Green. There Jonathan conceded defeat. As far as the eye could see the street was cross-hatched by flaccid hoses.

'Sorry, Pip, this is as far as I can go. The engine's

overheating, and there's too many pitfalls. You might be lucky enough to get on the Underground from here.'

There had been long winding queues at the entrances to the few London Transport stations they had passed.

'I'll walk,' she said.

Smoke still drifted over the wreckage. The smell of smouldering wood and charred brickwork filled her lungs. Looking above her at the sky she saw the sun as through a dirty glass dome and had to remind herself that it was still the merry month of May and that in other parts of the country bluebells and cowslips were in blossom, larks soaring and cuckoos calling, and more fortunate housewives were cleaning their cosy little houses, not weeping beside pathetic mounds of glass and rubble. The 'London can take it' spirit was being sorely tested.

She passed a small group of firemen at rest on the pavement. One sat with his hands on his knees, his head bowed. The soot that blacked their faces could not disguise the marks of fatigue. She heard one say to another, 'I've been so busy over the weekend, mate, I forgot to check my football coupons.'

'Bugger Hitler,' she thought, and immediately felt better. It was the first time she had said that word, even to herself.

The City seemed eerie without traffic. Just stationary fire-engines, and ambulances nosing a passageway through glass and loose bricks, rubble, and dormant hoses. She felt she was walking through a battlefield, which in a way she was, and everyone she passed seemed to have the dazed look of someone waking up from a nightmare. Everyone too must have shared her dread of what they might find when they reached their destination.

Dust and smoke still lingered in Leadenhall Street. She turned into a side-street, and the same pungent smell of charred wood and brickwork she had first encountered at Bethnal Green caught her by the throat. Only half of Brundle's remained standing. At first she thought it had escaped the fate of those other buildings she had passed, but as she got nearer she saw it was mainly a shell. It was hard to take it in. Brundle's, that old established bank, that magnificent building of mahogany and marble, Italian tiling and intricate plasterwork. She had always thought it too good for a place of commerce. With all that workmanship it could have passed for a mansion. What a waste. What a wicked, wicked waste.

Tears trickled slowly down her cheeks. She wiped them away, feeling ashamed of crying for a building when thousands of people lay dead. She took a long, shuddering breath and walked on.

Among a group of fire-fighters, wardens and other officials, she recognised one of the senior members of staff whose name she could never remember, still wearing his steel hat and carrying his gas-mask. She guessed from his appearance that he had been on fire-watch all night, perhaps all weekend. He was a short, thin, fussy little man normally, now he looked anything but fussy. He trotted over to her.

'I'm sorry I'm late,' she said stupidly. 'I couldn't get through . . .'

She was surprised to see his eyes water.

'I don't think there'll be much work for you today, Miss Byrd,' he said with an attempt at humour. It was characteristic of him that he should know her name. 'I should imagine your ledger is buried – just about there – wouldn't you? Why don't you go and get yourself a cup of coffee. You'll find some of your colleagues in the tea-shop in Gracechurch Street. Then get off home as best as you can. We'll be in touch.'

She stared up at the jagged edge of the building outlined against the drifting smoke. Much of the coping was hanging loose. There was a pressing question that had to be asked.

'The – the Fullers . . . Are they all right?'

'They are still digging for them.' He turned away and walked back to his group and immediately began to issue orders like someone in dire need of keeping busy.

Every table in Lyons was occupied. A subdued but unbroken hum of conversation filled the room. Philippa longed to become part of it, to feel normality close around her, but there was no vacant chair. Normally she was shy of strangers, but there were no strangers today. Everyone was part of a large community sharing a common grief. She saw four of the other girls from her department drinking coffee, talking spasmodically, but just as often staring vacantly into space. She roused herself. A small queue had started at the till but she didn't join it. There was an Express Dairy not far away, she tried there, but that was also full. She thought every City worker must be drinking coffee, until she noticed the time and realised that the coffee break had extended to include the lunch hour.

She got her coffee finally in the refreshment room on Fenchurch Street station along with a railway bun which was difficult to swallow. Everything would have tasted like chalk today, she suspected. She wasn't hungry and left most of it on her plate. A pale-faced girl sitting opposite her kept staring anxiously at the door. Finally she was rewarded. A middle-aged man entered who made straight for their table and sat down beside her. They exchanged thin, melancholy smiles.

'Daddy, the office has gone – the whole block. I haven't got a job any longer. . . .' The girl's eyes brimmed over.

'Me too,' the man said. 'I've been sent home indefinitely. Oh my dear, what shall we tell Mummy?'

Philippa left, unwilling to intrude on their private misery. I'm one of the fortunate ones, she thought as she went down the station steps to ground level. She knew the bank would go on paying her salary until they found alternative premises. She'd had quite a tussle with her father when she first left school, for he saw no necessity for her to go to work. She insisted. She wanted independence, but the greater incentive was the chance of seeing more of Leo if she too went daily up to London.

Now of course, it wasn't so much a question of independence as obligation. Perhaps compulsory in time for there was talk of conscripting women to help the war effort. Those among the young juniors at Brundle's who belonged to some form of Territorial Army – and most of them did because the bank encouraged it – had been called up within days of war being declared. As in the last war, Brundle's went back to recruiting temporary staff to take their place, even married women, and – shock-horror for some of the old die-hards – girls from council schools!

Her homeward journey was less fraught than the one going in that morning. Most of the rubble had been cleared from the roads and transport was once more on the move. The first thing Philippa noticed as she entered the house was a letter from Leo on the hall table. She fell on it with joy for she had not heard from him for over a week and his previous letter had left her in tears. She took it into the kitchen to read. Mrs Mooney had been, bless her. Even the blitz couldn't keep her away. Everything was clean and in its rightful place. A note from her father read, 'Gone to Stratford to help clear up the mess. Won't be late.' Philippa filled the kettle, plugged it in, and opened her letter.

'My dear Philippa,
    Just as I thought I was settled in at Endlesbrough, I've now been told I'm to join the ack-ack boys north of the Tees at a village called Coopen on the outskirts of Stockley. It appears their present MO has had a sudden posting abroad. I sometimes feel that ever since I came to the north-east, I have been caught up in a game of general post. When I first reported at Newcastle I was told the division extended from the Cheviots, includes Northumberland and Cumberland and goes as far south as Scarborough. I'm beginning to think that before the army is finished with me I may well have seen all of it.
    I'm sorry I have done nothing yet about finding a place for you to stay when you come up here. I'm waiting until I can be sure of some leave so that we can explore the surrounding countryside together. Everything in this part of the world is industrial – in fact, the only non-military object is probably me. But a few miles out there are breathtaking views and some fine walks over the hills.
    How are you keeping? Regardless of what you think, you are constantly in my thoughts and I worry about you a lot. I've felt easier about you

lately as there's been no mention of heavy raids on London for several weeks. Please dear, you must believe that I miss you as much as you miss me. It is such a different life in the army from that in civvy street, so many vicissitudes I wasn't prepared for . . . Give me time.'

Dear Leo, she thought, putting the letter to her lips. He never uses a word of one syllable when one of five would do just as well. By now he would have heard as much about the latest raid as the censor would allow and that would be enough to shatter his peace of mind. She tried the phone but it was still out of order. All over the south-east telephone cables were grounded. She returned to the kitchen.

The kettle boiled and she made the tea, and while drinking it she reread Leo's letter dwelling on the passage, 'you are constantly in my thoughts'. Such sentiments as that were rare from Leo so all the more to be savoured. His previous letter she had torn up, but couldn't blot it out of her memory . . . 'You seem to take the attitude that nothing can be forecast in war so snatch the few things that one can and trust to luck. It's hard to be parted when single. How much more so when married? A single girl or a single man can fend easily for themselves, but marriage in wartime increases the difficulties which married couples normally go through. I'm not suggesting that no one should marry in wartime but merely advocating that one should not rush into it . . .'

Rush into it! That was when she had lost her temper and torn the letter to pieces and immediately regretted it. She had tried to put the pieces together again, but she had done the job too thoroughly, so had no idea how it ended. She didn't answer the letter by return which she normally did, but kept him waiting for three days which at least had the effect of jolting him into phoning her to see if she was all right. Just the sound of his anxious voice guaranteed that she was.

In February he had been posted to a military hospital in Yorkshire where within a few weeks he swapped his role as medical officer for that of patient and was confined to one of the wards with a kidney infection. When he was well enough he was sent home on a week's leave, but a week shared out between his mother and father, sister and brothers had been spread very thin.

All three brothers were exempt from military duty: James because he was above the present age of call-up; George, a draughtsman with an aircraft company was in a reserved occupation; Godfrey on medical grounds because of a hammer toe. Only Phoebe, tired of teaching and craving action, had shown any desire to follow her youngest brother into uniform. She had applied to the ATS and was awaiting an answer. All were anxious to hear first-hand Leo's experiences of army life. The Brookes, Philippa discovered, were a clannish lot and she was not yet one of the clan.

As soon as Leo recovered he was dispatched to Endlesbrough. From there his letters began again. 'It's like being in general practice, except that my patients are all men. I hold sick parades in the drill hall every morning, followed by rounds of the gun-sites. I have a car at my disposal and a driver. Even if I knew how to drive I wouldn't be allowed to. Just another of the nonsenses I keep coming up against. Spencer, my corporal, is an excellent driver and is giving me driving lessons. Now that the restrictions on learner drivers have been lifted I can go off and practise on my own. Do you remember my dreams of having a little three-wheeled Morgan? Of taking you for runs instead of walks. Ah, happy days . . .'

Her father arrived, hollow-eyed and coated in dust. 'Any tea in that pot, Pip?'

'I'll make you some fresh.' And while she did she told him what had awaited her in the City. They exchanged despairing glances.

'How are things at Stratford now?' she said.

'Bloody awful. What can you say to somebody who's lost their entire family? What can you do when a young mother is dug out with a dead infant in her arms? I tell you, Pippa, one more raid like that and London will be on its knees.'

London was not brought to its knees for there were no more raids like that, lasting eight hours or more with bombers coming over in wave after wave. They did not know then and would not know for some time the reason for the sudden lull. Hitler was massing his troops for an attack on Russia. The Luftwaffe was needed elsewhere.

In the meantime, Philippa had heard from the bank. They were negotiating for premises in Norwich and were hoping to be in business again by June. She greeted this news with mixed feelings. It meant going into digs. It meant seeing less of her father and Aunt Dot. On the other hand she would be that much nearer to Leo, but whether quicker was another matter. Norfolk was considered a bit of a backwater, right off the map, without a decent road in the county and no mainline trains. She thought it strange that Brundle's should decide to evacuate there until she remembered it was at Norwich that the bank had been founded early in the eighteenth century.

There had been a water-colour painting of the original premises, half timbered and thatch roofed, hanging in the boardroom at Brundle's. That she suspected had gone the way of the ledger department and the ladies' locker room. She felt quite a rush of affection for her old ledger, forgetting the hours of anguish it had caused when she was unable to balance it.

She paid a visit to Aunt Dot later that month, to discuss her move to Norfolk but mostly because her father insisted. 'We must try and visit the old lady more often. One never knows, at her age . . .'

'I was there for Easter . . .'

'That's nearly six weeks ago. You used to love going to Leigh.'

'I still do, but I enjoy working at Byrd's too.'

With time on her hands she had helped out at the family firm, going backwards and forwards to Stratford with her father, working in the office and trying to keep the accounts up to the standard set by Mr Billings. He was seventy; he had stayed on when the younger man he was grooming to take his place had left to join the army. A combination of the blitz, difficult travelling conditions and his wife's failing health had forced him to a reluctant decision to retire. He tutored Philippa for two days in the rudiments of bookkeeping, and then she was on her own, and just getting the hang of it when her father came up with the suggestion to visit Aunt Dot.

'Actually,' her father said, 'I'm interviewing someone tomorrow for Mr Billings's job. A widow, in her early forties, and if her references are anything to go by, a phenomenon. She was head of the accounts department at the celluloid factory until it closed down. I shall be lucky to get her.'

'She'll be the lucky one coming to work in this darling little place after a celluloid factory . . .'

Aunt Dorothy was waiting for her, watching from the window in the sitting room. Philippa had walked up from the station, stopping to look back at the view as she always did. The sentries had gone, but the beaches were still wired off. Across the still waters came the gentle put-put-put of a cockle bawley coming in with the tide. Aunt Dot was eager to show her something.

'There,' she said proudly, 'what do you think of my latest acquisition?'

It looked like a pamphlet in a narrow oak frame. Philippa went closer to investigate. It *was* a pamphlet in a narrow oak frame. 'Gracious. It's an invasion notice.'

It was headed, 'What you should know about INVASION DANGER', and went on:

> You will shortly receive a leaflet 'Beating the Invader', issued to all householders in the country, telling you what to do should invasion come. If invasion finds you in this town, and you are not ordered to leave, you must act on the instructions to stand firm. But you can help to defeat the invader by leaving now if you can be spared and have somewhere to go.
> *THIS APPLIES PARTICULARLY TO –*
> *SCHOOL CHILDREN*
> *MOTHERS WITH YOUNG CHILDREN*
> *AGED AND INFIRM PERSONS*
> *PERSONS LIVING ON PENSIONS*
> *PERSONS WITHOUT OCCUPATION OR*

'When did you get this? The threat of invasion has long since passed.'

'A few weeks ago. There is more on the other side, but I would need another leaflet to make a pair, and I can't get one because nobody I know will part with theirs. They want to keep them as souvenirs.'

'But why send out invasion notices now when the danger is over? Do you think the government knows something we don't? Aunt Dot, do you realise that you qualify for each of the last four categories? You really should have your bag packed ready for emergencies . . .'

'Impertinence, miss. I don't consider myself aged and infirm – not yet. I grant you the other three apply. Now come and sit here with me, and tell me more about this nonsense of being evacuated to Norfolk.'

It was funny to think of herself as an evacuee. It was something she would not have considered a few weeks ago but now the matter had been taken out of her hands.

Aunt Dot went on, 'I don't approve of running away, you know that. It is quite unnecessary now that the raids seem to have stopped, and in any case how will your dear father manage without you?'

'He can manage a lot better than I can, especially when it comes to cooking.' She had put up such a fight with her father to be allowed to stay. She had wanted to leave the bank and find another job. There was no shortage of vacancies now. Firms were offering all sorts of bribes to poach staff away from each other.

Then Jonathan had casually mentioned that his mother had been the daughter of a Norfolk farmer farming in the Broadland area at a place called Thornmere. This would be a great opportunity, he said, to seek out their family roots, something he had always intended to do himself but never got around to.

Philippa already knew that her grandmother had died when her little son was just a baby, but she had never been told before that she came from Norfolk. Not that it would have made any impression on her if she had been told, for it was all so long ago it seemed like ancient history. But now she had a vested interest, as it were, and her interest was kindled. She wanted to know more about her rural roots.

'Roots, what roots?' Aunt Dot retorted. 'Any roots there were withered long ago.' The lines of her face softened. 'I remember Lydia very well though I haven't given her a thought for years. Lovely little thing she was, not a bit as you would expect a farmer's daughter to look. She was such a petite dark little thing, not one of your buxom country lasses with rosy cheeks. She was full of life, always so enthusiastic about everything. She went through that musty old house at Woodside like a breath of fresh air. Down came all the old dark hangings; up went muslins and lace and cretonnes. She loved the forest. "Nothing like it in Norfolk," she said. "Only woodlands and those all private."' Aunt Dot sighed. 'I owe her such a debt of gratitude. She left me a baby to look after. You may well smile, Philippa. You will never know how much I wanted a baby, but in order to have a baby one had to have a husband, and no one showed the slightest inclination to marry me.'

'And no one kept in touch with grandmother's family?'

'No, unfortunately. When Lydia died my brother nearly went out of his mind; turned into a bit of a recluse. And Lydia's father, old Mr Bowyer – he didn't get married until he was sixty. He was too old to travel. They kept up a spasmodic correspondence, but even that fizzled out in time.'

Philippa mused. She said, 'Do you think there are Bowyers still living in – where was it you called it – Thornmere? I could pay them a visit. Introduce myself as a long-lost cousin. That would be a surprise for them.'

Aunt Dot sadly shook her head. 'There are no Bowyers living at Manor Farm now. They died out some years ago. I saw the obituary in the *Daily Telegraph*. Now, tell me the latest news from Leo. Have you heard from him recently?'

'Yes, he likes it very much where he is now. Says he hopes it lasts longer than his other postings. He's looking round for somewhere for me to stay when I go up to see him. I hope it'll be soon, before the bank sends for me.'

'Does he still write?'

'Of course.'

'I thought perhaps he might phone instead.'

They were wary of the phone since the occasion Leo called to tell her about his move to Coopen. The operator had broken in the minute he used the word 'posting'. 'No careless talk, please,' she said, and pulled the plug on them.

'No Careless Talk' ... 'Is your journey really necessary?' ... 'Be like Dad, keep Mum' ... 'Dig for Victory'. Exhortations such as these stared down at them from every vacant wall and hoarding. Philippa took exception to 'Be like Dad, keep Mum', for she knew of many Mums who were keeping Dad. Mrs Mooney for one, who kept her workshy husband in beer and cigarettes with her charring money.

'I suppose you haven't brought any of Leo's letters

with you? If you feel like reading one out to me, I wouldn't object,' said Aunt Dot coaxingly.

'I don't show Leo's letters to anybody, any more...'

'Not even to your father?'

'Particularly not to my father.'

'Becoming too lovey-dovey?'

Hesitation. 'You could say that.'

'I don't get many letters myself these days,' Aunt Dot lamented. 'Not since you persuaded me to have the telephone connected. My dear, I can't tell you how pleased I am you talked me round. I don't know now what I'd do without my telephone. I'm never lonely. If I do feel a fit of loneliness coming on I just pick up my telephone and call up one of my friends and have a lovely long chat. Some I haven't seen for years, and we have such a lot of news to catch up on. Philippa dear, I owe it all to you. I would never have thought of it on my own.'

Aunt Dot's friends, all as long-lived as herself, lived in such places as Cheltenham and Torquay and Harrogate, and one whose bridesmaid she had been, in Edinburgh. Philippa could imagine Aunt Dot and her cosy little chats in the middle of the morning or afternoon when time hung heavily on her hands. She devoutly hoped that when the bills arrived, she herself would be in Norfolk safely out of reach of recrimination.

Four

Later that month Philippa received a surprise phone call from Leo. After the usual greetings he asked her if she had anything booked for the following weekend.

'Nothing very exciting. And you?'

'I have Sunday free and was rather hoping that a certain young lady I'm extremely fond of might come walking over the hills with me?'

Jonathan, listening to the nine o'clock news, heard a sudden shrill cry of pleasure. Minutes later Philippa came dashing into the room. 'You don't have to tell me – I can guess,' he said. 'Leo has got forty-eight hours' leave.'

'Nearly as good. He's just found out that there's a guest house in Coopen right opposite the drill hall. Small but highly recommended, he said, and he wants me to go up there this coming weekend. Do you mind, Dad?'

'When have I minded anything that you do?'

'You didn't think much of my perm...'

'Let's not get back to that subject. Anyhow, time has solved that little problem. Of course I don't mind, I'm pleased for you. I'll stop off at the station tomorrow and get your ticket.'

When she arrived at King's Cross station the following Friday and saw the crush of waiting passengers, Philippa wondered how many like herself considered their journey not only necessary but essential. These days, everybody seemed to be on the move. It was understandable with His Majesty's forces but why so many civilians? Because there was no petrol for the use of cars or other transport? Or, with the threat of death forever hovering, was there this urgent need to keep in constant touch with friends and relatives? Her train that day was completely packed. She was late arriving but was fortunate enough to get the last seat in a compartment and squeezed in between two large gentlemen, one in uniform, the other in tweeds.

The train had hardly drawn away from the outer suburbs of north London before she began to suffer hunger pangs. She had been too excited to eat breakfast, and not far-seeing enough to bring sandwiches like most of the other occupants who were now unwrapping and munching. To make matters worse the tweedy gentleman on her right had fallen asleep with his head on her shoulder.

She was released from this embarrassment at Peterborough when the elderly clergyman sitting in the window seat departed. Before anybody from the corridor saw their chance she had taken his place.

Everybody was asleep. She was too hungry to sleep. It was now well into the afternoon. The refreshment car would be open for afternoon tea but there was no way she could reach it. The corridor was blocked with servicemen and their kitbags. They were now travelling through the placid green valleys and gentle uplands of the Lincolshire Wolds – a landscape new to her. Though she was familiar with many of the beauty spots of Europe, she was totally ignorant of parts of her own country. Her first sight of the industrial north therefore, came as a revelation. She tried to take in everything she saw for she knew her father would question her on her return, and there would be the familiar 'Eyes and No-eyes' routine.

She woke fitfully when the motion of the train ceased. She couldn't remember falling asleep. She had no idea where they were until she saw the noticeboard. York. The merchant seaman and the civilian got up, stretched and left. Two young sailors took their seats, spread a newspaper across their knees and produced a pack of cards. They played for money. Philippa soon lost interest and drifted back to sleep.

She awoke again when the train came to another sudden halt. This time it was not a station; the signals were against them. She yawned, roused herself and sat up, pulling down her skirt which had ridden up above her knees. Only then did she look out of the window and on to a foreign landscape that at first sight appalled her.

Belching chimneys, cooling towers, blast furnaces. She didn't know the correct term for half of these grim works of iron and steel rolling slowly past the windows as the train got up steam again. Are these the dark satanic mills? she asked herself, and for once the words made sense to her.

She tried to remember all she had ever read about the Industrial Revolution. It had made romantic reading at school and she swelled with pride to think that her country was then the workshop of the world, when anything stamped 'Made in Britain' carried its own guarantee. But now her pride took something of a dent. In reality there was nothing at all romantic about an industrial landscape. It was ugly, dirty and menacing. It depressed her to think that people were born, lived, worked and died in such an environment. By the time the train steamed into Stockley she was feeling tired and rather low in spirits.

But the sight of Leo waiting on the platform changed all that. He helped her from the carriage, took her case and gave her such a hug it left her breathless. The old Leo would not have done that, or kissed her so ardently in public. She was touched to see tears in his eyes. Tears were in her eyes also.

He released her reluctantly. 'The train was so late, I was beginning to think you hadn't made it. What time did you leave London?'

She told him.

'Ye gods! You must be starving.'

'Ravenous.'

He took her arm. 'I'm glad of that. Come along, I've got a taxi waiting.'

It was just a short drive from the station to the marketplace, a large cobbled square flanked by shops and hotels and a cinema in front of which a queue stretched out of sight and round a corner. The taxi dropped them outside an attractive half-timbered coaching inn with the date 1776 carved in the lintel of the door.

'The grill room here,' Leo said, 'is reputed to be the best in the county.'

A table had been reserved for them within sight and smell of a blazing fire over which two chefs were busy turning steaks and cutlets, kidneys and mushrooms. Philippa's mouth began to water and she could barely tear herself away. 'I must have a wash and brush-up first.

I was confined in my compartment all the way from King's Cross.'

'Before you go, tell me what to order if the waiter comes. Beefsteak? Lobster? I can recommend the steak. I don't know about the lobster – but I expect you can get all the shellfish you want when you visit your Aunt Dorothy.'

Philippa laughed at the idea. 'You've been to Old Leigh. Did you ever see lobster on the cockle stalls! I'll have the steak, I haven't tasted steak since meat was rationed.'

The reflection staring back at her from the mirror in the powder room looked rather startled. Well it might, she thought. No colour, and eyes sunken with fatigue. Grubby too, but she could soon put that right. There was a plentiful supply of hot water and soap and the towels were soft and fluffy. She was applying fresh make-up when the attendant who had been watching, said, 'Petal, if I had a complexion like yours I wouldn't cover it up with all tha' ole mook,' which Philippa thought deserved a two-shilling tip at least.

Leo watched her as she came back through the swing doors trawling many admiring glances. She had a graceful way of walking and held her head at an angle that those who didn't know her might have thought an affectation but which was nature's way of correcting her slight astigmatism. These past few months had brought home to him how precious she really was. In the past he had taken her for granted for she was always there when he wanted her. But now she wasn't there, and the fear had grown that he might not be able to keep her – that someone with more verve and daring, qualities that he lacked – might entice her from him. Solid, hard-working, conscientious; those attributes had been said or written about him, but they weren't the qualities that would sweep a girl off her feet.

Yet she had always been so loyal to him; waiting all through his long student years, spending her leisure hours, when other girls were having fun, embroidering household linen for her bottom drawer. He had thought this quaint and old-fashioned at the time but was secretly pleased that she had something to keep her occupied when he could not.

This girl, he knew, would go out of her way to please him, but now, he asked himself, what had he ever done to please her? He only did what pleased her if it happened to please himself also. It gave him no comfort to realise he had inherited most of his father's traits, solid, conscientious, hard-working – his father was all that too. But also unimaginative, and completely unable to see another person's point of view. Physician, heal thyself – but when had he ever given heed to that old saw.

'You're looking very thoughtful,' said Philippa as she joined him. 'Something on your mind?'

'I was just thinking how that colour green suits you. I like your outfit, very splosh.'

Not much of a compliment as compliments go, but coming from the source it did, it delighted her. Splosh was one of Leo's made-up words – a homespun version of chic.

'I bought it originally for going away in,' she said.

'Going away? You bought something *special* to travel up here in?'

She laughed. 'No, you darling chump. For going away on our honeymoon.'

Their eyes met. A misplaced word now and the whole

evening could fall apart. Neither wanted that. Leo cleared his throat. 'A suit that style will never date,' he said.

'That's why I chose it in the first place.'

The wine waiter came. Leo made his choice. She knew he hated going through this ritual, the uncorking, pouring out, tasting, assenting; unlike her father who would have no qualms in rejecting a poor wine, Leo wouldn't know the difference.

The firelight brought out the golden flecks in his eyes. Tawny like a lion's, she thought. Leo the lion. When they had first met she had asked him whether Leo was short for Leonard. He said no, he had been named after the month in which he had been born. The first four young Brookes got two names each, but by the time he was born his parents had either run out of ideas or interest, until his mother, looking through her copy of *Napoleon's Book of Fate* had come upon the signs of the zodiac, and his own fate was sealed. He had thanked his stars ever since, he said, that he hadn't been born under the sign of Capricorn.

Philippa never knew whether to take him seriously or not. He had the ability to pull her leg in a very straight-faced way, though his eyes sometimes betrayed him. They were expressive eyes and they were alert now with a look of expectancy that quickened her heart. 'At last,' he said, 'I think this is our order coming.'

Her steak was put before her. Medium rare as she preferred it, with sauté potatoes, wild mushrooms and a green salad. She said, 'It appears I have come to a land of plenty.'

Leo looked up from his burnt offering. He liked his steak well done.

'It wasn't always, you know. Eight or nine years ago,

there was real hunger up here. We thought down south that we were hit badly enough by the Depression – what I saw in the East End when I was a student would wring the hardest heart – but compared to some of the stories I've been told lately, I'm not so sure. I told you about the Red Cross nurses who help out in the sick bay? There's one in particular, Mrs Mortimer, a kind-hearted little body who goes out of her way to fuss over me. I think she feels I miss my home comforts, and often has me back to her house for a meal. Her husband likes nothing better than a good argument – north versus south, mostly. He thinks we're an effete lot down south. We're just the shop window, he says, for the manufactured goods of the north. Up here they do all the work, down there we take all the profits. It's a deep-rooted opinion that many in these parts hold. Makes you wonder if there isn't some truth in it.'

He paused to help himself to more vegetables.

'He's a manager with one of the ship-building works, one that was badly hit during the Depression. His job was secure, but a lot of his workers were put off. It angered him to see good workers thrown on the scrap heap and it's given him a kind of guilt complex that he now vents on the south. It's taken a war, he said to me only last week, to bring full employment back to the north, but what's going to happen after the war? Another three million unemployed?'

'Leo, I understand all that, I really do, but you and I are not to blame for the Depression so why are you making me feel so guilty.'

'Do I make I you feel guilty?'

'I'm not enjoying this meal as well as I thought I would.'

'We can't have that. I'd better shut up.'

'Oh, no, don't. I love to hear you talk. But please, choose a more cheerful subject.'

Leo thought hard. 'Well, what with the Germans doing so well in Crete, and HMS *Hood* being sunk, there's not much cheer about at the moment.'

They walked from the market-place to the village of Coopen, a matter of about three miles. They needed that walk after the meal they had eaten. A meal to remember, thought Philippa, and remember it she would in days to come when shortages cut deeper and meals were often augmented with dried egg omelettes and American fat bacon which had only one thing in its favour – it was unrationed, and no wonder, there was hardly any lean to it.

They strolled rather than walked, making the most of the long summer twilight. Double summer time meant that at this time of year it kept light until ten o'clock. The sky in the west was the colour of aquamarine against which a few rose-tipped clouds drifted lazily. Philippa suddenly clutched Leo's arm.

'Look, up there. That cloud. In the shape of a V – a large vee. V for Victory. Do you think it's an omen? A sign?'

He usually scoffed at any hint of superstition on her part, but not tonight. 'Are you going to wish on it?'

'It's too serious for a mere wish.'

'Then pray.'

She was alerted by the tone of his voice. 'Leo, you haven't any doubt, have you, about us winning?' She herself had never doubted for a minute.

He did not answer immediately. In silence they watched the V-shaped cloud disperse and fade into a darkening sky. He said, 'I'd feel more sure about victory if we had just one ally.'

'We have the Empire.'

'Oh, I wasn't forgetting the Empire. A pity it's such a hell of a way off though.'

The nearer they got to Coopen the more open the outlook. Heavy industry was only a matter of miles behind them but there was no evidence of it here in the outer fringes of Stockley. Coopen itself was a delightful surprise to her; a village of charming old stonework houses clustered around the traditional green, with the church at one end and a rustic old inn at the other. The only building that did not blend in with its surroundings was the drill hall, and that stuck out like a sore thumb.

They stopped at the entrance to a house with tall Georgian windows and a mounting block at one side of its solid double door. There was just sufficient daylight for Philippa to read the name Kimberley Lodge painted on a wooden plaque fixed to the wall.

'You're coming in with me?' she said, suddenly overcome by shyness.

'Just to introduce you to Mrs Daniels. There's a couple of patients waiting for me in the sick-bay.'

'Then let's say good night, here. I can't kiss you good night in front of a lot of strangers.'

But even that was denied them. The door opened almost immediately and a friendly and welcoming voice invited them in.

Philippa had convinced herself that nothing would keep her awake that night for all through the evening she could hardly keep her eyes open: but the happy anticipation of seeing Leo again, the exhaustion of the journey, the reunion at the station, the rich and satisfying meal at the White Hart grill, her introduction to the other guests, all this combined to keep her mind so occupied that sleep was out of the question.

Physically she was so weary that she had nearly crawled into bed without a bath, until at the last minute she remembered Mrs Daniels's warning; 'If you want a bath, honey, you'd better take the opportunity now. There's usually a rush for the bathroom in the morning.'

The word 'honey' was not a borrowed Americanism as she thought at first. It was a word much used in these parts, along with other expressions like 'petal' and 'flower', a pleasant and flattering form of address that was strangely at odds with the grim surroundings. Much nicer though than the 'ducks' or 'luvs' in constant use by London bus conductors.

They had all been waiting for her in the sitting room after Leo had taken his leave, Mrs Daniels and her husband (as lugubrious as his wife was cheerful), and the six house guests. These were Mrs and Miss Fletcher, Mr Morley, Mrs Burrell, Miss Shaw (about her own age, pretty and plump and smiling) and a Mr Pryer, a wizened little gnome of a man who did not offer to shake hands, but scowled malevolently from behind the smokescreen of his pipe.

'I'll never remember all their names,' she confided to Mrs Daniels as she was shown upstairs to her room. 'I'm not very good with names.'

'Don't worry, honey.' Philippa had the impression that worry was something that Mrs Daniels carefully avoided. She was a well-preserved woman in her late fifties with an inattentive manner that was quite misleading. 'What you need is a few tips to help your memory. Let me see how I can suggest something... Miss Fletcher is the one with the woolly hat. I rather suspect she has alopecia. Her mother is the painfully thin lady with a whiff of mothballs about her. Mrs Burrell is the one with the jewellery. She has been twice widowed and is looking for a third husband. She was disappointed when she heard that it was a young lady from London was taking my vacant room, and not a —'

'Essex, actually.'

'It's one and the same to me, honey. Now where was I? Ah yes. Miss Shaw. She works at the council offices and comes from Nottingham where the girls, I am told, are the prettiest in the country. I expect you recognised her accent, slight as it is.'

Philippa, who could not tell one accent from another, unless it was instantly recognisable as Scots, Irish, Welsh or Cockney, held her tongue.

'That leaves the two men. Mr Morley, the tall gentleman. He has just been appointed manager to a shoe shop in the market-place, and comes from Mansfield, of course (why of course? wondered Philippa). And last, Mr Pryer...' Here, Mrs Daniels gave just a hint of a sigh. 'Yes indeed, Mr Pryer. A thorn in my poor husband's flesh, but very prompt with his payments. Well, here we are honey, this is your room.'

The only remarkable thing about the room was that it was divided from the one next door by a partitioned wall that stopped short within eighteen inches of the ceiling. This didn't worry Philippa too much at first – after all she was only here for three nights – until she heard the unpleasant sound of hawking and spitting, and caught a whiff of pipe tobacco. Mr Pryer!

Cocoa and biscuits were served in the sitting room

before the guests retired for the night, and it was then Philippa understood why Mr Pryer was a thorn in Mr Daniels's flesh. He would be a thorn in the flesh of anyone who had to tidy up after him, and Mr Daniels she was quick to realise was the main tidier-upper in that household.

Mr Pryer was the first to leave, nodding to everyone in turn. Philippa was sitting near the door. No good night nod for her, no glance her way even, just a vindictive hiss from the side of his mouth. 'You folk down south know nought about work. Too scared o' getting your hands dirty.'

Later, coming from the bathroom she passed him on the landing. Another and louder hiss. 'Can't cook, buy everything ready made. Buy flour a quarter of a pound at a time. Not much you can do wi' that!' And away he scuttled before she could think up a crushing answer.

And now she could hear him coughing his lungs out in the room next door, and any minute now his head might appear over the top of the partition and aim another verbal dart in her direction. He would have to stand on a chair to do so, she thought, perhaps even a chair on the bed, but she wouldn't put that past him. It wasn't until she heard the creaking of bed springs followed soon afterwards by prolonged and catarrhal snores that she was finally able to relax and drift off to sleep herself.

She had her first introduction to black pudding next morning when it was served up at breakfast with bacon and tomatoes. She pushed it to one side and when she thought no one was looking fed it to the ancient and fat retriever who padded hopefully behind the yawning fourteen-year-old maid.

Miss Shaw sitting opposite caught her eye and said, 'Did you sleep well?'

'Eventually.'

'No alerts, thank goodness. We get a lot of those.'

'I expect you do.'

'You've had a bad time in London, haven't you?'

'Yes. Poor London has had it rather rough.'

Everybody turned sympathetic eyes upon her except Mr Pryer who growled into his cup. Mrs Daniels appeared with a message from Leo. He had been called to an emergency at a gun-site near West Hartlepool. He hoped to be back by the afternoon.

Philippa swallowed her disappointment, aware that once again all eyes were upon her. Leo and she had so little time together and now a whole morning lost. You'd better get used to this sort of thing, she warned herself. It was one of the hazards of being a doctor's wife.

Mr Pryer was the first to leave the table. He looked down its length at Philippa, leered, mouthed the word 'Coventry' at her, then left.

'What has Mr Pryer got against London?' Philippa asked when she and Miss Shaw were alone together. 'Has he ever been there?'

'Only once. Swore he would never go again. Said it was an evil city. That's what I was told anyway. Mr Daniels thinks he was palmed off with a forged pound note. He said anyone who could put one over on Mr Pryer deserved a medal. He can't stand Mr Pryer, as I expect you've noticed. Mr Pryer doesn't like Mr Daniels either. He calls him Mrs Daniels's Abigail. I wonder what he means by that.'

'I think Abigail is an old-time word for housemaid or maid.'

'Fancy Mr Pryer knowing that! Well, I'm away out. It's my morning off and I don't intend wasting it indoors this weather. What do you plan to do?'

'Leo, my – er – boyfriend was planning to take me over the transporter bridge to Endlesbrough, but that's off now. I think I'll explore locally. I didn't see much of Coopen last night.'

'I'll take you to Endlesbrough if you like. I intended to do some shopping. We could have lunch in one of the stores then catch the bus back to Stockley. Do the round trip. Does that appeal to you?'

In the light of Miss Shaw's friendliness it seemed churlish to refuse though she had hoped to dawdle around Coopen in case Leo returned unexpectedly. 'Give me ten minutes and I'll be ready,' she said.

Outside the drill hall they caught the bus which for the first few miles took them through a grey and depressing countryside that had no similarity whatsoever to the inspiring descriptions in Leo's letters. Where were the deep valleys and high hills? Here was nothing but flatness and greyness. Even the fleeces of the sheep were grey. Everything was grey.

'I've never seen sheep that colour before,' Philippa said. 'Is it something to do with the atmosphere?'

'Everything to do with the atmosphere I should say, though around here they call it the synthetic.'

'Synthetic?'

'You'll see.'

Suddenly they came upon a wall of solid yellow smoke hanging across the road like a barrier. Philippa half expected the bus to stop. It didn't, it plunged straight on. She could almost imagine she was back in London in the midst of a pea souper. The only difference was that London fog eventually dispersed. This, she gathered, did not.

'Is this what you call the synthetic?'

'Yes. It comes from the chemical works up the road. See these houses we're passing? You can't see their sparkling windows or shining brass doorsteps can you? You could, if it weren't for the synthetic, for the women here clean them every day. What a waste of energy. But they are a houseproud lot in the north.'

'Why do they stay here, living under these conditions?'

'Because they are company houses, and their menfolk work for the company, and the rent's dirt cheap!'

'They would have to pay me to live here,' said Philippa with feeling, 'and then I'd refuse.'

Her companion chuckled. 'You get used to it. I work at the Council Offices – look, we're just coming to it on your left.' Out of the gloom there arose and passed a large and unremarkable building. 'I don't mind it so much in winter for then the synthetic is hardly distinguishable from the natural gloom, but in summer it's insufferable. We dare not have a window open.'

'Whatever makes you stay?'

Miss Shaw gave another chuckle. 'I suppose you could call it love. My fiancé is an industrial chemist and works for the company responsible for all this. We knew each other at Nottingham. We both worked for the same cosmetic firm, Dave in the laboratory, me in the office. When the Manpower Board sent Dave up here, I followed and got myself a job with the council.'

'I think you're a heroine,' said Philippa sincerely.

'No, I just like to keep my eye on my private property

that's all.' Again one of those throaty chuckles. Miss Shaw's sense of humour had a very short fuse, decided Philippa. 'There it is, the famous chemical works. Enormous isn't it?'

Philippa thought it a blot on the landscape, even *this* landscape. The plant was almost obscured by the filth it was pumping out from its towers. As she could think of nothing nice to say about it she kept silent.

'Would you believe it employs about twenty thousand people?' Miss Shaw was out to impress.

Philippa was impressed. Her father employed just thirty but then he was only producing books, not noxious substances.

Once they had passed the chemical works the synthetic gradually thinned out and soon they were in what would pass in that area for fresh air. They were now approaching the docks, a place of cranes and gantrys, seedy-looking public houses and run-down shops and houses. Smitten by the Depression, then lifted up by the requirements of war, with no time in between to repair, improve or rebuild, it was a far cry from Coopen. Philippa, lost in thought, was suddenly aware that Miss Shaw was still discoursing about the chemical works.

' . . . That's why my Dave says to me – "Don't knock the synthetic. It's helping to buy us a house." '

Philippa was all attention now. 'You're buying a house?'

'We hope to when the war is over. Property is the best security a man can have, Dave says. We don't want to burden ourselves with a mortgage either, so we're both saving like mad. That's why Dave lives in the hostel, it's cheaper than digs. Of course, when we get married we'll have to look out for a furnished flat or something then . . .'

It all sounded very prosaic and matter-of-fact. Nothing that even verged on the romantic, yet Philippa envied the other girl from the bottom of her heart.

'You'll not be waiting until after the war to get married?'

'Good gracious, no. What's the point in that? We'll be getting married next time we go home. Just a quiet registry office affair and a little family get-together afterwards. No fuss, that costs money. It's only a question of legalising our union, anyway,' she added casually. 'We've been sleeping together for years. It'll be a relief to get married though – no matter how careful you are there's always that risk—' She gave Philippa a quick glance. 'Am I boring you with all this? I do get carried away sometimes.'

'I'm anything but bored.'

'You're sleeping with your boyfriend, aren't you? Everybody's doing it these days – it's the war. Mind you, Dave and I started before the war, but what's a few months between friends.'

'I don't,' said Philippa after a pause.

'Don't what?'

'Sleep with my boyfriend.'

Miss Shaw fell silent, but not for long, that would have been against nature. 'How long have you known him?'

'Getting on for eight years.'

'Good Lord. There must be something wrong with him or with you or with both of you. What a waste of good effing time,' a word which even in its diminutive form left Philippa speechless.

'There's nothing wrong with either of us,' she said when she recovered. She was about to qualify that with, 'It's a question of principle,' but that she knew was not strictly honest so changed it to, 'It's just that I've set my heart on a white wedding.'

'What on earth has that got to do with it.'

Philippa reminded her what white stood for and Miss Shaw stared back at her incredulously. 'My Godfathers! I thought ideas like that went out with the last war. My cousin walked up the aisle in white satin, six months pregnant, and carrying a bouquet large enough to hide the bulge. She wasn't the only one in the family, either. D'you know what my mother used to say. "Bad girls don't have babies." You can't win either way, can you?'

By now they had reached the bus terminal and the transporter awaited them. If I were a man or a schoolboy, I'd appreciate this engineering feat in the way it deserves, thought Philippa as she followed Miss Shaw into an enormous kind of cable car capable of carrying several vehicles and hundreds of passengers each trip, so her companion informed her. She pointed out that the car was suspended by steel ropes from a trolley running on the underside of the bridge, and like a cable car there was a slight motion as it moved which gave Philippa a queasy feeling, not because she was afraid of heights but because it seemed unnatural to have a bridge that went overhead instead of underneath.

And on that trip they stopped addressing each other formally and fell easily into Jean and Philippa for it seemed foolish to keep on with formality after such intimate revelations.

Philippa had expected a lot from Endlesbrough, for its attractions included a fine shopping centre, several cinemas, a theatre, a concert hall and a famous town hall. Her first view of it therefore was disappointing, for there was little difference to be seen between the dockside area they had just left on the north side of the river and the one that greeted them on the south. But once past this and into the residential and then the business part of the town the outlook improved, and the shopping centre, she admitted to Jean, though not quite Oxford Circus was nearly as good.

She was surprised, however, by the lack of colour. Both men and women looked drab. She remarked on this. 'I can understand it in the men considering the kind of work they do, but not the women. So many of them are in trousers and wearing turbans – almost as if it were a kind of uniform.'

'Which in a sense it is,' Jean said. 'What's the point of them getting dressed up to go and work in a factory or workshop or shipyard, then coming home to catch up with cleaning and washing and making the weekly batch of bread; they never skimp on that no matter how hard they work at their paid job. They're a hard-working breed up here.'

'We work quite hard in the south too!'

Jean smiled. 'Not the way they work up here. You'll never see a southerner in dirty overalls.'

'It occurs to me,' said Philippa coldly, 'that you and Mr Pryer must have come out of the same stable.'

They queued for lunch in the crowded restaurant of a department store and by the time they were shown to their seats the slight frost that had arisen between them had thawed. They both ordered the toad-in-the-hole, which when served turned out to be ten per cent toad and ninety per cent batter pudding. But a batter pudding which melted in the mouth, not like some Philippa had eaten with the texture of cardboard, which she was fair enough to mention to Jean. They finished their meal with coffee served with one cube of sugar in each saucer and cakes filled with ersatz cream.

They browsed around the store later. Philippa bought a packet of hair grips which were unobtainable at home and a pair of very fine artificial silk stockings. Not fully fashioned of course, that was expecting too much, but what a luxury after lisle or heavy rayon.

'Are you going to wear those tomorrow? asked Jean who had bought a more practical pair of lisle for herself.

'Certainly not. I'm keeping these for my trousseau,' which remark for some reason caused Jean to blow a fuse.

They both stopped to admire a short-sleeved summer jumper in a pale shade of lavender. 'That would go beautifully with your suit,' said Jean.

Philippa was tempted to buy it, then looked at the price ticket and decided against. A decision she was bitterly to regret a week later.

They returned by a bus that took them over a road bridge across the Tees to Stockley, where Philippa saw the market-place that had been empty the night before now packed tight with stalls and shoppers; then on to Coopen. Leo was waiting for her in the guests' sitting room making polite conversation with Mrs Fletcher.

She introduced Jean and told him excitedly about the events of the morning. He didn't say much but she sensed his disappointment, for he had wanted to be the one to take her over the transporter and explain how it worked. She was about to take him to her room where they could talk in private, but changed her mind when she caught Jean's eye which winked at her.

They walked through the village and out along an unmade road until they came to open country. By now the sky was clouding over and as they were about to climb a stile into a buttercup meadow the first few drops of rain began to fall. They hurriedly retraced their steps as far as the bus stop and finished up in a cinema in Stockley watching Bette Davis in *The Old Maid*, a film that did nothing for Philippa's ego. She wondered when or if they would ever get the chance to be on their own together.

But things improved on Sunday. The weather was fine, the outlook good. They left early, changed buses twice, and by mid-morning were deep in the North Yorkshire countryside heading for the Cleveland Hills.

'Now will you stop lamenting about the industrial landscape as you call it,' Leo said. 'Just feast your eyes on that view. Not a factory in sight.'

They had been climbing for some time and were now high up on the hillside. The wind was fresh and untainted by smoke or soot, yet she was so happy to be alone with him that if a dozen tall chimneys had suddenly appeared she would not have cared. It was other people who were unwanted. Here was nothing but space and silence. The only moving objects in sight were the sheep that grazed the lower slopes.

A sudden gust of wind whipped Philippa's hair into her eyes and snatched Leo's forage cap and sent it bowling along the ground. He ran for it, caught it, folded it and put it away in an inside pocket. Laughingly, he rejoined her.

It was the first time she had seen him in battle dress. It gave him a jaunty look, reminding her poignantly of the boy she used to know. Thinking of those carefree days before the war clouds gathered, she was overwhelmed by a sudden rush of affection for him. I'll do anything he wants, she thought.

He too was assailed by sudden memories. She had been so much a part of his life this slender girl; first as a gauche and leggy schoolgirl in a short drill slip; and now as a desirable woman so much part of his life that it had taken this parting to bring home to him the fact that he was only half a man without her. The half that mattered – the heart, the spirit, the emotions – only began to function properly when she was near.

He had always seen himself as her protector. He had kept a masterly control of his feelings for many years, for she was a girl of impulses, never stopping to think of the consequences, which meant that their fate was in his hands. She was in his care, he was responsible for her, he must never ever drop his guard, so he was telling himself, when she turned the force of her misty eyes upon him and said imploringly, 'We've walked miles, Leo. Couldn't we rest now for a little while,' and all his good intentions were blown away with the wind.

In the shelter of a massive outcrop of stone was a green and spongy patch of grass and here Leo spread out his raincoat. As he lowered himself on this and drew Philippa gently down beside him, a pair of buzzards appeared and soared high overhead uttering high-pitched haunting cries. They could have been singing, 'Gentle maiden, do not trust him,' for all the attention Philippa paid to them, for Leo was kissing her in a way she had never been kissed before.

'Was that what they call a French kiss?' she asked.

'What do *you* know about French kisses!'

'Only what a girl at the bank told me. She said it was wet and messy and she didn't like it.'

'Come here!'

He released her. 'Was that wet and messy?'

'Oh, indeed not...' And when he kissed her like that again her own good intentions followed close upon his, down the long wind.

If the inevitable had to happen, she thought, what better place than this? Out in this great expanse of open space amidst crags and endless vistas, and the buzzards above serenading them with plaintive cries. Leo's kisses were becoming more urgent. Philippa closed her eyes. She always closed her eyes when in a state of bliss like being kissed or listening to Richard Tauber singing 'You are my heart's delight'. Suddenly the kissing ceased.

Slowly she opened her eyes again and saw that Leo's gaze was not riveted on her but on something just beyond. She turned her head to see what it was and found herself looking straight into the empty eye sockets of a dead sheep. Her screams could have been heard in Endlesbrough.

Leo was on his feet in an instant and lacking the tenderness with which he had pulled her down he pulled her up. 'For God's sake, Philippa, control yourself,' he said.

She turned on him. 'Didn't you notice the sheep before we sat down!'

'Would I have chosen that spot if I had?' A moment before they had been perilously near to losing their virtue; now they were perilously near to losing their tempers. They stared at each other aghast, then Philippa burst into tears. Instantly Leo's arms were around her, cradling her to him, wiping the tears from her cheeks.

'It's my fault, darling. I should have noticed. If the bally sheep had been on the ground, I would have done, but up there on that crag... Roughly the same colour, too. I was in too much of a hurry,' he added lamely.

They were hailed from above by two soldiers on the shoulder of the hill. They spotted Leo's two pips and saluted smartly. 'Sorry, sir. Didn't recognise you, sir. We were the other side of the hill an' we heard the screams an' came to see if anyone needed help.'

Leo, who had sprung from Philippa's side with the agility of a goat, returned their salute with a bungled one of his own. The crumpled raincoat on the ground, the bits of grass on his trousers, her own dishevelled appearance had not gone unnoticed by the two young gunners who exchanged significant glances.

'My – my...' Leo cleared his throat. 'My friend here was frightened by that sheep.'

'Want us to clear it away for you, sir?'

'That won't be necessary. The crows have already made a start.'

'It does rather pong, sir. You didn't notice?'

'The wind was in our favour,' said Leo briskly. The soldiers lingered. They're enjoying this, thought Philippa.

Leo said, 'Well, we won't detain you. Sanders. Hardy. Thank you for your offer of help.'

'Glad to be of help, sir. Miss.' They saluted, turned smartly and resumed their interrupted climb. The wind brought back echoes of their laughter.

'You know them?'

'They're from Jay site – buddies of the chap who was taken ill with appendicitis yesterday. What rotten luck. This will be all round the camp tomorrow.'

'I wish a big hole would open and swallow me up,' said Philippa miserably.

Leo drew her to him again. 'Darling, I'm sorry. It's all

my fault. I'm such a bumbling idiot. I should have scouted around and found a more sheltered spot...'

It was so unusual for Leo to admit he was wrong that Philippa's spirits revived considerably. This was a more tender, sweeter Leo than she had ever known before and for some unknown reason it made her think of the story of Samson and the lion (she was well versed with the Bible, Aunt Dot having seen to that). Then, sweetness had come forth from a dead lion. Now it had come forth through a dead sheep. She rested her head against Leo's shoulder and began to shake.

'Sweetheart, don't cry.'

'I'm not crying, you darling chump – I'm laughing.'

They were both laughing then, clinging to each other, laughing until their sides ached. Laughter that washed away any sense of embarrassment – any lingering shame.

'What are we going to do about ourselves?' said Leo, wiping his eyes. 'What a pair of star-crossed lovers we are to be sure. Any suggestions?'

'Get married?' she said hopefully, thinking how lovely it would be to make love under licence and with no fear of interruption.

'You may have something there,' he said, then lapsed into a thoughtful silence and Philippa did not pursue the subject, quoting instead to herself, ' "Sufficient unto the day... thereof" Matthew; 6.34.'

Walking was easier though no less tiring once they had left the hills behind and continued over rough moorland. Philippa's feet were aching. She had exchanged her high heels for a pair of sandals comfortable to wear but unsuitable for walking. Leo, of course, was wearing army boots and seemed tireless. Long before they reached the road, he was helping her along, taking her weight with his arm round her, sometimes lifting her clear of the ground, encouraging her with promises.

'Bear up, sweet. Only another few yards and you'll see light at the end of the tunnel.'

The light in this case was what he described as an inn in a farmyard, and renowned for its Sunday lunches. 'Are you hungry?'

'I am rather. I couldn't eat my breakfast.'

'Oh. Why was that? Too much for you?'

'No; it was kidneys on toast, and I can't stand offal at any price.' Words that came back to Leo when later he went to the bar to order lunch.

They had been shown into a small but gloomy room at the back of the premises, spotlessly clean but cheerless. There had been a fire in the bar in the front, and old oak settles, spittoons, and pewter tankards hanging from hooks in the ceiling. It looked very cheerful and cosy and peopled mostly by ruddy-cheeked countrymen with their dogs. Leo and Philippa, not knowing any better, had taken a seat by the fire for the wind blowing across the moors had chilled them to the bone, but no sooner had they got settled than they'd been asked to leave as no females were allowed in the smoke room.

'I bet some of those dogs are bitches,' Leo had muttered as they left. 'What will you have, darling?'

'Anything that's on offer.'

'I mean to drink.'

'A cup of coffee for preference.'

Never had coffee been requested at the inn before. The woman behind the bar looked nonplussed. 'No coffee, sir, I'm afraid. I suppose we could stretch a point and make the lady a pot of tea. What will you be having to eat? There's a choice between giblet pie or sweetbreads.'

Leo took the bad news back to Philippa. 'But all is not lost. They keep chickens here. They're willing to make you an omelette.'

Her eyes widened. 'Fresh eggs! It's ages since I had a fresh egg. Just a boiled egg would be heavenly.'

She was served two, done just as she liked them, with homemade bread and a generous pat of butter; afterwards apple pie with a slice of Wensleydale cheese. Leo, ploughing through a generous helping of giblet pie, mashed swedes and boiled potatoes drowning in a lake of rich brown gravy, loosened his belt.

'I shall remember this day for the rest of my life,' said Philippa, sipping her second cup of tea. 'Even the bits that made me cry at the time,' and even now tears stood in her eyes, but they were tears of laughter.

'And there's the rest of today and part of tomorrow yet. Oh God, sweetheart, it's going to be hell when you have gone.'

On the train returning to London the following afternoon, Philippa had time to relive the weekend all over again. She was too keyed up to read, too sick at heart to relax and enjoy the view from the window, though once past the industrial heartland and into the shires it was a view worth watching. The train was less crowded than on Friday; less like a troop train. There were only two servicemen in her compartment; a restless young air cadet biting his nails, and a mature army sergeant deeply engrossed in *Jude the Obscure*. Philippa closed her eyes, willing herself back to the day before. It was about this time twenty-four hours ago that she was getting herself ready for a drinks party at the mess.

Leo had brought the invitation over from Major Baxter Sunday afternoon and it had taken a lot of persuasion on his part to get her to accept. She had squirmed at the idea of meeting his fellow officers after the affair of the sheep.

He had laughed her fears away. 'They wouldn't have heard about that. That was a yarn for the ranks only. They are decent chaps, good company too. They treat me like one of their own.'

'But you are one of them.'

Leo shrugged. 'Not quite. They are regular army, I'm conscripted. They are professional fighters, I'm a non-combatant. They went through Dunkirk together, I've never heard a gun fired in anger. There is a difference, but they don't let it show. And you won't be the only female there,' he went on. 'Some of the chaps have their wives living in the area, in rooms or digs. They'll all be there this evening as well as Mrs Baxter. You'll get on famously with Mrs Baxter – she's your kind of person.'

Philippa knew exactly what Leo meant by that as soon as Mrs Baxter introduced herself, seeking Philippa out where she sat on her own, her glass of sherry warming in her hand.

In spite of Leo's reassurances, in spite of the major's warm welcome, this visit to the mess was not destined to become a highlight in her memory. She watched Leo at the far end of the room indulging in some good-natured verbal sparring with his fellow officers. They were all on Christian-name terms except for Leo whom they referred to as 'Doc'. The ladies were more formal, addressing him as Mr Brooke.

Everybody had been charming to her, yet she still felt the odd one out as if the others belonged to a sectarian club from which she was excluded. They spoke a different language; they shared common memories. Some of the wives had tried to draw her into their circle but had come up against the barrier of her shyness. Finally, excusing herself on the strength of her tiredness after the walk that morning, she had escaped to the sofa in the corner.

She envied Leo his easy manner and lack of self-consciousness until it dawned on her that he was only like that with the men; not their wives with whom he was as ill-at-ease and as tongue-tied as she herself. He was certainly not a ladies' man and she got a certain comfort from that until it raised a doubtful question in her mind.

Had Leo remained faithful to her all these years because he was too shy to go after anyone else? Was Aunt Dot right when she said they had become a habit to each other? Not with her, he hadn't! She had only been fifteen when they first met but had known straight away that there could never be anyone else in her life, and she had always assumed that Leo felt the same. Now she wondered. Then across the room their eyes met and something in the way he looked at her banished all doubt. She was glad after all that they had waited for their wedding night. She still wanted to go to him as a bride in white.

'Would you mind if I joined you?' A younger version of Aunt Dot beamed down at her. Was that why Leo thought Mrs Baxter was her kind of person? She certainly had Aunt Dot's gift of putting people at their ease.

Once seated she produced some knitting from a

capacious handbag, and went to work on a sock even more shapeless than anything Aunt Dot produced.

'You don't object to me knitting, dear? Some do, especially in the cinema. I do so want to get this pair of socks finished this evening. I have a pattern for a cable-knit cardigan I'm dying to start on. Well now, my dear,' she continued. 'Tell me all about yourself.' Which Philippa did without any difficulty or restraint. 'And now tell me about your charming young man. Leo, such an unusual name.'

Philippa found herself explaining about that too. Mrs Baxter had no need to ask questions. She was the sort of person people unburdened themselves to.

'Leos are considered to be leaders of men. Is your Leo a leader of men? A man's man rather than a ladies' man?'

'Definitely a man's man,' said Philippa smugly.

'I am pleased to hear that for your sake, my dear, for he is very attractive to the other sex. All the Red Cross ladies are in love with him, even those old enough to be his mother.'

'What on earth did you and Mrs Baxter find to talk about?' said Leo as late that night he escorted Philippa back across the green. 'Every time I looked across at you your tongues were going nineteen to the dozen.'

'This and that, and cabbages and kings,' Philippa said, smiling secretly. 'She also showed me how to knit a sock without a heel.'

'Great Scott! Do you mean to say people actually knit socks with holes in them?

Philippa spluttered with laughter. 'Oh, you precious idiot. I didn't mean heel-less in that way – I mean knitted like a tube; it takes the shape of the foot. Aunt Dot will love it, she hates turning heels.'

'Did Mrs Baxter mention anything else? Such as a move . . .?'

'What kind of move?'

'A posting. Going overseas . . .?'

Philippa suffered a moment's panic. 'We didn't discuss the army at all. I don't think she would have said anything even if she'd known. Would she?'

'No, you're right. She's an army wife. It's just that – well, there've been rumours. I wondered, that's all.'

Philippa clutched his arm. 'Leo, even if this lot are posted overseas, it doesn't mean you'd have to go with them?'

He didn't answer immediately. They had reached Kimberley Lodge which was in darkness except for a pinhole light above the keyhole. Leo put his hands on her shoulders and gazed intently into her eyes.

All cats look grey in the moonlight, thought Philippa irrelevantly, all eyes look dark. There was no moon but searchlights lit the sky. Not sufficiently, however, to read the expression on Leo's face.

He said with confidence. 'I shan't be going overseas with this bunch, sweetheart. I'm RAMC, not Royal Artillery. I'm just one of the odds and bods the army mucks about a bit and there'll be a lot of mucking about before I'm finally sent overseas.' Words which comforted her until she woke up at three a.m. in a sudden panic, wondering if he was being less than honest.

As she was about to enter her bedroom Mr Pryer came out of the bathroom. He was wearing a striped nightshirt that came just below his knees, and was, for once, without his pipe. He looked her up and down.

'Been out enjoyin' yoursel' agen. That's all you Londoners ever think about, hevin' a good time, going off to night-clubs an' sich . . .'

She had said her goodbyes the following morning, written down her address for Jean, and was sitting in the hall waiting for Leo when Mrs Daniels approached her. 'Just a little something to eat on the train, honey. I know what these long journeys are like. Don't forget what I said earlier – I'll always find a bed for you, any time you feel like coming up again. By the way, Mr Pryer won't be down to say goodbye, he's feeling rather poorly . . .'

That was a relief. The last person she wanted to see that morning was Mr Pryer; then she had second thoughts. Why should he get away with it, the old goat. His rudeness, his insults – and now he hadn't the guts to say goodbye. She'd show him what Londoners were really made of.

She was up the stairs and in his room before she could have second thoughts. He was still in bed, a breakfast tray on his lap and his mouth full. His jaw dropped at the sight of her and a piece of sausage fell on his plate. He was not an attractive sight.

'I've come to say goodbye, Mr Pryer. You'll be pleased to hear that I am going home this morning so you won't have to think up any more unkind things to hiss at me. I just want to get a few things straight before I go. First, I have never been to a night-club in my life and I don't suppose ninety per cent of Londoners have either. They are too busy working to keep alive. It may not be such heavy work as the work up here, but they stick at it, and they stuck at it all through the blitz. They are English just the same as you are, so if you want to abuse somebody, abuse the Germans – they are the enemy, not us down in the south. And another thing. We don't buy our flour a quarter of a pound at a time, we buy it in quarten bags – which is three pounds to you, you miserable old ignoramus.' And then she was gone, leaving him spluttering and coughing.

She had only gone a few steps when she stopped, sighed, and retraced her steps. He was still coughing. He glared at her over the top of his handkerchief, unable to speak.

'I've come back to apologise,' she said, 'I shouldn't have said what I did. I didn't want to leave you with the impression that we haven't any manners in the south. I was brought up to show respect for my elders. I have a father and an aunt who would be very disappointed in me. I'm very sorry.'

She left hurriedly then and was almost at the bottom of the stairs when she was hailed by a loud, 'Hi!'. She stopped and turned. Here it comes, she thought, more abuse. Mr Pryer was standing at the top of the stairwell, his hairy legs exposed, and grinning toothlessly.

'I like a lass with a bit of backbone,' he yelled. 'Didna' think you had any down south. Coom and see us agen, soon. I've enjoyed your visit. It's cheered me oop.'

The train which had been stopping and starting for most of the journey now stopped again. The young air cadet opposite lost his patience.

'Golly. How much longer is this journey going to take. A plane would have done the job in fifteen minutes. What a waste of time, just sitting here doing nothing.'

The sergeant looked at him over the top of his book.

'Oh, for an iron horse with wings,' he said quietly.

'Eh – what?'

'A misquote from *Cymbeline*, my dear chap.'
'Eh?'
'Shakespeare.'

'Silly fool,' muttered the cadet. Philippa tittered to herself. She was glad the army had scored over the Air Force for once. The Air Force had been getting all the kudos lately. The poor patient army was only mentioned in defeat.

Her father was waiting for her on King's Cross station. An unexpected and delightful surprise. 'How did you know what time I'd be here,' she said, exchanging a hug and a kiss.

'Leo phoned me, warned me the train was running late. He said he'd phone again later. He has some news for you.'

But she had only left Leo that morning. What could have happened since? In the army, anything. She thought of a possible posting, and her blood ran cold.

'Did he sound kind of – well, down-hearted?'

'On the contrary. If anything, rather pleased with himself.'

'Oh Dad, I wish we had a magic carpet. I can't wait to get home.'

'I've got the next best thing. My old jalopy, parked round the corner.'

'But how did you manage to get hold of petrol?'

'I scrounged an egg-cupful here and an egg-cupful there – just enough to get me to London and back.'

She was carefully measuring powdered coffee into cups when the phone rang. She flew to the hall and within minutes she was back again, her cheeks pink with excitement.

'That was quick,' said her father.

'Yes, Leo couldn't spare the time, he was on his way to headquarters. Oh Dad, guess what? He's being sent to Edinburgh next week on a four-day course on gas warfare and wants me to join him.'

'And of course, you said yes.'

'What else!'

'What would you do if the bank wanted you to start next week?'

She didn't hesitate. 'Tell them they could whistle for me.'

Five

Philippa travelled to Edinburgh wearing the same green suit in which she had travelled to Stockley and which she had originally intended for her honeymoon. Such was not her intention. She had seen a smart blue and white outfit in Bourne and Hollingsworth which she had set her heart on but the day before she planned to go up West to buy it clothes were suddenly rationed. It was a terrible blow, and quite underhanded of the government, she considered. A last-minute decision, obviously, as there had been no time to issue clothing coupons and so for the time being margarine coupons would have to do instead.

She thought too with regret of the delicate and lacy jumper she could have bought in Endlesbrough. That would have added a stylish touch to freshen up her old green suit, but no good regretting it now. She had hesitated over packing one of her trousseau nighties, the apricot silk trimmed with coffee-coloured lace which had been a twenty-first birthday present from the girls at the bank (Leo had given her an enormous box of Yardley's toiletries), but decided not to and packed her rayon pyjamas and a cotton nightie instead, for who would see her at that time of morning. Only the chambermaid when she brought in morning tea.

Leo had written to say he had booked two single rooms in a hotel within equidistance of the castle and Princes Street, two of the city's main attractions, and had enclosed a voucher for a first-class seat on the express to Edinburgh which he was joining at Newcastle. It was a booked seat, so there would be no possibility of them missing each other.

Everything went off as planned. She had the window seat and spotted Leo wearing a broad grin as they steamed into Newcastle. He looked very trim with his cane tucked under one arm, and his canvas holdall by his feet. A porter carried the holdall in for him and hoisted it on to the rack. Leo tipped him and took the vacant seat beside her.

There had been no kiss on greeting, just a quick squeeze of her shoulder as he had reached up to put his hat and stick with his bag. His eyes said all that was necessary. She knew what put him off as she had been put off when she joined the train at King's Cross – the age and rank of her fellow passengers. None of them below the rank of major, one with red tabs. She fancied they wore disapproving looks as she took her place trying to make herself as inconspicuous as possible. For a minute she had wished she was travelling third class where the atmosphere would have been more congenial, even noisy if there were children aboard, for it was the silence, except for the occasional rustle of a newspaper, that daunted her. Like being in a men's club, she thought, not that she had ever been in one, but her father had.

The comfort was sublime compared to the last time she had travelled north. Far more room for each passenger. No danger of one's next-door neighbour falling asleep and lolling against one's shoulder. She smiled at the memory and the elderly colonel opposite returned her smile in the nicest possible way. Her spirits rose.

And now she had Leo sitting beside her, and even with the arm rest between them she could feel his closeness. She felt sure that if it weren't for the proximity of six senior officers he would have lifted the arm rest and snuggled closer still. As it was they held hands under the cover of the raincoat he had draped across his lap.

'Good journey so far?'

'Luxurious. I do like travelling first class, Leo, it could grow on me.'

'Please don't let it. I won't be able to afford first class in civvy street.'

They were at lunch in the restaurant car when they crossed the Tweed at Berwick, and from then the scenery which had entranced Philippa throughout Northumberland grew even more spectacular. Her squeals of delight brought indulgent smiles from nearby diners.

'Please do lower your voice,' Leo begged in a whisper. 'You're attracting attention.'

'I can't help it, it's all so – so wonderful. Leo! Look – look, a waterfall. Oh, what a darling little waterfall. I've seen bigger ones in Norway but none so pretty. Are they fir trees? No. Pine trees – Scotch pines of course. The real McCoy.' She laughed and choked into her soup, and after that was much subdued. Even a second glass of wine couldn't renew her enthusiasm.

'I felt such an utter fool,' she confided to Leo when they returned to their compartment.

'You get so excited about things.'

'I can't help it, I've always been like that. You would rather I was like that than sitting there with a long face not appreciating anything.'

'You sounded as if you were drunk.'

'I *was* drunk. I was drunk on excitement and the journey and the scenery, and the prospect of having you all to myself for four whole days. I was gloriously drunk.'

Leo looked helplessly around him. The only other occupant of the compartment was a Royal Artillery brigadier, and he was asleep or pretending to be. Leo relaxed. Lowering his voice, he said, 'You realise I shall be tied up at the castle from nine until five?'

'We'll have the evenings together.'

'Yes,' he conceded, 'we'll have the evenings.'

The foyer of the hotel was crowded, mostly with young men in uniform. 'I thought you said this was a family hotel,' Philippa whispered. 'It's anything but. Very swish though.'

There was a queue at reception. Leo joined it. 'You'd better find somewhere to sit while I book us in.'

She found an empty seat behind a palm tree where she could observe all that what was going on without herself being observed. From the direction of Princes Street came the muted sound of traffic; the clanging whine of trams and the rumble of buses. The foyer buzzed loudly with voices. There was a constant to-ing and fro-ing through the revolving doors and the queue at reception grew longer. Philippa's mouth was dry and she longed for tea but was too timid to summon a waiter.

Leo finally joined her. His expression was that of a small boy given an unexpected surprise.

'What's the matter?' she said.

He looked shamefaced. 'You're never going to believe this,' he said.

Her spirits plummeted. 'They've double-booked our rooms.'

'Not quite as bad as that, but they have made a mistake about the booking. They've reserved a double room with single beds instead of two single rooms. They've given me five minutes to take it or leave it. They're besieged by requests for beds.'

Colour rushed into her face. Even her forehead was blushing.

'Leo! You did this on purpose.'

'I guessed you'd think that.' He looked sufficiently contrite for her to realise he had not. He stood up. 'So you want me to cancel.'

'No, wait. Oh dear, I can't think. Leo, what are we to do. Is there a chance do you think of another hotel?'

'Judging by some of the horror stories I heard while I was queuing, I gather not.'

She suppressed a nervous giggle. Her biggest regret was that she had left her silk nightgown behind. She wouldn't have minded Leo seeing her in that for it was prettier than either of her dance dresses. But the skimpy cotton nightie or washed-out stockingette pyjamas! She went cold at the thought.

'But they'll know we're not married,' she wailed. 'The names on our ration books are different.'

'The girl was too rushed to bother about them, or perhaps under four days they're not needed. We'll worry about that problem when it confronts us. In the meantime, darling – what is it to be?'

'If it's all the same to you,' she said, 'I'd love a cup of tea.'

Room 204 was enormous, dwarfing the two high iron-framed bedsteads standing several feet apart. One window looked over a cobbled road and the other over a park. Two solid Victorian wardrobes, a round table of the same period, two large chintz covered chairs and two smaller upright ones, and a boxed-in wash-hand basin completed the furnishings but still left enough floor space in which to dance the polka if they felt so inclined.

'There's enough room here for two more beds,' said Philippa without thinking.

'One's enough.'

'Oh!'

He walked across and took her hands. 'Look darling, if you have second thoughts just say so. I wouldn't do anything you didn't want me to. You only have to say no.'

She looked away, her eyes downcast. 'You don't know how hard it would be for me to say no.'

He gave a shout of laughter. 'Not as hard as it would be for me to take no for an answer.'

They spent the evening exploring Princes Street. The shops were closed of course and, though there was nothing Philippa liked better than window shopping, if the real thing were not available tonight it was a torment to her. With all these beautiful things on display, she had not the means in cash or coupons to make a purchase even if the doors were open. Gazing was not enough, especially not with lingerie that made her mouth water; she turned away. When Leo suggested they should take a climb up to Arthur's Seat before the daylight faded she readily agreed.

They sat there in the hills as twilight closed around them, quietly absorbing the panoramic view spread out below, sitting close and holding hands, somewhat shy and a little overcome by the events that had overtaken them.

Leo broke the silence. 'If it were peacetime,' he said, 'we'd be looking not at a city in darkness but at a city of lights. Who was it said when the last war started that "The lights of Europe are going out one by one"?'

'Lord Grey, I think.'

'I'm overwhelmed by your historical expertise.'

'You needn't be. It's just something I remembered that came out of what my father calls his "rag-bag" of general knowledge.' She gave a sigh. 'I wonder what my father would say about us sharing a room.'

He noticed she said sharing a room rather than sleeping together. He wondered if the time was opportune to give her a little something he had been carrying around with him all day. He withdrew from his pocket a small chamois leather draw-string bag no larger than a fingerstall and watched Philippa's eyes widen with delight and surprise as he revealed what it contained.

'Oh Leo, where and when did you get that pretty little ring?'

He remembered only too well. It was the day he went up to central London to take his final exam. He had arrived at Queen Square with an hour to spare, and rather than kick his heels about in the gardens had wandered off in the direction of Tottenham Court Road and that's how he came across a little second-hand shop tucked away in one of the cobbled alleyways common in that part of the capital.

In the window was a tray of antique jewellery and among the jet and amber necklaces and chandelier-type earrings he spotted the pearl and amethyst ring, its stones arranged in such a way as to suggest a flower – a violet perhaps. Violets were Philippa's favourite flowers. On an impulse (his first impulsive act for many years and not to be repeated for many more years to come) he stepped down into the musty little shop and put down a small deposit for he only had enough on him to pay for his lunch and a packet of Players.

By the time he had paid off the amount still owing he was a registered medical practitioner, his country was at war and the ring, in broad daylight, didn't look the bargain he had thought it. One of the tiny seed pearls was missing, and the amethysts themselves on closer inspection were not whole stones at all, but only chips of stones cunningly clustered together. He put the ring away and tried also to put it out of his mind for Philippa deserved something better than that. Diamonds when he could afford them.

He told Philippa this story now as they sat on Arthur's Seat in the fading daylight. Tiny specks of light began to flicker in the city streets marking the progress of dimmed-out vehicles.

'I don't want you to think I'm using this ring as a sort of bribe,' he said earnestly. 'I thought I would give it to you now if you want it, as I have every intention of buying you a proper engagement ring tomorrow. We could choose it together because I'm hopeless at that sort of thing.'

Philippa did not answer immediately. She's either holding back her tears or her temper or both thought Leo sadly. He was beginning to wish he had let sleeping dogs lie. This one was likely to bite him.

'All these months – nearly two years, when I've been hinting and nudging, and deliberately dragging you past jewellers and pointing out rings I liked. And you so implacable, just staring and not saying a word...' She smothered a sob.

'I was stunned by the prices half the time...'

'That's because you were only looking at the diamonds. I never did like those ugly great solitaires, or those half-hoops. I don't like diamonds – they look so cold. I like pretty stones and pretty colours, particularly I love amethysts. I love this dear, sweet little ring and you've hidden it from me all this time, you beast. And now when you *have* given it to me it's too dark to see it properly – and it doesn't fit. It's too big even for my thumb. Oh, you stupid, adorable chump, why do you do such things to me,' and she collapsed in a fit of tears.

By the time Leo had consoled her, kissed away her tears, wedged the ring on her finger with a page torn out of his diary, and promised he would take it to a jeweller first thing in the morning to be altered, his need to take her to bed had become acute.

As they walked away, arm in arm, she turned and looked back.

'What now?'

'Just savouring. Just thinking that Arthur's Seat is a great improvement on Cleopatra's Needle.'

He was at a loss.

'I'll explain one day,' she said, hugging him gleefully.

*

Leo carefully pulled back the bedclothes exposing Philippa in all her appealing nudity. She was asleep, curled up like a child, her back towards him and one hand tucked under her cheek. She was small-boned and finely sculptured – small breasts, narrow hips, smoothly rounded flanks. All this delectable symmetry hidden from sight and it could have been all his these past two years.

He cursed himself for a fool, for putting caution before their need of each other, for fearing to venture into marriage. And where had it got him? In a single bed in a hotel room in a strange city at the start of a clandestine affair! He smiled ruefully. The first thing he'd do as soon as he got back to barracks was put in for leave; the second, obtain a marriage licence; the third, bring her back here if at all possible.

Philippa stirred but didn't wake. Carefully he replaced the cover. He recalled, with another more rueful smile, her frantic efforts to prevent him removing her nightgown.

'Put the light out! Put the light out!'

'But darling, I've seen many a naked woman. I've been studying anatomy since I was twenty; there isn't anything I don't know about you.'

'Oh yes there is. You may know all about my body, but you don't know what's in my mind. You haven't an idea what I'm thinking. Leo, put the light out, *please*.'

So they had made love in the dark, fumbling and inept at first for they were both virgins, but it came right in the end and afterwards they had fallen asleep in each other's arms. When daylight began to edge round the curtains he had gone back to his own bed and slept on and off for the next few hours waking each time to an awareness that he had taken on a commitment – a precious commitment – and his life would never be the same again. A thought that gave him a great deal of pleasure.

Philippa's eyes were open, the pupils so enlarged her eyes looked all black. She smiled shyly. 'Have you been here all night?'

'No. I went back to my own bed for a little while, but I missed you and came back. Any regrets, darling?'

She shook her head. 'You?'

'Good God, no!'

'Perhaps there is just one teeny weeny one. . . .'

'What's that?'

'I shan't be able to have a white wedding now. I don't qualify any more. I'm no longer a virgin.' She was serious, but he laughed uproariously. He was in fine fettle this morning. He looked young and boyish and carefree.

'Well, I promise not to tell anyone if you don't, so go ahead and have your white wedding. Anyway, you'll always be a virgin to me.'

It was the nicest thing he had ever said to her, and the most romantic. Secretly she was relieved to be rid of her virginity. Goodness knows it had been hard enough to keep it all this time, but she couldn't tell Leo that.

She looked at the clock. 'What time have you got to be at the castle?'

'Nine o'clock.'

'Oh dear, I suppose we had better get up.'

'No time for a little more practice first?'

The room was getting lighter, her nightie was on the floor out of reach. Oh, what the heck.

'Lock the door first,' she said, but time had run out. There came a rattle of a tea-trolley, a discreet tap on the door. She heard Leo's muttered, 'Coitus bally interruptus,' as he made it with seconds to spare to his own bed. She smothered her laughter under the eiderdown.

Edinburgh was all hers for the next three days. She left the hotel with Leo, walked with him to the castle entrance and then was off on her own wearing that seeking, expectant look common with tourists. She spent most of that first morning in Princes Street, visiting first the National Gallery where she lingered over the French Impressionists and then on to the Royal Scottish Academy, then showing an exhibition of Polish art. She enjoyed the old masters more than she did the modern painters, though it was the pictures of war and devastation painted by a refugee that haunted her for the rest of the day.

She went out into the sunshine, and walked aimlessly for a while, happily absorbing the sights about her. It was a perfect place to be on a day like this at this milestone in her life. She did not feel guilty about being Leo's mistress, for that in the eyes of the world was exactly what she was (she did wonder where she would stand in the eyes of her father and Aunt Dot but didn't linger over that thought for long. She was amazed how quickly she was losing her prudish tendencies). She wished Leo were with her to share her delight as she walked the Royal Mile, the old-time route taken by the kings and queens of Scotland between the castle and the Palace of Holyrood House. She looked up at the castle perched on its volcanic crag, high above Princes Street, and wondered what Leo was doing at that precise moment. Listening to some dull lecture, no doubt, with the smoke from his cigarette drifting up into his eyes. Was she as much on his mind as he was on hers? She blushed thinking of the events of the night. It hadn't been at all easy; as a matter of fact it had been rather painful at first, but it had come right in the end, or nearly right. As Leo said, what they needed was more practice.

Only two more nights of practice. She sighed. Of course, they did not necessarily have to wait for night-time, but she couldn't see herself undressing in front of Leo in broad daylight. For one thing there was nothing very elegant in a woman shrugging out of a pair of roll-ons, and in any case Leo had other ideas when he arrived back at the hotel.

He too wanted to do some sight-seeing, and there were only the evenings to do it in. Philippa groaned inwardly as he outlined his plans. She had walked her feet down to the bones that day. The morning in Princes Street, the afternoon exploring the Old Town and visiting the many places of interest crammed within its narrow precincts and finishing up at Holyrood House which did not interest her half as much as some of the more humble dwellings.

Leo slipped the ring on her finger that evening. The jeweller had done a wonderful job of cleaning and burnishing and replacing the missing stone. They were back where they left off the night before. In the gloaming at Arthur's Seat.

'I shall treasure this all the days of my life,' she said, twisting her hand this way and that so that the stones caught fire in the dying light.

'It will do as a stand-in until I replace it with the real thing.'

She protested at such a suggestion.

'I don't want a replacement. I don't want any ring but this.' She held it to her lips and kissed it. 'There, I've put my seal on it,' she said. 'Now I'll put my seal on you,' and she leant forward and kissed him on the lips. It was too much for Leo. He made a grab at her, but she wriggled out of reach.

'Not here, Leo, oh, darling, not here. Somebody might come along. Besides it's not respectable – out in the open . . .'

'Right then, let's get back to the hotel and be as respectable as we like.'

She didn't go so mad the next day. She saved her feet by taking a bus out to the zoo, and reached there ten minutes before opening time. She had the place to herself for the first half-hour and wandered about at will, taking as much interest in the shrubs and flowers as she did the animals for she always felt slightly uncomfortable about wild animals penned up in cages. Not that these animals were all in cages. Going along one of the narrow sidepaths, she suddenly came upon a chimpanzee sitting on a low stone wall enjoying a quiet smoke.

They eyed each other warily. If it had been a large and ferocious-looking dog she would have said, 'Good dog. Good dog' in an appeasing way because she had heard it said that dogs could smell fear. That seemed hardly appropriate in this case so she said a friendly 'Good morning' instead. The chimpanzee regarded her with the eyes of a solemn and thoughtful old man and went on smoking. After that she kept to the main walks where there was always a keeper in sight.

Another trip was to Queensferry to see the Forth Bridge, a sight nobody visiting Edinburgh could afford to miss. She had seen it many times on film, three times in *The Thirty-nine Steps*, though the attraction there had not been the bridge as much as Robert Donat. Seeing the bridge now in reality, straddling the sparkling blue waters of the Firth against a background of gentle hills, she admitted reluctantly that sometimes man could rival nature in producing something to marvel at.

'Oh, you should see it,' she told Leo later, welling with enthusiasm as she always did when something had touched her deeply. 'I've always thought it a bit of a joke, you know – because of that old chestnut – taking so long to paint the Forth Bridge that when they reach the end the men have to start at the beginning again. Oh, I wish you could have been with me instead of being shut up in that grisly old castle.'

'It is an extremely interesting castle, and I should have thought with your love of history you would have added it to your list of musts. It has a very fine example of an artesian well.'

She had no idea what an artesian well was and didn't ask because she felt the explanation might take up precious time. 'All castles are grisly as far as I'm concerned,' she said. 'The only ones I like are the ones in ruins. Every time I go past the Tower of London I shudder to think of all the poor souls who have been tortured or murdered or beheaded there. If the stones could weep they'd weep blood. You can keep your old castles – I'd rather have a thatched-roof cottage.'

'With roses round the door, death-watch beetle in the timbers, and a privy at the end of the garden?'

'Naturally.'

When she returned to Woodside her father asked her what she remembered most about Edinburgh. The obvious answer she could not give him but the one she did came straight from her heart. 'Feeding the squirrels in Princes Street Gardens.'

'Great Scott, girl. You can feed squirrels in Regent's Park any day of the week.'

'But they're not so pushy as the Edinburgh ones. I used to buy sandwiches for my lunch and take them to eat in the gardens and as soon as I sat down the squirrels were all over me. I loved it. It made me feel like St Francis of Assisi.'

But before then there was another magical day and night to come. Leo finished his course at midday and they went back to the hotel to lunch in the dining room. Philippa hoped he would suggest an afternoon of relaxation in their room, but he was bursting with energy and longing for fresh air after sniffing various gases all morning. And, too, he wanted to see all the sights for which Philippa's graphic descriptions had whetted his appetite. They took the bus to the zoological gardens, but being Friday afternoon, the zoo was full of visitors. No chimpanzee having a casual cigarette on the quiet – all animals were safe behind bars. 'Normally, I don't like seeing wild animals in cages,' Leo said. 'But I must admit these look a contented lot.'

After the zoo they went, by a different bus, to Queensferry, this time taking the ferry across the Firth and back which gave Leo ample opportunity for a good view of the bridge from all angles.

'Gosh, I wish I had a camera. Why didn't I think to bring my camera with me?'

'Even if you had I don't suppose you'd be able to get a film,' said Philippa, which was true enough. Rolls of film were fast disappearing off chemists' shelves. But the mention of a camera had given Leo an idea.

'I haven't got an up-to-date photograph of you. There's a photographer's on the way to the castle. I passed it this morning. Let's hurry back before it closes and see if he'll oblige us.'

'Without an appointment, I doubt it. I haven't got one of you in uniform, either. But oh, Leo, wouldn't it be wonderful if he could.'

He could, and did. It was nearly closing time. Both his assistant and receptionist had already left. His quota of film was almost exhausted, but one look at the earnest young officer and the girl with the misty grey eyes and his mind was made up.

'See that door?' he said to Philippa. 'Just through there and on your left if you want to do your hair.' To Leo: 'What time did you say your train leaves tomorrow?'

'Eleven hours.'

'I won't be able to show you proofs. And I can only let you have one copy each, but they will be ready for you by ten.'

That evening they took a last energetic walk to Arthur's Seat. It was a sad leave-taking with a few tears on Philippa's part. 'Promise me you'll bring me back to Edinburgh, one day.'

'Perhaps sooner than you think.' When she turned on him the full strength of her enquiring gaze he felt he had either said too much or not enough. 'Don't bank on it, darling. I don't want to raise your hopes unnecessarily, but I am hoping to get some leave soon – a week or ten days, perhaps. I know it's rushing things, but would you be prepared to get married then?'

She didn't know whether to laugh or cry. Rushing

things! Oh Leo. 'And come back here for our honeymoon?'

'Where else?'

So their last night together was one of joy rather than poignancy. When Leo said yet again, 'Any regrets, darling?' she had her answer pat.

'Yes, one rather big one – about two hundred feet high, and 287 steps to the top. That's why I jibbed. I was already down on my uppers. . . .'

'What on earth are you talking about?'

'The Scott Monument.'

'I see. You want to play games, do you!' So they did, gentle and loving games in the playing of which Philippa finally shed the remnants of her shyness.

All through breakfast she made plans. A white wedding was out of the question, so why not a dress to match her ring? She had seen some beautiful pale mauve shot silk in a store in Ilford, the last of their pre-war stock. She could have that made up into a princess-style dress and wear with it what she had always planned, a silver net snood.

'You're very preoccupied this morning,' said Leo, helping himself to the last piece of toast. Philippa had hardly touched her food. 'Not sad, are you?'

'Yes in one sense, but not in another. There's too much to look forward to.'

Her smile was one of simple contentment. Leo was smitten with doubt. He hoped to God he hadn't raised false hopes. She took everything to heart this unpredictable girl – hope, expectation, disappointment – each could smite her in a different way. He didn't want to see her so smitten – he didn't want to see her cast down. He said; 'Don't bank too much on it, sweetie. There's no certainty in wartime.'

'Or in peacetime. You never know when you're going to be knocked down by a bus or—' She couldn't bring herself to utter the most obvious – the threat from the sky. 'Or killed in a train crash.' She smiled reassuringly. 'Don't worry Leo, everything is going to turn out right. I know because my right palm was itching this morning.'

The photographs exceeded all expectation. They were good of them both, especially Leo for he was the more photogenic of the two. Philippa wished there had been time to have had her hair reset but at least she had had time to tidy it. She was a little disappointed the photographer had cut her off at the elbows because she was hoping to show off her ring. He had been more generous with Leo, showing off as much of his uniform as possible, and Leo as always looked at his best in uniform. They exchanged their photographs with due solemnity. Somehow it seemed symbolic, like exchanging vows.

Edinburgh. Old Reekie. Never to her she thought as they steamed out of the station. A city of history and culture and impressive vistas. Of dreams come true, and a lost virginity.

'What are you smiling at,' asked Leo.

'Nothing of consequence,' she answered.

Leo's first letter arrived two days after her arrival back at Woodside. There was no news of his pending leave, it was too soon yet to make enquiries he said, yet the letter itself sent her into transports of joy.

No longer beginning, 'My dear Philippa' but 'My

Beloved'. No longer finishing, 'Yours ever, Leo' but 'Your ever-grateful husband'.

So this is what happened when you lost a man's respect. He suddenly began to write love letters.

'Any news?' said her father.

'No. Just that he got back safely and found plenty of work waiting for him.'

'Am I not allowed to see his letter?'

She looked up with a whimsical smile. 'Not if you don't mind, Dad.'

'Why should I mind? I'm glad at last you've come to your senses.'

He had been very circumspect in his questioning of her stay in Edinburgh. He had admired her ring and enquired its history. He had put her through the eyes and no-eyes drill on the Forth Bridge, but not once had he asked about their hotel or sleeping arrangements. But he knew. She could tell by the way he sometimes looked at her that he had a shrewd idea what went on in Edinburgh.

She lived for the telephone. She knew as soon as Leo had news he would be in touch. Aunt Dot had taken to phoning quite often. She had nothing really to tell them, she just wanted to chat.

'The poor old lady is lonely. It's about time I went down to see her again,' Jonathan said one evening. 'As a matter of fact, I thought about running down this Sunday. Can't expect this fine spell to last much longer. Better take advantage while I can.'

She looked up. Her father was on the prowl – up and down the room in a straight line, hissing between his teeth, a sure sign of something on his mind. 'What about petrol?' she asked.

'Ursula's brother managed to get me some. He's a handy chap to know, Ursula's brother.'

Philippa lowered her book. 'Ursula?'

'Ursula Warwick – my new bookkeeper-cum-secretary. Get your grey cells working, girl.'

'Oh, Mrs Warwick. I didn't know she had a brother.'

'Neither did I until recently. He lives in Slough.'

'Oh.' Philippa read two more paragraphs then lowered her book again. 'And you're taking her to Leigh on Sunday?'

'W-ell . . . as she got me the petrol. I thought it would be a nice little afternoon run for her.' He paused by a small side-table, picked up a piece of Rockingham china and studied it as if it were something he had never seen before. 'I don't suppose you want to come with us?'

Put like that she had no option but to refuse. His obvious relief strengthened her suspicion. He sat down at last and rolled himself a cigarette. She took up her book. Neither relaxed. Jonathan was the first to break the silence.

'I was wondering . . . as you know, Ursula lives on her own and must get lonely at times. Would you mind if I asked her in for coffee one evening? It's time you two met.'

Philippa was not surprised that her father wanted her to meet his latest employee for with such a friendly little firm as Byrd's that was not unusual, but she was surprised that he should feel the need to ask her first. He seemed rather embarrassed too, which was a new experience for him.

'I shan't mind in the least,' she said, trying not to sound as if she did. 'Any evening you please.'

'Make it tomorrow evening then.' He rose. 'Well, too

late to start on the garden now. I think I'll call on Beckham and see if he'll come for a drink.' Beckham was their friendly neighbourhood forest-keeper. 'Don't wait up.'

Ursula? Not the sort of name that fitted the image of the efficient but reticent bookkeeper as her father had once described her. More of a name that befitted a traitress, somebody like Mata Hari who had been shot as a spy in the Great War and, so rumour had it, faced the firing squad wearing a fur coat and nothing else. She had seen Marlene Dietrich in the title role and had sat in the cinema on her own, crying copiously. But now her sympathy for the poor dead spy suddenly evaporated. How could her father fall for somebody like that! The telephone bell broke into her wandering thoughts. She flew to answer it.

'Leo, oh darling – any news?'

'Are you doing anything on 20 September?'

'Leo, that's three months away! Can't you make it sooner?'

'I tried, darling, but there's some kind of flap going on at present – everything at sixes and sevens. Anyway, the date my leave starts is official – 19 September. I'll be down that day and we'll get married the day after. All right with you? Good. And do you still want to go to Edinburgh for the honeymoon . . . and the same hotel? I guessed you would. But not that same room.'

'Darling, it was a lovely room,' she protested.

'But I think you'll find a double bed has its advantages.'

She hung up in a state of utter bliss. Her happiness spread out to embrace all others. Poor Dad, he wasn't that decrepit. It was only to be expected that he could still enjoy female company. He had kept faithful to her mother's memory for more than sixteen years. He deserved a break. And fancy taking exception to a name – she must have been mad. Ursula, a pretty name really, not a bit *femme fatale*ish when uttered slowly. What a lot of fuss about nothing, she thought, she ought to be ashamed of herself. She was. She hoped Ursula would turn out to be the motherly sort. Her father could do with a bit of spoiling.

So it was to be September after all, her thoughts ran on. It was fated that September should be earmarked as her wedding month. Postponed by war in 1939. Blitzed in 1940. Now September 1941 – third time lucky. She danced a little jig. First thing tomorrow she'd go off to Ilford and buy the lavender silk and take it to Mrs Downie to have it made up. Mrs Downie of South Woodside had the reputation of being a court dressmaker. Philippa wasn't sure what the difference was between that and an ordinary dressmaker, she only knew that whenever she went to Mrs Downie for a fitting she knew she was in the hands of an expert.

Her father and Ursula Warwick arrived just before nine o'clock. She watched them from the window of the drawing room as they walked slowly along the garden path, stopping now and then to admire the border of shrub roses. A blackbird who had a nest close by clucked nervously. This was no Mata Hari she thought, studying the tall spare figure as she bent over to smell one of the roses – or one of the motherly sorts, either. For no reason that she could fathom, she shivered.

They met in the hall and eyed each other like two protagonists in a ring. Under the eye of the referee they shook hands and exchanged polite greetings. Philippa took the first opportunity to wipe her hand on her skirt.

She felt as if a cold, dead fish had rested momentarily on her palm. She couldn't remember taking such an instant dislike to anybody before and wondered how she would survive the evening.

For her father's sake she did her best to make their guest feel welcome. Jonathan's cellar had diminished rapidly since the beginning of war, but even so there was enough sherry left to colour a Waterford decanter. She poured out a glass for Mrs Warwick and eyed her surreptitiously as she sipped it.

Some people might call her handsome if they liked that hollow-cheeked, narrow-faced, prominent-chin type of beauty. Another forty years and she'll look like a witch, thought Philippa with pleasure. She had an abundance of light brown hair worn in a becoming style, centre parted, and coiled in a bun at the nape of her neck.

She was plainly but smartly dressed in dark colours, her only ornament a diamanté clip in the lapel of her jacket. There was no wedding ring on her left hand, Philippa noted, but she found that unsurprising. Many widows left off their rings if or when resuming work, it made for happier staff relations. Her eyes were unusual, almost milk-coloured. Philippa found them so disconcerting she kept her own averted.

Only once did Ursula directly address her again, and that was when Jonathan asked her to show off her engagement ring. Reluctantly, she did so, and Mrs Warwick made the necessary responses though all the time, Philippa thought, she was pinpointing with her opaque eyes the mismatched pearl and tiny non-precious stones.

'Very quaint,' she said, smiling enigmatically. 'So refreshing to see an old-fashioned ring on the finger of a modern girl.'

There were a lot of retorts Philippa could have answered to that, and would have done if her father had not been present. Instead she went to the kitchen and took her temper out on the coffee pot.

When Jonathan returned from running his guest home, he came looking for Philippa and found her in the kitchen, washing up.

'You didn't exactly make Mrs Warwick feel welcome.'

Philippa thought that remark unfair. 'I made her a cup of coffee. I offered her a piece of my Victoria sponge.'

'Yes, but saying you made it with liquid paraffin was enough to put anybody off.'

'It didn't put *you* off. You said you wouldn't have noticed it hadn't been made with marge if I hadn't told you.'

'Philippa, why do you dislike Mrs Warwick?'

She looked away not wanting to see the hurt in his face. 'I don't dislike her – I just don't like her. There's something about her. It's her eyes, I think.' She latched on to this idea as if it were a lifeline. 'They're such a weird colour – like opals. It quite put me off.'

'You can't blame Ursula for the colour of her eyes. Would you be put off by a hunchback or a club foot or a harelip?'

'What a perfectly beastly thing to say.' Philippa was close to tears.

Her father could see that; his expression softened. 'Philippa is it that you don't want anybody to take your mother's place?'

She turned on him instantly. 'You wouldn't say that if it wasn't already in your mind. You're thinking of marriage, aren't you! Oh Dad, how could you. You hardly know her.'

'I'm not thinking of marriage,' he said wearily. 'I just want company. I get lonely, Pippa. I was lonely when you went off to Edinburgh. I was dreading you going off to Norfolk. Now you are thinking of joining the band of camp followers. Where do your loyalties lie? With Leo, or with the bank, or with me?'

He had turned the tables with a vengeance.

'Oh Dad, I'm all churned up inside. Naturally, I want to be with Leo, but if I join him up north I'll be letting the bank down – after they've been paying my salary all this time, too. And leaving you. I don't want to leave you all on your own. . . .' Especially not now with Mrs Warwick waiting in the wings, she could have added.

'Well now, Norwich is not all that far away, and there's a good train service I understand to Liverpool Street. And don't worry about me – I've got enough to keep me busy. I won't be lonely.'

I bet you won't, thought Philippa with venom, her good sense flying out of the window. 'Dad, I must warn you. That wo – that Mrs Warwick – she's out to catch you. She's a schemer . . . she'll stop at nothing—'

'*Philippa!*' His mood changed. His voice was like thunder. 'I want no more of this sort of talk. Do you understand!'

'Yes, Father.'

There was an abyss between them that lasted until Sunday, when they heard on the wireless that Hitler's troops had invaded Russia.

'We have an ally again,' said her father with obvious relish.

She stared at him. 'But what good will they be all that way away? In any case, how can they hold out against

Germany when they couldn't even hold out against a little country like Finland?'

'Don't underestimate the Russians,' her father said. 'That was the mistake Napoleon made.' He took out his tobacco pouch and rolled a cigarette. It took him longer to light it than to make it, but it was alight at last. He drew on it with a sigh of contentment. 'This is a momentous day, Pip, 22 June – remember that. The day Hitler made his second fatal mistake.'

'When was his first?'

'The day he invaded Poland.'

Sometimes, Philippa mused, her father seemed to be talking in riddles. 'Will you still be going to Leigh this afternoon?' she enquired casually.

'Of course, why not? We can't stop the course of events by staying at home.' He rose from his chair and went to the window, looking out. 'It's a lovely day for an outing. Sure you won't change your mind and come?'

Leo mostly phoned on a Sunday. 'No, but thanks all the same. Give my love to Aunt Dot, and tell her I'll be writing.' She decided it was time to offer an olive branch, hypocritical though it made her feel. 'I hope it keeps fine for you. Have a good time – the two of you.'

He turned. He looked pleased. 'Thanks, Pippa. I'm sure we will.'

The day turned into a scorcher. Philippa only allowed herself fleeting thoughts of the two enjoying salt sea breezes. By mid-afternoon the drawing room was unbearable, getting the full force of the sun even though she had drawn the curtains and opened wide the windows and French doors. She would have decamped to the garden but the part near the house was in full sunshine and the shady part at the bottom was out of earshot of the phone.

She had skipped lunch as it was too hot to eat, but now she was beginning to suffer hunger pangs. There was the remains of a rather limp salad in the larder and a tin of Spam she was keeping for her father's supper. She smiled to herself, thinking of one of her father's classic sayings: 'If we only had some eggs we could have eggs and bacon if we only had some bacon.'

She didn't know the origin of that remark but her father would often quote it if she began a moan that started with, 'If we only had. . . .' Dear old Dad, she wondered how he was getting on with that harpy. Not too well, she hoped.

She found at the back of the larder, a bit rusty with age, a tin of sardines. She opened the tin with difficulty and sniffed at them. They smelled all right, but then she had never come across a bad sardine before so had nothing to go by. They tasted good too with the salad and a slice of bread spread with the remains of the week's butter. Tomorrow she would join the queue for another weekly supply of rations. Sunday was always Oliver Twist time in their household. Perhaps other housewives managed better. She never could.

She was dozing over the Sunday paper when the ringing of the phone shattered her dream of Leo in a kilt walking hand in hand with her across the Forth Bridge. In her hurry to reach it before it went dead she lost a shoe.

'Leo – Oh, darling,' she cried. 'I was just dreaming of you.'

'You can dream of me for a change,' said Aunt Dot. 'What I want to know, miss, is why didn't you come with your father instead of sending that dreadful woman with the white eyes. . . .'

'Aunt Dot, have they left?'

'Of course they've left, otherwise I wouldn't be talking like this. Philippa, how could you do that to me? I was expecting you and there she was instead, and your poor father like a dog with two tails. She is nothing but an adventuress. Did you know she is out to ruin your father?'

'Aunt Dot!'

'She has got *plans* for Byrd's. She wants your father to branch out. She says there is no call for fine art books in wartime, that the public want escapism and as books are about the only thing not rationed there will be a much greater demand for them. She a schemer, Philippa, a manipulator, and I never thought your father could be so taken in. Didn't you try to warn him?'

'Yes, and got my head bitten off.'

'Philippa, if you don't do something, she'll be getting control of the firm. That's what she's after. She has some hare-brained idea of publishing popular fiction. Light romance even. *Romance*.' Aunt Dot's voice rose. 'Philippa, your great-great-grandfather must be turning in his grave. . . .'

Philippa felt it only fair to break in here.

'Well, actually Aunt Dot that was Dad's idea. No, not publishing romance but branching out into general fiction. It's becoming more and more difficult to get hold of the expensive paper Byrd's have always used. When the present stock goes there'll be no more forthcoming. In fact, Dad says, there will be only one type of paper available if the war goes on for long. He has seen samples of it. Like recycled cornflake packets, he said, but you know Dad. . . .'

'I thought I did until today, but now I'm not so sure.' A troubled sigh came over the wires. 'So Byrd's will be publishing a sort of *Comic Cuts* for adults in future, is that it?'

'Not as bad as that. There will still be a demand for serious fiction, and reprints of the classics. I think that's what Dad has in mind.'

'I hope you are right, my dear, but I have my doubts. Philippa, please come down and see me soon. I am feeling extremely low. Oh dear, there was something else on my mind that I wanted to tell you, but it has gone now. Never mind, it couldn't have been important. . . .'

Philippa had just retrieved her shoe when the phone summoned her again. Aunt Dot must have remembered what it was she wanted to say. But it was Leo, sounding like a tired old man, who answered her. She knew at once something had gone dreadfully wrong and the hairs on the back of her neck rose.

'I've been trying to get you all day, but the switchboard's been jammed this end. I haven't got long, darling. Just a minute or two – just long enough to say goodbye.'

She couldn't marshal her thoughts. 'Why goodbye? It isn't anything to do with—?' She was about to say 'anything to do with Russia', then remembered the ever-vigilant operator and altered it to 'the events of today?'

'No connection. There's been a flap on all week but I didn't think I was part of it. Now it appears I am. We move out tonight. I'm allowed one letter which I'll post to you from the docks if I get the chance.'

Her ears filled with a great rushing sound which almost drowned his voice. She grabbed at the table as she felt the floor tremble beneath her feet. 'The docks! Leo, you don't mean you're being sent overseas . . . *Leo*. . . .'

'No careless talk, please.'

She screamed, 'Don't cut us off. Oh, please – please – don't cut us off. . . .' But all was silence.

Six

Norfolk became her salvation, her refuge. In those long weeks before the first of Leo's letters arrived, she slowly and painfully carved out a new life for herself in a city that was to become her second home.

It was here in mid July that the first news of Leo reached her in a letter her father had forwarded from Woodside. It was unstamped and censored, carrying the words 'Examiner 7909'. It was also brief.

'Darling sweetheart,
As you no doubt realise, I'm on board a ship which I may not describe to you or even hint where it is. You've probably noticed I haven't even dated this letter. It goes in a special envelope, taken ashore, and then delivered to the Base Censor.
I am finding it difficult to know what to write. There is so much I want to say and so much I can't. Now that I am on board I feel I must and can brace up to the fact that we are going to be

parted – maybe for years. We have had so many partings but since they have all been followed by happy reunions we must look forward to an even happier reunion when I return.

Sweetheart, try not to be despondent. Think of the memories we share – Epping Forest, the dances at the Chantry, Coopen, Edinburgh, and our many visits to the Odeon. Keep smiling, pet, just like in that lovely photograph you had taken in Edinburgh. I must say "cheerio" for now. There is only one table in this cabin and three other chaps waiting to use it.'

She had cried so much since Leo's phone call that she had thought it impossible to cry any more but now tears flowed without effort. Wearily she wiped them away and went in search of her writing-case. In that was the code she and Leo had devised during her stay at Coopen.

Thinking then that should he be shunted off without warning (which neither of them thought likely, poor innocents) it was a way of letting her know his destination. A simple code using cinema titles for theatres of war or military bases. Odeon headed the list and that stood for India. India – thousands of miles away. Oh God, it could be months before she heard from Leo again.

It could have been worse, she mused, trying to chivvy herself out of her depression. He could have been sent to Singapore, Malaya, Hong Kong – distance was only relative. They had been torn apart, and what fate had put asunder could not be joined together again by a young RAMC officer or a heart-sick girl.

And heart-sick she certainly was on that fateful Sunday

in June when her father, arriving home, stopped dead at the sight of his daughter hunched on the bottom stair with a chalk-white face and swollen, reddened eyes.

'Philippa! Why aren't you in bed?' For she had got as far as changing into pyjamas and dressing-gown. 'What on earth are you doing there?'

'Waiting for you,' she said, dully lifting her head.

'Great Scott, child, you look perished. How long have you been waiting?'

'I don't know – hours, I think. I couldn't get to sleep. I was worried about you not coming home. I was beginning to think I was going to lose you too. Losing everybody. . . .' Her voice broke. 'Oh Dad, I've had a phone call from Leo. He only had time to tell me he was being posted when the beastly operator cut us off. . . .'

'Overseas?'

'I think so, judging by his voice. He sounded dreadful. Oh, Dad, I don't know when I shall see him again.'

He wanted so much to comfort her as he used to when she was a child, sitting her on his knee and stroking her hair as she sobbed out her latest heartbreak. Her best friend wouldn't play with her any more, or the kitten, or rabbit, or guinea-pig, or stick insect, whatever, had just died. But only one person was capable of comforting her now, and God knows where Leo was bound for.

'Didn't Aunt Dot warn you that I would be late home?' he said, gingerly lowering himself on the stair beside her. 'I told her that Ursula and I were stopping off for a meal at that new Road House on the Arterial Road. She promised to phone you.'

'She did phone, but she didn't say anything about you staying out late. There was something she wanted to tell me but couldn't remember. I expect that's what it was.'

'Poor old Dot, she's becoming forgetful in her old age. Her behaviour today was odd to say the least.' He rose and helped Philippa to her feet. She was shivering. 'Come along, child, it's cold out here. What you need is something to warm you up.'

Facing her father across the kitchen table, sipping the cocoa he had generously laced with brandy, Philippa felt her emotions beginning to thaw and with the thaw came a deluge of resentment – a resentment that drove her to make a spirited attack against all wars in general and the present war in particular.

'I didn't know they could send somebody abroad just like that. I always thought servicemen got embarkation leave,' she said bitterly.

'Ninety-nine times out of a hundred they do, but there's always the one that slips through the net. Leo was unlucky. I expect they needed an extra MO to make up a draft. Here was a likely young chap – no ties, unmarried... Which in the circumstances I suppose is just as well.'

She bristled. 'What do you mean... just as well?'

'What if you had been married? What if you were pregnant? How would you have felt losing your husband just at the time you needed him most? Not knowing when you'd see him again, or if at all. How would you like to be in that position?'

But Philippa wasn't in the mood to be comforted. 'At least I would have had his child – I would have had part of him to love.' The tears started again, spurting uncontrollably. Her father stretched across the table and touched her hand.

'What you need now is something to keep you occupied. A job. I wish to goodness you could hear from the bank. It's about time you did.'

She looked at him with streaming eyes. 'I'm being punished,' she whimpered. 'Losing Leo is my punishment. I was hateful to your Mrs Warwick, and now I'm paying for it.'

He sighed. 'Oh, child. When are you going to grow out of this footling superstition?'

Her father got his wish. A few days later Philippa received an official notice from the London branch of Brundle's Bank, now established in its new headquarters at Ludgate Hill. Enclosed in the envelope were details of the newly formed Norwich branch, and also a list of recommended accommodation for those who hadn't already made their own arrangements. For unattached female staff (unattached from what, wondered Philippa peevishly, still too down at heart to see anything to smile at in the bank's arcane language) there was the hostel in Riversway supervised by Miss Jolly, and with a local woman, a Mrs Toser, acting as housekeeper. There were double rooms and single rooms available, and as there was likely to be a demand for single rooms immediate application was advisable.

Philippa put in her application at once. As much as she liked Miss Jolly, and was delighted to learn that she had opted to come to Norwich rather than to Ludgate Hill, she had no wish to share a room with her. She had no wish to share a room with anybody. She was a girl who willingly shared her joys but kept her sorrows to herself and she needed a private room for that.

This was not the first news she had received of the bank since the devastating raid in May. Daphne James, also from the ledger department, had kept in touch. It was she who had put Philippa's mind at rest about the fate of the caretaker and his wife.

'They were dug out alive,' she wrote. 'They were saved by a crossbeam that took the weight of the falling masonry. Poor Mrs Fuller was in a state of shock and taken to hospital, but as soon as she had had a cup of tea and a hot bath she insisted on discharging herself. They are caretaking at the Ludgate Hill premises now. You would never believe,' the letter continued, 'how normal it looks now around Gracechurch Street. Do you remember that awful morning when it looked like something from Dante's *Inferno*? I thought then, and so did everybody else, that that part of the City was written off completely. Well, it's working again, or most of it is. The scars remain, but there are not so many as were thought at first when everything was obscured by smoke. Unfortunately, our old bank is too badly damaged for temporary repairs. It's going to be pulled down and rebuilt when the war is over. You'll be pleased to hear that that little shoe shop opposite, the one where we could buy a pair of silk stockings for one and eleven (not fully fashioned of course) has survived. Also Fuller's cake shop, and the jewellers in Leadenhall Street where you spent so much of your lunchtime gazing into the window. . . .'

Daphne wasn't coming to Norfolk, she informed Philippa in another letter. 'I'm a real Londoner, not one of your ersatz kind. My father was a Methodist minister in the East End and I was brought up within the sound of Bow Bells. I'd rather be bombed in London than bored to death in the country, so I'm sorry, Philippa, but I won't be joining you in Norfolk. I'm starting at the Ludgate Hill branch on Monday. I understand they have installed one of the new photo copiers and in future everything is going to be duplicated and triplicated and dispatched around the country for safety. I wouldn't mind having a bash at that. All one does is sit there feeding it with documents, letters and paying-in slips – just up my street. There are rumours floating around that all females between the ages of eighteen and thirty will soon be conscripted for National Service unless, of course, they work in a reserved occupation. Is banking a reserved occupation, do you think? Not for lowly clerks like us, you bet.'

When Philippa got her first glance of Norwich cathedral she hardly gave it a second look. Carrying only an overnight case, for her main luggage had been sent on in advance, she made her way through the barrier at Thorpe station and approached the taxi rank in the station forecourt.

'Riversway, please.'

The driver gave her a quizzical look. 'You ever been to Norwich before?'

'My first visit.'

'Well let me make it easy for you, miss. If I was to tell you that do you get in the cab on this side and I was to do a U-turn, and then you stepped out on the other side, you'd be in it.'

'You mean Riversway is just across the street?'

'That's about it, but I'd hate to think of you getting lost so just hop in.'

It was a little more than just across the street. It was crossing the line of traffic which in spite of the shortage of petrol was surprisingly busy. A short but leisurely drive alongside a river placid and sparkling beneath drooping trees aroused her from her apathy. She sat up and took notice.

The journey from Liverpool Street had been long and tedious with the train stopping and starting all the way, and her mind was still full with memories of that other happier journey to Edinburgh. She could not but compare the scenery then to the boredom of the flat East Anglian landscape rolling slowly past the windows.

But now, looking out of the cab and seeing as a whole a picture of a shimmering river amid water meadows, and beyond that the slender and graceful spire of the cathedral against a milky sky, her spirits received a much-needed lift. Not quite a Constable, she thought, but it could have been if he had visited Norwich instead of Salisbury, and the first tiny seed of what was to grow into a deep and abiding love for Norfolk took root.

Mrs Toser was quite a surprise. Mrs Daniels had set the pattern for what to expect of a boarding house landlady and Mrs Toser didn't quite fit. But then, Mrs Toser didn't fit anything, certainly not the dress she was wearing which only fitted where it touched her bony figure.

She regarded Philippa with pale blue eyes from beneath a furrowed brow almost eclipsed by a greying fringe of scanty hair. The expression on her long sallow face was that of a martyr.

'You caught me at an awkward time,' she complained. 'You said you'd be here at three.'

Philippa apologised and explained about the train being delayed but her excuses fell on deaf ears. Her spirits began to flag again. She was led up two flights of stairs to the top of the house and then shown into an attic room which changed her whole perspective. She, who had arrived determined not to be cheered, now found herself being cheered considerably.

'Oh, what a pretty little room,' she cried. 'It's charming, it really is. And a view of the river – it's got everything!'

Not quite everything. No carpet for one thing. But the floor boards were painted in a glossy paint that reflected in large flickering pools the sunshine that streamed through the window. And from the windows there was an uninterrupted view of the river, and lush water meadows and the cathedral; a living picture that could change its mood and colours daily. She gave a heartfelt sigh.

'I used to dream of a room like this when I was a child,' she said. 'One with a sloping ceiling and dormer windows, dainty wickerwork furniture and rose-patterned wallpaper – just like this. At home I have a heavy old-fashioned mahogany bedroom suite and navy-blue Grecian urns on the wallpaper.'

Mrs Toser sniffed. 'You'll freeze in winter and fry in summer and the water cistern in the room next door will keep you awake at night. You'll be singing a different song before long.'

Philippa looked at her. 'I slept in a cellar for five months,' she said. 'Sometimes I froze and sometimes I fried and often I couldn't sleep because of the noise of gunfire or of bombs dropping. After that I think I could sleep anywhere.'

The first crack appeared in Mrs Toser's face. 'Would you like a cup of tea, my little woman?'

By the time August arrived, bringing with it a second flush of roses in the garden, bees droning amid the lavender and the odd butterfly on the buddleia, Philippa was well established in her new home. Wimborne House had started life as two semi-detached Victorian villas but sometime in the twenties they had become attached and converted into a commercial hotel that soon became popular with travelling salesmen. The Depression brought a loss of custom and since then its fortunes had waxed and waned until now, leased to the bank, it was more or less back to hotel status. It had been redecorated and refurbished, and in the capable hands of Mrs Toser and a handyman known as Red, soon earned for itself the reputation of comfort, a free-and-easy routine, and plentiful food. Those members of the staff who had turned up their noses at the idea of a hostel-type life and opted for bedsitters or furnished rooms instead went around with the aggrieved look of one who had drawn a short straw. Every week Miss Jolly added yet another name to the Wimborne waiting list which tellingly never grew shorter.

Miss Jolly's main function was the care of the female staff. She had had her own office at the old Brundle's and though 'Welfare Officer' was not a term often used that, in effect, was what she was. She was also responsible for arranging holidays and was in charge of the Widows' and Orphans' fund and that side of her work kept her more occupied as the war ground on. She took a keen interest in all her 'girls' and never failed to enquire after Leo and looked out for a letter from him as keenly as Philippa did herself.

One day Miss Jolly was rewarded. She had arrived back at Wimborne House early and was hovering near the front door waiting when Philippa arrived. 'For you,' she said. 'It must have come by the second post.'

Philippa pounced on it, saw in one glance 'ON

ACTIVE SERVICE' written across the top in Leo's firm capitals and in one corner, rubber stamped, 'Passed by censor'.

She was already on the stairs before Miss Jolly could stop her. 'You're going to your room to read it?'

Philippa nodded, too full at that moment to speak.

'Philippa, don't you think you should spend more time with the others? You are inclined to shut yourself away too much. We're a jolly crowd, you know. We play cards, talk, sometimes have a sing-song round the piano. Give it a try. You wouldn't feel so lonely. . . .'

'You can be lonely in a crowded room,' Philippa answered.

Miss Jolly sighed. 'You're too young to have learnt that already.' Philippa looked at her. Miss Jolly, who had always before lived up to her name, now frequently looked sad. Philippa would often see, for no apparent reason, tears fill her eyes. Miss Watson had not joined her friend in Norwich. She had left the bank altogether and was working in the office of a West End store. Miss Jolly felt the parting keenly though she tried not to let it show. Philippa could understand that a woman might miss another woman, especially if they had been close friends, but she could not see there was any comparison with the heartbroken longing of a woman for the man she loved. To her Miss Jolly's tears were inexplicable.

'I go to my room to write letters,' she said, though this was only partly true. She preferred her own company to that downstairs.

'Every night?'

'I write to Leo every day.'

'Oh Philippa, I didn't know. Join us later then.'

She opened the letter carefully, and unfolded several

pages of flimsy paper. Leo's name and number at the top, and his address c/o Army Post Office, 4040, beneath. The date had been neatly snipped out by the censor, the words 'At sea' left in.

She read it through several times. The first time, she was so blinded by tears, she couldn't focus clearly. It was only when she had taken the contents in as a whole that she went back and reread it word by word. Knowing Leo, there might be one or two clues. There were.

'I started many letters to you when we first sailed but as none would pass the censor I tore them up. . . . There's a rumour we may be able to go ashore at the next port of call. To walk on dry land, have a fresh-water bath, see a good show and order a good meal. Gee, what a thought! . . . I've been soaked in perspiration for some time now and I sleep with only a sheet over me and that's too hot . . . everything one wears becomes soaked. Last night we had a quiet game of solo-whist. No energy required but perspiration trickled down my face, down my chest and legs, and into my shoes so that when I got up my shoes squelched. To think that at the beginning of this trip I was pleased to have my greatcoat. It seems impossible that I was ever cold. . . . We have plenty of hot or cold sea water to bath or bathe in but only cold (now tepid) fresh water for a couple of hours a day. . . . If we do go ashore I'll make straight for a bar and have a long cool beer, but I don't suppose it will taste as good as the drinks at the bar of the Ritz. . . .'

She reached for the code. Ritz . . . South Africa. He had written that letter in the tropics but was now heading south. How long would it take for his ship to reach a South African port, she wondered. How long, dear God, before another letter?

She wiped the last of her tears away, combed her hair, and dabbed her nose with powder. Miss Jolly was right. She was doing herself no good moping up here. She'd go downstairs, join the others, read them snippets of her letter which she felt would interest them just as she used to for her father. Not all the letter of course. Some parts were for her eyes only.

The next morning she received two more letters, one a continuation of the other with description of life on board ship in greater detail.

'Just to make you jealous,' he wrote, 'among the goods available on board – real Mackintosh's Quality Street in tins; boiled sweets in half-pound jars; chocolate (slabs) as many as you like.... I wish I could send some to you. Heaven knows, sweetheart, when you'll receive this letter. We get very little news on board. There's a bulletin posted up each day which is the official BBC news bulletin. It doesn't give one much idea of what's happening so when you write you really must pass on all the news.'

When I write! thought Philippa with a sense of helplessness. She must have written over forty letters already. There'd be a sackful waiting for him when he reached his destination, that is if the army post office was doing its job properly. If to her it felt as if she were writing to a brick wall, what must it feel like to Leo?

His second letter included a description of the means by which he and his companions kept fit. Working out in the gymnasium, walking the decks, swimming daily in the pool. He finished with, 'Last night, one of the fellows in the draft – an Indian – read the palm of my hand, and this is what he told me: Life line – very good, no serious illnesses. Heart – one love and one love only throughout my life and that I would never love any woman other than one I loved at present (maybe he's a thought-reader). Head line – very steady, unswerving and faithful (it's not for me to question that!). Fortune – I would never be rich but from the age of thirty-five I'd have no more financial problems (that will make a nice change!). Children – I'll have two. At least darling, that means we'll be together again. This chap read several other palms and apparently brought out some remarkable truths which he couldn't have known about. But, of course, one has to remember we have all lived together in close contact for a long time and naturally he has picked up a hint or two about our lives. Let's hope he's a hundred per cent right about us, sweetheart, it's given me something to hang on to – and I was the one who used to tease you about being superstitious!'

It was a satisfying letter in many respects and, again, the only bit censored was the date. What was so significant about the date? she wondered. What could the date tell the enemy should it fall into their hands? It couldn't be half as important to them as it was to her. She looked at the calendar on the wall – it was getting dangerously near the time they had planned to marry. She didn't want to be on her own on that day. She couldn't bear the thought of sitting in her room brooding. She'd go home to Woodside. She had only been home once since coming to Norwich and then she had had to share her father with Mrs Warwick. She supposed she'd have to get used to that but it wouldn't be easy for her.

In mid August, after the historic meeting of Franklin Roosevelt with Winston Churchill on shipboard somewhere off the coast of America to discuss the fundamental principles of the post-war world, headscarves printed with the clauses of the Atlantic Charter were in all the stores. Philippa bought a green-and-tan-coloured one and wore it over her green suit which was beginning to look a little jaded now after almost daily wear, and needed something fresh to liven it up.

Red, the handyman-cum-gardener of Wimborne House, had pinned a large map of the Eastern Front on the kitchen wall, a source of great irritation to Mrs Toser. Not that she wasn't as interested in the fate of their ally as the rest of them but she objected to it on principle as she objected to anything that originated with Red. Her annoyance was water off a duck's back as far as he was concerned. He enjoyed teasing her and for that reason always called her Bones. She didn't call him anything at all if she could avoid it.

Philippa had assumed that Red got his nickname from the colour of his hair which not only grew profusely on his head and down the back of his neck, but also in his nostrils and ears. Either that or because he was never seen in anything but a red pullover, stencilled with the letters USSR on the back. Philippa asked Miss Jolly the reason why.

'To show his allegiance to the Soviet Union,' said Miss Jolly with a chuckle. Red was a constant source of amusement to her.

'We all feel allegiance these days, but we don't go around wearing red pullovers with USSR painted on them to show it.'

'Ah, but his allegiance goes back to the days when we looked for Reds under our beds.'

'Oh, I see.' Philippa was intrigued. 'You mean he's a communist?'

Miss Jolly's silent laughter was almost uncontrollable.

'Not the sort of communist acceptable to the Party. He is a dedicated reader of the the *Daily Worker* and he believes in many of its policies, but he believes just as deeply in the church and the Royal Family so I don't know where he draws the line. Mrs Toser says he's tenpence-ha'penny for a shilling, a common enough saying in these parts, but I don't accept that for a minute. He's just an oddity, a rare old mixture, and a sweetie. I love him.'

'*Miss Jolly!*'

'You know what I mean.'

Philippa watched Red closely from then on. This was easy on a Sunday as he always joined them, unasked, in the drawing room to listen to the nine o'clock news. It had become the custom, following the news, for each of the national anthems of occupied countries to be played in turn. Red sprang up and stood to attention when Russia's anthem was played, but as he jumped to his feet and stood to attention for all the anthems they could hardly hold it against him. However, some of the lodgers took offence when he sang the words of the 'Internationale'. That he sang 'God Save the King' with equal fervour went unremarked.

Philippa's one big disappointment at this time was that none of the girls she had known at the old bank had made the transition to Norfolk with her. Two had transferred to Ludgate Hill, like Daphne James, and the two others had married and followed their husbands to their service quarters. None of the new girls who had taken their place had had any experience of working on ledger machines and to her dismay Philippa found herself assigned the task of instructing them. It was, she wrote to her father, rather like teaching learners to drive by someone who had never passed the driving test.

However, on this particular Friday everything had gone smoothly; they had balanced early and she was free to leave the bank by half past four, in addition to which it was her Saturday morning off. On an impulse she decided to go home for the weekend, and not to phone her father first but surprise him.

Four hours later she was approaching Byrd's House by the short cut from the station, taking a footpath that led through part of the forest, which at this time of year, when birds were moulting, was comparatively silent. The soporific cooing of pigeons and one lone robin practising a few bars of his winter song was part consolation. She missed the forest. As yet she had seen no trees in Norfolk to compare with those of Epping Forest.

There was a dusty, tired look about the trees now, however. They had lost their early summer freshness. Mr Beckham, the forest-keeper, had once said, 'Give any tree in the forest a good shake and you'll get showered in soot.' She believed him. Once as a child she had walked bare-footed through the bracken and had had to give her feet a hard scrub before putting on her socks again. Smoke from the factories of the East End and from the houses of the crowded suburbs had left a residue on every branch and twig. It would require a monsoon, she thought, to wash the forest clean again.

From this angle Byrd's House looked shabby and neglected, but nothing a team of painters and decorators couldn't put right. And the garden was a wilderness with the grass nearly knee high, for their gardener had been called up. It would be better Philippa thought, to turn it over to vegetables and dig for victory like many others, but she knew her father had little time for that for his business took priority. Business or Mrs Warwick? One and the same, came an unhappy thought.

But shabby as it looked it was her home and her heart lifted as she stepped into the kitchen sniffing those homely and familiar smells that always greeted her on her return. A mixture of stored apples and spices, dried lavender and beeswax with which Mrs Mooney polished the wood-block floors. But now there was an added and unpleasant smell. She sniffed again. Something was burning, but not here in the kitchen. Not in the hall either. The drawing-room door was ajar. 'Dad?' she cried as she pushed it open.

Lying asleep on her great-great-grandmother's *chaise-longue* with *his feet up on the brocade* was a stranger, and there smouldering away on his tie, obviously fallen from his mouth, was a half-smoked cigar. Another minute or two and the tie would have been on fire.

Philippa was tempted to walk away and leave him to his fate, but it could be the fate of the sofa too so she picked up the soda siphon from the drinks trolley and sprayed him liberally. Tie, chin, open mouth, eyes – the lot. That will teach him to put his shoes on great-great-grandmother's *chaise-longue*, she thought.

The stranger spluttered and sat up, drops of soda dripping from his nose and chin.

'What the hell's going on,' he said, slurring his words. He opened one eye and stared at Philippa, then swung his legs to the ground, buried his face in his hands and groaned.

He was too well-dressed for a vagrant and Philippa had never heard of a house-breaker getting sloshed then sleeping it off on his unwitting host's sofa. A fifth columnist? She dismissed that idea with scorn. She had always been sceptical of the 'spies dressed as nuns' stories. 'Should I know you?' she said frigidly.

He raised his head and stared at her with bloodshot eyes. 'I don't see any reason why you should.' He took out his handkerchief and mopped his face, before adding ruefully, 'If you'd known how much that siphon of soda cost you wouldn't have been so generous with it. Just as well you didn't use the whisky instead. Not only did it cost a damn sight more but I might have gone up in flames.'

'Pity I didn't think of it.'

He chortled. 'You must be old Jonathan's girl. My sister said you were a prickly little b . . . er . . . beauty.'

She regarded him from the top of his coal-black hair to the tips of his patent-leather shoes. So this was Mrs Warwick's brother. The one who could conjure up with the click of his nicotine-stained fingers anything that was in short supply. She could see no familial likeness to Mrs Warwick. Even their colouring was at odds. He was swarthy, and she had no colour at all to speak of.

He returned Philippa's gaze with a twinkling one of his own. 'I can guess what you're thinking, girlie. That you can't see any likeness to my sister. It's not so uncommon. I'm either a throwback to some gypsy ancestor or my old mum had a roving eye.'

'You are the brother from Slough?' said Philippa, still unconvinced.

'That's me.' He grinned, and put on an exaggerated East End accent. 'Charlie Ford is my moniker, an' the Trading Estate Slough, Bucks, England will find me any day of the week.' He pronounced Slough to rhyme with enough in an attempt to bring a smile to her face perhaps, but without success.

'And what do you mean by falling asleep on my great-great-grandmother's *chaise-longue*!'

'On her chez what?'

'The sofa – that sofa you're sitting on. It's not for sitting on really. It's an antique – reputed to have belonged to Marie-Antoinette.'

For such a heavy man he was nifty getting to his feet. He studied the *chaise-longue* with added interest. 'Antique, eh? Marie-Antoinette? It must be worth a nicker or two.'

'We don't put that kind of value on it,' she said loftily. 'Money isn't everything.'

He raised one eyebrow. 'If you think that, it's obvious you've never gone short of it.'

It was belittling carrying on this conversation, she thought. She cut it short by going to the kitchen in search of something to eat. He followed.

'I see to it that your father doesn't go hungry,' he said. 'Take a dekko in the larder.'

She ignored him, and pretended not to notice the tins and groceries stacked on the top shelf. She'd rather starve than eat anything this man provided. She ignored too an unopened packet of coffee, even though she hadn't tasted real coffee for months. She spooned out Nescafé into a cup, toasted bread and spread it with Marmite, conscious all the time that he watched her every move.

'There's some eggs in the fridge,' he said.

'Thank you, I'm quite satisfied with what I've got.' She placed cup and saucer, plate and knife on a tray. 'Just what are you doing in my father's house, anyway?'

'Well, it's like this. Jonathan wanted to take Ursula for

a spin down to the South Coast, but it was a question of petrol. So I borrowed his car, took it over to Slough, filled up the tank, drove it back here and he took over. Now I'm waiting for them to get back so I can drive myself back to Slough.'

'What's wrong with the train?'

'At eleven o'clock at night? Everything, I should say. In any case I've promised my sister a lift back to her flat.'

Her heart sank. So her father wasn't expected home until eleven. 'I'll say good night,' she said.

'You're not going to bed?' He sounded disappointed.

'I'm tired. . . .'

'Let me carry your tray for you.'

'Thank you, I can manage.'

The toast had gone cold, the coffee tepid, but she finished both, had her bath and got into bed, locking her door first. She didn't think he would attempt to ravage her in her father's house, but she was taking no chances. She hoped to goodness he didn't start on the whisky again. She listened for any sound of movement, but the house was too solidly built to allow for noise to carry. Presently she slept.

The sound of an engine being revved woke her. Voices, muted – a woman's laughter, then the swish of tyres on shingle as the car juddered along the drive. Not her father driving, he didn't slip the clutch like that. She was fully awake now and sitting up in bed, hoping her father would come up and say good night. He didn't disappoint her. A gentle tap on the door. A quiet 'Philippa, are you awake?' She switched on the bedside lamp and pulled her dressing-jacket around her shoulders.

Her first thought was how well her father looked and how much younger. He seemed to have shed years since her last visit. 'This is a lovely surprise,' he said. 'But why in the Dickens didn't you warn me.'

'I wanted to surprise you, but it was I who got the surprise.'

He laughed. 'Yes, I heard about that. Charlie nearly set himself on fire.'

'He could have set the house on fire. And Dad, he was sprawled on the Marie-Antoinette sofa *with his feet up*.'

Though her father pulled a face, laughter still crinkled the skin around his eyes. She felt she hadn't made her point. 'He's not house-trained,' she said.

'That's a bit unfair, Pip. I grant you he's a bit of a rough diamond, but he means well. Anyway, you've made a conquest there. He thinks you're the tops – whatever that may mean.'

She etched a pattern on the bedspread with her fingernail. Her father, sitting near her feet, shifted slightly. 'I know that look,' he said. 'What's on your mind, Philippa?'

'Dad, he's a black marketeer. . . .'

'You're wrong there, Pip. He's not making money out of it. He fiddles a bit on the side, that's all, and only for his friends. It goes on all the time and likely to get worse before this war is over. . . .'

'Because other people do it doesn't make it right. The idea of rationing is so we all get fair shares, rich and poor alike. I think it's all wrong to fiddle on the side, as you call it.'

'You do do you.' Her father rose. No trace of laughter in his face now. 'Since when have you adopted this holier than thou attitude, Philippa? I don't remember you saying anything against Mrs Toser for fiddling.'

'Father!' Philippa looked shocked. 'She does no such thing. She wouldn't know how, anyway.'

'No? Then what about her visits to all these cousins in the country? A dairyman cousin here, a kitchen-garden cousin there, a farming cousin somewhere else. The only cousin she doesn't seem to have is one in the clothing business.'

'She comes from a large family. And they're spread all over. . . .' But Philippa's interruption was ignored. Her father had got himself thoroughly wound up.

'You write and tell me about her bringing home plump little chickens, sometimes a duck or rabbit, eggs, butter, dripping, and sausages – now what was it you said about the sausages. "Made from real pork, not bread like in the shops." You're kidding yourself if you think she's not dabbling in the black market.'

'She can't get tea or sugar,' said Philippa miserably. 'And she doesn't bring things home *every* week. And Dad, it's not a fiddle, it's fair exchange. She goes scouting around in Norwich for things they can't get in the country, like batteries and nails and razor blades and toilet rolls.'

'Yes, I can understand how some would think that a toilet roll is a fair exchange for a chicken.'

There was silence, then, 'Are we quarrelling, Dad?'

'We're very near to it, Pip.'

She jumped out of bed, padded across to him and slipped her arm through his. 'I'm sorry . . . I was just . . . I don't know. I was disappointed at not finding you home – and then finding *him* here instead, and . . .' She lowered her head against her father's shoulder. 'I'm sorry, Dad, I'm truly sorry. He was your guest and I know you think it unforgivable to be rude to a guest, and I was.'

He returned her hug. 'Don't worry about that – Charlie's skin is thick enough. It's just... well, don't always be too quick to pass judgement. He's been a good friend to me, Philippa, in more ways than you realise, and perhaps I'm a bit too touchy myself. There... end of first lesson. Now, hop back to bed and I'll bring you a cup of Ovaltine – bought fair and square across the counter with my ration book.'

They were having breakfast when the post arrived. The weekend spread before her, full of promise, for her father had just revealed that Mrs Warwick had gone back to Slough with her brother, the best news Philippa had heard in a long time.

'She does occasionally – to give his place a good going over and wash his clothes....'

'He hasn't got a wife to do that for him?'

Jonathan smiled. 'So that's what a wife is for, is it? I often wondered. No, he hasn't got a wife, but he doesn't exactly live the life of a monk either.'

'Dad, what would you say to us going to the Moletrap on Sunday – for old times' sake?'

'I'd say it was a damn good idea.' It was then they heard the postman's rap-a-tap-tap.

'Anything for me?' Philippa looked up eagerly as her father returned with some letters. 'Anything from Leo?'

'Yes, a nice fat letter for you, from overseas. But not in Leo's handwriting, and no censor's stamp, either.'

Philippa examined the letter, turned it over, felt it, all but sniffed it. It was in a woman's hand, the postmark was smudged but the stamp was South African. Her father laughed. 'I can see you're dying to open it. Run off and read it in peace. I'll see to the dishes.'

Her bed was not yet made. She curled on top of the turned-back covers and slit the envelope. Another letter fell out. That, addressed to her in Leo's handwriting, was unstamped and uncensored. She picked up the sheet of paper that was with it. It carried a Durban address and a July date.

'Dear Miss Byrd,
   Lieut. Brooke has asked me to send you the enclosed. I sincerely hope it reaches you safely, one can't be sure these days. My husband and I have spent a very enjoyable weekend in his company and I feel I now know you very well. I hope it won't be long before this wretched war is over and you two young people are together again. Your fiancé left some money with me to buy you cosmetics, but I am afraid they may take a little longer to reach you than this letter will.
   Very best wishes for your future.
   Yours sincerely,
      Laura Richards'

Laura Richards? Who was this Laura Richards? An angel in disguise? – a fairy godmother? – a life saver? All three in Philippa's opinion. By this time she had got Leo's letter open, tearing the envelope in her haste. At last a date. It had taken just over a month to reach her. By now, perhaps, Leo had already landed in India.

'My darling sweetheart,
   I'm taking a risk with this letter, and no doubt Mrs Richards is too, but it was her idea, and she

says if the censor does open it he'll only destroy it. There'll be no action taken against her.

Well, my pet, we landed here at Durban three days ago. I can't tell you what it felt like to be on firm ground again. The people here are so helpful and friendly. I was introduced almost immediately to Mrs Richards who is on the committee of a group of ladies who take pity on homesick soldiers like me and invite them to their homes. The first thing Mr and Mrs Richards did was to take me and Captain Newman, one of my cabin mates, out for a drive. They took us about twenty miles into the country where we stopped at a sort of café, and it was lovely sitting in the shade having tea and cream scones just like in peacetime England. They drove us back by a different route showing us sugar cane, banana plantations and orange groves, and some beautiful trees I've forgotten the name of. There were some magnificent-looking strawberries but we were warned not to eat any because of the unhygienic way in which they are grown.

The Richards have a son in the army serving in North Africa, in Tobruk. It is an awful time for them, waiting for news, wondering when and if Tobruk will ever be relieved. Being in this beautiful and peaceful place it is difficult to remember there is a war on. They insisted Newman and I spent the weekend with them and I must say, to bath in fresh water instead of salt, and to sleep in a bed that stays level is my idea of Heaven.

Just a few details about the journey out. We were holed up in Liverpool for days – so frustrating when I couldn't get ashore to phone you – there was a flap on as it was thought there was a U-boat lurking just outside the harbour. We weren't a large convoy, just the one troop ship which in peacetime was a luxury liner – the rest, a mixed bunch of cargo ships and an escort of gunboats. We had another U-boat scare just off the Azores and went almost across to the West Indies to avoid trouble. Then back to Freetown, where we stopped for about twenty-four hours putting down anchor behind a U-boat barrier that guarded the harbour. We weren't allowed to go ashore, but our mail was picked up by tender.

Darling, as soon as I get to India, I'll cable you. I'm sending your letters to Woodside because I don't know your Norwich address. I know you have written to me, perhaps even cabled me, but of course I've received nothing yet. I live in hope, my sweet. I dream of you constantly and think of you all the time. When we're married I'm taking you on three separate honeymoons. To Edinburgh, of course, and the Scillies, and then here to Durban. I shall feel so knowledgeable showing you round with the air of a Cook's guide. Darling, I get choked up just thinking of it. Remember me, always.'

As if I could forget you, she thought, watching as a tear fell on to the page and trickled off the edge leaving a trail of smudged ink behind. Carefully she folded the letter and replaced it in its envelope to be put away and read and reread later. Each time she did so she would hear Leo's voice coming to her from the paper.

It was a satisfactory beginning to a satisfactory weekend. She spent the rest of Saturday morning helping her father cut the lawns. There were three of them broken up by flowerbeds and fruit trees, and at the present they resembled hayfields. There was no petrol for the motor mower so while she pushed away at the hand mower her father went to work with a scythe. It was hard work and by lunchtime they were both ready to cry quits.

'What about that walk to the Moletrap now,' Jonathan suggested. 'If we're lucky, they might even be able to rustle up a sandwich.'

They repeated the walk the following morning, more decorously dressed. Even so, Philippa's conscience smote her when they passed families going off to church. Her father had always been casual about religion perhaps because of the compulsory church attendance when he was young and from which he rebelled in adolescence. Consequently (and to Aunt Dot's horror) he allowed Philippa to please herself whether she went or not, which she did, going alternately to Matins and Evensong, until Leo came into her life, when she swopped churchgoing for walks in the forest or over Chingford Plain. She still worshipped God, but on her own and preferably in the garden.

'You're quiet,' said her father.

'I was just thinking I haven't been to church for ages and I've so much to be thankful for. . . .'

'We could go to Evensong tonight if you like.'

'Dad, would you! Oh, I'd love that.' Her face dropped. 'But that would mean getting up at the crack of dawn tomorrow to catch the early train.'

'It's up to you.'

'I'll stay.'

It was like dipping back into the past sitting in that

old musty church again, sniffing in the familiar smell of candle grease, flowers and dust, joining in the responses, and the beautiful words of Mary's song of praise. She emerged into the evening sunshine feeling as if her spiritual batteries had been recharged. She was more hopeful than she had been for weeks, both for herself and her country. She left her father to walk home on his own while she walked on to Belle Vue Road, not to call on the Brookes for they had already left for their annual holiday in Penzance which not even a war could interrupt, but just to have a good look round the garden so that she could describe it all to Leo in her next letter.

The day she dreaded was coming nearer and nearer. Only she now remembered. Her father had obviously forgotten for he had written to say he was spending the weekend at Brighton with Mrs Warwick and her brother. Aunt Dot's memory was unreliable so she wouldn't remember, which left only her and Leo to mourn their lost wedding day.

His letters were now arriving more frequently; those he had posted in Durban she guessed, though they still had 'At Sea' written across the heading. Any day now she expected a cable to say he had arrived in India. She didn't know yet whether she dreaded or welcomed that news. At least he'd be safe in India, miles away from any enemy, though months away by letter.

As if in mockery, the sun shone brilliantly on 20 September. The same in Essex too, she suspected. She couldn't check for weather forecasts were another casualty of the war. She thought of the lavender silk dress hanging under a sheet in her wardrobe, and the three lace-trimmed nightgowns in her bottom drawer, and hoped they wouldn't have rotted by the time her wedding day finally arrived.

She dreaded going into the kitchen these days for the postage-stamp-size swastikas on Red's map of Europe were creeping nearer and nearer to Moscow. Kiev had fallen. She could no longer bear to read about the German offensive for the newspapers bore graphic descriptions of the atrocities committed against Russian women and children. The only hopeful news was the valiant stand the Russians were making at Leningrad, but at a heartbreaking cost.

'What are you doing moping here all by yourself,' said Mrs Toser coming into the drawing room with fresh flowers. Mrs Toser was Norfolk born and bred but her accent wasn't so broad as Red's. Only words such as 'stew' and 'tube' and 'beautiful' gave her trouble. Norfolk folk, thought Philippa, like Americans seemed incapable of pronouncing their 'u's, but she loved the way they spoke. Red's Broad Norfolk was music to her ears even though it was completely incomprehensible.

'You should be out of doors on a lovely day like this,' grumbled Mrs Toser. 'Sure as fate the next time do you want to go out it'll be raining.'

'It's too fine to go to the cinema and there's no point in going to Lowestoft or Yarmouth as I won't be able to get near the beach, and I don't feel like traipsing all the way to Mousehold Heath.'

'You are in a fair ole mood, aren't you? What about those people you were telling me about – related to your grandmother, weren't they? – had a farm at Thornmere, you said. Give me half an hour to get ready an' I'll come with you. My cousin Alice keeps the post office at

Thornmere. Her greengages should be more than ripe for picking by now.'

So Philippa went to her room and changed into a neat little navy blue and white twopiece which she had bought through the classified ads in *The Lady*, for that paper was now a respectable mart for the purchase of second-hand bargains, and as she put the last touches to her makeup and flicked her bob into place she had no inkling, for how could she, that this sudden decision was to alter the whole course of her life.

Seven

Philippa's former acquaintance with farms (on holiday in Devon) had led her to believe that, without exception, all were marooned within a sea of mud churned to the consistency of batter pudding by the to-ing and fro-ing of cows to the milking pens. Therefore her first sight of Manor Farm was quite a revelation.

What she now saw at the top of a well-kept drive was a long, low, pink-washed, white-shuttered house that looked anything but a farmstead. There was not a chicken in sight or a dog straining at a leash. There was, however, curled up on a mound of catmint, a handsome Siamese cat who watched her approach with squinting blue eyes.

The barn had been converted into a garage and parked outside this was a silver-grey Rolls of uncertain age and an assortment of bikes, some of them apparently as old as the car. One of the ground-floor windows was open and from this came the sound of laughter and chatter against the muted strains of boogie-woogie being played on a piano.

Philippa's immediate impulse was to turn and flee. She couldn't barge in on a private party. She couldn't knock on the door with the feeble excuse that her grandmother had been born in this house and could she please see over it? Country folk were incredibly hospitable, but this place didn't give the impression of belonging to country folk – more likely townees who had spent a small fortune converting a centuries-old farmhouse into an idyllic country retreat.

The traditionalist in her was slightly put off. What would her grandmother's father think to see the old house turned into a showpiece? Yet it made such a charming picture, merging as it did into its background of manicured lawns and ornamental trees, that she could not help but admire it.

What would she do with herself until Mrs Toser appeared, for Mrs Toser had arranged to pick her up in two hours' time (more out of curiosity to see what Manor Farm now looked like than for any altruistic purpose, Philippa suspected), and while she stood there pondering whether to knock or not, the Siamese cat did it for her.

It jumped with ease on to the cast-iron boot scraper at the side of the door and from there reached up to the latch and rattled it. The door opened almost immediately.

'There you are, Mitzi – on the dot as usual.' A woman in white flannel slacks bent down and ran her hand along the sleek length of Mitzi's back, who in turn leant ecstatically against the woman's leg and rumbled like a two-stroke engine. Philippa went unnoticed until the woman straightened up.

'Oh, I am so sorry – I didn't see you there.' She was in her early forties, slim, with sad dark eyes completely at odds with her friendly smile. 'Have you been waiting long?'

Her tone gave Philippa courage.

'I'm sorry to barge in like this, especially when you seem to be having a party, but it's just that...' She hesitated, then out it came in a rush. 'My grandmother was born in this farmhouse – I don't know when – sometime in the middle of the last century, I think. She died when my father was a baby so I don't know much about her... I couldn't resist, I mean – I would so love to—'

'You're curious to see her old home? Of course. Do come in.'

'But you have visitors.... If it isn't convenient...'

'Of course it's convenient – any time is convenient, Saturday afternoons especially.' Philippa found herself drawn into a small white-washed lobby, and then into a hall where several forage caps, both army and air force were strewn on a cushioned window-seat. The strains of 'In the Mood' could now be heard quite plainly. Automatically, she tilted her head and listened.

'He plays well, our young pianist,' the woman said. 'Don't worry, it's not a party – just one of my usual Saturday-afternoon gatherings. By the way, I'm Evelyn Smith.'

'Philippa Byrd.'

The woman smiled. 'Byrd? I like it – a great improvement on Smith. Well now, come along and join the scrum – don't be shy – they're all young boys, mostly air force though there are some soldiers from the local gun-site. We're open house to the forces on Saturday afternoons....' A shadow crossed her face. Her voice was not now so steady. 'We have a son in the RAF. He was shot down in flames... he's now...' Just for a second or two she hesitated, 'He now qualifies for the Guinea-pig Club.' She tried to say it on a light note, but failed. 'They can do marvels with plastic surgery now, can't they.' Her eyes filled and she hastily produced a handkerchief.

'Oh, my dear, I shouldn't have inflicted this on you. I do get so emotional at times, and blurt it out to the first victim who comes along.' A lock of dark hair had fallen across her brow and she pushed that back. She said, 'Robin is still convalescing – in Kent, in a special place they keep for cases like his. He doesn't want us to see him until his scars begin to heal. The scars of the plastic surgery, I mean.' She paused, then gave a self-mocking, weary little smile. 'Everybody thinks I'm wonderful opening my home to strange young servicemen like this. What nobody knows is that I need them more than they need me. It helps, you know, keeping busy.' Another pause, then in a brighter tone. 'I couldn't help noticing your ring, it's so unusual. Engagement?'

Philippa's face lit up. 'To my childhood sweetheart. He's a doctor now, in the RAMC.'

'Overseas?'

'He should have landed in India by now.' For a short time she had been able to forget which day it was, now it all came back and with it a rush of tears. Not triggered off so much from self-pity but out of compassion for this other woman. She too groped for her handkerchief.

'I should have been married today,' she wept.

Mrs Smith took her arm. 'It's difficult being a woman at a time like this, isn't it? Stiff upper lip and all that. There's nothing worse than sitting at home waiting. Unless it's sitting at home with no one to wait for. Ready now? Then let's face the mob. The one with grey hair and an old face is Clive, my husband.'

There was instant silence when they entered the room. All eyes turned in their direction. Mitzi made her sinuous way to the nearest sofa and leapt lightly on to the lap of the middle-aged man. He instantly dislodged her by standing up and came over with hand extended. His face wasn't old but it was heavily lined. Lines of suffering, Philippa thought. She took his hand. He had a powerful grip, like Leo. 'This is a pleasant surprise,' he said. 'Where did Eve find you?'

Eve made the introductions and when she gave the reason for Philippa's visit there was an instant rush of volunteers to be her guide.

'That's my honour,' said Clive. 'I know the history of this place and you lot don't. If you want something to do, help Eve prepare the grub.'

Softly the music started again, something sweet and romantic that Philippa couldn't put a name to. She looked towards the pianist, a broad, stocky figure leaning forward over the keys. A young airman with short curly black hair who at that moment turned his head in her direction. His eyes, a brilliant blue under heavy black brows held her gaze for longer than was necessary then, smiling to himself, he looked away.

Philippa coloured up. He looked far too pleased with himself for her liking. She overlooked the suffering of Eve and Clive Smith. She forgot, temporarily, the unknown Robin convalescing in Kent. Her latent prejudice rose to the surface. Fighter pilots! The glamour boys of the forces! She always did think the RAF too cocky by half.

'Don't blame us for the so-called improvements,' Clive was saying. 'We inherited them from the previous owners three years ago when we bought this joint. They had bought it from an old farmer whose family had farmed here for generations. Bowyer – any relation of your ancestor? He wasn't married, had no heir, and when he died a neighbouring farmer bought the land and this house was put on the market. Our predecessors said they got it for practically nothing as it needed so much doing to it. The improvements cost more than the purchase price, so they said. Apparently old Mr Bowyer beggared himself when he bought the freehold in the early twenties from the Massingham estate and was either too poor or too old to bother about repairs.'

Philippa had never heard of the Massinghams. Clive Smith enlightened her. 'It was the family who used to own Thornmere Hall. The squirearchy, if you like, though that sounds quaint these days. The new squire,' and here Clive laughed, 'who took over the Hall when the estate was split up was a Great War profiteer. So I was told, anyway. Actually, he did a lot for the village. He built the Memorial Hall and founded the cricket club. We never met him. By the time we got settled in here the second war had started and the army had requisitioned the Hall and park.

'D'you know what happens to a place once the army takes over?' he went on. 'You must go and take a look sometime. There used to be a grand avenue of elms – they've mostly disappeared, either for fuel or to make room for the barrels of the anti-aircraft guns. Still, one can't blame the army for the loss of a magnificent pair of wrought-iron gates. They were taken for salvage. Vandalism I call it. But look here, I'm doing all the talking.

What about you having a turn. What relationship were you to old man Bowyer?'

Philippa found this hard to answer. A quick bit of mental arithmetic led her to think that he could have been her grandmother's brother. 'I really don't know anything about the family. I only learnt that I had a grandmother who came from Norfolk a few months ago.'

'Well, I'll tell you what. I'll take you to see the bedrooms and you can pick out the one you like best and pretend that was your grandmother's.'

Except for the master bedroom, the three other bedrooms had no independent doors. Each one led out of the other. The ceilings like the ones downstairs were beamed and the floors uneven, but the furniture, in fumed oak or burr walnut, was modern. It was a compromise that did not clash for it had been done with taste.

Philippa said, 'I wouldn't like to make a choice, they're all equally splendid. Perhaps I'd plump for the one with lilac-patterned curtains because mauve is my favourite colour, but that's the only reason. But what an odd arrangement, the rooms all communicating – was it to save space?'

Clive's expression was droll. 'Originally I think so that the farmer and his wife could keep an eye on their daughters. No suitors sneaking up the back stairs; no slipping out for midnight trysts. Anything untoward, they would soon know about.'

'Not very trusting of them, I must say. What about sons? Did they have to keep an eye on them too?'

'Oh, I shouldn't think they worried too much about sons. Sons can look after themselves. . . .' His voice suddenly cracked. He did then look old. Philippa bit her lip.

'I'm sorry,' she said awkwardly. 'Your wife told me

about your son. I'm sorry. . . .' She hesitated, for words of condolence did not come easy to her.

He smiled thinly. 'We've got over the worst of it. At least, the essential Robin – the inner Robin – he's still alive. The body is only a shell, isn't it? In this case it was a damn good-looking shell.' Philippa thought he would break down then, but he pulled himself together. 'Only sometimes it hits us afresh, then we go to pieces. But not today. We look forward to Saturdays. We love having visitors, we like young people around us. Well now, my dear,' he assumed again his false hail-fellow-well-met manner. 'Have you seen all you want to up here? I'll take you down by the back stairs and show you the kitchen quarters, a great barn of a kitchen it is too. And the pantry I've had made into an office. I'm fortunate, I'm an accountant and able to work from home, but I won't show you in there. Eve calls it my dug-out. Do be careful on these stairs – it's like descending a corkscrew.'

Downstairs the music had changed. No more boogie-woogie, no more sentimental swing, but something that caught Philippa by the throat. 'That's beautiful,' she said. 'What is it?'

' "Liebestraum". Liszt, one of Eve's favourite pieces. Joe always finishes his recital with that.'

'Joe?'

'Joe Gilbert – our talented young sergeant-pilot. By the way, if you want to know more about the history of Thornmere Hall he's the one to talk to. It was his god-father, a Daniel Harker, who bought the big house from the Massingham estate. Now let's come and join the bun fight.'

Mrs Toser arrived before time and to her gratification she was invited in and offered a cup of tea. 'I've already had my tea but I wouldn't say no to another cup. But we can only spare ten minutes. Our train goes at half past six and it's a fair ole walk to the station.'

'I could give you a lift on my cross bar,' said one young soldier who looked no more than sixteen. Mrs Toser tittered and turned pink. With the exception of Red, she was always susceptible to the attentions of the opposite sex.

'And I could take Miss Byrd on mine,' said another. Immediately a clamour arose.

'On that old bone-shaker! She wouldn't be safe.'

'She wouldn't be safe with him, anyway.'

'Miss Byrd, try mine. It's nearly new.'

'Mine's newer. Dynamo brakes and three gears. It'll be a more comfortable ride.'

'He'll have you in the ditch in no time. Miss Byrd, please allow me to escort you to the station.'

'If there's anybody doing any escorting around here, it's me,' said Clive. 'I have just enough petrol to get me to the station. Some of you can come along too if you like and push me back again.' There were no offers. Clive winked at Philippa.

In the ensuing ten minutes they were entertained by Mrs Toser's account of her role of chatelaine at Wimborne House, the reason why it had come about and a short character sketch of each of her lodgers. Philippa came out best.

'She's the only one who knows how to make a bed properly, tucks in the corners just like a trained nurse and doesn't leave any hairs in the wash-basin. I can't abide hairs in the wash-basin. Doesn't leave her undies dripping on the bathroom airer, either. There's nothing worse than having drips on your back when you're bending over cleaning the bath.'

'Mrs Toser,' Eve broke in. 'Would you like to try a piece of my carrot cake.'

Philippa, red to the tip of her ears, raised her eyes and met the amused blue gaze of Sergeant-Pilot Joe Gilbert. He, like all the others, was grinning broadly.

Said Clive soberly, 'I gather you had a pretty rotten time in London, Miss Byrd.'

'It wasn't very pleasant at the time, but the raids seem to have eased up since then,' she added, for she didn't want talk of air raids to sour the occasion.

'You're safe enough now. Norwich is an undefended city. I don't think even the Luftwaffe would sink that low, to bomb an undefended city.'

'There have been raids – houses and buildings destroyed and people killed,' objected Evelyn.

'But nothing compared to London or Coventry. The East Coast ports have taken a lot of punishment, but the raids on Norwich have been little more than nuisance raids. Let's hope it stays like that.' Clive gave a quick look round. 'Any more tea, anybody?'

'My cousin in Horning had a pig killed by a piece of shrapnel,' said Mrs Toser proffering her cup. 'You never know what dirty tricks that Hitler will think up next.'

Philippa's life now took on a regular pattern. She began to live for Saturday afternoons as she had once lived for Leo's letters. Not that she didn't still live for his letters, and grieved when she went days without hearing, but now, because her life was so full of interest, she found the waiting bearable.

His cable telling of his safe arrival reached her at the

end of September. His next letter, still addressed to Woodside, told her of his posting to an Indian Military hospital in Meerut. She now wrote to him c/o Lloyds Bank Ltd in Bombay, and wondered how long before she received a letter addressed to her in Norwich for then she would know that at long last her letters had caught up with him.

Sometimes his letters sent on from Woodside were readdressed in a feminine hand. She hated the thought of Mrs Warwick even handling them let alone addressing them on to her for that implied an intimacy which did not exist. She accepted it as inevitable now that her father would marry Ursula Warwick, but buried that thought along with other worrying thoughts in her subconscious.

She tried to tell herself that she only went to Manor Farm for the company and the music – mostly the music – but she knew it was more than that. Every time she entered the long, low living room hazy with cigarette smoke her eyes went straight to the piano stool, and if it were Evelyn Smith sitting there and not Joe Gilbert, her heart would sink. She even tried to kid herself that though Eve was a competent pianist she lacked Joe's magic touch and that was the reason for her disappointment. But in her heart she knew that was just self-deception.

Joe had been absent at the Smith gatherings for the two last Saturdays as too had Bob Fellowes, a Flight-Lieutenant in the same squadron, which rather suggested they were out on escort duty or had been posted elsewhere. There had lately been talk in the press of a RAF unit arriving in Russia to aid the Soviet air force. Would that include fighters, she wondered, turning cold at the thought. She told herself it wasn't Joe she was worrying about so much as all those other eager young fighters anxious to have a bash at the enemy without thought of their own danger, knowing all the time she was indulging in yet another little game of self-deception – a game she played once too often for retribution quickly followed.

Recently, she had stopped wearing her ring to work. It was still slightly loose and she was frightened of losing it as had happened to a recently engaged girl, and they had spent nearly all morning searching for it and finding it finally among the accounts in the filing cabinet. Now for safety she left her ring in one of the small drawers in her dressing-table, wearing it only in her leisure hours.

This particular late October day she dawdled home in the half-light, for with summertime in operation all the year round it didn't get really dark until seven o'clock. She had grown to love the walk from Riversway to the bank in Tombland. Sometimes she took the longer way round by road. At other times, when the weather was fine, she crossed the river by Foundry Bridge, backtracking over the rough grass until she came to Pulls Ferry, the ancient monument that had orginally been the gateway to the canal along which the stone to build the cathedral was hauled, then through the cathedral precincts into Tombland where in her fancy she felt she was stepping back into history, and on to the rather cramped quarters of Brundle's Bank.

Cramped they might be but where else, she asked herself, could she work in an office that overlooked a medieval market-place, a Tudor hostelry and a cathedral rising out of a spread of trees which at this time were rich in autumn colours? Now, homeward bound, she loitered, feeling well pleased with herself and her surroundings, until arriving at her room she discovered that her ring was missing.

She remembered now she had not put it away in her drawer last night but on the pin tray, meaning to put that right in the morning. But she had overslept and forgotten. Could she have knocked it on the floor when she was dressing? Panic gripped her.

She was on her knees searching under the bed when a knock came on the door and Mrs Toser entered. One look at her face was sufficient.

Sick at heart Philippa pulled herself to her feet.

'If you're looking for your ring, Red's got it.' The tone of Mrs Toser's voice was more appropriate to a funeral parlour.

'*Red!*'

'It's getting chilly o' nights, now. I sent Red up this afternoon to light you a little fire. He said when he stepped back he heard something crunch and thought he had stepped on a piece of coal . . . But . . .'

Philippa closed her eyes. 'Please, don't say any more, Mrs Toser. I can guess.'

'He's ever so upset. I never thought to see a man of his size crying. He thinks a lot of you. He wouldn't hurt you for the world. He's in the woodshed. He won't come out. He's been there all afternoon chopping up kindling. He's chopped enough kindling to last me through two winters — there won't be anything left to chop soon. Besides, it's getting dark. He'll have to come in, but he can't face you. . . .'

'I'll go and have a word with him.'

It was too dark to see his face. Just his bulk, and the sound of his axe.

'Red, it's all right. It wasn't your fault. It was my own

fault – my own stupid carelessness. Please, Red, you must believe me . . . I don't blame you one bit.'

She could hear him shuffling his feet, then blowing his nose. He said something which sounded like 'having it mended'.

'No, don't worry about that. I'll take it to a jeweller's – I'm sure they can do something with it. Come in for supper now, you must be hungry.'

He didn't answer, just dropped the ring into her hand. She could tell by the feel of it that it was flattened, and it took all her self-control not to exclaim aloud. Miserably she returned to her room and standing under the overhead light she opened her palm. It was then her grief exploded.

By the time she had washed all traces of tears away and changed into something more casual than the clothes she wore for work, she had pulled herself together. Nothing could repair her ring. Some of the pieces of amethyst were missing as well as two of the pearls. She accepted with a sense of fatalism that this was her punishment for betraying Leo in her thoughts. The problem facing her now was should she or should she not confess to him? Not about her thoughts, of course, that was out of the question, but about her carelessness. I won't worry about that now, I'll worry about that tomorrow, she said, unwittingly echoing the words of one of her favourite heroines of fiction.

But of course she worried, even in her sleep, and woke unrefreshed the next morning, remembering as she opened her eyes that it was Saturday. I'll stay away she thought – this is a warning. If I ignore it something worse might happen.

On Tuesday she received a note from Evelyn Smith.

'Do wish you were on the phone – can't you drop a hint to whoever's in charge of the privy purse? Missed you on Saturday. Please don't fail me this Saturday. I need your support. Two lone females against all these hearty young chaps – not that there will be so many this week. The gunners are on the move. Another lot taking over. Come early.'

She could have phoned and made her excuses. She was quite determined to do so, but somehow her resolve petered out by Wednesday. She so looked forward to Saturdays. Why should she give them up because of a pair of magnetic blue eyes – because that's all it boiled down to. A stupid schoolgirl crush, that's all it was; the way she had had a crush on Errol Flynn and later on Robert Donat, neither of which had diminished her love for Leo. Her love for Leo was unassailable.

As Evelyn requested, she arrived at Manor Farm early, but Joe was earlier. He was sitting on the arm of one of the easy-chairs reading the paper, and immediately stood up when she entered. Evelyn left them to go and prepare tea, refusing their offers of help. There was an awkward silence in which Philippa sat down on the sofa beside Mitzi. Mitzi opened one eye, saw who it was, climbed into Philippa's lap and pushed at her hand with her wet nose in a demanding way. She was asking to be stroked and Philippa obliged. It was comforting to them both.

Joe lazily strolled over and took a chair opposite.

'Eve has been telling me about your fiancé. An army doc – is that right?'

Philippa nodded and, immediately conscious of her ringless finger, removed her hand. Mitzi stretched, dug her claws in Philippa's knees, dropped lightly to the ground and walked away with tail upraised, affronted.

'We call them saw-bones in the Raf,' Joe said, then dropped his bantering tone. 'Hard luck about him being posted abroad, just when you planned to get married too. . . .'

Oh Eve, is nothing sacred.

'Tough on you both.'

'Yes.'

Another silence. 'I see you're not wearing your ring today.'

'No . . . it – it got broken.'

'What, the engagement?'

She gave him a withering look. A long unnatural silence which Joe finally broke.

'You don't like me, do you?' he said.

'What on earth makes you think that?'

'The way you chaff with the other chaps, but never with me. The way you avoid looking at me when I speak to you, as you are now. Come clean. Philippa – you don't mind me calling you, Philippa? Good. Well, whatever it is you dislike about me, be honest about it and I'll try and put it right.'

Come clean! How could she do that when she couldn't even come clean with herself? How could she confess that she avoided his eyes for fear that there might be something in hers she did not wish him to see? How could she explain, even to herself, why he was ever in her thoughts encroaching upon that one secret place that had been forever Leo's? How could she tell him that to her he was torment, yet not to see him was a greater torment? How to say all this without giving him the impression that she was in love with him, which was such a ridiculous idea it made her want to laugh. Or cry.

'I've hurt your feelings,' he said.

'Nonsense!'

'Your eyes are wet.'

'Please play something,' she said quickly. 'That piece that always makes Eve cry.'

There was something unnerving about the look on his face as he went slowly across to the piano. 'An apt choice in the circumstances,' he said.

The strains of 'Liebestraum' brought Evelyn from the kitchen. 'That's not fair,' she said indignantly. 'You usually save that for last.'

'By special request,' said Joe, looking across at Philippa.

At once Evelyn noticed Philippa's flushed cheeks and troubled eyes. 'Philippa, come and give me a hand with the sandwiches, dear.'

It wasn't until the loaf had been sliced and Philippa was mixing a small amount of butter into a large amount of margarine that Evelyn said, 'Do you know what "Liebestraum" means?'

'No I'm afraid not. It's German, isn't it?'

'In English it means "Dream of Love".'

Philippa dropped her knife, looked up aghast. 'Oh, no – oh, not that . . . I didn't know.'

Evelyn's expression was pensive. 'You know what they say about a moth who flies too near the flame? Philippa, my dear, beware of getting your wings singed.'

Protecting her wings cost Philippa more than she cared to pay. After one long tedious weekend when it had rained the whole time and the queues stretched endlessly outside every cinema, and every seat in the theatres was booked, she decided to spend the next weekend at home. She went to the station to phone her father.

'Philippa, why couldn't you have said before. It's Ursula's birthday and we're going to Henley for the weekend. I've booked in at a hotel overlooking the river....'

Scorpio. Yes, she looked a Scorpio, thought Philippa sourly, conveniently overlooking the fact that she herself was born under the sign of the Scorpion.

'Could you make it the weekend after?' her father was saying. 'It will be your birthday then. Perhaps Charlie could get hold of a birthday cake. What's it like up in Norfolk?'

'Cold.'

'Same here. Any news of Leo? I haven't forwarded on any letters lately.'

She became more animated. 'He's received my letters at last. A whole bunch of them. He'll be writing to me here, in future.' The operator broke in with a request for more money. Philippa had no more change. She said a quick goodbye, gave a promise to write, then hung up. She was loath to go back to her lonely room. She had posted a letter to Leo only that morning. There was nothing new to tell him. She lingered in the station watching late-comers (mostly in uniform) hurrying for the London-bound train, and had to fight back an impulse to join them. She was suddenly overcome with homesickness for Woodside. She wanted the solid comfort of that old house. She wanted to walk through the forest which at this time of year would be as colourful as an artist's palette. She wanted to lie in bed and listen to the tawny owls. She wanted to be home.

I'll go, she thought, I'll go this weekend even if Dad

isn't there. I'll walk over to Belle Vue Road and call on the Brookes. They'll be pleased to see me. I might have more up-to-date news of Leo for them. She wanted desperately to talk about Leo to someone. Talking about him might bring him nearer. She was fearful of him fading.

She caught an early train on Friday evening. The new manager, a local man, was generous with Saturday mornings. He had instigated a rota for everyone to have one Saturday morning off a month. His keenness for a game of golf had nothing to do with it, said Miss Jolly with a wink. The staff could, if they liked, swap Saturdays with a willing colleague as long as it was recorded in the attendance book. Philippa swapped hers with a girl who wanted to go to a wedding the following Saturday. So now, she was snug in her window seat, the anticipation of a weekend of solitude before her in which she hoped to come to terms with the many problems robbing her of sleep. And wrapped in tissue paper in her handbag was Leo's ring, for she knew of a jeweller in Woodside who was a wizard with intricate repairs and he just might be able to do something about it. She was suddenly aroused from her reverie by a tap at the window. She looked round and there, grinning at her through the pane of glass was Sergeant-Pilot Joe Gilbert. She stared back disbelievingly.

'That was a stroke of luck,' he said. He flung his holdall on the rack above and made himself comfortable beside her. 'I didn't even think I'd find a seat, let alone an agreeable travelling companion. And where are you bound for?'

The whistle blew, the train juddered, steam hissed,

wheels clanged, and they were off into the twilight. The overhead lights came on; tiny, dim circles of filtered light that only gave sufficient illumination in which to find a seat. Philippa was thankful it wasn't enough to reveal her expression. Joe was a living, breathing presence beside her and her heart was pounding.

'Where are you heading for?' he said again.

'Woodside.'

'Woodside!' His surprise was just a mite overdone. 'I live at Chingford. D'you know Chingford?'

'Of course I do.'

'D'you know those little weather-boarded cottages on the green? My mother lives in one of them.'

She conjured up a childhood image of that tiny corner of the original village. The green, the church, a row of old Essex cottages, and a blacksmith's shop on the other side of the road. Chingford now was fast becoming a dormitory town of London but she could recall the days when an ancient four-wheeled fly with a tired old horse between the shafts waited in the station yard for a likely fare. She remembered Holiday Mondays, the hawkers with baskets of rock or bags of peanuts, streamers and windmills, touting for custom in the station forecourt, and trippers from East London pouring out of the trains and spreading in wide, colourful swaths over Chingford Plain. The Bank Holiday fair at Chingford had become a tradition like Guy Fawkes Night or the Lord Mayor's Show. She wondered if it would survive the war. She doubted it.

'That was a very deep sigh,' Joe said.

'I was just remembering Chingford as it used to be. Just wondering if the fair still comes on holiday weekends.'

'I'll ask my mother. Not that she is one for fairs. She's deaf and dumb, or rather, because she is deaf she has never learnt to speak. She tries to – oh, how she tries. Sometimes, I wish she wouldn't.'

'She has never heard you play!'

'She watches me. She feels the vibrations. She was rather upset when I left the academy but I think that was on Uncle Dan's account, knowing how disappointed he'd be. But you don't want to hear about that.'

'But I do,' she said, for listening to him would be easier than talking to him and she could relax in the half-light and conjure up thoughts of Leo for the mention of Chingford Plain had revived other memories: Leo winning a coconut at the shies and digging holes in the end with his penknife so that they could drink the sweet, nutty fluid; Leo rowing her on Connaught Waters and laughing until he cried when her attempt at the oars took them round in a circle; Leo sitting astride a log, carving their initials. Leo . . . But Leo suddenly bid her adieu for something Joe said caught her attention.

'When you say Dan Harker, do you mean the Mr Harker who owned Thornmere Hall?'

'That's the one. Closer to me in a way than my own father. He was also deaf and dumb.'

She took a sharp intake of breath. 'D'you mean to say that neither of your parents could hear? Have never heard a note of music in their lives – yet you were born so gifted! Where did you get that gift from?'

'Gift!' he laughed. 'A tyrannical mistress more like it. No, that's too strong – more of a driving force, I should say. A hard taskmaster sometimes, but a comfort at others.'

He told her then of his decision to give up music and

join the air force, that was in 1939, and the only time he and his godfather did not see eye to eye.

'Though I had another year at the academy before I got my diploma I knew by then I would never make it as a concert pianist – and where did that leave me? Teaching? Perish the thought. Orchestral work? Very few openings for pianists. A dance band? I was suddenly dissatisfied with the whole idea of music as a career, so I joined the RAF instead.'

In spite of her determination to keep on strictly impersonal terms Philippa found herself laughing with him. 'It seems such a strange transition – from music to flying.'

'Not for me it wasn't. I'd always wanted to fly since the day Uncle Dan took me to a flying circus and we had a five-shilling flip in one of the old biplanes – a Tiger Moth it must have been. I was only up in the air a few minutes but long enough to get bitten by the flying bug. I must have been about twelve at the time, just the right age to dream of becoming an aviator. It was Uncle Dan who was anxious for me to study music. When I realised I could never make it as a virtuoso, I thought seriously of that other ambition, and what with that and the threat of war, I joined the air force.'

'Not as an officer?'

'No. All I wanted to do was fly and the easiest way, it seemed to me at the time, was to apply to a Flying Training School. I was taken on and here I am.'

Yes, here he was, sitting very close, and she becoming every minute more uncomfortably aware of his presence. Suddenly the lights went out, and the train put on speed. Nobody spoke; everybody was too intent on listening. Above the rattle of wheels the whining of a siren could be heard. Philippa shrank back in her seat. She hated being caught in a train during a raid. Black-out precautions seemed futile to her for the fire-box was a giveaway. She dreaded the possibility of a bomber taking careful aim or diving low to rake the train with machine-gun fire. She had yet to hear of someone being killed in a train during a raid, but there was always a first time.

'Nervous?' Joe whispered.

'Aren't you?' she whispered back.

'I'd rather be up there taking a pot-shot at them than sitting here waiting for them to take a pot-shot at me.' He reached for and found her hand. Her first instinct was to draw it away but his clasp gave her the confidence she needed.

His hand was warm whereas, even in the heat of summer, Leo's was always cold. 'Cold hand – warm heart. Warm hand – cold heart,' Leo would say. But no way could she believe that this amiable young man beside her was cold-hearted.

The All Clear was sounding as they drew into Liverpool Street. People were emerging from shelters, hurrying for trains. They had come in on Platform Twelve and had to cross by the footbridge to get to the suburban lines. Here their ways diverged.

'Let me see you home,' Joe said. 'I don't like the idea of you travelling on alone in the black-out. I could easily get a bus from Woodside to Chingford, or even walk it. It's a fine night.'

'My father will be waiting for me at Woodside station,' she answered glibly.

'Oh.' He was clearly disappointed. 'Well, perhaps I could see you sometime during the weekend. I've got a forty-eight hour pass.'

'I – I don't know what plans my father might have made.'

'We'll leave it to Kismet then, shall we?'

'Yes, Kismet,' she said, using the word as goodbye.

The ringing of the telephone dragged her reluctantly from a heavy sleep. The black-out curtains were still drawn, the room was in darkness. She switched on her torch. Half past eight! Whoever was calling her at this unearthly hour! Who knew she was at home? Mrs Toser? But Mrs Toser wouldn't use a phone to save her life. She decided to ignore it but the ringing went on and on. Muttering to herself she pulled on a dressing-gown and pattered downstairs.

'Hello,' she said shortly.

A breezy 'Good morning, good morning, rise and shine and all the rest of it . . .' banished a coming yawn. She was fully awake now.

'Is this Kismet,' she said sarcastically.

'No. Kismet was a washout so I had to do the job myself. Pity to waste a lovely morning like this indoors . . . come for a walk.'

She leaned over and pulled aside the curtain at the hall window. It was not yet light. 'Beautiful morning, ha ha!'

'It's not raining and the stars are out. . . .'

'Are you phoning from your mother's?'

'Now what use would my mother have for a phone? I'm speaking from a telephone kiosk near the church and for once there's no one outside waiting.'

'How did you get my number?' she said suspiciously.

'How does one usually find a subscriber's number – the telephone directory of course. . . .'

So no conspiracy, but she couldn't get it out of her mind that his appearance on the train had not been exactly coincidental.

He said, 'What about me coming over there to see you?'

'No!' She didn't want him to discover she was on her own. She hesitated. She felt if she didn't comply with his wishes, he would come, anyway. 'I'll come over to Chingford. I'll get a bus and meet you at the station.'

'What time?'

'Say eleven?'

'What shall we do?'

'You could always take me for a row on Connaught Waters.' She said it flippantly, without giving a thought to the consequences, then could have bitten her tongue out for he took her seriously. Now what on earth made her say a thing like that! Connaught Waters belonged to Leo. Perhaps boats were no longer available, perhaps they were stored for the duration. What a fool she was. Why had she said such a thing? Perhaps because in some indefinable way he reminded her of Leo. Not physically, there was no physical likeness between them, but in his use of schoolboy slang and the swift, sudden smile that illuminated the whole of his face.

Yet her misgivings hardly survived the short bus ride to Chingford station. Relief to get out from that cold and silent house vanquished them. She had anticipated silence, in fact had welcomed it after the noise of Wimborne House for there there was either someone's radio playing or Mrs Toser giving voice, which she did often and vociferously if it were Red who was at fault. But the cold was another matter.

The electric fire had made little difference and she had

been too tired to light a fire. She had opened a tin of soup and that, piping hot with toast, had been sufficient for her supper. Then she had gone to bed with two hot-water bottles. Her bedroom had been like ice. However, she found it warmer out of doors than indoors this morning. Joe's prediction had come true for it was one of those sunny, sparkling days that sometimes come as a delightful bonus in early November. She began to feel glad she had come home, after all.

And at Chingford station Joe was waiting for her, still in uniform. She had changed into a pair of navy-blue slacks and a cream polo-necked jumper and over that the Burberry her father had bought her when she first started at Brundle's Bank. In her estimation it was now middle aged, but still looked good she thought, and Joe must have thought so too for he looked her up and down with approval. 'Just the thing for boating,' he said.

It delighted her to find that Joe was no better with the oars than she herself. In fact she was better, for under Leo's tutorship she no longer rowed in circles. Joe did.

'I hope you are better with a plane that you are with a boat,' she said.

'It's that left hand technique of mine,' he retorted with a wicked grin. 'It lets me down every time. One of the reasons I knew I'd never make it as a virtuoso.'

They had the lake to themselves. The few fishermen on the bank watched their antics with amused contempt.

'Have you ever known a fisherman to take a catch out of Connaught Waters?' Joe asked.

'Never. My father calls them the Band of Hope.'

He looked at his watch. 'It's nearly time for us to go in.'

'I shouldn't worry. It isn't as if there are any other customers waiting.'

'One more circuit then we'd better think about lunch.'

She hadn't realised that lunch was on the agenda. She wished now she had put on something more in keeping. She hoped he wasn't taking her back to meet his mother. She wasn't dressed for social calls.

'I've booked a table at the Forest Arms for one o'clock,' he said.

Her heart sank. Leo had taken her there once to a dinner dance. It was all gilt and plush and cut glass chandeliers. That was in peacetime of course, but still . . .

'The Forest Arms of all places!' she wailed. 'And I'm in trousers.'

'Very sensible wear these days. You never know when you may have to dive head first into an air-raid shelter.'

This was little consolation to Philippa who liked to look her best for any occasion. That the exercise on the lake had given her a colour, that her hair shone like pale gold in the sunlight, that there was an extra lustre to her splendid eyes was lost on her, but not on the elderly waiter or indeed on Joe who, when she wasn't looking his way, feasted his eyes on her.

They sat over their lunch exchanging inconsequential chatter, until the wine Philippa had taken freed her from inhibitions.

'Have you got a girlfriend or anything?'

He looked at her from under his brows. 'If by anything you mean a wife, the answer is no.'

'A girlfriend?'

'At present no but I'm always open to suggestions.'

Philippa wasn't sure how to take that. She wasn't that

befuddled not to see the danger in pursuing this kind of raillery. She said, 'Would you mind ordering coffee?'

Coffee arrived and with it the offer of a cigar for Joe. He waved it away.

'Don't you smoke?'

'Never felt the urge, which makes me very popular back on base.'

They finished coffee, Joe paid the bill, and they went outside. The sky had greyed over and there was a decided threat of frost in the air. Up here on high ground on a fine day it was possible to see for miles but now mist was obscuring the distant view. The open space in front of the hotel was a bus terminal. Joe turned to her.

'Do you want to wait for a bus or walk across the Plain to the village?'

'Let's walk. I've eaten so much, I could do with the exercise.'

It seemed natural that he should take her hand. There was nothing objectionable in holding hands. If he had put his arm around her as Leo did when they walked together, that would have been a different matter. There were few people about at this side of Chingford. No golfers as in peacetime. Only a few cows exercising their owners' 'commoners rights', grazed the rabbit-bitten turf.

They walked in silence, but a comfortable silence. Philippa found her mind roving. Could she risk asking him home to tea? No, that was out of the question. Yet she felt she ought to repay his hospitality. Goodness knows what the bill had come to, though she had deliberately chosen one of the cheapest dishes on the menu. She had no idea how he was off for money. She had no idea how much a sergeant-pilot in the RAF earned. His mother lived in a tiny cottage so they couldn't be that well-off. Her conscience began to worry her. Should she offer to pay half the bill? She and Leo had always gone Dutch during his student years. But another look at Joe's pugnacious profile decided her against it.

He said, 'I would love to take you home to introduce you to my mother. Unfortunately, she has an old school friend staying with her. They were both pupils at the Margate School for the Deaf for a time. When those two get together their fingers go at it like knitting needles. I can't keep up with them and I consider myself quite good at the deaf and dumb language. I should be, I started early enough. Good practice for me in later years though, kept my fingers limber.'

'I can't understand how you can talk about your mother's affliction in such a casual way,' she said.

He stared at her in amazement. 'Affliction! My mother! Great Scott, I've never thought of my mother as being afflicted. She is just like anybody else's mother except that she cannot hear. That doesn't worry her. She loses out in some ways but she gains in others. She's never heard an unkind word in her life. She loves life, too. Has a great gift for making the most of things. The only time I saw her give in was when my father died. He had worked for Daniel Harker for years – long before he married my mother, and when it was time for him to retire, Uncle Dan bought them this cottage in Chingford. Poor Dad, he didn't live long enough to enjoy it. I thought Mum was going to follow him, but she pulled herself together and came fighting back.

'She's a wonderful old lady, really. I got a right ticking off for not telling her I'd be home this weekend. She wouldn't have invited Annie if she'd known.' He chuckled softly. 'When she ticks me off she does it with her fists – it's like being tickled with a feather duster.' A pleading note came into his voice. 'Come home with me, please. I'd so much like you to meet her.'

Philippa really wanted to say yes. So far Joe had done all the giving and she wanted to give him something in return, but she shrank at the idea of meeting his mother. Not because of Mrs Gilbert's disability; she could have coped with that, clumsily perhaps, but with tact and understanding she hoped. But by accepting Joe's invitation to visit his home, to be introduced to his mother, might it not start a precedent? She had enough on her conscience as it was. What about her intention of calling on Leo's parents? How could she disregard them yet find time to visit the mother of a comparative stranger? I'll visit them tomorrow, she told herself, and at the time meant it. To Joe she made the excuse that she wasn't dressed for visiting, that it wouldn't be fair to call on his mother without warning.

He accepted her excuses with a shrug. He wasn't surprised. He could tell by the struggle she had with herself what the outcome would be. But he was not one to be put off so easily.

'As you won't come home to meet my mother what about me coming over to Woodside to meet your father? I've got no such qualms about what I'm wearing.

'Go on, be a sport,' he said, and as she hesitated. 'Would you have such a thing as a piano in your house?' A joke. For he knew well enough that everybody of their generation, except the extremely poor, had access to a piano. Nearly every young person had had to undergo piano lessons, though many, like Philippa, had fallen by the wayside.

Still she hesitated. 'There is a piano,' she said slowly. 'But it hasn't been tuned for donkey's years.'

'You don't suppose I could exchange an hour or two at your warm fireside in exchange for a little light tickling of the keys?'

She couldn't quite meet his eyes. 'Warm fireside, that's a laugh – the place is like an ice-box. The fires haven't been lit since Thursday.'

'But—'

'I lied to you. My father is away for the weekend. I knew before I left Norwich that he would be.' Her voice trailed off.

Joe looked puzzled for a moment or two, then a slow smile spread across his face. 'If this is confession time,' he said, 'I have one to make too. I knew you'd be on that train. I wrung the information out of Evelyn, and it took some wringing. But I promise you I didn't know about your father being away.'

Neither did Evelyn, Philippa thought, otherwise he would have wrung that out of her too. It was decision time. She knew now she had to say yes or no and if she said yes, might have to face the consequences. But surely she had willpower enough to say no if the occasion warranted it. She wasn't that weak-willed.

'I'd certainly appreciate having a fire,' she said, 'I'm hopeless at lighting fires.'

Joe's eyes twinkled. 'I'm a knockout at lighting fires.'

He was as good as his word. In no time at all he had a blaze roaring up the chimney.

'My fires always smoulder and then go out. What did you use to light it with?' Philippa asked.

'A bone,' was all the answer she got.

They knelt by the fire warming their hands. Firelight flickered over the walnut casing of the piano. Mrs Mooney polished it regularly. It looked good. It was good. 'Pity it's been so woefully neglected,' said Joe when he first examined it. 'A Bechstein too.' The keys were turning yellow, some remained silent when depressed.

'My Great-Aunt Dorothy was the last to play it, and goodness knows how long ago that was. We never use this room, it gets so little sun.'

It was a small room at the back of the house completely overshadowed by trees. It had started life as a music-room and was still referred to as that, but over the years it had become a depository for discarded objects from other rooms. There was very little room to sit, even the two easy-chairs were taken up by books.

'I'll make us a cup of tea,' said Philippa. 'Could you eat something?'

'Good heavens, no.'

'Perhaps later.'

'Supper?'

'Certainly not!'

The kitchen was some distance from the music-room so she didn't hear the catchy melody emanating from there until she was out in the hall. Considering the state of the piano it could still make a pleasant sound, she thought.

'I like that,' she said, making room for her tray on a pedestal table. 'I could Charleston to that. What's it called?'

' "Chicago". Come on, let's see you Charleston.'

'And have you laugh at me. Certainly not.'

They sat on the fur rug by the hearth and drank their

tea. There was nowhere else to sit. The fire was throwing out real heat now. Joe unbuttoned his tunic.

Philippa stared dreamily at the flames. 'Why does Eve like "Liebestraum" so much,' she said.

'Something to do with their courting days, I believe.'

'Then why does it make her cry?'

'Not all tears are unhappy tears,' said Joe.

She looked away. When he smiled at her like that she felt her blood turning to water. He was so near, inching nearer. 'Play "Liebestraum" for me,' she said desperately. But that was a mistake too. The first few notes made her realise how susceptible she was.

She rose. 'I'd better draw the black-out curtains. This fire is lighting up the room.'

She stayed by the window, clutching the curtains as if reluctant to let go. The playing stopped. She heard the piano lid being closed, the legs of the piano stool scraping against the floor, his tread as he came across to her, and shivered with anticipation as his arms went round her.

'I'll leave now if you want me to,' he said, his cheek against hers.

Oh Leo, please help me – please rescue me, she cried inwardly. But Leo was thousands of miles away and there was only her self-control to protect her.

Years ago while still at school, she had in company with the other girls in her class paid out twopence to a budding gymslipped entrepreneur for the loan of Elinor Glyn's notorious *Three Weeks*, which she read, clandestinely and guiltily in bed, never dreaming that the day would come when she herself would follow in the footsteps of Elinor Glyn's heroine. Making love not on a tiger skin as such, but on a fur rug.

She should have been ashamed of herself. She *was*

ashamed of herself, but she was also in such a state of confused and blissful happiness that shame took second place in her consciousness.

The fire had died down to glowing embers but still gave out considerable heat which was just as well as she was wearing nothing. They had discarded their clothes ('unnecessary obstacles,' said Joe) long before. He lay beside her asleep, one arm across her waist. His chest was covered with the same wiry, thick, black hair as on his head. Once the thought of sleeping with a man with a hairy chest would have appalled her. She had been relieved to discover in Edinburgh that Leo had not a hair on his chest. But she didn't want to think about Leo, not when she was lying in Joe's arms.

But Leo would persist in being thought about. After all she had thought of nobody else during the past five months, and try as she might she couldn't dismiss an image of his reproachful hazel eyes. He had been a gentle and considerate lover. Joe, though not ungentle, had fired in her an exciting and compulsive response. He had said earlier, she now remembered, 'I'm a knockout at lighting fires.' He had certainly lit a fire within her. He had taught her, in the past hour, more about her own sexuality than anything she had learnt during her three nights with Leo. There was no shyness with Joe, no nonsense about modesty. Just the assumption that the pleasure they gave each other was a natural outcome of their chance encounter.

'The minute you walked through the door with Eve, I knew I had met my fate,' he said.

'You mean Kismet.'

'Call it what you like. You led me to it.'

She pondered on this now as he slept peacefully beside

her. Was there such a thing as predestination? Did it go as far back as the bomb that destroyed the London branch of Brundle's Bank which in turn led her to Norwich and then to Manor Farm and hence to Joe? Or even further back still to the unknown grandmother who left the farm at Thornmere to go to Woodside and marry Philippa's grandfather? Was it all written down in some imaginary ledger – that the paths of differing individuals would cross at some future time and date? No, she couldn't accept that for that would abnegate one's wrongdoings. Like standing in the dock and whining, 'I wasn't responsible for my actions, my Lord, it was all written down in the Book of Fate before I was born.'

That would make it all too easy – would wipe away all responsibilities for one's misdeeds. She had sinned in the sight of God. She had wronged Leo. Suddenly she was overwhelmed by such a rush of guilt and self-hatred she could have wept from the pain, yet a few minutes later when Joe stirred and drowsily kissed her shoulder, she readily turned to him.

Eight

Sunday, 7 December 1941. Pearl Harbor. A name unheard of among the vast majority of the British public until the sudden attack by the Japanese air force on the US naval base. A name that would go down in history, like Waterloo, Gettysburg, and the Somme. Philippa heard the news the following morning on the blue-cased portable radio her father had given her as an early Christmas present.

She was stunned. It was hard to believe that the Americans had been so unprepared. Inwardly, and she was ashamed of feeling it, she rejoiced. Not that she didn't regret their heavy losses, but the thought of having someone else in the war with them came as a tremendous fillip. Lately there hadn't been much reason for rejoicing. In November, the Italians had torpedoed the *Ark Royal*, and every day Hitler's troops were inching nearer to Moscow. The Americans had done all they could to help the Allies' cause without actually taking up arms. Now perhaps, they had no choice.

She was meeting Joe that night. Just a quick hello and

goodbye, a half-hour or so of stolen pleasure, for to go long without sight of each other was becoming unendurable. They met this time in the refreshment room on Thorpe station and sat, cups of untouched coffee before them, holding hands under the solid mahogany table.

'Will this bring America into the war?' said Philippa, for that was the main topic of conversation, even for lovers, at the moment.

'She's already in it whether she likes it or not. We've got another ally, Phil, and it's going to make a hell of a difference to our lives.'

'We've got another enemy, too.'

'I'll back the Yanks against the Japs, any day.'

Philippa didn't answer. She was thinking of the Russians' present ally. Winter. The Russian winter was killing the Germans in their thousands.

Joe stirred his coffee, his thoughts miles away while her gaze wandered lovingly over his face. Nobody could call Joe handsome. None of his features matched and his nose was badly out of joint, a legacy from his childhood when he had been kicked in the face by a horse. She couldn't imagine Joe with a straight nose – it wouldn't go with the rest of his face. His crooked nose and boyish grin, his unruly hair and short, stubby, workmanlike hands were all part of the image she carried around with her.

'I always thought pianists had long sensitive fingers,' she once remarked.

'So they do in fiction, but in real life they're worn down to the knuckles with practising.' He took a delight in teasing her.

When she had asked him how he got his nose he had told her about Sam, the one remaining horse at Daniel

Harker's canning factory after mechanisation of the delivery vans.

'My father had had charge of the horses for years. Then of course the time came for modernisation. The horses had to go, all except Sam, Uncle Dan kept him back out of sentimental reasons, or so he said. The real reason of course was to placate my father who was heartbroken at losing his old friends. Anyway, Sam stayed and was treated like a household pet until the day he kicked out at me. Nobody knew why except me, and I wasn't saying.'

'Tell me.'

Joe chuckled. 'I dropped a fire-cracker behind his tail. My only excuse is that I was too young to know what I was doing, I wanted to see Sam jump – and by jolly, he did too – with his back legs! I landed up in hospital and poor old Sam in the knacker's yard. Philippa, don't look at me like that. It's been on my conscience ever since.'

'I don't believe you know what a conscience is. Didn't anybody find out?'

'I think Uncle Dan suspected but he didn't let on. I've learnt my lesson, Phil. I've never dropped a fire-cracker behind a horse since.' She could tell by his voice that he was laughing. It was too dark to see him clearly for at the time they were occupying two seats in the back row of a cinema, the last resort for frustrated lovers.

But there was no chance of heated and passionate embraces in the refreshment room, just wistful looks across the table. The chance to kiss might come later, in some deeply recessed shop doorway. Philippa hated having to come down to this. It made her feel degraded, and it was difficult sometimes to contain Joe's ardour, and just as difficult to contain her own. It was then

Evelyn's words came back to haunt her. 'Philippa, my dear, beware of getting your wings singed.' Singed! If only it were that simple. She was consumed by a fire that no words of warning, her own common sense, sense of propriety, or the thought of the wrong she was doing Leo, could put out.

Joe broke into her thoughts. 'If I could wangle next weekend off, and there's every chance I might, would you come away with me? What about Cromer – that's not too far, and at this time of year there'll be plenty of accommodation.'

'It's cold at Cromer. The wind comes straight from the Arctic.'

His eyes sought hers. 'Was that just a piece of information or are you having another attack of conscience?'

'No – no, it's just that . . .' But she couldn't tell him about the letter she'd had from Leo that morning. She couldn't begin to explain the feeling of self-disgust that tormented her at times. Her eyes misted over, looking moist and appealing in the dim lighting. Joe felt his heart turn over. God, how this girl got under his skin. 'I won't pester you if you don't want to come,' he said.

'But I do want to.'

When she got back to her room that night, she reread Leo's letter. She always flipped through his letters quickly and if there was anything that would cause her pangs of conscience she would put it aside and not bring it out again until she felt strong enough to take it. These days Leo's letters caused her more suffering than joy. Just the sight of his bold, upright writing was sufficient to bring her face to face with her duplicity. Reading his letters was an ongoing torture. The more he told her he loved her or recalled the happy times they had had together, the greater her pain. It wouldn't hurt so much if he no longer meant so much to her, but he did. You couldn't love somebody for years and then substitute that love with indifference. *She* couldn't anyway. Leo was too much a part of her life for that.

Just one small passage in this particular letter guaranteed another white night. 'All the time my thoughts are with you. I'm always working out Greenwich mean time and wondering what you were doing at any particular time.'

'I'll tell you what I was doing,' came her silent, savage response. 'I was whoring with a another man. Yes me, Leo – your sweet, untarnished, bashful, little hypocrite. The one you said you would always think of as a virgin. I lost my innocence Leo – not with you, but with another man, a man I hardly knew. . . .' But she couldn't keep it up. Railing at herself didn't solve anything. She resorted to tears, fat scalding tears that rolled down her cheeks and on to the paper. Go on, cry, she said. Crying costs nothing – you're crying out of self-pity, anyway. Bitter thoughts that stuck in her conscience like burrs.

Wearily, when her tears were spent, she got off the bed and looked at herself in the glass. She couldn't go downstairs looking like that. Everybody would be too polite to say anything but eyebrows would be raised and remarks passed behind her back. She undressed, washed, and got back into bed, ready for sleep this time, knowing that sleep would be a long time in the coming.

What she needed was a friend, someone who would give her the right kind of advice. Only two names occurred to her – Mrs Toser and Evelyn. Miss Jolly was always available, and nobody would be wiser or kinder than she, but Miss Jolly had never been in love so wouldn't have the right kind of understanding. Mrs Toser hadn't had much experience of love either. Her husband had left her and their four young children and gone off with another woman which Mrs Toser said was the kindest thing he had ever done for her, so how could she know anything about a love so consuming it could destroy in the end. It might even embarrass her to discuss it. That left Evelyn who knew all there was to know about love and the suffering and joy it brought in its wake, but was far too involved with both herself and Joe to give an objective answer. So that, of course, left her father, who had never let her down where advice was concerned. But when would she ever have the chance again to speak to her father on his own?

She thought that chance might come over the Christmas holiday, but even that small hope was denied her. As Charlie had supplied the turkey it was only right he should be invited to come and help eat it, and he was already installed at Byrd's House when she arrived. Just for a short while on Christmas morning was she alone with her father for Mrs Warwick and her brother had shut themselves in the kitchen and issued orders not to be disturbed.

The sitting room looked very Christmassy. Mrs Warwick had used greenery from the garden with very good effect. The topmost branches off a fir tree made a good stand-in for a Christmas tree (what, no Christmas tree, thought Philippa when she saw it, Charlie had slipped up there). A log fire blazed in the hearth and the drinks trolley was loaded. But – there were other things missing. There were gaps in the display cabinet, and on the mantelpiece the only things on display were Christmas cards.

'What's happened to the Chinese vases, and the French enamels and the little Rockingham shepherdess and the other bits of family china?' she asked.

Her father, sipping his sherry, didn't answer immediately. He had, Philippa thought when she first arrived, looked pale and over-tired, but now looked more rested and certainly had a better colour, though that might have been due to the fire or the second sherry. He slowly looked up. 'Oh, those. They've been put away for safe-keeping . . . in case of raids. It was Charlie's idea.'

'They survived the blitz. And there hasn't been a serious raid since that ended.'

'That doesn't mean there won't be another. And with all this talk of Hitler's secret weapon . . .' Jonathan spoke irritably. 'Oh, for goodness sake, Pippa, you're here for such a short time, don't let's spoil it by arguing.'

She curled up on the sofa beside him and tucked her arm through his. He squeezed her hand. 'I didn't mean to snap, but I don't like being badgered – especially not by my own daughter.'

'I'm sorry Dad, but I couldn't help wondering. I've known those family treasures all my life . . . they are *part* of my life. I'm worried about them. Aren't you?'

'No, because I know they're safe. They have been put away in a safe-deposit box in the vault of some broker Charlie knows. Way outside the danger zone. We decided that was safer than with my bank at Stratford.'

Philippa held her tongue. As her father said, they didn't want to spend her short stay in argument, so would this be the right time, she wondered to introduce Joe into the conversation?

The door opened and Charlie stood on the threshold

wearing a drying-up cloth tied round his middle, and a paper hat tilted over one eye. 'Come and get it,' he said.

The dinner couldn't be faulted. Ursula and her brother had taken a lot of trouble with the preparations and the cooking. The turkey was tender without being dry, and there was no lack of pre-war accompaniments. Chestnut stuffing, bread sauce, cranberry jelly, bacon rolls and chipolata sausages. And Christmas pud and mince pies waiting in the wings no doubt, thought Philippa sourly. She looked at her plate, wishing she had the strength of mind to plead lack of appetite, but hunger overruled her scruples. Her father, she noticed, ate very little, and Ursula only ever picked at her food. Charlie Ford made up for both of them. He packed the back of his fork with a little of everything, patting it all down with his knife until he had made room for another layer, and finishing it off with a mound of mashed potato.

He'll never get all that down at once, thought Philippa, watching with unwilling fascination. But he did. The corners of his mouth unlocked as if hinged, his gape opened wide and into it without any difficulty went the loaded fork. A bite, a gulp, a swallow and the packing started up again. Philippa turned her head away with disgust and as she did so she met the amused and cynical gaze of Ursula Warwick. Philippa was the one who blushed.

She arrived back at Riversway late on the evening of Boxing Day, tired and bitterly disappointed for she had hoped for a telephone call from Joe or to see his jaunty figure watching out for her on Thorpe station. No word from him either when she got to Wimborne House. Some late Christmas cards and a letter addressed to her had been delivered on Christmas Day, but nothing from Joe.

She took them to her room, where someone (Red, she guessed) had lit a fire. The cards were from old friends, from school and the bank, and the letter from Jean Dickson, Jean Shaw that was, from Coopen.

Jean had married her industrial chemist in October, sending Philippa a taste of her wedding cake 'for luck'.... 'It's good to have that little gold band on my finger at last,' she wrote at the time. 'Dave can't get away now, ha ha.' Now she wrote to say she was pregnant which Philippa found surprising, for Jean had always said she wouldn't dream of starting a family in wartime.

'This is no time to have a baby,' she'd written in a previous letter. 'Apart from the danger – I want to be able to walk into a shop and buy all the baby things I need, not have to worry about stupid coupons. Do you know it's impossible to get hold of a baby's potty now? My sister told me; she scoured the shops for one where she lives. She says she's driven to using a pudding basin....'

But now Jean herself was pregnant it was a different story. Her delight shone through every word. 'I won't be able to travel much after baby comes and I would so like to see you before then. Could I come and stay with you for a few days? I'd love to see Norwich after all you've said about it. I want to see if it measures up to Nottingham. Dave insists I go back to Nottingham when the baby comes, but I shan't of course. Where he is, there stay I.'

Philippa folded the letter with a sigh of envy. Not so much for Jean's marital status which mattered little to her these days, or her good news, but for her clear-minded attitude to life. Not for Jean the pangs of guilt that prevented sleep. Not for her the vacillations between right and wrong or love and loyalty. Jean knew what she wanted and went for it.

Yes, a visit from Jean was just what she needed. Jean, with her cool-headed common sense undiluted by sentiment, was the very confidante she required.

But where was Joe? Except for a Christmas card bearing the RAF insignia she hadn't heard from or of him since their snatched weekend in Cromer. There, they had stood on the cliff-top braving the full force of the Arctic wind until cold drove them back to shelter. They had thawed out in front of a roaring fire while a solicitous landlady served them buttered toast ('Butter in name only,' she said apologetically). That night they made love in a sagging bed whose ancient springs protested noisily at every move they made, and when they lay spent, gave a last, sudden, drawn-out and untuneful twang that reduced them both to helpless laughter.

Late on the Sunday night when they arrived back in Norwich, Joe had walked with her from the station to Wimborne House, but she didn't ask him in for a nightcap. The other residents knew about Leo, were always enquiring after him, so how could she now face them with Joe. Where was Joe, anyway? Why hadn't he been in touch?

She discovered the answer to that on her next visit to Manor Farm. Joe had been posted to an airfield in Scotland, flying on escort duty. Escorting the bombers attacking the Nazi air bases in Norway.

'Has he written to you?' said Philippa with a nonchalance she was far from feeling.

'What, Joe!' Evelyn laughed. 'He's one of the world's worst letter-writers. He can express himself better in his music.'

Jean came for her promised visit in March, a bit sooner than she had said in her letter and Philippa could see the reason as soon as she met her at the station. Jean was well advanced in pregnancy. At once Philippa realised that the camp-bed Mrs Toser had made up for her would not do. 'You don't mind sleeping in with me, do you?' she said, taking Jean's case. 'There are no other rooms available.'

'I'd love to share with you. Give us a chance of a natter – I love a natter. That's what I miss most since giving up my job. Keeping house is such a lonely occupation – still, it has its points, I can put my feet up when I feel like it.'

Mrs Toser brought their supper on trays. 'Wouldn't be wise do your friend traipse up and down those stairs too often,' she said in an audible whisper to Philippa, adding, 'Thought you said she was only five months gone. She look a lot more'n that to me.'

They stifled their laughter until the door closed behind her. 'She look more'n that to me,' said Jean making an attempt at the Norfolk accent. 'Anyway, what gave you the idea I was only five months gone?'

'October... March... I just assumed...'

'You assumed it was a honeymoon conception. Oh Philippa, you innocent! I was three months pregnant then – all Dave's fault. But I'll tell you about that later. Could we eat now, I'm starving.'

It was cosy and deliciously warm in the attic with the fire flickering up the chimney and their nightgowns warming in the hearth. They were replete and rather sleepy but loath to go to bed when they had so much to tell each other.

'What did you mean about it being Dave's fault?' said Philippa. 'It takes two to make a baby.'

'Oh, so you know that much do you?' In the firelight Jean's eyes gleamed wickedly. Pregnancy suited her. Her hair had thickened and curled becomingly around her face. She was always pretty, now she looked beautiful. Philippa felt scrawny by comparison.

'It was Dave's fault in as much as he would insist on trying out this new preventative that came out of a tube, horrible messy stuff it was too. We'd been doing all right for years on the old method, and then – shock-horror – I was suddenly pregnant. I'm quite pleased now that I've got used to the idea, and Dave's tickled pink.' Then with one of her well-remembered chuckles, 'Dave says if it's a girl we'll have to call her Miss Conception. Get it?'

Philippa got it.

There was quite an argument over who should have the camp-bed, which Philippa won and was in possession of before Jean started to undress. Philippa had discreetly undressed under cover of her nightgown. Jean stood up and stripped off in front of the fire and was now down to her bra and knickers, the like of which Philippa had never seen before. In spite of her careful upbringing she couldn't help blurting out, 'Where on earth did you get those enormous things.'

'You mean my outsize knickers?' Jean grinned unself-consciously. 'Latest in maternity wear, and my own invention. Actually, they're a pair of Dave's old pants. I stitched up the opening and trimmed the legs with lace just to make them look a little more feminine. I'd grown out of all mine and I wasn't going to waste my coupons buying bloomers that wouldn't fit me once the baby was born. I wore these for the first time on one of my visits to the doctor. Unfortunately, he decided to give me an examination that day. I went red with mortification, but Dr Miles kept a perfectly straight face. It was his finest hour. . . .'

Philippa, weak with laughter, wiped her eyes. 'I knew your visit would do me good,' she said. 'I'm feeling better already.'

Previous to Jean's visit she had compiled a list of things they should see and do, completely overlooking Jean's addiction to street markets. They got as far as Norwich's famous market and that was it.

'Do come along. This is not the first market you've seen.'

'It's the only one with little striped awnings on the stalls, and a castle in the background.'

At the haberdashery stall, Philippa met her Waterloo, for with a squeal of delight Jean fell upon a tray of pale pink two-ply Shetland wool done up in small skeins and being passed off as darning wool. Darning wool was not on coupons. Jean bought the entire stock.

'Enough here to knit a pram set,' she said triumphantly.

'In two-ply! It'll take you for ever. Anyway, supposing you have a boy.'

'He'll just have to wear pink then, won't he?'

They did do a little sight-seeing, especially around the more medieval parts of the city, but Jean utterly refused to step inside a church or a museum.

'I'm not here for culture,' she said flatly. 'I'm here to buy something to fit me once I've lost this bulge. Other people's shops always seem to have better goods available, have you noticed that?'

So Philippa took her to London Street, a narrow, busy

thoroughfare with some fine shops where Jean found something to her satisfaction.

'I expect Dave will have a fit when he finds out how much I forked out for it, but it's ages since I wore anything half so pretty. Do you like it?'

Philippa could truthfully say she did though she thought a high neckline and a zipped-up opening at the back rather impractical for a nursing mother but she didn't intend to spoil Jean's pleasure by saying so. All too soon the weekend passed. It rained hard all Sunday morning, but after lunch a watery sun broke through the clouds and Jean expressed a wish to see the cathedral.

They went by the route alongside the river, past Pulls Ferry and through the close where gracious houses and an avenue of trees made a fitting approach to the cathedral itself.

Jean stood still and looked around her, her expression solemn. 'It's a far cry from the chemical works at Teesside. Do you believe what they say about the environment having on effect on one's character?'

'Most certainly.'

'Hm. Then I should come and have my baby down here.'

'Mrs Toser is fearful that you might.'

Which made Jean laugh, but softly, for to make a noise in that setting seemed a sacrilege. Worshippers were entering the cathedral. 'Is there something going on?' she asked.

'The three o'clock nave service. I sometimes go to it.' Usually after receiving one of Leo's letters, hoping that prayer might help to ease her guilty conscience. When it did not she put it down to a lack of faith.

'I'd love to go,' said Jean surprisingly. 'But I've never

attended a service in a cathedral before, so give me a nudge if I do anything wrong, won't you.'

Philippa walked Jean to the station on Monday morning; her train went soon after eight o'clock. When it was time to say goodbye Philippa was surprised to see Jean in tears. Bright, breezy, self-sufficient Jean in tears!

'Yes, I know,' said Jean sniffing. 'I'm a sentimental fool, but I have so enjoyed this weekend, Philippa. I wish I could stay on a bit longer. Thank you for giving me such a lovely time – thank Mrs Toser again for me. Tell her I think she's a jewel. Tell Red that if I wasn't already married I'd be setting my cap at him. I love big muscular men with red hair. Seriously though, Philippa, I've been waiting all weekend for you to open your heart to me, for I had a strong feeling you wanted to. Nothing on your mind, is there?'

'Nothing I can't deal with,' said Philippa, kissing her. She waved until the train rounded the bend on the first lap of Jean's long and tiring journey back to County Durham. She could have spoken out many times during the course of Jean's short stay. More than once she had been on the brink of doing so but the thought of something Jean had said soon after her arrival prevented her.

She had asked after Leo, had wanted to know the latest news of him. Then suddenly, to Philippa's discomfiture had said, 'I never let on at the time, but I could have fallen for your Leo. Not for his looks or his position, but because he is such a decent sort of chap. Someone you could rely on, utterly dependable. I hope you realise how lucky you are, Philippa.'

Had Jean got an inkling, Philippa wondered. Did it show on her face – this new awareness of love? Did she go around unconsciously telling the world at large that she was a woman possessed?

'Of course I appreciate him,' she said. 'Of course I know his worth.' But it was of Joe she dreamt at night. Joe, where are you? was her constant and inward refrain. Why don't you write?

She had no intention of going to the farm that Saturday. But at the last minute she changed her mind and dashed out just in time to catch a later train to Thornmere Halt.

The sun felt warm on her back as she took a shortcut along Gypsy Lane. A female blackbird flew across her path carrying a beakful of nesting material. Far off across the fields a pheasant called. Fresh shoots were greening the hawthorn hedges, and celandines flowered at their roots. Spring was in the air, and a spring was in her step. She felt more contented than she had for weeks, so it was not a complete surprise as she neared the house to hear the strains of 'Liebestraum' being played as only Joe could play it.

Even so she took a moment or two to compose herself. Her mouth had gone dry but worse than that she had come out without makeup. While she frantically searched her bag for compact and lipstick, the door opened and Clive beamed down on her. 'I spotted you coming along the drive,' he said, and bestowed on her one of his fatherly kisses. 'Welcome stranger. . . . Guess who's here?'

'I know. I heard him. . . .'

Evelyn appeared. 'Come in, do come in. We were just talking about you, willing you to come.'

It was just like that first time back in September. The cigarette smoke, the smiling faces, the mix of uniforms and Joe at the piano looking over his shoulder, the stunning blueness of his gaze surprising her anew. Joy such as she hadn't experienced in weeks surged over her.

Evelyn said, 'Philippa dear, before you take off your coat, would you mind getting me some chives for the salad.'

Philippa went, not unwillingly, for all those grinning faces looking in her direction quite unnerved her. Had they guessed?

Footsteps on the gravel behind her. She knew that tread. She turned and waited for him, fighting against the urge to fling herself into his arms. 'You could have written,' she said reproachfully.

He didn't answer. He took her in his arms and kissed her in such a manner that left no doubt of his intention to anyone who might be watching from the house. She stepped back, breathless. 'You could have written,' she repeated, but less accusingly this time. 'If you had only known the agony you've put me through.'

'I did write – every day. . . .'

'I didn't get them. Not one of them. Oh, Joe.'

'Because I didn't post them. They sounded such drivel when I read them over. I'm no good at writing letters. I composed a piece of music for you instead.'

She was only partially mollified. 'I imagined all sorts of things happening to you. I feared the worst. . . .'

'You would have heard if the worst had happened. Bob Fellowes has been briefed about that. I'll do the same for him should it be necessary. But we won't waste time talking about what didn't happen. Come along, there's things to do.'

'That's not the way to the herb garden.'

'No, it's the way to the barn and in that barn is a

roomy and accommodating Rolls-Royce. Have you ever been made love to in a Rolls-Royce?'

'Oh no, Joe . . . !'

'But, oh yes, Philippa.'

'I must go and pick the chives for Evelyn. She'll wonder what I'm up to.' They were lying, out of necessity, very close, on the back seat of the Rolls, at peace with themselves and the world.

'She knows jolly well what you're up to. You don't think she really sent you after chives, do you? That was just a ruse to give us a chance to be alone. Good sport, Evelyn.'

Traitress Evelyn – after all her warnings! Joe must have got round her. Darling Joe. It was dark in the barn with the door closed. She could only just make out the pugnacious thrust of his chin, the crooked line of his nose. She nestled closer against his shoulder and as he turned his face to her, his eyes glinted like twin points of fire.

'I missed you, you gorgeous beast,' he said. 'It was hell for me just thinking about you. And there was I stuck in this inaccessible place and no females within miles.'

She stirred uneasily. Did that mean that if a woman had been available . . .? 'Were where you, Joe?'

'In training for some rather sticky operations and that's all I intend to say about it. . . .'

'Anything to do with Russia? Anything to do with the Arctic convoys?'

He whistled a few bars of 'Tell me the old old story'.

She tried another tack. 'Do you think you may return to your old base at Beckton?'

'I doubt it. I think there's a likelihood that the Yanks

will take over most of the air bases in East Anglia. Never mind, you'll have me for the next two days . . . I'm spending my leave with Eve and Clive.'

'Will you play the piece you wrote for me?'

'Not until I've polished it up a bit more.'

'What have you called it?'

'I had problems with that, and finally decided on "Parted". I thought it apt under the circumstances.'

She was horrified at this suggestion. 'You can't do that – that's the title of one of Peter Dawson's songs.' Also one of the ballads Leo had sung to her years ago during their trysting days in Epping Forest.

'There is no copyright in titles,' said Joe, adding with a wicked-sounding chuckle, 'There's no copyright in love, either.'

Her father and Ursula had at last settled on a date for the wedding – Wednesday, 29 April, which choice irritated Philippa out of all proportion. She telephoned her father after receiving this information.

'Why pick midweek? So thoughtless of you. Didn't it occur to you that I might not be able to get time off? Why couldn't you have picked a Saturday like everybody else?'

'For one thing we didn't want to be like everybody else and, for another, it's the only day Charlie has free that week and for many weeks to come. The lucky chap has just landed a government order, a large one too, and he can't afford to let such a prize slip through his fingers.'

Philippa was not in the mood to discuss Charlie Ford, but she was curious to know what his business was apart from black marketeering. That bit she left unsaid when she asked her father.

'He manufactures precision tools, in a very small way as yet, but this order could be the first step towards expansion.' Jonathan's tone could not hide his own disappointment. The Stationery Office was inundated with work – pamplets, directives, ration books, coupons, leaflets. To ease the load the government had invited tenders from outside printers. It was just what Jonathan needed to put Byrd's back on its feet again but he lost out to a larger and more commercial firm of printers. Now with paper severely rationed his firm was barely covering expenses. Concern for his employees, concern for the future of his business had taken its toll. It had always been said of him that he looked young for his age. Alas, she thought, not any longer.

She found Miss Jolly in her office with all the signs of an incipient cold. Watery eyes and the snivels. She was blowing her nose into a man-size handkerchief when Philippa entered.

'Anything I can do for you, dear?'

'First of all I owe the bank for a call I've just put through to my father. I timed it – it was just under four minutes, long distance. And secondly, could I please have Wednesday 29 April off to go to his wedding?'

Miss Jolly looked thoroughly taken aback, but quickly pulled herself together and was then all watery smiles. 'Of course, of course. You couldn't possibly miss your father's wedding. Oh dear, please do congratulate him for me.' Her handkerchief came into play again, this time to mop her eyes. 'Now, let me see. . . .' She turned the pages of the holiday book. 'Wednesday 29, you said. I don't see why not – that week is free. You can have the whole week off if you like. Count it as part of your annual leave.'

Philippa couldn't believe her luck. A chance to be alone with her father, perhaps. A visit to Mr and Mrs Brooke and a few days with Aunt Dot whom she had not seen since a brief visit in late winter.

'Well, that's settled, then.' Miss Jolly wrote Philippa's name in the empty space and replaced the book in its drawer. 'Weddings seem to be in the air,' she said wistfully. 'It must be something to do with spring. I had a letter from Miss Watson this morning. You remember Miss Watson? She's getting married too, in June – to a widower with a nice home in Berkshire. Quite a feather in her cap.'

If that expression had come from anyone but Miss Jolly Philippa would have thought it sprang from pique. Miss Watson yes – pique to her was second nature. But Miss Jolly? They were so dissimilar in every way that Philippa had often wondered how they ever became such close friends in the first place. Suddenly, she wondered no longer and with her newfound knowledge saw clearly that Miss Jolly's tears were not the sign of a coming cold but the sign of acute distress. Embarrassed, she turned to go.

'Just one moment, dear.' Miss Jolly rose from her chair. 'I meant to ask you earlier. Have you heard from Leo lately?'

'Not for three days.' Sometimes she went days without hearing from him then a whole bunch of his letters came at once. His latest one contained the news that several casualty clearing stations were being formed and there was a possibility he might join one. She told Miss Jolly this.

'Oh dear, does that mean he may be sent to Burma?'

The news from the Far East wasn't good. Ever since

the fall of Singapore in February the Japanese had had things much their own way. Now that they had broken through in Burma, even India wasn't safe from invasion.

Philippa shut her mind to any thought that Leo might be in danger. India was a vast country and medical officers were never right in the thick of things, were they? She only asked that question of herself, never of anybody who could have given her a different answer. Her guilt was hard enough to bear without the thought of Leo being caught up in the fighting. I can't break my heart over two men at the same time, she thought, and wondered then if some of the emotion that was tearing her apart was noticeable for Miss Jolly was looking at her with compassion.

'Isn't love bloody?' she said, her eyes watering afresh.

The opportunity to talk things over with her father came on Tuesday, the day before the wedding. They had the house to themselves as Ursula had decided to spend that day at her flat. There were still things to be done, she said, to leave it in readiness for the incoming tenant.

Philippa had suggested a visit to the Moletrap, hoping that during a walk in the solitude of the forest she might find the courage to bring up the subject of Joe. But it was not to be; her father showed little enthusiasm. They were having breakfast at the time, and outside the morning-room window, a great tit was trilling his familiar '*teechu-teechu-teechu*'. To Philippa it sounded alarmingly like a see-saw version of *traitress-traitress-traitress*.

Her father said, 'Let's just have a restful day at home. These days, I don't find it so easy to take long walks. I get breathless.'

Philippa looked up in alarm. 'Dad! There's nothing wrong?'

'Certainly not.' He was a little too touchy. 'Just a sign of *anno Domini*, that's all. I'm the wrong side of sixty now, you realise.'

Neither was in the mood to pursue that subject. Philippa asked if she were allowed to know where the honeymoon was being spent? Her father laughed.

'It's no big secret – no honeymoon either; just a short break until the summer comes, then we may go further afield. The Park Hotel – just for a few nights, to catch up with the latest shows and give Ursula a chance to buy some new clothes.'

Lucky Ursula, Philippa thought. No doubt her brother had supplied the necessary coupons or her father had given up his. As for herself she'd have to fall back on her green twopiece. She needed new shoes. If she could get a pair smart enough to 'tart up' her outfit, (as Jean would say), she could get away with it being nearly three years old.

She was lucky enough to find just what she wanted, a pair of navy-blue patent court shoes, and to go with them a navy and green spotted scarf. Hats were unrationed; they either came very expensive and looking it or very cheap and looking it even more so. Women, and younger women especially, were resorting more and more to scarves, worn peasant fashion or as turbans. The turban style flattered Philippa exceedingly.

Out of courtesy she had asked Ursula if she was superstitious about colours. 'I mean, you won't think me wearing green at your wedding will bring you bad luck?'

Ursula had fixed her with her colourless eyes and said

with amusement, 'My dear, it wouldn't worry me what colour you chose to wear. I make my own luck.'

Her father was staring glumly at the empty marmalade jar. 'Any more marmalade, Pip?'

'Sorry Dad, not until next week's rations.'

'Bugger the war!'

The telephone trilled. Philippa went off to answer it. She wasn't gone long. She came back, sat down, and stared with stricken eyes at her father. All the colour had gone from her face. 'That was Evelyn Smith on the phone. Norwich was heavily bombed last night. She phoned to tell me that Riversway wasn't hit, that everyone at Wimborne House was safe – shaken but safe; those were her words.'

'Many killed?'

'Oh yes, and a lot of damage too. . . .' Philippa's voice faltered. First Exeter, then Bath, and now Norwich. Baedeker raids the papers were calling them. Revenge for the devastation the RAF had inflicted on the Baltic port of Lübeck.

Her father banged his fist on the table. 'Spite raids, that's what they are. Hitting back at undefended towns and cities. Lübeck, Essen – they were legitimate targets and heavily defended. How is the destruction of Exeter or Bath or Norwich going to help the Nazi war effort, tell me that!'

That wasn't intended as a question, just an utterance to vent his anger and frustration. He rose, leaving his second cup of tea untouched. 'I'm decamping to the sitting room. If there's anything I can help you with just give me a call.'

He went, taking the newspaper and his cigarette-making things with him. Philippa knew that the scarring of another beautiful and sacrosanct city was not entirely the reason for his anger and distress; he had always considered Philippa safe in a place like Norwich, now that certainty had been swept away. Poor Dad, it was hard on his generation, having to suffer total war twice in a lifetime.

She kept herself busy with small household tasks, her mind all the time on Norwich. Evelyn had had very little information to give about the damage caused as so many roads were closed to the public but, of course, rumours abounded. Fears that what had happened to Coventry Cathedral might also have happened to the cathedral of Norwich haunted Philippa. She raged inwardly at the wanton destruction of people and places. For the first time she was glad that Joe belonged to Fighter Command and was not a member of a bomber crew. What must it feel like to drop bombs on sleeping civilians? – On sleeping children? Bugger the war! her father had said. Bugger the war, indeed.

When she took mid-morning coffee into the sitting room her mind was made up. No more deviation, no more sweeping feelings of guilt and deceit under the carpet, no more pretence. The time had come.

She sat in her favourite spot, the corner of the chintz-covered chesterfield, her coffee cup in her hand and told it just as it was – her affair with Joe.

Her father put aside his newspaper and stared at her. 'I've been waiting for this,' he said. 'I knew there was something eating away at you. I imagined all sorts of things – but the last thing I would have dreamed was that you had betrayed Leo. You of all people.'

She put her untouched cup on a nearby table. She could not trust herself to hold it steadily any longer.

She had hoped for understanding, instead she was getting anger and disapproval.

'I can't help it, Dad. I didn't ask to fall in love with another man.'

'That excuse has been used by lovers since time immemorial,' he said impatiently. 'How far have things gone with your Spitfire pilot? Are you planning to get married?'

'We've never talked about marriage, we just don't think about the future at all. We only live for the present – that's all we've got.'

Her eyes, drenched in tears, reminded him painfully of her mother. His anger left him as suddenly as it had come. Poor kid, she was in the grip of something she couldn't handle. She had no one to advise her, no one but him to turn to. When he spoke again it was with compunction.

'What you mistake for love could just be sexual attraction. Have you considered that?'

As close as she was to her father sex was a subject she had never been able to discuss with him. She looked now like a cornered animal.

Jonathan persisted. 'That sort of love burns itself out in time – it's not a basis on which to get married. You and Leo were meant for each other. You made a perfect couple.'

'Oh Dad, I've already said – there's no plans for Joe and me to get married. We've never given it a thought.'

'Has he had other affairs?'

'I expect so – I've never asked.' She didn't have to ask. Joe was an accomplished lover. She came out with a sudden anguished cry. 'I love him, Dad ... I love him madly. I couldn't live without him. ...'

Her father was unconvinced. 'You were just as ardent about Leo, I remember. For years you thought of nothing else but marriage to him. Yet, he's hardly gone out of your life before you think yourself in love with someone else. I hope you haven't told Leo about Joe.'

'Not yet – I keep putting it off because I'm a coward. But I must, it's not fair to go on deceiving him like this.'

'For God's sake *no*, woman!' Jonathan's voice was like a whiplash. 'I saw what happened to the men in the last war whose wives or women friends felt it was only *fair* to unburden themselves to them. I didn't think it was any coincidence that soon after some of them got in the way of enemy bullets. I don't say they did it deliberately, they just took risks they wouldn't have done previously. They became indifferent – lethargic even. I could always tell by a man's eyes what private hell he was going through. Don't put Leo through that same hell. Leave him his fool's paradise a little longer. Who knows, this obsession you have for this other fellow might peter out. I hope to God it does.'

He stopped, realising he had said too much. She was no longer a child, she was a woman with a woman's right to make her own decisions. Yet now she looked all child, and like a child was crying unrestrainedly, and like a child he comforted her. When she had quietened down and returned to him his sodden handkerchief he suggested they had a drink to cheer them up. It was too far to the Moletrap, but the Traveller's Rest was only ten minutes' walk away.

'What do you say, Pip? Shall we go and drown our sorrows?'

She gave him a half-hearted smile. 'I think mine are immune to drowning.'

'Well then, let's try giving them a damn good ducking instead.'

Next morning she stood besides Charlie Ford in the registry office witnessing the marriage between her father and his sister, and inadvertently intercepted the look that passed between them. There was love and trust in her father's eyes and an unusual warmth in Ursula's. Always an easy prey to sentiment Philippa felt her eyes filling, and as the ring was slipped on to the bride's finger one tear escaped and rolled slowly down her cheek.

Charlie bent towards her. 'Bear up, kid,' he whispered. 'You haven't lost a father; you've gained a stepmother.'

A special lunch had been put on for them at a restaurant belonging to one of Charlie's acquaintances, and included in the menu was sole mornay, an almost forgotten luxury. Also champagne – of unknown vintage, but with the same effects, then home in good spirits to cut the cake.

It went without saying that that was also provided by the indefatigable Charlie – a real wedding cake too, not just a plain fruit cake with fake icing. And what was more, Philippa discovered as soon as she bit into it, the marzipan was genuine and not made with almond-flavoured soya flour.

Then the moment of departure. A bridal car had been arranged to take the newlyweds to London. Out came the confetti. Goodbyes were said. Philippa had feared some coarse *bon mot* from Charlie, but he was strangely quiet. Again she intercepted a look, this time between brother and sister and one that left her puzzled and rather disturbed. Jonathan was the only one of the wedding party who looked as if he were thoroughly enjoying it.

The house echoed with silence when the wedding car had driven away trailing an old bucket behind it. Charlie surveyed the disorderly table, the wrapping paper strewn around, the wilting flowers, and muttered something about giving her a hand. She politely refused.

'I'll be glad to have something to keep me occupied,' she said.

Charlie's gloom did not lift. He surveyed the cake with despondency. 'I'll collect that another time,' he said. 'If you know anyone who'd like a wedge, be my guest.'

For herself she would have said no, but Mrs Mooney deserved a little something on top of the payment for the way she had cleaned the house from top to bottom in readiness for the wedding. And what about a slice each for Mr and Mrs Brooke when she visited Belle Vue Road later?

'I'll be off, then – unless you'd like me to take you out somewhere?' She felt he had been instructed to make that offer. She could tell the idea appealed to him even less than it appealed to her. For the first time during their acquaintance her manner towards him warmed a little. She found it impossible to dislike anyone who looked so abject. 'Bear up,' she said. 'You haven't lost a sister, you've found a brother-in-law,' but he couldn't even raise a smile.

He was gone at last and she had the house to herself and she was going to make the most of it. From now on Ursula was the true mistress of Byrd's House and though a flag of truce was now flying over their relationship, Philippa had a strong feeling it wouldn't be long before it was lowered to half-mast.

Later that afternoon, armed with some tulips from the garden, a tin of Spam and another of golden syrup, for these days the most appreciated gifts were those that could be eaten, and not forgetting an extremely large wedge of wedding cake, Philippa made her way to Belle Vue Road.

She felt her ring must have awakened Mrs Brooke from her afternoon nap. She opened the door in her stockinged feet with one large toe protruding through a sizeable hole, and her hair looking like an unfinished bird's nest.

'Philippa! I didn't know you were in Woodside. I thought you were in Norwich – I was worried when I heard about the raid last night. What's brought you home? Nothing wrong with your father I hope?'

Mrs Brooke had forgotten about the wedding. She was annoyed with herself for having forgotten, but when presented with the tins of Spam and golden syrup and then the slab of wedding cake her face lit up like a child's. 'I'll be able to make Dad a treacle pudding. He loves treacle pudding – so does Leo. Have you heard from Leo, lately? I had another of his food parcels yesterday – and now these. This must be my lucky week.'

One of the first things that Leo had arranged as soon as he got settled at Meerut was the sending of food parcels to Philippa, his mother and sisters-in-law.

They were always the same – a tin of butter, a packet of tea, and a parcel of dried fruit. The butter was too rancid to eat on bread but made lovely cakes. The dried fruit needed several washes before it was free of dirt. Mrs Toser, to whom Philippa gave her food parcels, decided it came over loose in the ship's hold and was swept up by stevedores. Not that she was complaining, she hastened to add; butter, dried fruit and tea were some of the commodities not available from her cousins. The leaves of the tea were at least half-an-inch long; lovely for telling fortunes, said Miss Jolly.

Personal parcels came too, but those only for Philippa: brass from Benares; a pure silk sari; mother o' pearl buttons; silver bangles; a carved ivory letter-knife. It seemed to her as if Leo were trying to make up for all the years he had been too poor to buy her anything.

Every undeserving gift that came from him she put away untouched in the drawer where she kept his letters and the amethyst ring still wrapped in its screw of tissue paper. The Woodside jeweller had sadly shaken his head over it. 'I'm afraid I'm just a humble jeweller not a miracle worker,' he had said.

She came back to the present to find Mrs Brooke regarding her. 'I said, have you heard from Leo, lately?'

'Yes, I had a letter from him just before I left Norwich.'

'Did he say anything to you about Burma?'

'He expects to be sent there soon.'

Mrs Brooke sighed deeply. 'The two children who made less trouble for me than the other three put together are now making my life miserable just worrying about them. Leo can't help it, he was conscripted. But there was no need for Phoebe to go off and join the ATS. She wouldn't have been called up, she was doing an important job. I don't hold with women going in the army or wearing uniform – it defeminises them.'

Philippa wasn't sure if there was such a word as defeminised, but it explained just what Mrs Brooke meant. That Phoebe wore size nine shoes and rode a powerful motor bike was beside the point.

They had tea in the kitchen for it was the sunniest room in the house at this time of day. The table had to be cleared before they could sit down at it. Mrs Brooke had obviously been employed cleaning the brass and silver before succumbing to sleep for some of the pieces were still encrusted with paste. Unceremoniously she dumped the lot in the sink. 'I'll finish those later,' she said.

Philippa had grown quite fond of Mrs Brooke since finding she wasn't quite the paragon Leo held her up to be. She had discovered too a rich vein of sardonic humour hidden behind a perpetual air of vagueness, a vagueness that was more in evidence when she was visited by her daughters-in-law, of whom Philippa suspected she was rather in awe.

Philippa had met them on one occasion, all three at once, and they had certainly overawed her. Hilda had been the first to arrive. No sooner had she taken off her hat and coat than she had grabbed a duster and dusted everything that needed dusting (everything did), then dashed off holding the duster as if it were a bomb likely to go off any minute. Once in the garden she had given it a good shake, saying, 'I got the top layer of dust off, anyway.'

Madeleine and Daisy were much the same; all three sisters-in-law were perfect housewives and superb cooks. 'I'm only happy when I'm working in my little kitchen,' trilled Hilda. 'You'll never find my James having to resort to indigestion tablets.'

'Mother,' said Madeleine who had a more subtle way of going about things, 'you really ought to replace Mrs Dicks. This is far too big a house for you to cope with on your own.'

Mrs Dicks had left to go to work in a factory where the money was better. 'But why should I bother when you girls are so willing to clean it for me,' answered Mrs

Brooke mildly. She caught Philippa's eye and Philippa saw in hers a look of ironic mischief. It was then she began to warm towards Leo's mother.

Now she took the cup that Mrs Brooke handed to her. Floating on the top were several tea leaves like logs in a whirlpool. She spooned them out one by one.

'I know I've got a tea strainer somewhere, but I can't think where. . . .' Mrs Brooke gazed wistfully at the wedding cake.

'Why don't you have a piece.'

'No, I'll save it for Dad. It's not often he gets a treat these days, and he always comes in so tired.'

Before his retirement Mr Brooke had been the company secretary at the London branch of a Scottish insurance company. With half their staff in the forces, they had begged him to return for the duration of the war.

'Will you stay to see him?'

Philippa looked at her watch. 'I think I'd better get back. I'm going down to Leigh tomorrow and I want to write to Leo tonight.'

At last she had something to write about, something she could write with an easy conscience – her father's marriage, the raid on Norwich, tea with his mother. Her recent letters had been scanty and circumspect.

She finished the letter to Leo, all six pages, by ten o'clock. She had started it three times before she had got it right. A light-hearted approach seemed the wisest course with just enough fondness showing through to stop him wondering. The fondness was genuine, she couldn't think of Leo in any other way, but to have written about undying love would have been downright hypocritical. She felt hypocritical enough as it was. It was strange, she thought, that Joe showed no jealousy of Leo – showed no interest in him whatsoever, as if he was beyond consideration, which attitude she found hurtful at times. He was based in Scotland again and on 'sheep-dog duty' as he called it, defending the small cargo boats and coasters that plied their trade among the east coast ports between Aberdeen and the Thames Estuary. From something Bob Fellowes had let drop during a recent leave, she thought she knew now what Joe was at during his long silence.

She had read in the papers that Spitfires had escorted the new RAF four-engined bombers on raids on industrial installations in northern France and it seemed awful to her at the time that Britain had found it necessary to bomb a former ally. Well, that was the nature of war, she thought, but she still couldn't understand why Joe had been so secretive about it. Instructions? It seemed strange to her that Joe should be so careful about keeping to the rules, and Leo so lax.

She didn't hurry to get up the next morning. She felt lethargic and rather flat after all the excitement of yesterday. She was having a late leisurely breakfast when the phone rang. This time it was Miss Jolly. Last night Norwich had suffered another Baedeker raid and the bank had been hit.

'Nobody killed – nobody was in the bank at the time fortunately and the two fire-watchers had a miraculous escape. You don't have to hurry back,' she said, 'though we could do with an extra pair of hands at Wimborne House. Poor Mrs Toser is fit for nothing – her nerves seem to have gone to pieces. You won't believe this but she wears a tin hat all the time – won't be parted from it. You will come? Oh, good. I'll expect you when I see you then. Take care.'

It was disappointing having to cancel her trip. She had looked forward to seeing Aunt Dot again, but she no longer worried about her. She now had living with her as a housekeeper a pleasant young woman from Dagenham whose husband was with the Eighth Army, and whose home had been damaged by a landmine. It was Doreen who answered the phone.

'Don't worry, Miss Byrd, I'll explain to your aunt, she'll understand. She takes things very calmly these days.'

'Give her my love, Doreen, and tell her I'll be down to see her as soon as I can.'

'Leave it to me, Miss Byrd.'

When she stepped out of the train that afternoon and the pungent smell of charred wood and smoking rubble hit her nostrils, Philippa was taken back in time and place to that last savage raid of the London blitz a year ago. And 'the blitz' the Baedeker raids became to those who lived through them.

Yet a week later the sun shone down on a still beautiful though scarred city, and a cathedral whose slender spire still dominated the Norwich skyline, and life went on very much as usual.

But of course there were differences. Gaping holes where once had stood old established businesses, ancient monuments and well-loved landmarks. Homes too. Whole sections of terraced houses as well as gracious Georgian residences were gone. Bombs fell indiscriminately on rich and poor alike.

Philippa's first walk through the city after her return brought her mixed feelings of joy and grief. St Peter Mancroft, that beautiful church next to the market-place which many visitors mistook for the cathedral had survived, as too had the ancient Guildhall and castle. But Chapel Field Gardens, that tranquil and leafy memorial to an earlier monastery garden, was a scene of devastation. She felt ashamed of crying over a garden when there were hundreds lying dead, but she didn't know the dead and she did know and love the garden where she had often sat in solitude to wrestle with her conscience.

But it could be mended. Trees would be replanted, flowerbeds remade. Old men would come back to sun themselves there, and children to play. It was a sign of Germany's weakness to turn their might against the lightly defended cities, she thought, as if they weren't up to the task of attacking heavily defended military targets. She took what little comfort there was from that.

Mrs Toser, in apron and slippers and still wearing her tin helmet, was watching out for her. Every time Philippa saw her afresh in this weird get-up she was hard put to it not to laugh, even though there was nothing to laugh at, really.

'A telegram for you,' Mrs Toser said, pulling a long face. 'I 'spect it's more bad news.'

Philippa went cold. Her fingers shook so she could hardly tear the buff envelope open, but once she had taken in the contents colour swiftly returned to her face.

'It's from Jean,' she said joyfully. 'She's got a little boy – big boy actually, he weighs ten pounds. She's naming him after me, Philip. Isn't that lovely?'

Mrs Toser was just as delighted but wouldn't show it. 'You'd have thought she'd have more sense than sending a telegram and frightening the life out of us,' she grumbled, but a moment later she was all smiles. Good news came so rarely these days it seemed a pity to waste it.

'What about wetting the baby's head? I've got some of my sloe gin left over from Christmas. Just you and me before the others get back. To wish little Philip luck.'

The bank was back in business before another week was out. Looking a bit like one of 'the ruins that Cromwell knocked about a bit', as Miss Jolly said. She was in much better spirits these days having come to terms, Philippa thought, with the fact of Miss Watson's marriage, and was much taken up with wondering what to wear.

And at last Mrs Toser discarded her helmet, complaining that the blessed old thing gave her a headache. But she kept it handy just in case, upturned like a bowl on the dresser where in the course of time it became a repository for odd buttons, pencil stubs, bits of strings, safety pins and unwanted farthings. The Baedeker raids went on spasmodically, both York and Canterbury becoming victims in turn, but by the end of June the 'spite' raids had petered out, but not before having another bash at Norwich – and the cathedral in particular.

Red went off to help with the fire-fighting and returned in the early hours of the morning with bloodshot eyes, smelling of smoke, begrimed with soot, but triumphant. 'We saved 'er,' he said.

September again. The third anniversary of the outbreak of war. The Smiths had closed up Manor Farm and were temporarily renting a cottage in Kent to be near their son. Evelyn wrote, 'The medics have done all they can for Robin, now they say it is up to him. Clive thinks his scars are as much psychological as physical. I wanted him to come to Norfolk but he shrinks from the idea – it's the thought of seeing strangers, or rather, of having strangers seeing him. So we are going down to Kent, and hoping that we might in time persuade him to come back into society. Remember us in your prayers, Philippa.'

Except for a war of attrition going on between Mrs Toser and Red since the latter had taken part in a second front campaign, marching well to the fore and proudly displaying a placard which read, 'WHAT DOES HITLER FEAR? A SECOND FRONT. TIME TO PUT THE WIND UP HITLER', life for Philippa, that summer, was fairly uneventful.

'Silly ole fule,' said Mrs Toser at the time. 'If he had to take part why couldn't he have done it respectfully, like the others. Everybody else was carrying banners what said, 'SECOND FRONT NOW'. He had to go one better. I bet he couldn't even read what he'd writ, if he writ it, which I doubt. I bet that Mr Summersfield put him up to it.'

Quentin Summersfield had recently left school and was filling in the time before call-up working at the bank. The female-only rule that prevailed at Wimborne House had been waived in his favour, and room had been found for him. A courteous and pleasant-mannered young man, and the son of a country vicar, Mrs Toser felt he was quite a feather in her cap until she discovered she was harbouring another revolutionary.

'It's all the fault of this blessed war,' she wailed to Philippa. 'It's turning everything upside down.'

Leo was writing from Burma now and had received

his captaincy, routine procedure after a year's service in the RAMC. Philippa filled her letters to him with anecdotes of everyday happenings, amusing or interesting gossip about the bank or Wimborne House. She made the story of Red and the second front campaign spread to a whole page.

And still the war went on, taking its toll in heartbreak and suffering. Joe was still based in Scotland. His letters were scrappy and completely lacking in news but she treasured them because they were so rare. Leo's, unless they were airmail letter cards, ran to four or five pages. It was agony for her to read through them, but she made herself do it. That was part of her punishment.

Then came the news that brought rejoicing to her heart. Joe was back in East Anglia, posted to Suffolk, and due for leave.

'How would you like a holiday on the Broads?' he asked her.

'Are they still letting out boats in wartime?'

'I'm not thinking of a cruiser. I've been told of a houseboat for hire on the River Bure. Could you put up with me for seven days? In early October?'

There was a subtle change in Joe she could not quite put a finger on. He was thinner but then she had noticed that when he first returned from his long absence. He was quieter too and often lapsed into thoughtful silences. He needs a holiday, she told herself. He looked tired, and she herself was ready for a break. She had saved up the remaining week's leave owing to her. Now she claimed it.

The *Melody*, a long, low, squarish vessel more like a floating bungalow than a boat, was tucked away in a small inlet off the main river and almost completely screened by overhanging trees.

'What better place for a clandestine honeymoon,' said Joe with a wolfish grin. He was busy unloading his kitbag of some clandestine tins at the time and didn't see Philippa flinch. She didn't want to be reminded of that other unofficial honeymoon in Edinburgh. She wished, and not for the first time, that a conscience could be removed like a rotten tooth. It might hurt in the pulling, but oh, the relief afterwards.

They were lucky with the weather. At times it was as warm as at midsummer. Of course, it got dark early, but that didn't bother them. The lamps were lit, the curtains drawn, a meal prepared. Sometimes they walked up to the village inn with torches to light the way, but mainly they preferred their own company. One evening Joe produced a piece of well-handled paper. A sheet of music handwritten in pencil.

'My song,' she cried, 'I thought you'd forgotten all about it.'

'I meant to get it printed out, but printers who specialise in music are a bit thin on the ground where I've been. I could whistle it to you, if you like. That will give you some idea what it sounds like.'

Whatever it sounded like would have been sweet music to her ears, for it was written especially for her by the man she loved, but it stood on its own merits, haunting, nostalgic and unforgettable. She heard the melody ringing in her ears long after Joe had stopped whistling.

She could only speak with difficulty for her voice was thick with tears. 'Oh Joe, that was beautiful – and you wrote it for me, I feel so proud . . . so *humble*.'

One side of his mouth went up in a crooked smile. 'Well, actually, Liszt wrote it – well, most of it....'

It had the same emotional effect on her as did 'Liebestraum', but otherwise there was no similarity. 'It doesn't sound a bit like Liszt to me.'

'Well, no, it wouldn't – I've juggled with the notes a bit, shifted some passages from left to right or from right to left, turned other notes upside down. It's not a new idea. Famous composers have done the same sort of thing much better than I ever could, and given the result such titles as "Variations on a theme by so and so"... I've decided against "Parted" as a title, I wanted something more in keeping. What about "Love Song for Philippa"?'

Her eyes filled with tears. 'Whistle it again, please Joe.'

It was on the afternoon of their last day that Joe filled in the gaps of his long absence. They were lying stretched out on the top of the houseboat. It wasn't warm enough for sunbathing by any means, but warm enough to bask in the sun that filtered down on them through autumn-tinted leaves. All was silence except for the gentle lap of the water against the sides of the boat and the occasional cry of a coot. Philippa felt drowsy, could easily have slipped away into blissful unconsciousness but came instantly awake when Joe began to tell her, somewhat diffidently, about the time he was shot down off the coast of France.

She sat up, stared down at him. 'Shot down! *Shot down.*' She began to cry.

He chaffed her, told her she was weeping over an empty stable long after the horse had bolted to safety. With his arms around her he told her about the bullet that had pierced his lung and the eight hours in the sea before being rescued.

'Luckily I was spotted by one of ours and not one of them,' he said. 'Otherwise I'd be in Stalag something or other, by now.'

Or dead, she thought morbidly, listening with horror at his account of his long battle back to health. She could tell, as much as he made light of it, that it had left its mark. She knew now the reason for the change in him.

'And where were you all that time?'

'Lincoln – first in a RAF hospital, then a convalescent home.'

'Lincoln! You told me you were inaccessible....'

'So I was. You should have seen the dragon of a matron who was guarding me.'

'And no females within miles!'

He grinned. 'Yes, I did bend the truth a little there. I was surrounded by females. Very efficient, Queen Alexandra nurses – but they weren't you. I didn't want you to see me ill, Philippa. I didn't want my mother to see me ill either, and I swore Bob Fellowes to secrecy. I'm fully recovered now. I'm coming off "sheep-dog" trials at last, thank God, and getting back to some real work for a change. Don't worry, nothing's going to happen to me again. I pranged my kite once, I won't do it twice, there's the law of averages against that.'

He tilted her face to his. 'Don't look like that. I tell you, I've had my lot – it won't happen again. We'll live to celebrate our golden wedding, you see if we don't. That's better. You've got a lovely smile.'

'I didn't know you had marriage in mind.'

'I didn't know myself until recently, and now I can't think of anything else. Do say yes, Philippa.'

'Let me think about it, Joe.'

'Don't take too long.' He felt her shiver. 'Come along, time to go below. What about an early night? A long, long night. It might be ages before I get the chance to see you again.'

The November days were getting shorter. Philippa walked through ankle-deep fallen leaves on her way home from the bank that evening. It wasn't cold but the mist curling off the river was chilling. Nevertheless she lingered, not too anxious to get back to Wimborne House with the black-out curtains drawn and the inevitable evening of talk or listening to the wireless, knitting or playing cards. She had much on her mind and she wanted to savour it in solitude. A nearly full moon was riding above the rooftops and Venus overhead was keeping pace with her, it seemed, as she walked.

She was happy and contented and at peace with herself for once. Joe was hoping to get leave again soon and said he was taking her to Chingford to meet his mother which seemed significant. A week ago the bells of Norwich had rung out for the victory at El Alamein. The tide of war had changed. She had everything to live for.

As always she went straight to the kitchen. Mrs Toser was pink-cheeked from exertion and scolding Red who was in the scullery peeling potatoes in a manner not to her liking. There was nothing unusual in that. Philippa removed her coat and hung it on the back of the kitchen door. 'Anything I can do to help?'

'Yes please, dear. Could you beat up a batter for me. It's Spam pancakes tonight once I can get started. My cousin from Thornmere has been here all afternoon talking me to a standstill, and now I'm late with the supper.'

Mrs Toser, slicing tomatoes, chopping onions, struggling with a pre-war tin-opener past its prime, hardly paused for breath. Most of the gossip gleaned from her cousin went over Philippa's head until the name Smith was mentioned, then she looked up.

'You mean the Smiths of Manor Farm? Coming home?'

'That's what Alice say. Mrs Smith put a call through to the post office. Asked for someone to go over to the house and get the boiler started and to light the fires. They'll be home next week and bringing their son with them. They wanted to be home for Christmas, Mrs Smith say. I thought that would please you.'

'Oh it does, it does.' Philippa resumed her beating with renewed vigour. 'Any other news of Thornmere?'

'Not that I can recall. Oh yes, wait a bit, I nearly forgot. There was something else Alice told me. Not about Thornmere exactly, but there is a connection. D'you remember that young RAF chap who played the piano? He was there the first time you went to the Smiths – when I came and called for you afterwards. Remember? Cheeky young beggar I thought him the way he grinned every time I opened my mouth. Well, he's been shot down and is presumed dead, so Alice say. Isn't it awful? It seems worse somehow when it's someone you know. Him so talented an' all. . . .'

Red, digging eyes out of the last of the potatoes, heard a sudden awesome cry, followed by the sound of crockery breaking and someone falling. Before he had the chance to investigate, Mrs Toser was at the scullery door her face the colour of putty.

'Quick Red,' she said, in panic, 'get off and fetch the

doctor. Miss Byrd has fainted, or had a fit or something, and there's batter all over my kitchen floor.'

Nine

On a crisp but sunny January day, Dr Clarke sat warming himself by the fire in his surgery at Thornmere. It wasn't his surgery as such, only for the duration. He was standing in as locum to its rightful incumbent, a promising young doctor who if he hadn't been so eager to get into the war might still be here in his rightful place instead of somewhere in the Pacific acting as a medical officer on board one of His Majesty's ships. And he, Cecil Clarke, instead of shivering before an inadequate fire, could have been shivering in comfort in his own house in his own favourite part of Norfolk.

Not that Dr Clarke had anything against Thornmere, where the folk seemed a resilient and healthy breed, not given to overburdening him with work. But the area was flat and uninspiring, unlike north Norfolk where the villages were tucked into the folds of gentle hills which sheltered the sturdy flint cottages from the cold north winds that blew straight down from the Arctic in winter.

Poppyland it was known as, that stretch of beautiful countryside on the north-east tip of the county, scarlet with poppies in summer, bracing and healthy enough to give rise to such quips as 'folk around these parts doan't die, they hev to be culled'.

Dr Clarke thought he himself might have to be culled when his time came. He was rising eighty and had only just retired to his north Norfolk cottage and was more than ready to hang up his stethoscope when war came and duty and conscience combined put him back into harness. Not that he minded work, he was well used to it after a busy Norwich practice, the trouble was he didn't get enough of it to keep him busy. They were a funny lot in Thornmere. Even newcomers from another part of the county were looked upon as 'furriners'.

A bell pinged. He knocked out his pipe, eased himself out of his chair and opened the communicating door between the waiting room and the surgery. A young woman had entered, and he recognised her immediately as the girl who was staying with the Smiths, convalescing after a nervous breakdown.

He beckoned her into the room, placed a chair for her and took his place at the desk, contemplating beneath his brows awhile for he was always appreciative of a pretty girl, and this girl was deucedly pretty in spite of her unhealthy pallor. And her eyes were stunning. Pregnant, he suspected, though she lacked the glow that usually came with early pregnancy, which was not surprising in the circumstances. He noticed at once that she was not wearing a wedding ring. The old old story and always more so in wartime.

She returned his look with one of apprehension tinged with a faint defiance. 'I believe I'm pregnant,' she said.

He twinkled kindly. 'I bow to your superior knowledge, my dear, but just to get the record straight let me ask you a few questions.' When he did, and she had answered to his satisfaction, he agreed with her diagnosis. 'I'll wait another month before making sure. No point in putting you through that unnecessarily. Have you made any plans for your confinement? No, of course you haven't; it's far too early though they do say that in order to get a bed in a hospital or a nursing home these days you have to give ten months' notice.'

He chuckled alone. Philippa could barely raise a smile. 'It's not so far-fetched as you think. Most of the big hospitals in the country have closed down their maternity wards in case the beds are needed for air-raid casualties. Some of the old local authority hospitals have reserved a few for maternity cases, but to qualify for one of those you'd have to be an emergency, or live in overcrowded conditions which I don't think is so in your case?'

He knew it wasn't. Even with four of them living at Manor Farm there was still plenty of space available.

'There is another alternative. Bardney Place, a lovely old hall up on the north coast, the home of Brigadier and Mrs Abbott. They have given up part of their house to be used as an emergency maternity home. You've never heard of it? I'm not surprised – it's thirty-odd miles from here. Lovely part of the country, but then I'm biased – I own a cottage nearby. To tell you the truth I was loath to leave it. I'd only just retired when Dr Morley asked me to locum for him. I couldn't very well refuse – apart from anything else, he's my godson.'

'Bardney Place,' she said thoughtfully. 'That's an odd name for a house.'

'Odd sort of house it is too at present – half maternity home and half private residence. I don't think the servants approve, especially not the footman. I've always thought Place was a corruption of palace, but I may be wrong. Well, my dear, would you like to hear more about it?'

Philippa had made her home with Evelyn and Clive since her illness. Many times she had suggested she was well enough to return to work but they wouldn't hear of it. They begged her to stay for Robin's sake, she was one of the few people Robin did not shrink from meeting. Once she thought she'd never have the courage to face him, fearful that she wouldn't be able to hide her feelings, but now she felt that they had much in common. He was another victim, like herself, of the war. Her scars did not show but they were just as painful to live with.

During the period of her recovery when her spirits were so low she didn't care whether she lived or died, Evelyn took matters into her own hands and transported her and all her belongings to the old farmstead.

'This is your home from now on,' she said, 'and no argument about it. Honestly though, Philippa, you'd be doing us a favour. You're company for me and the difference in Robin since you came is nothing less than miraculous.'

And nothing less than miraculous too for Philippa to find that life still held something to live for. Not at first. She even resented their over-tactful efforts to say or do nothing that might remind her of Joe for what she wanted more than anything was to talk about him. Pretending he had never existed was nearly as bad as knowing him dead. Once she heard Robin stumbling through 'Liebestraum', no doubt to please his mother, but when she entered the room he stopped immediately.

'Please go on,' she begged.

'I can't play. I haven't practised in years.'

'Then practise now.'

After that the restraint gradually lifted. Old anecdotes were revived and Joe was quite often mentioned now as if he were still a presence among them which in some ways he was.

Philippa found Evelyn in the kitchen preparing a winter salad. She looked up as Philippa entered. 'You're pregnant?'

'Yes I am. . . . Leastways, Dr Clarke thinks I am. He's giving me a proper examination next month.' She took off her coat and scarf and threw them on to a chair. 'He's charming, but I just wish he wasn't so old. Methods have changed since his days.'

'But having babies hasn't, and you need have no qualms about Dr Clarke. He ran a very successful surgery in Norwich before he retired. In any case, he won't be delivering your baby, will he. Unless you decide to have it here.'

'Dr Clarke is going to arrange for me to go to Bardney Place. Except that it is a very old mansion on the north Norfolk coast, I know nothing about it. Do you?'

Evelyn's knowledge was scanty too. 'I think the best idea would be for you and me to pay it a visit, then if you don't like the idea of going all the way up there, you can have your baby here. I could turn the fourth bedroom into a nursery.'

Philippa sat, staring blankly before her. 'I wonder what Joe would think about his baby being born in a palace. He would have laughed himself silly.'

'If you don't like the idea . . .'

'No, it's not that . . . oh Evelyn, please be patient with me. I feel so – so lost. I've lost all those I loved – perhaps it would be just as well if I lost the baby too.'

Though Evelyn felt a desperate pity for the girl she did not intend to let her wallow in such morbid fancies. 'How can you even think such a thing? Philippa, you're not well. You are definitely not well. And what do you mean "losing all those you've loved"? You've lost Joe in person, that's true, but his spirit will live on in his child. Your father loves you. He may have married again, but that hasn't stopped him loving you, you little goose. And whether you want him or not, you still have Leo – faithful Leo. He writes constantly, and he's always sending you little gifts. Philippa, it's about time you stopped feeling sorry for yourself and started counting your blessings.'

Philippa had never known Evelyn so outspoken. It made her stop and think.

'I do count my blessings,' she said. 'I am blessed having you and Clive for friends – and Leo,' she added tearfully. 'I haven't been honest with him. I suppose because I'm a coward, but also because I can't bear the thought of hurting him. I try not to think about him too much, but just lately I'm constantly getting reminders of him. Only last week his mother sent me a photo taken when he was away at camp with the Officer Cadets Training Unit. Perhaps if he hadn't joined the beastly OCTU in the first place he wouldn't have been called up, and then I might never have met Joe and I wouldn't be in the mess I am now....'

'Are you telling me you wish you'd never met Joe!'

Philippa's eyes flashed at her. 'Of course not – it's just that...' She collapsed with her head in her arms. 'Oh Evelyn, what shall I do?'

'Stop crying,' said the ever practical Evelyn. 'Unless you want a grizzly baby. Besides...'

But Philippa never did learn what the 'besides' was

leading up to for at that moment the telephone rang and Evelyn went off to answer it. In a few minutes she was back again looking a bit pinched about the mouth.

'That was Miss Jolly. The police called at Wimborne House with a message for you. Your father has suffered a stroke and been admitted to hospital. Your stepmother thinks you should go to him as soon as possible. Oh Philippa, my dear, what can I say?'

Philippa rose slowly from the table. She swayed a little but otherwise showed no emotion. 'I'd better get a few things together,' she said, and walked as if in a daze out of the room. Evelyn flew out to look for Clive and found him in the garage. He listened imperturbably as she told him about Jonathan. He said, 'You want me to run Philippa to Woodside?'

'Have you got enough petrol?'

'Just about, but not enough to get us back again. However, we'll worry about that when the time comes. I can be ready in ten minutes, what about you?'

'I may take a little longer, I'll have to leave something for Robin's evening meal. Clive, I'm worried sick about Philippa, she took it too calmly. It's not natural – it's got to come out or she'll have another breakdown.'

It came out in a storm of tears a few miles south of Norwich as they were crossing the old pack horse bridge at Cringleford. Clive, hearing what sounded like a smothered mewing coming from the back, thought at first that Mitzi had stowed away for there was nothing she liked better than travelling in the car stretched out along the top of the back seat, surveying the retreating world through her oblique blue eyes. Looking in the driving mirror, however, he realised the whimpering came not from Mitzi but from Philippa whom Eve was cradling in her arms. When all was quiet he stopped the car and Eve joined him in the front.

'She's sleeping now,' Eve said. 'With luck she'll sleep for the rest of the journey. Oh Clive, what more will that poor girl have to take? I'm beginning to believe what she says about fate. That it's got it in for her.' She told him about Philippa's visit to the doctor, and the outcome.

Clive surprised her by taking this very calmly.

'Just what she needs – a child to look after.'

Evelyn exploded. 'A child to look after! *She's* the one who needs looking after. What she needs is a decent and reliable man to take care of her – someone like Leo. But I'm afraid she's lost all chance of that now.'

'I dunno. Perhaps he loves her enough to marry her.'

'Clive, when I said a decent and reliable man, I didn't stipulate a saint!'

He didn't answer. He knew her irritation was directed more towards herself than to him. She had encouraged the flirtation between Philippa and Joe, never dreaming it would blow up into an all-consuming passion. They were two young and attractive people whose youth had been overshadowed by threats of war, then war itself, and they deserved a little fun, she had convinced herself. But the fun had turned to tragedy and Evelyn was blaming herself for that.

Jonathan Byrd had improved sufficiently to be removed from the dangerously ill list by the end of the week. All that time Philippa had hardly moved from his bedside, only giving up her place when Ursula came to keep watch in turn. Evelyn and Clive stayed with friends the other side of London, driving over to Woodside daily, making themselves useful in any way they knew how which would not have been possible without Charlie's help. He supplied the petrol.

'I saw the way that Charlie Ford was eyeing the Rolls,' remarked Evelyn on their homeward journey. There was nothing more they could do at Woodside and Robin needed them at home.

'He was very taken with it.'

'I bet he was. Did he make an offer?'

'Yes, but I told him I'd rather part with you.'

Evelyn wasn't in the mood for banter. She had just parted from a heartbroken girl and she wasn't happy at leaving her with that dodgy pair. She could see now why Philippa had never liked Charlie Ford, but for Ursula she had reservations. Her concern for her husband seemed genuine enough.

'I didn't care much for that brother,' she said. 'A spivvy kind of individual, he appeared to me.'

'Oh?' Clive seemed surprised. 'I found him quite a congenial chap, myself.'

'Sometimes you exasperate me beyond measure,' she said crossly.

Jonathan was home and installed in what was the old music-room. During his spell in hospital Ursula had completely transformed it. The Bechstein and other pieces of heavy furniture had gone and in their place were choice bits from other rooms including his grandmother's *chaise-longue*. Philippa had to admit her stepmother had good taste. She knew how to blend things together so that they formed a homogeneous and pleasing whole. Surprisingly, some of the valuable trinkets had reappeared and were displayed artistically around the room. The only item that remained from the original furnishings was the fur rug at the hearth. For Philippa each fresh sight of it meant an agonising stab of pain. Finally she asked Ursula to remove it.

Her stepmother raised questioning eyebrows. 'You don't like the rug?'

'I don't think it looks right for the room as it is now. It's too heavy.'

The fur rug went to Jonathan's study which was now his bedroom, and a slim Chinese rug took its place, which in turn became a nuisance because it 'travelled' and tripped up the unwary. But anything was better than being daily reminded of that passionate awakening with Joe.

So life went on and a routine was established. A nurse arrived early to bath and dress Jonathan and with Ursula's help get him into his wheelchair; they would then, according to the weather, wheel him into his sitting room or on to the verandah. The extent of his disability was now apparent. He had lost the use of his legs and one arm and his powers of speech. This, for Philippa, was the worst part. Never to hear her father's voice again. Never to hear him praise or admonish, tease or scold in his characteristic way. His eyes had dulled over too, only coming to life when Ursula came into sight.

In the few weeks that followed her father's homecoming, Philippa, much against her will, had to review her opinion of Ursula's brother. He had made himself invaluable. He gave up his flat in Slough and moved in with them, taking over the care of Jonathan at night when the nurse went home. He was a powerful man and it was no effort for him to lift Jonathan bodily while the bed was straightened under him. Philippa went out of the room on these occasions, not being able to bear seeing her father treated like a helpless child. That he had now become a helpless child was a reality she closed her mind to.

March was blossoming into April. Soon she would begin to 'show'. Already she imagined Ursula's pale eyes scrutinising her every movement. She had sent in her notice to the bank, giving her father's health as the excuse and had received a warm-hearted response from Miss Jolly assuring her, as she put it, 'the back door of Brundle's will always be left open for you'.

Then again there was the problem of Aunt Dot. She had been notified of her nephew's stroke, but not in too much detail. She had given up writing letters now that she had the phone, but it was Doreen who rang regularly to enquire after Jonathan. One day Philippa decided to go down to see for herself how things were at that old cliff-top house at Leigh-on-Sea.

It was a fine breezy day and the well-remembered smell of brine and seaweed and the much-maligned ozone greeted her as she left the station. The tide was out and acres of oozing mud shone like a vast sheet of polished black glass. She noted with pleasure that a small part of the beach had been opened to the public; the barbed wire rolled back and a narrow opening made for easy access.

There were mothers with babies sitting on the beach. Children with pudding bowls and wooden spoons in lieu of buckets and spades, now unobtainable, were building castles in the sand. Even the news a few days ago that Churchill had lifted the ban on the ringing of church bells did not gladden her heart as much as the sight and sound of those happy children.

She continued on her way to Cliff Cottage deep in

thought. The sight of the children brought her face to face with the reality of her condition. During her father's illness she had pushed it to the back of her mind as a problem to be settled later. She could not think of the future when the present was so fraught with anxiety but now that her father was out of danger she must begin to plan.

There was no question of living at Byrd's House again though that possibility had never been a serious option. The state of truce that existed between Ursula and herself would not survive a permanent relationship which she admitted was more her fault than her stepmother's. She couldn't bear the thought of Ursula's veiled looks and secret smiles should she turn up on the doorstep with an illegitimate child. Neither could she plant herself indefinitely on Evelyn and Clive, and to return to Wimborne House in her present condition was unthinkable. That only left Aunt Dot and she had her doubts about that. To visit Leigh occasionally could be a delight – but to live there in wartime, cut off from her friends in what was literally a war zone... for now the War Office had established a naval base at Westcliff, closing off most of the promenade, erecting Nissen huts and requisitioning all the large houses along the front. HMS *Westcliff* and the sailors based there were now very much a presence in the borough.

But life went on as usual. Some of the schools had reopened as the fear of invasion had passed, and the air raids were more of a nuisance than a threat. So was this a suitable place in which to rear a child? she asked herself.

Decidedly, yes. The children on the beach were the answer to that. How bonny they all looked. The air was clean, free of London dirt and soot, and a closeness existed between the civilians that had not been there before. It was as if those who remained belonged to an exclusive club of which she could if she wished become a life member.

Doreen opened the door, for once unsmilingly. Normally Doreen was a cheerful little body, but not today. There were signs of recent tears.

'My aunt not giving you trouble, I hope,' enquired Philippa anxiously.

'Oh, miss, if only it were as simple as that. No, it's my Perce – he's been wounded. He was taking part in a round-up of Germans prisoners who were hiding out in the mountains, and got shot in the leg. Just fancy, he was in the thick of it all at El Alamein and didn't get a scratch, now in a little local skirmish he goes and gets himself wounded. He's in a hospital in Cairo, and writes quite cheerfully, but I can't help worrying, and I do miss him so. I haven't seen him for five years. He was in the Regular Army and stationed out in Palestine and I was just about to join him when war started. I'm just hoping like mad that they give him sick leave before they send him back into action again. Oh, wouldn't it be heavenly to see my dear old Percy again.' She lowered her voice. 'I haven't said anything about this to your aunt or told her any more about your father. She does get so worked up about things. Fortunately, miss, she doesn't know what's going on half the time. She lives in a world of her own.'

Philippa digested this with a sinking heart. Common sense told her that she couldn't expect her aunt to remain ageless. She was well into her eighties now, and though prone to the vagaries of old age, her agile mind had always made her appear much younger than her years.

To think of her becoming senile was almost as bad as seeing her father in a wheelchair.

'Take me to her,' she said. 'And please, Doreen, don't keep calling me "miss", it makes me feel like a schoolmarm. "Philippa" sounds much more friendly. How would you like me to call you Mrs Smellie all the time?'

'The Lord forbid! I didn't marry Perce for his name, that's for sure.'

Except for some loss of weight, Aunt Dot looked little changed since Philippa's last visit. Yet there was something different about her that Philippa could not quite put a finger on. Perhaps it was the faraway look in her eyes as if she were seeing something that wasn't there. Her voice too was fainter, becoming at times little more than a whisper, but there was nothing lacking in her welcome.

She cupped Philippa's face in her hands and kissed her effusively. 'Oh, my darling girl, I'm so delighted to see you. Mind you, I was expecting you; I thought such a fine day would bring you both down. I said to myself this morning, "What a lovely day for a sail." But where's Jonathan?' Which question she answered herself. 'I expect he's gone down to the mooring to check on his boat. Whenever he comes to visit me he always goes to check up on his boat first. I don't know what he'd do if anything happened to that precious boat of his.'

Doreen caught Philippa's eye and pulled a wry face. 'I'll go and put the kettle on,' she said briskly.

When later Philippa noticed that a small brass bolt had been fixed to the outside of her aunt's door, she asked Doreen about it.

'I had to do it for her own sake, miss – er, Philippa. She's inclined to wander at night and I'm always scared she might fall down the stairs. She's not very steady on her feet at the best of times.' Which explanation left Philippa unreasonably distressed.

'I won't have my aunt locked in. She's not a child, she's just a tired old lady. Please Doreen, never bolt her door again.'

In the early hours of the morning Philippa was awakened by the sound of rustling outside her door. She switched on the light, hastily slipped into a dressing-gown and went to investigate.

Aunt Dot was tottering along the passage in her night-gown, bare-footed, and her thin white hair loose about her shoulders. She looked lost and bewildered. Philippa gently took her arm.

'Let me take you back to your room, Aunt Dot.'

'I can't go back there . . . it's a forbidden zone.'

'Let's go and check.'

But at the door to her bedroom Aunt Dot stopped dead and all Philippa's powers of persuasion couldn't budge her. 'I can't go in there — there's a soldier in my bed, and look, he has left his helmet on my dressing-table. . . .'

Philippa could see that anyone with a strong imagination or poor eyesight might think that by the way the bed covers were bunched in the middle there might be someone lying beneath them. And the handbag Aunt Dot had left on the dressing-table could in this poor light be mistaken for a helmet. She just didn't want to face the possibility that this rambling old lady beside her was the same eccentric but reliable person to whom she had always turned when in trouble. Now that same person pulled away, and glared petulantly at her.

'I want Doreen,' she said. And when Doreen came:

'Who's this bossy woman? What's she doing in my house? Tell her to go away.'

Later, when after some difficulty they got Aunt Dot back to bed, they took comfort in that old panacea for all troubles, a cup of tea taken black as the last of the milk had gone to making Aunt Dot a hot malty drink in which Doreen dissolved a small white tablet.

'It's something the doctor prescribed to make her sleep. I don't give them to her often as they make her so woozy all next day she keeps falling about.'

'Oh, Doreen, why didn't you tell me things had got as bad as this.'

'It's come on so gradual like, I didn't really notice. It doesn't bother me. I can manage, really I can, miss – er, Philippa.'

'Oh no, you can't. I can see that looking after my aunt is one person's job and you've got enough to do with the housework and shopping and the everlasting queuing. I'm going to arrange for a nurse to call. Just to get Aunt Dot up of a morning, and get her to bed at night. That will take some of the pressure off you.'

Doreen stared into her cup. 'Do you know how much a private nurse costs these days?'

'More than Aunt Dot can afford, I expect, but she's not spending much money otherwise. She gets a good allowance from her father's estate. I know the firm isn't doing too well at present, what with the shortage of paper and other restrictions, but there should be more than enough to pay for a nurse.'

An expression of embarrassment crossed Doreen's face. She toyed with her teaspoon for a moment then put it down and looked up with wary eyes.

'I was hoping I wouldn't have to tell you this. I was

hoping it was an oversight that would be put right when discovered. I'm sorry, Philippa, but the allowance was stopped two months ago. That doesn't mean to say that your aunt is going short of anything,' she added hastily, seeing the colour drain from Philippa's cheeks. 'She's still got a nice little bit behind her, but you know what happens when you start drawing on your savings. I have to deal with all that sort of thing for Miss Byrd now, so I can't help noticing how things are.... Oh dear – what is it?' Philippa had pushed her chair aside and was making for the door.

'I'm going to put a call through to my stepmother. I don't care if I do get her out of bed. I want to know what's going on – and I want to know right now!'

Evelyn was waiting on the platform at Thorpe station, her red dress making a bright splash of colour amid so much khaki. The station was thronged, as all stations seemed to be these days, with men in uniform. In this case, chiefly American GIs. The Yanks, as they were universally known, stood out among the other serving men. They were a lot smarter for one thing, and larger, and they had an air of self-confidence that bordered on cockiness. They were extremely popular with young women and children, and the streets of Norwich were full of them.

Evelyn came forward and gave Philippa a hug and a kiss.

'Clive is waiting in the car with Robin. Yes, we've managed to winkle him out of the house at last. It goes without saying that you were the bait.'

If Evelyn had expected a smile from Philippa in response to this, she was disappointed. Philippa had a listless look about her; her pallor was more marked and her eyes sunken. Evelyn took her arm and walked her towards the exit.

'I could hardly make out what you were saying over the phone. You sounded hysterical.'

'I was hysterical. If I'd stayed another minute in that house I would have had an attack of the screaming jeebees.'

Evelyn cheered up. Lackadaisical Philippa might be in appearance but not in spirit, and Norfolk air would soon put the colour back in her cheeks.

It was Byrd's House Philippa was referring to, not Aunt Dot's which she had left very early that morning. Still seething with anger when she arrived at Woodside, she was confronted by her stepmother not with trumped-up excuses as she had expected but with an excess of coolness which, paradoxically, put Philippa on the defensive. Ursula led her into the morning room where Charlie, with a glass in his hand, and his feet up on the arm of the sofa, eyed her cautiously.

'If your father could speak he would bear me out,' Ursula said, standing with one arm draped gracefully along the back of Charlie's chair. 'The firm has been failing for months; losses have far outstripped income. I can't remember the last time accounts were in the black. To go on like that would have been madness. The site is valuable, so too are the premises. I advised Jonathan to capitalise on them while he could. He signed the necessary papers just before we got married. . . .'

'How convenient for you,' Philippa's smile was bitter. 'He wouldn't be able to sign anything now, would he?' Immediately that was said, she wished it unsaid for it seemed to reflect on her father. Ursula seemed quite unconcerned.

'I have power of attorney,' she said.

The triumph in her voice was Philippa's undoing. She felt as if she were in some dark and unfathomable pit in which no matter how she struggled to get out she sank further in. 'And where will you find such a purchaser in wartime,' she said, unwilling to accept defeat.

Charlie, who had taken no part in the discussion, now chipped in.

'Someone with big ideas and not the space to put them into practice would see that site as a gift from the gods. Of course it will need a lot spent on it to bring it up to date, but it's got potential.' That was a quite a speech for Charlie who rarely used words of more than two syllables. An awful suspicion began to dawn in Philippa's mind.

She looked from sister to brother and back again. Both wore similar self-congratulatory smiles. Her self-control snapped. 'You two cooked up this scheme between you, didn't you! My father trusted you both and you cheated him.' She glared at Ursula, who looked serenely back. 'He was always on about your capability, that's why he left more and more of the running of the business to you, and that's just what you banked on. Right from day one you had it all worked out between you.'

She turned her wrath on Charlie. 'You're nothing but a pair of confidence tricksters. Run the place down, then buy it up cheap – that's an old dodge. A valuable site, *she* called it.' She refused to give Ursula the dignity of a name. 'I don't know how you can do this to my father. You, he thought his friend. . . .' She turned on Ursula again. 'And as for you . . .' But she had run out of likely insults, and was too wretched and sick at heart to fight on.

Ursula was studying her polished nails with rapt attention. She said without raising her voice, 'You had better beware of letting your tongue run away with you. I could sue you for slander for less than that.'

Philippa flared up again. 'Go on sue me, then. I'd love you to sue me, it would give me the chance to tell the world what sort of a person you really are.' She had no fear that the threat of slander would be carried out. Ursula had too much to lose.

Charlie gave a well-timed cough. He rose and sleeked back his hair with both hands. The smile he gave her was so painfully ingratiating that it made her squirm.

'See here love, if you're all het up on the old lady's behalf then you can forget it. She'll be taken care of as soon as everything is settled. It'll take time, switching over from printing to engineering, and it'll cost a mint of money but I'll see the old girl gets her allowance even if I have to pay it out of my own pocket. And that goes for the employees too. There's some only too ready to retire, and the others . . . well, if they don't want to stay and work for me, there's plenty of other openings. Nobody need be out of a job these days. And you won't be forgotten either, we'll see you right.'

'I'd rather cut my throat than take anything from you,' she said with more passion than logic. 'In any case, you can't give me what is already mine. What you don't know is that that business is willed to me.'

'And what you obviously don't know, my dear,' said Ursula with a voice like syrup, 'is that your father made a fresh will on the eve of our wedding.'

At this point Philippa gave up. She flew to the phone,

got through to Evelyn and told her she was coming back to Manor Farm that day.

Now it was just a question of shaking the dust from her feet before leaving her birthplace for ever, she told herself dramatically. First though, the awful pain of saying goodbye to her father. He was asleep. His head lolled unsupported and dribble escaped from the slack of his mouth. Gently she lifted his head back against the cushion, and gently she wiped the spittle from his chin, then sat beside him taking his useless hand in hers. Her touch woke him. Recognition came slowly. 'You do know me, don't you, Dad?' she pleaded.

He nodded, but looked beyond her at the door, looking for Ursula. Ursula was the only one he ever wanted. He tried to form a question but gave up exhausted. She wished he wouldn't attempt to speak, the contortions of his face as he strained to make himself understood were heartbreaking to witness. She didn't stay long. She knew it was just as painful for her father to go through this charade as it was for her. She kissed him goodbye, stopping at the door to look back once more. He was asleep again. Thank God for sleep, she thought. It was one way of escaping reality.

The hall was silent. She tiptoed through it hoping to make her own escape unnoticed. The door to the morning room was ajar, just wide enough to outline two figures standing so close they looked like one. Plotting more mischief, she thought as she hurried past, believing that rather than the alternative which was unthinkable.

But once away from the house her depression, never far away, returned in force. She felt too tired to resist any longer, too tired even to care what happened to the old family firm. The war had struck the first blow to its fortunes, now it was being finished off by a couple of crooks. There was only one gleam of light in the whole murky business. It couldn't hurt her father. He was beyond that now, encased in the protective shell of his ailment.

The Rolls was parked in the station yard with Clive at the wheel and Robin in the back. Clive got out, greeted her in his usual courtly fashion and helped her in beside Robin. It was the first time she had seen Robin in uniform, and thought how much it suited him. He looked the typical, jaunty, young RAF officer even to the unfastened top button of his jacket. Then one's eyes went to his face and the resemblance ceased. He smiled and a smile on those damaged lips seemed all the more poignant. She smiled back but felt more like crying. She could weep for all the damaged people of the world. For her father, for Aunt Dot, for Joe, for Leo as he would be when he learnt the truth, and for herself and her unborn child.

One evening in early June, Philippa sat reading the letters from Leo she had found awaiting her at Manor Farm and which Mrs Toser had brought over whenever she had visited her cousin. There were other letters she had received from Leo before she left for Woodside and which she had put away unread. Now she took them out of her writing case and spread them on the bed in order of date. Whether she wanted to or not she must read them, she owed that much to Leo.

Some had taken several months to reach her, some just a matter of weeks. The newly issued airmail letter cards had considerably speeded up the post. A strong hint in one of Leo's earlier letters gave her a good idea where he was now.

'I think I told you that Francis Brede and I had booked to go to a concert at the Carlton? At the last minute it was cancelled, some trouble with the conductor, I think. He wasn't much of a conductor by all accounts, and we've heard since that he has been replaced by someone more up to the job. I expect we'll get to the concert eventually.'

Carlton, she knew from her list of code names, stood for Burma; and conductor must mean the CO. This letter was written in March which meant that Leo could be in Burma by now. She knew he was attached to a Casualty Clearing Station along with Francis Brede, a fellow medical officer he had met on the troop ship going out East. She hoped that being a noncombatant, he was well away from the front line, if there was such a thing as a front line in the jungle. It amazed her that Leo's food parcels and personal gifts were still getting through, though they of course came from Bombay.

The monsoon figured large in his more recent letters, something they all welcomed ardently but which before long became an irritant when none of their possessions stayed dry for long. At first, Leo made light of it: 'After one of these monsoon storms the ground in our tent became awash with water,' he wrote. 'Bangali, our batman, overcame this by making a false floor of interwoven bamboo and rushes. He is a very adaptable fellow.' Later, his tone changed. 'Think of me sitting in my little canvas tub in the rain trying to clean off some of the dirt of this blooming awful country. . . .' But mostly he played down his troubles. If he was ever homesick or fed up with the conditions he was working under, he never spoke of it.

'I am now in the process of qualifying for all sorts of jobs when the war is over. Our BORs (British Other Ranks to you, sweet) have got sent off – temporarily I hope – so being rather short-staffed I took over looking after stores and the dispensary, and acting as general dogsbody. I even substitute in the laboratory. It's all good practice. The first thing I shall have to do when I'm demobbed is get a job – then we'll get married. . . .'

There were many loving bits which she tried to skip, but her conscience always made her go back and read them. 'Good night sweetest girl in the world', was his usual way of signing off, but once, more humorously: 'I'm just going to get into bed with my best friend – my mosquito net. I wish you were sharing it with me. Not with Francis in the tent, though, he snores like a grampus. You snore too, very softly in C minor. Have I made you blush? Oh darling, I miss you so.'

His letters had become a great solace to her. He was, after all, her oldest friend, but at other times reading them was a torture. She was collecting them together again when Evelyn came through from the next room holding a tumbler of hot milk.

'Here you are, something to help you sleep.' Philippa had been pacing the floor again last night, but Evelyn made no mention of this or of the small stack of letters on the bed, or in fact, of Philippa's puffy eyes. 'Do you mind if I stay on a bit, there's something I want to talk over with you.'

While Philippa had been away helping to nurse her father, Evelyn had made enquiries about Bardney Place. Through a friend who was a member of the Beckton

Red Cross she had got what she called the 'gen' on arrangements there, and now passed this on to Philippa.

'You should really decide where you're going to have your baby, Philippa. You can't leave it to the last minute, you know what Dr Clarke said about giving ten months' notice. I understand Bardney Place is becoming harder and harder to get into. My Red Cross friend says it's just like Buckingham Palace. I don't think she is familiar with Buckingham Palace but I know what she means.'

'It sounds expensive.' Philippa was loath to spend a penny more than necessary. She dreaded the time when she might have to go to Ursula with her begging bowl.

'That's the point, it's not. The maternity wing is run by the County Council and all the routine work is done by Red Cross nurses. Apart from the Red Cross there's a matron, three sisters, two of them midwives, a visiting doctor, and an obstetrician to call upon in an emergency. And no charge for those whose incomes fall below a certain level. And even those who can afford to pay are not charged more than about five pounds a week. You'd have to pay more than that in a private maternity home. I'm dying to see this place myself – it's in a beautiful part of Norfolk. What do you say to you and me paying it a visit? Perhaps Dr Clarke could make the appointment for us. . . .'

Dr Clarke did more than that. He arranged for Philippa to attend the monthly antenatal clinic at the same time. More than that, he gave Clive some of his carefully hoarded petrol coupons to spare the women the travail of the journey which meant a train to Cromer via Norwich and then a long and meandering ride by country bus.

'Are you sure you can manage?' asked Clive anxiously.

He never felt quite happy about Evelyn behind the wheel of the Rolls even though she was a competent driver. 'I'm willing to act as chauffeur. . . .'

'Men are surplus to this journey. Strictly for women only,' Evelyn retorted, delighted to get the chance for once to get behind the wheel of the Rolls.

It was a day designed for a journey through the countryside. Clear blue skies and just enough breeze coming through the open windows to prevent the car from heating up like an oven. The haymaking season had started and they passed meadow after meadow being harvested by farmhands and girls from the Women's Land Army. The fragrant smell of sun-warmed hay teased their senses. Once, in a narrow lane they had to give way to a loaded wagon. 'Straw,' said Philippa on a note of gloom.

'Has that any significance?'

'If you meet a load of hay it means a surprise, but if you meet a load of straw it means a disappointment. That was straw.'

'Philippa, why do you go around looking for trouble?'

'I don't have to look for it, it follows me.'

They reached Bardney Place about half past ten, just half an hour before the antenatal clinic started, giving them ample time to be shown over the maternity wing by one of the three sisters. A bouncing, 'jolly-jolly hockey-sticks' type of young woman.

She greeted them with the news that it was Matron's day off and as the other two sisters were occupied she would see them round.

'This is the smaller of the two wards.' She took them into a pleasant room, large and light with a high ornate ceiling. An immense bow window gave a view over parkland and a distant vista of trees. There were five beds with ample space between them and their occupants were all sitting up supported by several pillows. Each had a locker on one side of the bed and a baby in a cot on the other.

'These are the paying patients,' said Sister out of the side of her mouth. 'All they pay for really is a bit more elbow space, otherwise the treatment and the food is the same as in the other ward.'

The other ward was much larger, suggesting it might once have been the ballroom. It had an even grander vista of stone terraces and statuary, and a magnificent fountain that was not now, in wartime, functioning. This room held twenty beds, again, all occupied.

'Well, now that you've seen the wards I'll show you where the real work is done,' Sister Biddy was saying when she was interrupted by the arrival of another more ample figure in a sister's uniform. 'Ah, here is Sister Martin. I'd like you to stay and hear what she has to say.'

Sister Martin, the older of the two midwives, surveyed her patients with an indulgent smile. 'Ready mothers. . . . "Sit up like the letter L – guard those tender nipples well." ' This sing-song chant was followed by a shorter homily. 'Tummies, mummies.' Sister beamed. 'Now let's say it all together, shall we?'

'Ye gods,' said Evelyn under her breath.

Sister Martin came across to their little group.

'Ah, you must be Philippa Byrd. Sister Harvey is expecting you in the antenatal room. It's just beyond the staircase, you can't miss it.'

About ten other expectant mothers were already assembled, making as much noise as a cage of magpies, and the majority of them as busy with their knitting needles as they were with their tongues. The whole atmosphere of Bardney Place was one of easy-going tolerance which Evelyn found encouraging. How Philippa felt was hard to gauge as she hadn't spoken since they stepped over the threshold. Sister Harvey was occupied at the end of the room checking specimen bottles against names on a list. Hearing the door open, she looked up.

'Miss Byrd – Miss Philippa Byrd? – Will you come and sit here, in the front please.'

All conversation ceased. Every head turned and watched Philippa as she walked down the length of the room, her head bent. Evelyn seethed. Sister Harvey might be young and trim and decorative to look at but she lacked tact and sensitivity. Need she have used the word *miss*? But what was the alternative – not to use a prefix at all? That would have been even more noticeable. Evelyn sighed. This was only the beginning of what Philippa would have to get used to.

Sister disappeared into the ante-room taking the samples with her. Presently she reappeared carrying a small screw-top bottle.

'Mrs Timms?'

A woman in an advanced stage of pregnancy, red-faced and tittering stood up.

Sister Harvey held the bottle upside down and shook it vigorously. A few drops trickled out.

'Mrs Timms! For pity's sake! I know bottles are hard to come by these days, but this is ridiculous.' Her voice could hardly be heard above the sudden burst of laughter. Evelyn, at the back of the room stuffed her handkerchief into her mouth.

'Sonia, take her to the bathroom and get her to oblige,'

and Mrs Timms, still red-faced, still tittering, was led away by a Red Cross auxiliary.

Sister Harvey again referred to her list. 'Miss Byrd, will you come with me, please.'

The door behind Evelyn opened. 'Psst!' It was Sister Biddy. 'Could you down a cup of coffee? Follow me.'

It was an hour later before Evelyn saw Philippa again. She spent that hour in the grounds, mostly sitting by the lake half hypnotised by the play of sunbeams on the water. In a drowsy state she slowly made her way back to the house. Philippa was in the hall waiting for her.

'Where have you been all this time?' Both spoke together.

Evelyn laughed. Philippa said, 'I had to see the obstetrician, then I had an interview with Mrs Abbott.'

'Is that usual?'

'I wouldn't know. She was very nice. She showed me over the rest of the maternity wing. . . .'

'Sister Biddy took me,' said Evelyn, interrupting. 'What did you think of the communal labour ward? Cosy wasn't it? Twin beds – a fire if it gets chilly, pictures on the wall, and a lovely view of the lake. What more could a mother want.'

'Oblivion, perhaps.'

Evelyn decided to let that pass. The morning hadn't been easy for Philippa. 'When do they want to see you again?'

'Not until labour starts. They said Dr Clarke can keep an eye on me until then.'

'Did you know that he delivered both Mrs Abbott's children? A son who is a major in his father's old regiment, and a daughter married to an MP. Neither of them has children. That made me wonder if that's the reason why the Abbotts have installed a maternity home here – feeling a lack of grandchildren.'

'I should think it's more to do with wanting to help the war effort,' said Philippa indifferently.

They were walking towards the car, Evelyn with her arm through Philippa's. 'I expect you're right. It sounds more plausible. Better babies than soldiers, anyway. Look what's happened to Thornmere Hall since the army took over.' She gave a chuckle. 'Wasn't it a scream, that incident with the scent bottle? I can't wait to tell Clive, he'll laugh like a drain. Mrs Timms, the postmistress at Thornmere, has a daughter-in-law booked to come here. I wonder if it's the same woman.'

'I wouldn't know,' said Philippa, miles away. 'I've never been in Thornmere post office.'

'Well, now you might get the chance to become acquainted, if you're in the same ward. It would be nice for you to have someone from the village to talk to.'

'I'm having a room to myself, a single room on the first floor,' said Philippa expressionlessly. 'Mrs Abbott thought it would be better for me. It's a room they keep for mothers of stillborn babies. They keep them isolated so that they won't be upset by seeing the other mothers with their babies. In my case I suppose it's the other way round. I'm being isolated in case the sight of an illegitimate baby might embarrass the married mothers.'

Evelyn could have shaken her. Instead she gave Philippa a gentle hug. 'You're obviously suffering from vitamin deficiency. We'll stop for lunch on the way home, and I know the very place.'

They stopped at a fishing village which in days gone by had drawn artists both amateur and professional from all over Norfolk and beyond. It had changed little since then. The absence of a railway had prevented that saturation by speculative builders that had done so much to ruin the charm of other timeless villages. A group of fishermen unloading the crab boats at the quay turned to admire the Rolls as Evelyn parked in a space free from creels, coils of rope and crab-pots. The younger ones among the fishermen transferred their admiration from the car to Philippa, making Evelyn wonder if they were aware of the eight-month bulge hidden beneath the ample folds of Philippa's floral patterned smock.

'Along here, before the war, there was a very fine fish restaurant,' she said. 'Let's see if it's still in business.'

It was and could offer them crab straight from the sea, and salad fresh from the garden, and there might be a picking of strawberries, but alas, no cream to go with them.

'We're the only ones here,' said Evelyn, glancing about her. 'I remember when you couldn't get a table without booking, but of course that was before the war.'

It was pleasantly cool in the tiny dining room, for the sun could not penetrate the solid flint walls. Philippa seemed to throw off the pall of gloom that had descended upon her after leaving Bardney and even began to show some awareness of her surroundings. The white-washed walls were hung with fishing nets, two crossed oars were fixed above the mantelshelf, and a ship's figurehead in the corner had been adapted to form a hat rack. She said, 'I didn't realise I was so hungry – I could eat a horse.'

Evelyn laughed. 'There's only fish on the menu here, I'm afraid.'

They didn't hurry their meal for it was something to

savour and linger over. Philippa, for all her avowals of hunger, ate very little, but Evelyn tried not to dwell on that. There was something on the girl's mind other than her usual worries. Evelyn knew her well enough by now to see the signs. Give her time, she thought, get her in the right mood – she'll open up.

They took their coffee outside. There was a table there and a few weathered chairs, the sun looked alluring and they were chilled from sitting too long in the shadowy restaurant.

The fishermen had gone, presumably home for their lunch. A rough-haired terrier scratched lazily at one ear, and a flock of seagulls hovered noisily above some discarded crabs. Out at sea, a gunner on the bridge of a coastal vessel was the only reminder of the war.

'I can remember on June evenings when this whole stretch of coast was white with sails. This was a favourite holiday resort for yachtsmen.'

'Did you own a boat?' asked Philippa, thinking back to her father's dinghy and the good times they had had with it.

'No, alas. Clive wasn't interested in the sea, but we did promise to buy Robin a sailing dinghy for his twenty-first and then the war came.' Evelyn turned and looked fondly at the girl beside her. 'Whatever it is you've got on your mind, Philippa, share it with me.'

'Yes, I've put it off long enough. I've been wanting to tell you ever since we left Bardney Place but I couldn't pluck up courage.'

'Am I that much of an ogre?'

'No, of course you're not – it's just that I'm that much of a coward. That interview I had with Mrs Abbott, it wasn't a spur of the moment thing. Dr Clarke arranged it.'

'And you were frightened to tell me that!'

Philippa released a quivering sigh. 'Oh Evelyn, it's difficult enough to tell you without these interruptions. No more, promise?' Then out it came in a rush. 'Mrs Abbott wanted to see me about the adoption.'

'Adoption – what adoption?' Evelyn forgot her promise. She thought she couldn't have heard aright. 'Adoption,' she echoed feebly.

'I've been going over in my mind how to break the news to you all the way from Bardney Place. I had it all worked out, all very matter-of-factly and sounding quite reasonable, I thought, but now I can't remember a word of it. So please, don't say anything more until I've finished. It's not going to be easy for me as it is.'

So Evelyn kept quiet all through Philippa's stumbling explanation though what it cost her only Clive would know, that night, when she unburdened herself to him. What it amounted to was that Mrs Abbott knew of a couple who had for some time been looking out for a suitable child for adoption. They had appealed to her to help them, thinking like all desperate-to-be parents that among the babies being born at Bardney Place every week there might be one to spare, and Mrs Abbott in turn had appealed to Dr Clarke, and he had put the idea to Philippa on her last visit to him.

'I wouldn't consider the idea at first,' Philippa said, staring fixedly at the table. 'I was appalled that he could even mention it to me. But when I got home and thought over some of his arguments, I could see what he meant.

'I know you are asking yourself – how can I do this? How can I give up my child, Joe's child. What right have

I to make such a decision before even the baby is born. You couldn't ask me anything I haven't asked myself, or condemn me more than I condemn myself.' She paused here for her voice had begun to falter, but she quickly pulled herself together, and went on in the same flat monotone. 'But that was thinking with my heart, and Dr Clarke said I must try and think with my head. For weeks I have had this inner battle with myself. I haven't been able to sleep. I haven't been able to think straight. All I know is that that other side of me, the more rational, far-seeing side of me kept coming up with this more valid argument. How can I support a child? What kind of a home can I offer her? And what name could I give her?'

Here, Evelyn tried to interrupt again, but she was stopped with a heart-rending 'No, you promised . . . you promised. . . .' A pause then Philippa went on, her voice almost inaudible now. 'And something else kept nagging at me. Supposing I did give my baby away. Would she be any better off? How could I guarantee that she would go to a good home? Well, I got my answer today. Mrs Abbott gave it to me, in detail. They are wealthy – well-born – the baby would lack for nothing. They had given up hope of ever having a child of their own. They had so much love to give and no child to give it to. When Mrs Abbott said that, it settled the argument for me, for there was only one question left to ask and that of myself. Did I love my baby enough to give her up? And I decided – yes, I did.'

Silence fell. The dog had gone; the seagulls had settled down on the rooftops of a row of cottages; the sea lapped soundlessly against the wall of the quay. All was peace except in the minds of the two women.

'There is a lot I could say, but won't at present,' said

Evelyn at length. 'There is just one thing though. Why do you refer to your baby as she?'

'I've dreamt many times of having a little girl, but never of having a boy. I think that's an omen. I've given her a name – Jennifer Anne. I always think of her as Jennifer Anne.'

Evelyn stared at her. 'You intend to part with your baby, but you give it a name first. This is madness!'

'Yes, I think I am a little bit mad, at times. Oh, Evelyn, please don't scold, I feel so sick at heart.'

The woman from the restaurant came out to collect their coffee cups, but when she saw that the girl was crying and the older woman comforting her, went away again. Evelyn was saying, 'Would you let Clive and me adopt your baby? We've always longed for a daughter....'

Philippa grasped Evelyn's hand. 'That's so sweet of you. Such a kind thought – but no. You must see why. It's best I shouldn't know the adoptive parents.'

'Will you tell your father? After all, he is the baby's grandfather.'

Philippa gave another long-drawn-out sigh. 'My poor father, he's a stranger to me now... I'm a stranger to him. I write to him regularly but of course he never answers. He can't write, as you know, and I think Ursula reads my letters to him. I never put anything in them that I wouldn't want her to see.'

'He doesn't know about the baby, then?'

'Why add to his burden?'

Sadness settled on them like a cloud. Again it was Evelyn who broke the silence. 'Have you thought of the future? After the... I mean what do you intend to do with yourself? Go back to work? I'm just asking before you start making plans. You know you can always make your home with us. As I've said, we've always wanted a daughter.'

Philippa only knew she didn't want to go back to Byrd's House. She was reluctant to return to Wimborne House either, even though they had all turned up trumps, and sent her little presents for the baby as soon as Mrs Toser broke the news to them. Philippa couldn't explain her reluctance to pick up the strands of her old life, perhaps because the girl she had been then was no longer recognisable to her. She had been through the shadow of the valley of death and come forth a different person, one who wouldn't fit in with the old ways so easily. What she wanted was a refuge until her wounds healed and she could think of no better refuge than Aunt Dot's house at Leigh. At least, she would find there what she wanted most. Anonymity.

'I suppose I shall have to return them all now,' she said, thinking aloud.

'Return what?'

'All the little woollies and other presents that have been sent to me for the baby.'

'I should hang on for a bit in case you change your mind.'

'It's too late to change my mind. I made all the necessary arrangements with Mrs Abbott this morning.'

Clive was given a detailed account of this conversation at the end of the day when the two of them had a few precious moments together.

'You don't seem all that surprised,' Evelyn commented.

'I'm not surprised, but I am saddened,' said Clive, going to the drinks cupboard and looking wistfully at the half-inch of whisky left in the decanter. 'Share this with me?'

'No, you have it. Why aren't you surprised?'

'Her attitude, I suppose. The way she's walked about as if in a daze these past few weeks. She will need a lot of support when she comes out of the maternity home. We must be very gentle with her. What does she plan to do afterwards? Go back to the bank?'

'She says she is going to Leigh to look after her aunt. The housekeeper is leaving. She expects her husband back in England later in the summer. He was wounded in the leg and it's gone bolshie. He's in a hospital in Cairo at present, but the powers that be are shipping him back home for further treatment and naturally the wife wants to be near him. She has given in her notice but is willing to hang on until a replacement can be found.'

'And Philippa is offering herself as the replacement,' said Clive draining his glass.

'Not if I have anything to do with it.'

He lifted an admonishing finger. 'Eve, I warn you, beware of rushing in where angels fear to tread. Perhaps the best thing that could happen to Philippa when all this is over is to have someone dependent on her.'

Philippa, shelling peas in the garden, saw Robin coming towards her. His features, as yet, were not mobile enough to express his feelings but his demeanour reflected every mood, and this morning it reflected a determined resolve. Philippa, guessing his intentions, sighed inwardly as he drew up another chair alongside her.

'Don't say it, Robin, please. . . .'

'You don't know what I was going to say.'

'I think I do. I think you were girding yourself up to

ask me to marry you. Your mother put you up to it, didn't she? I've noticed the winks and nods she's been giving you lately, and I can guess why. Dear Evelyn, she'd do anything to prevent me giving my baby away – but to expect you to take on the responsibility.... How old are you Robin?'

'Nearly twenty-two, and you're all wrong about my mother,' he said despondently. 'She didn't have to push me into anything I didn't want to do, and now you have deprived me of the pleasure of proposing to you.'

'And I'm nearly twenty-five, and there's a whole lifetime's difference in our ages because a woman comes of age long before a man. You're far too young yet to lumber yourself with a wife and another man's child. You've got your whole life before you....'

'What life?' he broke in bitterly. 'Who would marry me except out of pity? I love you,' he said with sincerity. 'Mum had nothing to do with it. She knows I've loved you ever since I first saw you, but she never encouraged it because she didn't want to see me hurt. Now she thinks I might stand a chance. Do I, Philippa?'

Philippa went on shelling peas through a blur of tears. She was touched by Robin's offer, but not so morally weak that she could take advantage of it. 'Do you think pity is a good basis for marriage? Your pity for me and mine for you? Dear Robin....'

'I think concern would be a better choice of word than pity.'

She apologised for her clumsiness. 'But I still don't think concern is a basis for a happy marriage. I couldn't marry anyone I didn't love. I couldn't sleep with anyone I didn't love. I don't think you are really in love with me, Robin. You just think you are. We've been thrown together and become very close in these past few months, but you mustn't mistake that closeness for love. You haven't given yourself the chance to meet anyone else. You must give yourself that chance.'

'What, with a face like this!'

'Do you judge others by their looks alone?'

'Of course not.'

'Then why be so hard on yourself?'

A week later, again in the garden, now idling for she was near her time, she saw another well-known figure in uniform coming towards her. It was Bob Fellowes whom she had not seen since just after Joe's death. The one who she had always feared would be the bringer of bad news, instead of which it had been poor, unsuspecting Mrs Toser. She held out her hand in greeting.

'How nice to see you, Bob. I hope this visit isn't to ask me to marry you.'

He looked at her in alarm. When he saw her last she was hysterical and unbalanced. Had something tipped her over the edge?

She gave a brittle little laugh. 'I'm sorry, you obviously haven't a clue what I'm talking about. It's just that Evelyn is trying to find a husband for me – because of this,' and she patted her bulge.

He felt uncomfortable. Tears he could handle, but not this brittle flippancy. He said, 'I didn't see Evelyn or Robin, they are both out. Clive told me where to find you. I've come to give you this.'

He was carrying a cardboard tube from which he extracted a sheet of music. 'It was something Joe asked me to do on his last leave – get this printed for him. I'm sorry I've taken my time, but I've been on the move, and have now found myself posted to an air-field about fifty miles from here. I'm on my way back there now. I was in London recently, and took the opportunity to make enquiries about a printer who specialises in music. I can't read a note of music, so I can't tell if they've made a good job of it or not. Perhaps Eve would play it to us when she gets back. I'd like to hear it. I expect you would too.'

The little black notes were dancing before Philippa's eyes. The title – 'Love Song for Philippa' – swam in and out of focus. She was fighting hard to stop herself breaking down, not wanting to embarrass Bob even further. She wanted to run away and gloat over this most precious gift alone. She couldn't bear the idea of sharing it with anybody. Least of all she wanted anyone else to play it. She rolled it up and replaced it in its tube. 'I'll hear it another time,' she said.

Bob hid his disappointment. He knew some women acted strangely at times like this and allowances must be made for them, but he thought it a bit thick that after all the chasing about he had done to find a printer capable and willing to take on such a small order, he wasn't going to hear what it sounded like. But one look at Philippa's downcast face and all his annoyance vanished. Poor kid, why shouldn't she have her little quirks after all she had gone through – all she still had to go through. If it weren't for a certain sloe-eyed girl he had met on his last leave, he'd be almost tempted to ask her to marry him after all. He cleared his throat.

'While I was in London I called in to see Joe's mother. She's given up the cottage at Chingford and is living with her sister in Barking. . . .'

'How is she?'

'She'd taken Joe's death better than I expected. I think

she had half expected it since the day he joined the RAF. Did you ever meet her?'

'No. Joe was planning to take me to see her, but we left it too late, and there didn't seem any point afterwards. It would have been too embarrassing for both of us.' Philippa had been rolling the tube of cardboard restlessly between the palms of her hands. Now she laid it carefully on the ground by her feet.

'Talk to me about Joe,' she said. 'Say anything, I don't mind what it is. The others rarely mention him, not in my hearing, anyway. I think they are being tactful but they don't realise how I long to hear his name. Tell me something – anything that will remind me of him.'

Bob thought hard. He wasn't a very imaginative person and ideas didn't come easily.

'Did you ever hear about the time he turned down the chance of becoming an officer? He didn't want to be one and he made damn sure he wasn't made one. When the CO asked him why he hadn't put in for a commission, he answered, "Well sir, it's like this, sir. I prefer the conversation in the sergeants' mess to that in the officers' mess, it's on a higher plane, sir. No pun intended, sir." '

She smiled wistfully. 'I can just imagine him saying it – and getting enjoyment out of saying it. I'm surprised he wasn't thrown out.'

'He was too good a pilot to lose.'

'He shirked responsibility – that's why he didn't want a commission.' She lapsed into a thoughtful silence.

'He just loved flying. He told me once that he only felt free when he was way up there. It didn't matter a toss to him whether he wore stripes or rings. He just wanted to fly.'

'That's what I mean. He loved his freedom. I don't think marriage would have suited him.'

'With the right person I think he would have settled down very well. I also think he would have made a damn fine father.'

She flashed him a quick glance, then looked away. 'You don't know? No, why should you. I've arranged to have the baby adopted. It's for the best, Bob. There was no other way, so please don't condemn me.'

He couldn't hide his distress. He stumbled over his answer. 'I don't condemn you, I just think it's a great pity, that's all, but you know best.'

They sat lost for further things to say to each other. It was a relief to them when finally there came a call from the house. Evelyn was home. Tea was ready.

It was a nostalgic meal seated around that familiar table with ghosts from the past filling up the empty places. More than once Evelyn caught Philippa stealing a look at the piano. And more than once she caught Bob stealing a look at Philippa. Evelyn's hopes took a steep rise until she saw that Bob's look was not one of fondness but of regret and sadness. There was no romance between them, just friendship. Even so, when plans were put afoot to travel with him to Norwich to see him on to his train, she tried hard to persuade Philippa to join them.

'It will do you good,' she persisted. 'You never go out. There's a concert on at St Andrew's. We might catch the second half.'

But Philippa could not be persuaded. She yearned to be alone, and at last they were gone, sprinting up the lane to take the short cut to Thornmere Halt. Bob turned and gave her a final wave. She bit her lip, still feeling the warmth of his grasp when they said goodbye.

She shut the door. Just she and Mitzi now. Automatically she cleared the table, washed the dishes, watered the plants in the conservatory, then at last took Joe's music out and studied it.

She might just as well be staring at a page of Greek for all the sense it made to her. Oh, why hadn't she studied music when she had the chance, why didn't she learn to read music?

She sat at the piano, lifted the lid, and placed the sheet of music on the rack. If she could just remember a few easy notes she might be able to make something out of it. She knew middle C, couldn't she go from there? But she had forgotten the difference between a sharp and a flat. She didn't know a crotchet from a quaver. She was a failure, she knew nothing, she was an ignorant, addle-pated little fool who couldn't even keep a baby. She dropped her arms on the keyboard, crashing the chords, startling Mitzi, burying her face in her hands.

'Forgive, Joe,' she sobbed. 'Oh darling, Joe, forgive me.'

Ten

When Philippa saw the telegraph boy approaching along the track that led up from the station her heart gave a sudden lurch. The war had been over now for five months but the sight of that navy uniform and pill-box hat could still turn her bowels to water. Two telegrams in 1945 – one from Mrs Toser that shocked her with news of Miss Jolly's suicide, and later that same year another from Charlie Ford announcing her father's death – had fixed in her mind the firm conviction that a telegram was a notice of death.

So now she waited in trepidation for the telegraph boy to ring, her mind flicking through dire possibilities. Mrs Toser? Unlikely, she was still in her prime and with Red's help was now running Wimborne House as a private hotel. Jean in Nottingham or one of her children? No, Dave would ring. Robin? But Eve's last letter, only received last week, was full of Robin and his coming engagement. Ursula? No such luck.

The boy had propped his bicycle against the tree that marked the boundary of Aunt Dot's front garden and now approached the door with the cautious expression all telegraph boys wore unless the occasion marked a wedding. He handed her the dreaded buff envelope.

'All speed ahead, darling,' she read. 'Docking Clyde the 10th. See you soon. Leo.'

She gathered her wits. 'Stay there.' She ran into the kitchen, grabbed some loose change from the dresser, ran out and gave it to the boy and when alone read the telegram through again.

She had no need to look at the calendar to check the date, but she did. Today was the 9th January 1946. She had already ringed the 14th when she received Leo's first cable from Hong Kong telling her he had just embarked for home and giving her the date of his expected arrival. His airmail letter, dated 12 December had arrived on Christmas Day giving her further details.

'Can you believe it? I'm on a ship – an aircraft carrier – and we are due to sail tomorrow. Yippie! I'm hoping I can send this letter ashore to let you know. It all happened so suddenly. First, last Sunday I was told to stand by at two hours' notice. Then I was told I would embark today, and then I found my name crossed out. Then yesterday I was on the list again. These ups and downs put years on me, but now I'm actually on board and wild horses couldn't drag me off again. This is the programme as far as I know. Singapore, Columbo, Port Said, Gibraltar, Clyde – due in on 14 Jan. We're carrying mail so it's full speed ahead.'

Still feeling in a trance-like stupor, she went up to her room to take from her bureau drawer Leo's letters, all docketed and numbered in order of receipt.

His rise in rank had been rapid in the past two years. His majority in 1944, then promotion to Lieutenant-

Colonel a year later and in charge of a Casualty Clearing Station in Burma until, following the surrender of the Japanese, he had been posted to Hong Kong where for the past two months he had been in charge of a medical unit on the Kowloon frontier.

His parcels still came regularly, and still from Bombay. She had had rather a plaintive letter from him while he was still at Chittagong. 'Darling, are you being quite honest when you say it is so wonderful to receive the parcels of sweets, butter, sugar and tea I send you? This is what my father reports, mind you he's always pretty blunt – "Sweets are all damn paper, butter is nothing to rave over, sugar is only acceptable because it's rationed, but the tea isn't bad." Now darling, are you just being kind or is my father laying it on a bit thick? A little of each, I think.'

She had chuckled at the time of reading that and had wished so much that her father could have shared the joke with her, but she wasn't in the mood to laugh now for retribution was close, and what was his father's power to wound compared with hers. She had no doubt that Leo would stay only long enough at Belle Vue Road to dump his luggage before coming down to Leigh to her.

She had prepared herself and him for this. She had written a confession in the form of a letter several pages long, leaving nothing out. No pleas, no begging for forgiveness, no excuses – just the bare facts and ending by saying that she would be waiting at Aunt Dot's for him if he wanted to see her again, but if she didn't hear, she'd understand why. Then she had sealed it and registered it, and addressed it to Belle Vue Road. In a separate letter to Mrs Brooke she had asked her to keep the letter safe and give it to Leo as soon as he arrived.

So tomorrow he should be home and the letter placed in his hand, and if the phone did not ring, or he did not come to see her she'd know she had lost him. Suddenly the reaction set in and she began to cry. And why, she wondered. Contrition? Relief to get it off her conscience? Fear of how he might react? Oh God, she prayed, please help me.

There was a beautiful sunset that afternoon, as there sometimes is on a still, cold, January day. The sun low on the horizon had dazzled her with its brilliance when she fetched in the washing earlier. Aunt Dot made a lot of washing. Philippa didn't mind the washing, though getting it dry in winter was a problem. She had just draped the sheets over a wooden horse and put them to dry in front of the kitchen fire when the phone rang.

She didn't hurry to answer it. She guessed it was a call from Charlie Ford. He usually called at this time of the month making yet another excuse for the lateness of her aunt's allowance.

'Hallo,' she said on a note of resignation.

'Darling, it's me.'

She went rigid. She clutched hold of the telephone table as the room reeled. Panic swept over her. 'Leo, where are you?'

A chuckle. His voice hadn't changed. A little husky, perhaps, but that could be due to emotion. 'I'm down here at the station. I couldn't wait – I couldn't go home without seeing you first, so when I arrived at St Pancras I went on to Fenchurch Street and here I am. I'll be with you in five minutes.'

She slammed down the receiver. She grabbed a coat from the hall closet, an old one of Aunt Dot's, smelling of mothballs. She raced through the kitchen, out through the garden door, up the long straggling path to the gate on the upper road. From there, looking back she could see the wavering rear light on the guard's van of the train that had brought Leo from Fenchurch Street and was now making its way towards Westcliff. She turned and ran in the opposite direction, and did not stop when she reached Leigh Broadway but went on to the church and then down the steps to Old Leigh to find sanctuary in a shelter by the jetty.

She was out of breath and perspiring freely, not entirely from exertion. She felt hot and sticky outwardly, but inwardly she was shivering from the unnatural coldness that had gripped her when she first recognised Leo's voice. How was it he was here earlier than he had said? All that mattered was the fact that he *was* here and she'd rather die than face him.

The afterglow of the sunlight faded into a brief twilight. Another train rattled through the now defunct station of Old Leigh. The rush hour had started. The trains would now be coming through every five minutes or so, but no one was likely to come to the shelter. Old men sat there on sunny afternoons, holidaymakers in summer, courting couples in the evenings. But not winter evenings unless they were very hardy.

It was turning frosty. In the faint light from a nearby street-lamp she saw her breath as vapour drifting on the still night air, and she shivered, not now so much from tension as from cold, a cold that attacked from the outside and bit down to the bones. But still she sat on, feeling that Leo would wait for her until the last train back to Fenchurch Street was due.

Finally, she was ousted by a drunk. He came stumbling in and practically fell on top of her. When his hand came in contact with her yielding flesh he let out a yell that would have raised the dead. 'Holy Mary, mother of Jesus. Holy saints and all the apostles, if it's not the divil herself. . . .'

Philippa fled, racing homeward along the cinder track and only slowing down when the pain in her side became unbearable. A quarter moon gave just enough light to reveal the sea lapping against the breakers. It looked black and inviting, a way out from all her troubles? A coward's way out, she thought, but wasn't that what she was – a coward, running from someone who had been near and dear to her since she was a schoolgirl.

The church clock struck eleven. Surely Leo must have left by now, yet she was still reluctant to return home. She dawdled. The old cinder track evoked so many memories, it was a comfort to lose herself in them. It was along this track she had made for the swimming pool on warm summer days on holiday; it was along this track she had walked with her father to reach the boat, and it was along this same track one late June afternoon in 1944, coming back from Old Leigh with some shellfish for tea, she had seen a flying bomb coming up from the estuary, only two weeks after the Allies had landed on the Normandy beaches.

She was not surprised by the BBC announcement that morning of 6 June. She had been kept awake most of the night by the sound of airplanes flying overhead. A constant stream, plane after plane, throbbing and droning all night long. At first she wondered why the sirens hadn't sounded but quickly realised it was because they were not enemy planes (troop planes, she later discovered, towing gliders) and it didn't take much nous after that to put two and two together.

For weeks past, the residential roads in the district had been used as parking lots by army vehicles of every size and description. It didn't inconvenience those residents who still occupied houses there, but it did arouse their curiosity, and it was aroused to an even greater pitch when the men in charge of vehicles worked away coating all engine parts with what looked like red plasticine. One old gentleman of Aunt Dot's acquaintance asked a sergeant what his men were doing, and was told, not so politely, that they were frying sausages. He repeated this to Philippa.

'When I ask a civil question, I expect a civil answer,' he said, 'not to be put off with riddles.' He was quite huffed about it.

There was no excitement, no jubilation on that fateful day, just the grim hope that all would go well. It seemed ironic that Hitler had had sunshine all the way when he overran the Low Countries. But the Allies, fighting for a foothold on the beaches, had to contend with the cold and wet as well as the enemy fire.

It was only a week or two following that day that Philippa again had a sleepless night because of the constant drone of an unfamiliar engine overhead. This time the sirens did go, about eleven o'clock, a sound rarely heard since the raids of late winter – and what was more the All Clear didn't sound until 9.30 the following morning.

Not another blitz, oh dear God, not another blitz, she prayed, and it wasn't a blitz, it was something even more frightening for there was something sinister about these new weapons, something supernatural. They weren't traditional planes piloted by young airmen and dropping traditional bombs – one could fear that but accept it.

These were something else again, pilotless machines acting as bombs – Hitler's secret weapon. Suddenly, all the excitement of the second front was overshadowed by this new and malevolent threat, and once more the people were scurrying for their shelters and wondering what other secrets Hitler had up his sleeve.

But that June day in 1944 when she had been caught on the cinder track, powerless to move (and where was there to move to, for there was no shelter in sight?), listening as the last dying warble of the warning gave way to the noisy and lumbering approach of a doodlebug, she had no fear, just wonder.

She saw it quite clearly against a cloudless sky, much smaller than she had imagined, sluggish and low enough, she thought, to be picked off quite easily by an expert rifleman. It was certainly not a thing of beauty, yet she found herself fascinated, for there was something about these small metallic raiders that was beyond her imagination. Already, jokes about them had begun to circulate: an eagle flying alongside a doodlebug asked it why it was in such a hurry. 'So would you be in a hurry if your backside was on fire,' came the retort.

Philippa couldn't laugh when she heard this. She thought the joke was in poor taste and obviously thought up by someone far away from the scene. But now face to face with one, as it were, her fear gave way to a grudging admiration for the wonders of science, as she watched it carrying its deadly load on to London. Poor London. It had survived the blitz of 1940; it had survived the 'Little Blitz' of early 1944, and now, she had no doubt, it would survive the attack by flying bombs. But after five years of war the people no longer felt like taking it. They were tired and dispirited.

Not that there was any sign of that in May 1945. Jean had come to stay for a few days, leaving her husband Dave and the children in the care of her mother. The war with Europe was drawing towards its close. It actually ended during Jean's visit. They sat listening to Churchill's announcement over the radio, telling the people that the Germans had surrendered unconditionally, and the following day would be a holiday.

On the evening of VE Day they walked along the cinder track to Old Leigh in company with many other merrymakers. There was much to rejoice over. The war was over, the menace from the skies had ceased, the 'boys' were coming home. A massive bonfire was blazing on the foreshore, fuelled by old ships' timbers and the remains of a small dinghy. Excited children ran about with lighted sparklers, and the pubs ran out of beer and spirits, and – what was just as great a calamity – glasses. Jean, pushing through the throng came back with two tiny tots of cherry brandy. 'This is all that's left, I'm afraid, but it's better than nothing.'

They toasted the fighting men and women of the Allied Forces. They toasted the King and Queen and the two Princesses. They toasted each other, and finally gave a toast to a speedy end to war in the Far East.

'What are you going to tell Leo when he comes home?' asked Jean.

'I'll play it by ear,' said Philippa woodenly.

Three months later came VJ Day, but there was no rejoicing for Philippa. Her father had died two weeks previously and her grief still burned inside her. He had left everything to Ursula except the house which was hers as long as she lived, then reverted to Philippa. Also Philippa could take her pick of the household contents.

'Do you want anything in particular,' Ursula asked. 'It's all very old-fashioned stuff, and a lot of it is very shabby.'

And a lot of it very valuable, thought Philippa. So it was with as much expediency as sentiment that she claimed her great-grandmother's *chaise-longue* and the porcelain and ivory *objets d'art* from the cabinet in the drawing room, and other antiques. When funds fell low, as they had on more than one occasion, she could always raise money on them.

So VJ Day gave no cause for joy in Philippa's case, just a deep relief and, in common with most of her countrymen and women, a fear of the mushroom-shaped cloud that now overshadowed the future.

Now, putting such memories behind her, she hastened her step towards Cliff Cottage. The wind was keen and she was still shivering from the cold and damp of the shelter. Someone had been, there were lights on everywhere. She went round to the back of the house and in through the kitchen door. The room was empty and all was silent. The clothes horse had been pulled back from the fire – in case of an odd spark shooting out and catching the sheets alight? The sort of thing Leo would think of. She tiptoed into Aunt Dot's room. The fire had been made up and the guard replaced and her aunt was asleep.

On the bedside cabinet there stood the remains of a cup of warm milk where skin had formed, rippled like crinkly paper. Aunt Dot couldn't get out of bed to make it herself – Leo must have made it. Thoughtfully, Philippa returned to the kitchen, and immediately spotted what she had failed to notice before. A sheet of paper torn from the telephone pad, on the dresser. Her heart skipped a beat. Leo had left her a message.

'I was hurt and surprised to find you gone,' she read. 'What ever came over you? Not shyness, surely. I can imagine you doing such a thing when you were fifteen but not now. I went out in search of you, but didn't know where to look, and gave it up as hopeless. I disturbed your aunt, I'm afraid, when I searched the house but she settled down again once she had had a hot drink. I'll have to go to catch my train in a minute or two but I'll return tomorrow. Please, please, dear, don't be so foolish as to run away again. Surely, it wasn't shyness.

'Love, Leo.'

He was hurt, she thought, mortally hurt; one endearment and that only a dear. Automatically she washed out the milk saucepan and cup and saucer, left them to drain and went up to her freezing room to bed. Cuddling a hot-water bottle and weeping silently, she finally drifted off to sleep. And that night for the first time in many years, she dreamt not of Joe but of Leo.

He did not come the next day, or the day after, or next week or the week after that. She awaited each day with a hammering heart and sweaty palms and went to bed each night too depressed to sleep. Once she was driven to take one of Aunt Dot's sleeping pills, but never tried that short cut again because it induced a violent and erotic dream from which she suddenly awoke with her whole body on fire. She dreamt that Leo was thrashing her with his Sam Browne belt, and though she screamed for mercy she didn't want the pain to stop for it induced in her an orgasmic pleasure his lovemaking never had.

For several days Aunt Dot enquired after that 'kind

young doctor with the deep voice' and then forgot him. She had a chilblain. That preoccupied her mind and Philippa's time for another few days, then she forgot that too before slipping back into her twilight world where she was neither fully conscious nor fully asleep but just a troubled and confused old woman who had outlived her time.

Philippa spent her few leisure hours going through Leo's letters. At least they brought back to her the tender and thoughtful Leo she remembered. She wanted so much to recapture his other voice, his loving voice, and that she did every time she read through one of the flimsy airmail letter cards.

She always knew when he was on the move because then his letters were censored. Chittagong, Bangalore, Arakan, Rangoon, and finally Hong Kong where, the war now being over, all censorship had ceased. What was it like, she wondered, to travel with a Casualty Clearing Station? Something like moving a small travelling circus she suspected. No wonder Leo had had such rapid promotion, he was a born organiser.

'Darling,' he had written, soon after he arrived in Kowloon. 'I haven't written these last few days as we have been changing barracks. At present we have got the men in the family quarters of a peacetime barracks while our mess is in the old Kowloon Bowls Club. Everything was dirty and overgrown and derelict but the men have set to and cleaned the place up a treat. I've been round the shops again, and more and more are opening, but the prices are ridiculous. All the shopkeepers say that prices will come down as soon as they can buy food more cheaply. The only people who can afford to buy are the few Americans here. They pay in gold which has a great black market value, but even they don't buy much at such exorbitant prices. It will become more reasonable in a month or two and then I intend to buy some things for our future home. I heard rumours yesterday that the repatriation waiting time was going to be reduced. Keep your fingers crossed for me, sweetheart.

'The weather now (October) is perfect. Hot sun, dry, and a gentle breeze. Not sticky at all. A few days ago three Chinese turned up and said they were employed at the Bowls Club in peacetime and could we give them a job. It wasn't in our power to employ them so we said if they would like to help we'd give them food in lieu of pay. That delighted them as food is better pay than money. Today, two little girls of about thirteen or fourteen came and asked if they could work for their food. It was so pathetic we didn't know what to say, so at last I suggested they could make a start by mending my socks. Sure enough, those two little girls went through all my things and now there isn't a button missing or a hole anywhere. They are amazingly industrious and clean. Of course, everything is done in sign language, but they are as sharp as needles at understanding, whether one speaks in English or Urdu.'

At this point Philippa had to put down the letter as she could no longer read. It always happened no matter how many times she read that particular passage, which she had done over and over. The thought of those two hungry and industrious little girls and Leo patiently signing what he wanted them to do, reduced her to tears. But it went deeper than that. Any mention, any thought of a 'little girl' – any little girl – reopened old wounds.

She took up Leo's next letter, written in November. 'I'm afraid I've got behind with my letter-writing lately and feel very guilty about it so I'll start with making excuses. We are in the process of moving again to a place one and a half miles away where we will eventually open up the complete Casualty Clearing Station and close down our frontier section. We are treating all the local Chinese civilians. They've never had a hospital service before and some have awful injuries and wounds. My health is good but I have had a series of boils and sties and once those bally things get a hold of you they don't know when to stop. How are you, darling? You never tell me much about what you do with yourself these days. I suppose all your time is taken up with looking after your aunt. The rumours about repat. or demob. for doctors are gathering momentum. I don't care what I get first, as long as it comes soon.'

And then the last letter posted on land and dated 7 December. 'I got the surprise of my life today. I met the ADMS and he said, "Consider yourself at twelve hours' notice for embarkation to the UK." Then he rather dampened my spirits by adding, "Of course a ship might not come until the end of January." I've been like a cat on hot bricks ever since. Not having a second-in-command there is no one I can hand over to, but I'll get that sorted out. I feel like running down to the docks to see if any ships are coming in. You should see your husband-to-be being restrained from swimming out to the ships in the harbour. Thinking about weddings, darling, could you make all the arrangements your end? I don't want to waste a single day once I'm on English soil again.'

She bowed her head. Oh God, what have I done, she moaned.

Each wartime winter seemed to be harder and longer

than the one that preceded it. The winter of 1945/1946 was no exception even though it was the first winter in peacetime. The coal shortage was severe, the food rations were reduced. The fact that a shipment of bananas, the first for many years, arrived in the country, did not make up for the fact that the combined weekly fat ration, butter, marge, and lard had been cut from eight ounces to seven. Even an ounce made a whale of a difference to a people who had expected that once the war ended life would get back to normal. It did not. A world food shortage banished that dream. And Philippa, struggling to keep a large and poorly insulated house just reasonably warm, had an impossible battle on her hands.

All through winter she had kept only two fires going. The one in the stove in the kitchen, for that heated the water, and the one in Aunt Dot's room. She kept the other rooms shut up, for that saved electricity. There were hints that if the stocks of coal at the power stations fell any lower there would have to be compulsory power cuts. The thought of sitting for hours in the dark appalled her. Not able to read and not able to listen to the radio either if the battery went flat, and batteries were almost as scarce as fuel.

So it was that on this fine spring afternoon in early March, when the forsythia outside the drawing-room window made a glorious splash of colour and crocuses were poking up between the paving stones, Philippa was splitting logs on the only patch of level ground in the garden in the front of the house. She was not very proficient with an axe as anyone examining the bole of a tree she used as a chopping block could see – that had more splits in it than she had logs to split.

'I think I could make a better job of that than you,' said a well-remembered voice behind her.

Two thoughts flashed through her mind before her pulse began to slow down again. That she was wearing her oldest skirt and skimpiest jumper, and all she had for supper was a pound of sausages – 'Ah, sweet mysteries of life,' she thought illogically. That was how her father always referred to them. Even more mysterious since rationing. She turned.

He was in civvies. The same old Leo. He had hardly changed, except for a few more lines about his eyes and his unhealthy colour. Even under his tan the pallor was noticeable, and there were the remains of a sty on his left eye. He in his turn had been studying her.

'You are very thin. Too thin,' he said, unemotionally.

She looked away, unable to hold his gaze any longer, unable to fathom the expression in his tawny eyes. Not hostile, yet not overtly friendly either. Just neutral. 'I didn't expect to see you ever again,' she stammered.

He put down the suitcase and carrier bag he had been holding. 'Actually,' he said, 'I'm just as surprised as you to find myself here.'

She ignored that remark, it was no more than she deserved. 'I'm glad you came,' she said. 'It gives me the chance to apologise for the way I behaved that other time. I – I just didn't stop to think. I panicked and bolted.'

'Yes. I gathered that – later.'

Oh, the wealth of meaning in that word later. Oh yes of course, it took no great intellect to understand why she acted as she did once he had read her letter. She wanted him to say something regarding that letter, but he did not, and until he did they would continue like this – like automatons.

'Give me that axe, and I'll finish this off for you,' he said. 'Why are you chopping wood, anyway? Are you out of firewood?'

'It's not for lighting a fire with it's for keeping a fire in,' she explained. 'I'm not due for another delivery of coal until next week, and all I've got in the cellar is a little pile of dust. I don't mind for myself but Aunt Dot feels the cold so.'

Leo removed his coat and hung it over one of the palings of what had once been a picket fence that divided them from their neighbour. Most of the palings had long since gone to stoke the fires.

'My old man sometimes gets a hundredweight of coke from the local gas works. Have you thought of that?'

'Our nearest depot is at Southend and I don't think they'd let me on the bus with a sack of coke even if I could lift it.'

'I'll get you some when I've finished here.' She heard an echo of the old practical Leo in that remark. He handed her the carrier bag. 'I thought these might come in useful.'

She went into the house with the sound of the axe ringing in her ears. His blows were quick and rhythmic. I can't believe this is happening, she thought. But it was happening and it made her feel as if she were taking part in some silent film – farce or drama, it made no difference. Where were the angry words, the tears, the accusations and recriminations – the explanations and excuses, the pleading for forgiveness? Scenes she had lived through again and again in her imagination. Scenes more bearable in some ways than this unnatural civility.

The bag contained food. Butter, cheese, sugar, tea, a fruit cake, a large tin of ham and another of tongue, and several small minor groceries. She sat down at the table and wept. Not at the sight of such plenty but at the thoughtfulness behind the gift. Another man might have brought her chocolate or flowers. Joe had brought her music. Her tears flowed even faster. When the sound of chopping ceased, she went upstairs and washed her face, then went in to see if her aunt needed attention. She delayed a second encounter for as long as she could.

Leo was in the scullery washing his hands. The exercise or the sea breezes had put some colour into his cheeks, lending him an air of well-being which when she looked closer was entirely false. He said, 'D'you mind if I use your phone to call a cab? I'd like to get to the Gas Light and Coke Company office before it closes.'

She stared. Take a taxi to collect coke in! This certainly wasn't the Leo she knew who would have pushed it home in a wheelbarrow rather than spend money in such an irresponsible manner.

'That's how my father gets his,' he said. 'It costs him a guinea for the taxi and four and six for the coke, and all for the sake of his bally chrysanthemums.'

'You mean he uses it in the *greenhouse*. Is that allowed?'

'Provided it's off the ration, I don't think it matters.'

He donned his hat and coat. 'Won't you stay for a cup of tea before you go?' Their thoughtfulness to each other was unbelievable.

'Not now thank you, but I'll be glad of one when I return.'

He left. She had not overlooked the significance of the suitcase, standing now in the hall. She took it up to the spare bedroom and made up the bed. Then because the room hadn't been used in years and had a cold and musty feel about it she lit a fire in the grate using a mix of logs and coal dust and sacrificing two of her candles to get an instant blaze.

Only then did she change into something more flattering. A utility dress in a shade of dusty pink, unadorned and with its statutory number of pleats, but nevertheless quite pretty, which she kept for 'best'. Into the nightdress case on her pillow she put the unworn nightie Evelyn had sent her for Christmas, more practical than flattering with a Peter Pan collar and long sleeves. Her trousseau nightgowns were just a memory. She had given them away as presents when coupons or money was not available. In any case, they belonged to another person and another age. Things were different now.

She was still upstairs when she heard the taxi return. She had made up her aunt's fire and given her her customary bowl of bread and milk. In two hours' time the nurse would arrive to prepare her patient for bed and settle her for the night. Another nurse would take over in the morning to reverse the procedure. Mrs Arnold, their help, came two mornings a week, leaving Philippa free then to do her round of the queues. She had been that morning and would not come again until Monday for which Philippa was deeply thankful. She would not now have to introduce Leo to her for whom could she introduce him as? A family friend? An old flame? Her ex-fiancé? She quickly put such thoughts to rest. That was a bridge to cross when she came to it.

She heard Leo come into the house and go through the hall to the kitchen. Slowly she descended the stairs. He was in the scullery again rinsing his hands.

'I put clean towels in the bathroom,' she said.

'This'll do fine.' He rebuttoned his cuffs. 'I've tipped the coke through the coal hole. It should keep you going until your next quota arrives.'

'It ought to this time of year. Spring is just around the corner.' She listened to herself and marvelled at the steadiness of her voice considering her inner turmoil.

'One of the things I missed most was an English spring,' Leo said musingly. 'You don't really appreciate anything until you've lost it.'

'But you didn't lose it. It was here waiting for you.'

'But what about all those springs while I was away? I'll never find them again.'

She felt they were speaking in metaphors, and knew she couldn't keep it up. She said, 'I'm afraid that all I can offer you to eat is what you brought yourself.'

He looked at the table. She had set it with the fine bone china and burnished silver that had been put away when war started, and had put a vase of forsythia in the centre. It looked very festive and in spite of himself he was touched. 'I didn't come for this,' he said.

'Why did you come, Leo?' she cried desperately.

'I suppose because I couldn't keep away any longer.'

'Oh Leo, can't we talk like we used to? I feel I'm talking to someone I don't know.'

'I *know* I'm talking to someone I don't know.'

'But we don't have to be like this, do we? We only have to talk it out – clear the air. There's so much I must explain to you.'

'I don't think you have anything to explain. Your letter was extremely explicit.' For the first time there was a trace of bitterness in his voice, but also some sadness. 'If only you had been honest with me right from the beginning, I might have got over it by now. But to spring it on me like that, my first day home. That was extremely cruel.'

She looked appalled. 'I – I didn't think . . . I didn't see it like that. . . .'

'That was obvious.'

In the silence that followed, a bell chimed and Philippa started, brought back from the pain of her thoughts.

'That's the nurse for my aunt. I usually help her. Will you start. . . ?'

'I'll wait for you.'

When she returned he was sitting at the table reading the paper. He looked up. 'I see here that doctors have launched a £1 million fighting fund to oppose the plans for a national health service. Personally, I think a national health service is a very sound idea. Some of the young recruits who passed through my hands could have done with a good health scheme in their younger days.' He changed his tone. 'But I mustn't bore you with my pet hobby horse. Everything finished now?'

'I'll just make nurse a cup of coffee before she goes.'

When at last she was free to join him at the table, her uncertainty and constraint returned. His accusation of cruelty had shaken her. She had been thoughtless and not far-seeing enough, but not cruel, surely. There had been cruelty in her betrayal, she could accept that, but not in the way she had broken it to him. She stole a look at him under her lashes. He was enjoying his supper, eating with the old relish she remembered so well, going back time and again for another helping of the green tomato chutney she had made in the autumn. He didn't despise her, did he? Would he have taken the time and trouble to get the coke if he didn't retain some of his old fondness for her? Yes, he would because he was that sort of person, always ready with a helping hand. But could it not be possible that he still felt for her a little? She had forfeited his love and his respect, but he hadn't turned against her entirely, that was obvious. And he didn't appear that indifferent towards her either. So what did he feel? Pity? She flinched. Anything but that.

'I can't go on like this any longer,' she cried. 'We must talk – really talk. Not sit here like two stuffed dummies mouthing meaningless words.'

He looked surprised. 'I thought we were talking.'

'We are conversing – there's quite a difference. Would I be treading on your corns if I asked you what you have been doing with yourself these past two months?'

His expression was one of mild amusement. 'Rather a quaint way of putting it but I get what you mean.' He carefully placed his knife and fork together and pushed the plate away so that he could fold his arms on the table. 'There's not much to tell really. The journey home was uneventful. I think you must have gathered that from my letters I wrote at sea. The chief engineer was anxious to get his old job back. He knew his ship, a pre-war luxury liner, was docked at the Clyde, so he pulled out all the stops to get home before it sailed. That's how we got in a few days earlier than expected.'

She looked uncomfortable. 'I'm sorry I ran away. It was a stupid and childish thing to do, but I couldn't face you until you had read my letter.'

His face closed up. He had no intention of travelling along that road. He said, 'I had to report to RAMC headquarters at Aldershot and there I found myself demobbed on the spot. It was an excruciating experience, suddenly to find oneself without a job. They did give me a demob suit though,' he added somewhat whimsically.

'There are some very rude things being said about demob suits,' she said, entering into his mood with reluctance. Sweeping a problem under the carpet was storing it, not solving it.

'Then I visited my old teaching hospital. There I learnt of a government scheme to help medics like myself whose career had been interrupted by the war. I could put in a claim for a grant to keep me for a year while I worked for a higher degree or a diploma in a specialised subject. So I arranged to start at the hospital as a medical registrar on the first of May and study for a diploma in anaesthetics.'

'Won't that be something of a comedown for you after being a Lieutenant-Colonel?'

He shrugged. 'That's the least of my worries – the least I've had to come to terms with.' He let that sink in. Then, 'I'm just relieved I've got a job, and more than relieved to get back into medicine. Not that I wasn't doing medicine out East, but it was much of a muchness. Malaria, fevers, wounds, injuries.' He hesitated, then, 'Will you marry me, Philippa?'

Her breath caught in her throat. She couldn't speak. 'If – if you still want me,' she said stupidly.

'Oh, I want you. I wouldn't have come back if I didn't, but I can't promise it will be the same as before. It won't be the same for you either. You've had the great love of your life. I won't be able to measure up to that.'

'There are different aspects of love,' she murmured.

'I only happen to know one,' he said bluntly.

There were no kisses, no tenderness or satisfaction for

either of them. Just an urgent need on his part and a humiliation on hers. He came to her in his pyjamas and without removing them got into her bed. Ten interminable minutes later, not having uttered a word, he went back to his own room. She lay, as he had left her, wakeful, sore at heart, and weeping for Joe.

They were married a fortnight later at the registry office in Southend and left the following day for Norwich where Leo had booked a room for a week at an ancient hostelry in Tombland. Philippa wore a coffee-coloured woollen suit purchased with some coupons Leo had given her, and her only concession to the occasion was a bunch of violets pinned to her lapel. The lavender-coloured silk dress she had planned to marry in still hung unworn in her wardrobe, too cold for a March wedding, too reminiscent of old dreams to wear in comfort. Mrs Arnold, a clever needlewoman and the possessor of a powered sewing-machine, had made her a trousseau out of the two saris Leo had sent from India. Six yards of tussore and six of cream-coloured silk had gone a long way in Mrs Arnold's economical hands and she had cleverly used the embroidered edges as trimming on the nightgowns and underslips.

As for the reception, that had been more of a gathering of the Brooke clan. Except for Mrs Arnold and Doreen Smellie, who had taken a break from looking after her husband to look after Aunt Dot while Philippa was away, there was nobody from her side of the family to give support. Ursula and Charlie Ford might have come if she had invited them, but she didn't. Those she did, like some friends from the bank and Jean Shaw from Nottingham, couldn't make it at such short notice. And Evelyn and Clive Smith were on an extended tour of

Canada, staying with Eve's sister whom she hadn't seen since before the war. Philippa knew there was no point in inviting Robin for he never attended functions though his fiancée, a nurse, was already working miracles on his inhibitions.

They stayed the first night at Cliff Cottage and went on to Norwich on Sunday morning. Monday afternoon Philippa went on her own to call at Wimborne House.

Mrs Toser flung up her hands at the sight of her. 'Well, now, if this isn't a sight for sore eyes. Come in m'dear, and tell me what you've been adoing with yourself.'

'Getting married,' said Philippa bluntly.

'And didn't tell anyone! Sit you down there, I'll soon get the kettle on.'

Was she imagining it or had Mrs Toser filled out a little since she saw her last? She was still gaunt, her clothes still hung on her as if on a peg yet there was a roundness to her face as if the lines had been filled in with flesh-coloured putty.

'I miss the old days,' she said as she poured tea and cut a generous slice from a fruit loaf. 'I miss all the comings and goings of you young ones, and the things you used to get up to. Miss Birch and Miss Norton were hard to get on with but you others made up for them two old miseries. And that Miss Jolly,' here she sighed, 'she was as nice as pie – always ready for a laugh, not that she had much to laugh about towards the end. But what did she want to do that for? There would always have been a place here for her with me.'

'I thought the Coroner brought in a verdict of accidental death.'

Mrs Toser sniffed. 'That's all he knew about it. She took that overdose of sleeping tablets on purpose, I knew that. The bank asked her to take early retirement. They were cutting down on staff and transferring most of their business back to London. She sat where you're sitting now telling me all about it the night afore... afore she did it. "I got nothing to go back to London for, Tosie," she say. She always call me that. "I've lost touch with the friends I had down there. All my friends are here now, and they're leaving one by one." "This is your home for as long as you need it," I say, but she only gave a little smile. "I couldn't afford to stay here on a pension," she say. "But never mind, I'm sure to think of a way out." An' she did.'

Mrs Toser poked fiercely at the fire. 'Fancy her doing a thing like that. I wouldn't've turned her out. Mind you, it wasn't easy at first for Red an' me, running this place without any help from the bank. It wasn't as if we had anything behind us, but things be doing nicely, now. All the same,' she added darkly, 'I'd rather have you girls with all your untidy ways and traipsing mud all over my clean floor than some of the boarders I get now.

'You wouldn't believe this, but one guest come to me and claimed the chop I gave him was too small. He had saved the bone and showed it to me in a matchbox. "Look at that," he say. "Fancy serving up chops that size. What is this place, the Oliver Twist inn?" That got my pecker up. "That bone had a lot of meat on it afore you et it," I say. "And you can't get large chops off a small animal, an' a lamb's a small animal." "Norfolk lambs must belong to a bl— pygmy breed," he say, and he used a word I won't repeat. Well, you know Red won't have anything said against Norfolk. He got up then an' threw the man out and told him to go to Butlins, only he didn't say Butlins, he said something else tha' I won't repeat, either. Another cup of tea, m'dear.'

Philippa took the cup Mrs Toser handed her. 'Why don't you and Red get married? You seem so right for each other.'

Mrs Toser blushed and threw up her hands again, this time in mock horror. 'I got married once and didn't think much to it. And there's nothing silly like that between Red an' me, we're just good friends. Better friends than we used to be when he wore that silly red jumper.'

'He's not a communist any more, then,' said Philippa teasingly.

'Between you an' me, he never was, not a real communist, anyway. And I wouldn't mind if he was, for he's a good Christian. He's still got a soft spot for the Russians – the Russian people that is. And who wouldn't have, considering what they've been through? Well now, an' how's life treating you, m'dear, after all this time?'

'Better than I deserve. And you? and your family?'

Mrs Toser's three boys had served in the army throughout the war, and the daughter, a Land Army girl, had worked for a farmer in the Fens. Now, Philippa learned, the sons had all rejoined the army as they found civvy street too dull, and the daughter had married her boss and was expecting her first child.

Mrs Toser tittered. 'Fancy me a granny! I'll have to get me needles out and start knitting. I haven't knitted any baby clothes since that matinée coat I knitted for—' She caught the fleeting and despairing look that flashed across Philippa's face, and reddened.

'I'm sorry, dear, I didn't stop to think. But I must ask, an' I hope you won't take no offence.... Do you ever hear what happened to your little girl?'

Philippa shook her head.

'But you think of her?'

'All the time.'

Leo rescued her. He had fallen in with Red coming along Riversway and, recognising him from the many descriptions in Philippa's letters, had introduced himself. Having a better ear for dialects than Philippa, he found no difficulty in understanding the long and involved story that Red at once embarked upon.

Leo had only called in order to walk Philippa back to the hotel and couldn't be persuaded to stay for the inevitable cup of tea.

'I've managed to get two seats for the theatre tonight,' he explained. 'I think we'd better get back to the hotel to give ourselves plenty of time to change.'

'I prefer the pictures, myself,' Mrs Toser volunteered. 'I can hear better. What you going to see?'

'*Cavalleria Rusticana* and *I Pagliacci*.'

She looked blank. 'Oo-ah,' she said. When she came to kiss Philippa goodbye she whispered, 'He's not as young as he looks in his photo but he's got a lovely smile.' Leo's smiles were rare these days, and on the walk back to the hotel not in evidence at all.

They had a twin-bedded room with a bathroom *en suite*, a rarity in most hotels except the very exclusive. Their hotel was not exclusive, but extremely comfortable and looked out over the cobbled square and part of the cathedral. From the window Philippa could see the path she took all those years ago walking backwards and forwards to the bank. She could also see the building that had once been Brundle's and which was now a building society. Changes, she thought wistfully, nothing ever stays the same.

Leo came out of the bathroom in his vest and trousers, his braces hanging loose. He seemed broader than she remembered him, and his muscles rippled as he finished dressing. She was ashamed of the thoughts that went through her mind and when he caught her eye in the looking-glass she blushed. Such close intimacy with him she found painful considering that in bed there was no closeness or intimacy at all.

'Did we come to Norwich because of *Cav* and *Pag*?' she asked.

'No. That was an extra bonus I discovered when we got here. I came to Norwich because I was curious to see the city you thought so much of. Your letters were full of it. At one time I remember, it was the only subject you did write about.'

The dryness of his tone reminded her that there was a period when writing to Leo was such an ordeal she filled her letters with detailed minutiae. She had overlooked his powers of discernment, not realising how much she gave herself away, and he had played the waiting game until slowly, but never completely, her letters reverted to what they had been before Joe came into her life. Only when he read her full confession did he learn the true reason behind the lapse, and it must have hurt him deeply. She saw that hurt in his eyes still when she caught him off guard. Hurt and sometimes anger, and she wondered at the strength of the emotions simmering beneath the surface.

It was a newly formed touring company that was visiting Norwich, and their performance was excellent. Leo had managed to get two seats in the circle from where they could look straight down on to the stage. Because of her near-sightedness Philippa could not see the faces distinctly but that mattered little once she was caught up in the story. *Cavalleria Rusticana* was new to her though she had heard the beautiful 'Easter Hymn' before without knowing what she was listening to.

When the interval came Leo went off to get a drink. She refused, preferring to read the programme and refresh her memory of the story of *I Pagliacci*, and as she read she saw too clearly the parallel with Canio and his faithless wife and herself and Leo, and felt increasingly uneasy.

This is being ridiculous, she told herself. This is pandering to morbid fancies. Leo was no hot-blooded Italian, far from it. This visit to the theatre was no twisted act of revenge. Leo had known and loved *Pagliacci* from his boyhood, learning it by heart from his father's records. He had brought her to a performance because he had promised her he would years ago. It was a lucky coincidence that it should be showing the very week they were visiting Norwich.

The warning bell sounded. Leo was one of the last to return. As he bent down to take his seat she smelled whisky on his breath which surprised her for he wasn't one for hard liquor. Sherry or light ale were more in his line. Soon she was engrossed once more in the play-acting, giving herself whole-heartedly to the drama. She felt Leo's absorption, too, as he leant slightly forward with his eyes fixed on the stage. Only when the climax approached and Canio, stepping out of his part, sang the heart-rending 'Pagliaccio non son' did he relax and lean back in his seat. But Philippa was hardly aware of this, for she was Nedda up there on the stage trying to placate her jealous husband, and knowing what was about to happen felt a cold trickle of fear run down her spine.

'You got quite carried away at the end,' said Leo laconically as he helped her into her coat when the lights went up. 'I heard you gasp when Nedda was stabbed.'

'It was very realistic.' Her heart was still pounding, the perspiration clammy on her forehead. She took out her handkerchief and dabbed at her face. 'Is the bar still open? I could do with something to drink, water even, my mouth is very dry.'

'We'll get something at the hotel. It will be quicker than queuing here.'

They walked in silence through a silent city bright with street-lamps and illuminated shop windows. The last time Philippa had walked through Norwich at night the black-out was in force and she had found her way by a torch masked by several layers of brown paper. No such fear of tripping up kerbs or barging into other pedestrians this time, but no stars either. The stars in Norfolk seemed brighter than in any other place she had visited.

Back at the hotel Leo ordered a drink for her and one for himself and asked for them to be sent to their room.

'Red told me quite a tale this afternoon,' he said. 'About how he accidentally stepped on a ring belonging to you. It appears it's been plaguing him ever since, and he seemed relieved to get it off his chest. Is it true?'

God forgive her, she had forgotten all about it. So much water had gone under the bridge since then. So much tragedy, and heartbreak, and suffering. 'Yes,' she whispered, putting down her untouched drink.

'Why didn't you tell me?'

How could she admit she had forgotten it. She had done him enough harm as it was. 'I didn't want to hurt you,' she said, her excuse as hollow-sounding as her voice.

'It hurt more seeing you not wearing it. I thought perhaps it had been replaced.'

'No, nothing like that.'

'Ah. So, no engagement ring. A wedding ring, perhaps? That was something you omitted from your letter. Would there have been a wedding ring? Tell me.'

There was a madness in his eyes that frightened her. He was in a reckless mood induced by the realism of the performance, and the drink, plus his festering jealousy. She couldn't imagine him being violent, it wasn't in his nature, but then, she had never imagined herself having a passionate affair with another man.

'I asked you a question. Would you have married your paramour if he had lived?'

She lifted her head and stared him straight in the eyes. 'Yes.'

She thought he was going to strike her, but he turned away, picked up his empty glass and said, 'I'm going down for a refill. Be ready for me when I return.'

They hadn't made love, if love it could be called, since the night of his return. On their wedding night and last night they had slept in their separate beds, not even saying good night to each other. Not sleeping either. She had listened to his steady breathing and knew he was as wide awake as she. She had wondered what he would have done if she had gone across and got into his bed, but neither, seemingly, wanted a repeat of that painful reunion.

What did he mean by being ready for him, she wondered. She dreaded him seeing her unclothed for the signs of childbirth were all too evident. She hurriedly undressed and got into her bed wearing the cream silk nightgown made from a sari. There was something symbolic in that, she thought. It was the nearest she'd ever come to wearing a wedding dress.

He stayed away long enough to have more than one refill. She knew he was slightly drunk by the way he lurched towards her and threw back the bedclothes. 'Get up,' he said.

She obeyed, not wanting to goad him further.

'Take that off.'

'Leo, please. . . .'

'Take it off or I'll rip it off.'

She slipped it over her shoulders and it fell to her feet, a pool of shimmering silk. He looked at it and then at her and then his gaze moved slowly down the length of her body.

'There's one advantage to being a man,' he said with a bitter smile. 'A man can father as many bastards as he likes and it won't leave a mark.'

She began to weep and was still weeping uncontrollably as he picked her up and threw her on the bed.

Sun was streaming into the room when she awakened and the notes of a thrush's full-throated song serenaded her from the direction of the cathedral close. She had one moment of light-hearted forgetfulness before the events of the night came rushing back. She looked swiftly across to the other bed. It was empty, though it had been slept in, obviously. She wondered if she might have time to get dressed and escape before he came back, for she felt she would never find the strength to face him again. She could face him if it were only the violence and pain she had to contend with, but it was the way her own body had betrayed her that caused her the greatest humiliation. And he had known, for he had chuckled ironically when the moment came and her pleasure made itself evident. She felt she would hear that chuckle ringing in her ears until her dying day.

The door handle turned and Philippa hastily pulled the bedsheet up to her neck, and stared as one hypnotised as the door opened and Leo came in carrying of all things a tray of tea. She could hardly believe her eyes, but it was so typical of him, she almost laughed.

He looked awful. He looked as awful as she felt. His eyes were bloodshot and he wore a hang-dog expression.

'You slept through the first lot,' he said, avoiding her gaze. 'So I went down and got you some fresh.'

So this was it – the morning after the night before. The old natural politeness back in place, and life going on as usual. She felt rather disappointed. More than that, she felt cheated. She had hoped the passion and rage of the night had cleared the air. Obviously it had not.

'Thank you,' she said, and made a place for the tray on her bedside table.

'It promises to be a fine day. I thought perhaps you might like a trip on the Broads.'

'That would be very nice,' she said, determined not to be outdone in civility.

'I'll wait for you downstairs then.' But at the door he stopped and came back to her bedside, and this time did meet her eyes, and it was she who looked away.

'I want to apologise for my behaviour last night.' A tic had started up in his cheek. 'I wish I could blame it on the drink, but that wouldn't be honest because I got drunk deliberately so that I could go through with it. I said and did things that are unforgivable. I don't expect you to forgive me but I assure you it will never happen again. If you like, I'll move to another room.'

'There's no need for that. I will take you at your word.'

He went out. She slipped into a dressing-gown and went across to the dressing-table to see the damage. Her mouth was swollen and badly bruised but otherwise she was unmarked. There were other bruises unseen, those on her conscience, for she was deeply ashamed that she had driven this kindly and gentle man to such an act of violence. She sat on her bed and drank her tea and considered her position.

She could leave him of course. For his sake, rather than hers, for the very sight of her must now, she thought, be a torment to him. They could have the marriage annulled perhaps, but she didn't want that. She wanted the marriage to work, and she felt she could make it work, given the fact that it would be a loveless marriage.

Tears gathered in her eyes and rolled down her cheeks, and as fast as she wiped them away they gathered momentum. Some weeks later, checking through her diary, she realised that must have been the night that Leo's son was conceived.

Eleven

If anyone had told Philippa six, seven, even five months ago that she would be installed in a home of her own by September and that home in Thornmere she would have laughed, albeit ruefully. She was fully convinced that Aunt Dot was indestructible, for she had survived the war, the threat of invasion, the air raids, the V1s and V2s as well as minor troubles such as shortages and rationing. Yet she lingered on, living in her twilight world, cushioned from day-to-day annoyances by her many attendants, chief of those now being Leo, or Dr Leo as she always referred to him, having no understanding that he had any connection with Philippa but taking him as a substitute for Dr Campbell who was long retired.

Leo rarely got home from London before seven o'clock on weekdays and two o'clock on Saturdays and then once home there was the interminable studying, which he did in the old guest room, now his study-bedroom. It had been assumed without any discussion on the subject that he would make his home at Cliff Cottage. Everybody accepted that Philippa could not leave her aunt and as there was a good train service to and from London it was a rational solution to the problem.

They could have swapped the double bed in the guest room for the single bed in Philippa's, or alternatively the guest room could have become their bedroom, and Philippa's old room his study, but again without any discussion beforehand they left things as they were, neither appearing to feel strongly about it one way or the other.

Those occasions when Leo asserted his conjugal rights, as it was always referred to in the old-fashioned novels Philippa was fond of reading, were few and far between, becoming even fewer as his studies became more arduous and he sat up later over his books. When Philippa did hear that infrequent and hesitant tap on her door she would put down the book she was reading, and make room in her bed for him. There never was a repeat of that cold and clinical intercourse as on the night of their reunion, or the frenzy of the night of the opera, but a moderate and sometimes awkward intimacy lacking both passion and sentiment and which Philippa thought left Leo as unhappy as it did her. They had become two shy and remorseful people who could no longer communicate with each other.

And then, just as Philippa had discovered she was pregnant, Aunt Dot quietly began to die, making no bother about it, and finally flickering out like a candle on midsummer's day. She had outlived all her friends and, with the exception of Philippa, her relations too, so it was just a handful of people who followed the cortège to the cemetery at Prittlewell where she was buried in the same plot as her brother.

She left everything she possessed to Philippa which in

practice was not so impressive as it seemed on paper. The house, Philippa discovered, was leasehold, the ground belonging to one of the colleges of the London University. What was more there were only fifteen years before the lease expired.

'I doubt whether the house will last as long as that, anyway,' was the solicitor's dry comment. 'It has a bad subsidence. Underpinning will cost you more than the house is worth.'

For the first time since their marriage Philippa went voluntarily to Leo for advice.

'It's your house, you must do as you want with it,' he said.

'It's the only home we have at present.'

'I hope to put that right once I have my diploma.'

'I didn't mean . . .'

'I know you didn't.' He thought for a bit. 'I think we may as well stay put for the time being.'

For the first time in many months Philippa found time on her hands. She couldn't remember the last time she had only herself to think of. She passed the long, lonely hours spring-cleaning the house from top to bottom, then turning her energy on the garden. It struck her that she had no friends, not any within calling distance, anyway. She had given up all her time to her aunt and now that it had been returned to her she didn't know what to do with it.

She had the baby to prepare for of course, and had knitted one or two shapeless little garments, for like Aunt Dot she had no great skill as a knitter. But her heart wasn't in it. She had been through it all before, and now the memory of those fruitless months came back to haunt her. Was there another little Jennifer Anne growing in her womb? Would the coming baby expunge the guilt that was constantly gnawing at her conscience? She knew she would never be able to convince herself that she had done the right thing – that her baby was much better off with her adoptive parents than she would have been with her. She had given away Joe's daughter, and something within her had died in the giving. She would never allow herself to suffer in that way again and the best way to avoid such heartbreak was to look upon another child as a loan. This child she was bearing would, from the day it was born, she vowed, be its own person. She would make no claim upon it or consider it her possession. She would set it free.

The question of where to have the baby came up from time to time. Philippa wanted to have it at home, Leo didn't think much of that idea. He wanted her to attend the antenatal clinic, she said it was too soon to start yet. Like everything else the matter drifted unsolved between them, and the days went past.

She received a letter from Evelyn telling her that she and Clive were moving to Hampshire to be near Robin who was now working in the drawing office of an aircraft factory in the Southampton area. His fiancée was a staff nurse in a local hospital and they were planning to get married in August. As the girl had no family, Evelyn had taken over the planning of the wedding and couldn't disguise the satisfaction it was giving her.

'Just think,' her letter went, 'not having a daughter I never thought I'd ever be in this enviable position. Mother of the groom normally has nothing to say about the matter, now I'm having a say in everything. By the way, you wouldn't have any pre-war evening dresses you've grown out of, would you? It's so difficult getting

Felicity rigged out with a trousseau. I've kept my wedding dress wrapped in black tissue paper all these years, and it is still as good as new but it belongs to the period when dresses were worn above the knees and all we could get out of that is a slip or perhaps a pair of camiknicks. Any contribution that can be converted into a nightie or something similar will be gratefully received.'

Philippa sent off a pink chiffon, ankle-length dress lined with taffeta and received an ecstatic thank-you note by return.

'You don't honestly think we are going to cut this up for nightgowns do you? Felicity is overjoyed – it will do for her bridesmaid. We were all wondering how we were going to find sufficient coupons to kit the poor girl out. Your dress smells fragrantly of freesias and fits her like a dream. Felicity is very envious. She thinks her plain white crêpe dress will look extremely dull by contrast. She is a pet, Philippa, so right for Robin. In some ways she reminds me of you. Forgive me for being personal, dear, but how are things with you now? You should be happy. You have Leo, and a baby on the way, but I sometimes get an underlying sense of loneliness in your letters. . . .'

She had just replaced the pages in their envelope when she saw Leo coming up the track from the station. She was sitting out in the arbor at the side of the house soaking up the afternoon sun and he came across and sat himself beside her. Life was returning to normal. The sails of small pleasure boats fluttered like white moths upon the waters and the cries of children playing on the sands drifted on the salty air. It promised to be a mild and pleasant evening. On such an evening before the war she and Leo would have gone for a long tramp across the heathland at the back of the town. Now they never went on walks together.

'You're in early,' she said. 'I haven't got your supper ready yet.'

He was in a thoughtful mood. 'Would it break your heart to leave all this?'

'Leave what?' she said, her mind still back on pre-war days and the uncomplicated life she appeared to lead then.

'Leigh. This old house. The sea. Southend and its shops. Could you exchange all this for a village in Norfolk?'

She was taken by surprise at such an unexpected question, but nevertheless considered it. 'Yes, I think I would. I haven't any ties to keep me here now. But why ask?'

'I was smitten with Norfolk that week we spent there.' (He never referred to that time as their honeymoon.) 'I thought then I wouldn't mind living there. Last week I read in the *British Medical Journal* of a country practice for sale in a village in the Broads area. Thornmere. You knew Thornmere, didn't you?'

This was treading on dangerous ground and Philippa side-stepped carefully. 'Not all that well, I was more familiar with an old farmhouse two miles outside the village.'

'This particular practice covers Thornmere and the surrounding hamlets. Unfortunately, the house belongs to the late incumbent's mother and she's still in residence there, but there are quite a few houses for sale in the area. I've been up to Norwich today to see the solicitors who are acting for Mrs Morley. Her son was a naval medical officer and was lost at sea just before war ended. A tragic story. I met Mrs Morley too, a charming person.

She could have sold the practice before this but for her insistence on staying on at the house. She has her own flat at the top. An elderly doctor took over while her son went away, but he has since returned to his home in north Norfolk. There's a young locum holding the fort at present but he's anxious to get back to hospital work. He told me of a fine old house for sale not far from the surgery.... Am I boring you with all this?' For Philippa had gone very still.

'Not at all.'

'I had a look at the house while I was about it. It's a little gem. Queen Anne period, I believe. Funnily enough it's called "Rodings" – a familiar name in our part of Essex. I wonder if that's an omen.' A dig at her superstitious leanings, she thought. Or perhaps to kindle her interest.

'Are you serious about this?' she said at length.

'I am, very. I'd like to start somewhere afresh. I want to put down roots, have a place of my own.'

'But your hospital job – and your studies. Are you giving up your idea of becoming an anaesthetist?'

'No, I can carry on with my studies in Norfolk, and come down to London to take the exams when the time comes. Even if I don't practise as an anaesthetist, it will be a useful second string to my bow.'

'Can you afford to buy a practice?'

'No. Not if I intend to buy Rodings as well, but I can come to an arrangement with Mrs Morley about renting the premises for the time being. Hopefully I can arrange a mortgage for the house and my father is helping out with the deposit. He wants to sell up and move to Cornwall where he would have retired long before this if it hadn't been for the war. If and when he sells the Belle

Vue Road house, he intends to give us our legacies now, he says, instead of us waiting until he's dead. I'm hoping my whack will at least cover the deposit.'

'I could sell this house. That would help.'

For the first time since he had joined her on the bench he looked at her. She thought she saw something of his old affection kindling in his eyes, but it died before she could make sure.

'I don't think you'll get much for it, not with such a short lease. Better if you let it, as that will bring you in a little income, but be sure to do it through a reliable agent, and let it furnished otherwise you'll never be able to get the tenants out even if they should prove undesirable.'

She smiled to herself. The old, reliable, and cautious Leo was not completely extinct.

Nicholas Byrd Brooke was born at eight o'clock on the evening of Christmas day, 1946. A mild day, one of many such days before the full force of one of the coldest winters on record clamped down on the land, cutting off villages in many parts of the country, including Norfolk, causing shortages of fuel and compulsory power-cuts. When Mrs Toser heard of the birth she said, 'Poor little mite – now he's going to be done out of one lot of presents.'

Nicholas certainly didn't go short of anything that Christmas. The room he shared with his mother at the Carisbrooke Maternity Home of Beckton Market was quickly transformed into a floral bower. Once the post resumed after Boxing Day there soon wasn't space on the windowsill or mantelpiece to squeeze in another greetings card, and the shelf in the wardrobe was stacked with gifts.

He weighed eight and a half pounds and Philippa was in labour for just over two hours. 'Here's to the little mother who knows how to have babies,' boomed Dr Lucas when he visited her on Boxing Day morning. 'Leo been giving you lessons, eh?'

Dr Lucas was the Beckton GP Leo had entrusted her to. He was a big bluff man with a young and pretty wife whom he kept telling everybody he didn't deserve.

'He did better than that,' Philippa said. 'He bought me a book on natural childbirth and I read it so many times I knew it backwards.'

'I know that book, it caused quite a stir when it first came out. I gave Pat a copy and she threw it at me. She said she'd rather have old-fashioned chloroform. Now she's taking riding lessons to get back into shape again. Your tummy, Philippa, is beautifully flat.'

An image flashed on Philippa's inner eye of Sister Martin standing at the door of the long ward at Bardney Place beaming on her patients and chanting, 'Sit up like the letter L – guard those tender nipples well,' and 'Tummies, mummies.'

'What's this – tears?' Dr Lucas handed her his handkerchief. 'Can't have tears at a time like this.'

'It's just the reaction,' murmured Sister at his side. 'And the excitement – she's had far too many visitors.'

Leo had been the first, of course, coming hard on the phone call with the news. Fresh from the labour ward, washed, and smelling faintly of lavender talc, Philippa, sitting up in bed looking pink-cheeked and pretty in a fluffy bedjacket was awaiting his arrival with outward calm, and inward quaking.

When Nicholas was first put into her arms her immediate reaction was one of disappointment. For one thing she had wanted a girl and for another he was the image of her father-in-law. Later, back in her room, when he was given to her again, this time to be fed, he had been swabbed and dressed and the initial rawness had given way to a healthy pink, but he still looked like her father-in-law. Nurse Wentworth, coming in with yet more flowers, said, 'Having trouble, mother?'

'I can't wake him up, and Sister said I was to try and feed him.'

'It's not actually milk yet, but it's important that he gets it. Come along young man, your supper's waiting.'

Nicholas gave an enormous yawn, and the nurse, taking advantage of the gaping mouth hooked him on to his mother's breast. Philippa, unprepared, cried out in painful surprise. Nurse went 'Tch tch'.

'Surely you expected that – it always hurts the first few times. . . . Don't you remember from your first?'

'Unfortunately, I wasn't able to feed my first.'

The nurse, with a look at Philippa's face, thought it wiser not to pursue the subject. All she knew about her patient, and that only from her notes, was that she was the wife of a newly established general practitioner at Thornmere, and not a primigravida.

'Well, now that he's found it he's not going to let it go, is he,' she said cheerfully. 'My word, he's got powerful sucking pads – and a good appetite. He'll take some feeding, that one.'

'It runs in the family,' said Philippa with resignation. Now that the pain of suckling was easing up a warm and pleasant sensation took its place. Nurse stayed by the bedside smiling indulgently.

'That's right, you've got the hang of it. Now switch him to the other breast before he falls asleep again. Remember, the more he sucks the quicker your tummy will get back to normal.'

Philippa didn't mind in the least being instructed by a girl younger than herself. She liked having Rita Wentworth around her, and could put up with her bossiness because she was cheerful with it. Smugly she said, 'Dr Lucas thought my tummy had flattened very nicely.'

'And Dr Lucas is an expert on flat tummies – with his bay window?' They both giggled at that, and were still giggling when Leo walked in on them. Nurse Wentworth took the baby and Philippa hastily drew her dressing-gown across her exposed breast, an action not lost on the observant nurse.

'Let me hold him before you put him back in his cot,' said Leo. His expression as he took Nicholas in his arms was one of joyful pride. He examined his son's toes, his fingers, his ears, but had to forgo the eyes as they were now tightly shut. He even unpinned the nappy and had a good look in there too.

Nurse Wentworth sent a mischievous look in Philippa's direction. 'Anything missing, Doctor?'

'All present and correct,' Leo quipped. 'Poor little chap, he's had a rough ride.'

'He has not,' said Philippa indignantly. 'He had it jolly easy. . . .'

But Leo was too engrossed with his son to heed her, looking at him in the way he had once looked at her. She felt a thickening at the back of her throat, not a gathering of tears of sentiment so much as of self-pity. Was it expecting too much, she wondered, for Leo to show her a little attention too? Nurse tactfully took her leave, which

Philippa thought quite unnecessary. Nothing was likely to pass between Leo and herself that couldn't be said before strangers.

Sister was in her office enjoying a sherry. 'Christmas present from a grateful father,' she explained. 'Help yourself.'

Nurse Wentworth felt flattered. Rarely had she seen Sister in such a mellow mood. Must be the Christmas spirit, she thought, pouring herself a helping of sherry and hoping it wouldn't turn out to be too dry. It looked alarmingly pale.

She said, 'First time most new fathers come to visit their wives, they bring flowers, and are sometimes quite tearful, and always kiss them before they even look in the cot. But Dr Brooke seemed more interested in the baby than he did his wife. Don't you think that odd?'

Rita Wentworth, though young and not always mindful of her place, was an excellent and willing nurse, otherwise Sister would have reprimanded her for passing personal remarks about the patients.

'He's a doctor,' she said, as if that explained everything. 'I expect his interest in the baby was purely professional. He was keeping his non-professional attitude towards his wife until they were alone.'

It was true that once they were on their own Leo brought a chair up to the bed. 'I gather it was easy for you, too. No difficulties like last time?'

There, it had been said and with that hurdle behind them they could now converse like human beings.

'No difficulties at all,' Philippa answered lightly. But it had not been all that easy. The old cut had split open and had to be stitched up again. The doctor had given her Nicholas to hold while he got on with that job, and in the agony that followed she clung on to the small bundle as if for life.

'Hey,' Dr Lucas had boomed, 'don't take it out on your infant, take it out on me. I'm the one who's doing the hurting. . . .' But when it was all over he had patted her shoulder and said, 'I wish all my confinements were as easy as this one.'

Easy. *Easy*. A word flung about indiscriminately. Yes, it had been an easy passage for Nicholas, that pale little wraith of a sister had paved the way. Oh Jennifer Anne, where are you now?

Leo was watching her. 'What were you thinking about just then?'

'I – I don't think I was thinking about anything in particular.'

'You looked as if you were thinking about something extremely particular.' He rose. 'But you must be tired. It's been a long day for you and what you need now is sleep. I'll call in tomorrow morning – is that okay?'

'You know you don't have to ask.'

He bent over and kissed her on the forehead. 'Thank you for my son,' he said.

She was on her own and free now to give way to tears. It helps to cry, she had been told at Bardney Place, crying is part of the healing process. Obviously, she hadn't cried enough then for she certainly wasn't healed. She suspected that all the crying in the world wouldn't stem the aching loss of that other baby. But Nicholas might do that, given time.

Of all the visitors she had on Boxing Day the one who brought her the greatest joy was Nellie Timms, daughter-in-law of the postmistress of Thornmere.

That she found herself living in Thornmere of all

places was incredible enough to Philippa, but to find that the woman who served her stamps for the change of address cards she intended to send out was the same woman who had been her comfort and stay at Bardney seemed little less than a miracle.

They goggled at each other, speechless at first, then Nellie came running round the counter and gave her a tremendous hug.

'Philippa Byrd, of all people! I thought I was seeing things. Gosh, how long ago is it now? Just over three years – unbelievable! You haven't changed a scrap. Wish I could say the same.'

But Nellie hadn't changed, not in the way that mattered. A little more mature, perhaps, but still overflowing with the milk of human kindness. It showed in her eyes, her voice, and her large toothy smile.

'Brooke, now. Philippa Brooke,' Philippa informed her.

Nellie held her at arm's length. 'You don't mean to say you're the new doctor's wife! Well, I never. We've heard masses about him, but nothing about you except that you're expecting. Yes, I can see that is true.' She gave Philippa another hug, more carefully this time. 'I'm so happy for you. Congratulations. When is the great day?'

'Christmas.'

'Another three months... That will soon pass, and then bingo – Happy Christmas. It will be a happy Christmas won't it?' Her eyes held Philippa's for a moment, then looked away. Bless you, Philippa thought. Nellie was someone to be relied upon not to ask unwanted and embarrassing questions.

They walked back together to the red and white house at the north end of the village for as soon as Nellie heard that there was still some unpacking to do she insisted on coming to help do it.

'Ma-in-law will look after the shop, she likes to keep her hand in. I can't wait for Don's younger brother to finish his National Service. He'll be able to take over the post office store then and leave Don and me to look for a place of our own. Not that Mrs Timms doesn't make us welcome, but you know what it's like with three active youngsters about the place. . . . No, not yet you don't, but you will do. By the way, my Don is teaching at an elementary school in Beckton. I'd got so used to country life I didn't want to move back to London. And though he earns less than he would in London, there's other things that mean more.'

'Does that mean you'll be moving to Beckton, just when I've found you again?'

'Oh no, you wouldn't get my Don living on the job. We've put a deposit on one of the houses being built along School Lane, up past the pre-fabs. They haven't started the actual building yet but the plots are all sold. I'm not too happy about living on an estate, but at least it will be a brand new house and all our own. Not very big though. Did you know that new houses aren't allowed to be larger than a thousand square feet? I suppose there's a reason for it, shortage of bricks or manpower or whatever. I'm not grumbling, there's too many without homes at all. Two of Don's old army pals are squatting in empty Nissen huts. At least we won't have to come down to that.'

When they reached the Queen Anne house Nellie said, 'The times I've walked past this lovely little place and broken the commandment that says not to covet your neighbour's house and all the rest of it. A Miss Roseberry used to live here, according to Ma-in-law, and what she doesn't know about the inhabitants of this village could be written on the back of a ha'penny stamp. She, this Miss Roseberry, married a Mr Harker who owned the Hall – the big house the army has knocked about a bit. They had a son, or he did, though Ma-in-law says there's a bit of mystery about that, and they now live in America. He made his money first out of canning food, and now he's something to do with the frozen food industry. They go in for things like that in America, but I don't believe it will ever cotton on over here.'

Already, the ancient walnut tree in the small front garden was shedding its leaves. Autumn with its mellow days, its gold and red and sepia landscape, the smell of woodsmoke, and the farewell cries of pheasants was just around the corner. Philippa had always loved autumn, but autumn now brought painful memories. Nellie, seeing sadness cloud her face, said cautiously, 'Are you ready for this, living in Thornmere?'

Philippa did not immediately answer. There was a time when the thought of seeing Thornmere again would have been unthinkable. 'But it was like cutting off my nose to spite my face,' she told Nellie now. 'Some of my happiest memories are rooted in this village. This house coming on the market just when it did seemed as if it was meant to be.'

'So you've laid a few ghosts to rest?'

'Not all of them.'

'Let them go, Philippa. Let them go. Let them make way for a new generation.'

Now Nellie, seating herself on a chair near Philippa's bed, looked about for the latest member of that new generation and saw that the cot was empty.

'So where's the son and heir then?'

'Being changed. They'll bring him soon, he's due for a feed.'

Nellie loosened her scarf. It was cold outside and she looked as if she had had a battle with the wind and lost. Her hair was coming loose from her hat and her eyes were watering. There were about ten years difference in the ages of the two women but Nellie was one of those people who could adapt easily to any age group, and when with Philippa behaved like a slightly older and caring sister.

'Are they feeding you all right?' she said. 'I've brought you some butter and eggs in case you were going short, and a slab of chocolate I nicked from the shop.'

'Matron won't allow nursing mothers to have chocolate. She says it gives the babies sore tails.'

'What rubbish. They gave chocolate to the troops during the war and I don't remember Don complaining of a sore tail. Mind you, he complained about everything else. Do you remember the gorgeous food they gave us at Bardney Place?' A look of remembered bliss crossed her face. 'Rabbit pie, jugged hare, trout from the stream – all from the Bardney estate. Artichokes from the kitchen garden. Cream from their Jersey cow. We lived like Lords. Better – we lived like the family.' She brought herself up short. 'I'm sorry, I wasn't thinking. I don't suppose you remember.'

'I can remember everything about Bardney Place except the food.'

'Do you want me to stay? I seem to be saying all the wrong things.'

'Of course I want you to stay. Besides you haven't met Nicholas yet. Ah, that's him now.'

They could hear Nicholas long before he arrived. He cried on a deep baying note that distinguished him from the other babies in the nursery. 'He's got his father's voice,' said Nellie with a chuckle. 'Does he look like him too?'

'He's the image of my father-in-law.'

'Who wants him?' said Nurse Wentworth.

'Oh, let me.' Nellie held out her arms. 'Oh, the sweetie. It makes me feel quite broody holding a baby again.' She rocked him for a moment or two, making those unintelligible noises that all otherwise sensible women adopt when crooning to babies. 'How can you say that he looks like your father-in-law! Not that I know what your father-in-law looks like, but he couldn't possibly look as cherubic as this little one. Diddums, my pet, what are they saying about you, then.'

Nurse Wentworth had gone. Philippa leaned forward, her eyes anxiously fixed on Nellie's face. 'Do you see any likeness between him and little Jennifer Anne? Any at all?'

'Philippa, what a thing to ask me. I only saw her for a few minutes, and then she was wrapped in a shawl....'

'You said she was like a little doll and had the bluest eyes you'd ever seen....'

'All new-born babies have blue eyes.... I might have got carried away.'

'You are the only one who can tell me what she looked like. I was relying on you. Try. Oh, please try, Nellie. Any little thing you can remember.'

Anything Nell could have done she would have done to appease this unhappy woman, but pretend she could not. She placed Nicholas carefully in his mother's arms. 'You've got a lovely little boy, rejoice in that. Don't start looking for comparisons because that way leads to heartbreak.' She dropped a kiss on the top of the baby's head. 'Count yourself lucky, Philippa, that you have a fine, healthy son.'

'That's what I keep telling myself.'

'Then believe it.'

On her way out Nell was accosted by Sister who asked her into the office. 'You're a close friend of Mrs Brooke, I believe.'

'I haven't known her all that long, but yes, I suppose I am.'

'It's just that I'm wondering if there's anything on her mind – if she's fretting about something. I've seen that same look on the faces of mothers of stillborn infants, and it's made me think. Did she lose her first child?'

That was the assumption of all those who didn't know the full story behind Philippa's visit to Bardney Place, and to spare her feelings they had none of them gone further into the subject. Only the staff and Nellie herself and Evelyn and Clive Smith had known the details. Nellie had no compunction now in letting Sister assume the same.

Sister nodded. 'I guessed it was something like that. And now, of course, it's all come back to her. Still, there's compensation. She's got a lovely little boy, he'll take her mind off the one that she's lost.'

'That's what I've been trying to tell her,' said Nellie.

It was dark when Mrs Toser called carrying a gift wrapped in Christmas paper.

'Sorry about that,' she said. 'But it did seem a waste of money buying fresh paper when I had lots of that left over. It all finishes up in the dustbin, anyway. Everybody brings presents for the baby, so I thought I'd do different, as they say, and bring you something instead. I hope it fits you, I only just had enough wool.'

'It's beautiful. Such a pretty colour too,' said Philippa, saying nothing about the three other gift bedjackets in the wardrobe. 'Did you have a good Christmas?'

'Quiet, just Red and me. It'll be noisier tonight when my cousin from Horning and her brood come over for supper, so I mustn't stay long.' She had only just sat down, now she got up again as if fearful of making herself too comfortable. 'I left Red peeling the potatoes but I can't trust him to take the eyes out, so I'll have to go over them again.' She looked appraisingly around the room. 'This place do look a lot better than when I first saw it; brighter too. It were a dingy ole place in those days. It's been extended too, tha' makes a difference.'

'You had one of your babies here?'

Mrs Toser hooted. 'Me pay out good money to have a baby in someone else's bed! No, I'm talking about long afore it was a nursing home. I come here as a general help when it was a school. I didn't stay long, couldn't stand the vinegary ole maid tha' bossed me around. Uster run her handkerchief along the ledges to see if I'd dusted them properly, and once when I was short of time and hadn't turned her mattress she pulled all the bedding off the bed and dumped in on the floor. She and her father ran the school between them, but when the father died, way back in the twenties, she sold up and moved down south again. I didn't do myself much good in my next post either. I liked the work and I got on well with the cook I worked under, but it was there I met my husband 'cos he was the gardener, wasn't he. Worst day's work in my life when I married him.'

'But you wouldn't be without your family, Mrs Toser?'

'No, but it were a high price to pay.' Now, she adjusted her hat and replaced her gloves. 'Where's this baby? I must have a peek at him afore I go.'

'He's in the nursery. You can't mistake him, he's wearing a green matinée coat.'

'*Green*!'

'I bought the wool for its softness, not its colour.'

Nicky had been given his last feed of the day and was now back in his cot when Leo arrived, his eyes red-rimmed with fatigue. With the servicemen back from the war zones, the number of babies being born was booming and a country doctor in Leo's position, feeling his way in a new environment, was rushed off his feet. Then too his exams were looming so he had to squeeze in time at the end of the day for studying. Also, Philippa knew, he wasn't one to sit around when there were jobs crying out for attention. For the later part of the war the house had been used as an officers' mess and like most temporary and impersonal quarters had had to put up with a lot of misuse.

Philippa and Leo didn't grumble about this; it was because of its neglected condition that they had got the house at such a knockdown price, added to the fact that the owner, living at such a distance, had only been too pleased to be rid of it. They hoped in time to furnish it with period pieces but for the time being were grateful for anything they could get. The things Philippa had inherited from the Woodside house took pride of place in the drawing room, along with the Chinese rug and ivory ornaments Leo had bought in Hong Kong. The Bechstein, which Ursula did not want, was being renovated by a firm in Norwich before being installed in the smaller of the two sitting rooms, for Leo could play the piano, though not up to professional standard. The bedrooms were still rather sparse, but until they could afford better they were making do with the heavy old bedsteads from Cliff Cottage. Most of Aunt Dorothy's furniture, being riddled with woodworm, had been destroyed. The present tenant was quite happy to treat what remained.

Philippa felt that the joint interest and pleasure in their new home was welding a fresh bond between Leo and herself. It was the one subject they could talk about without restraint or fear of being misunderstood. Leo had ambitious plans. He wanted to convert the old stable block into a garage. He wanted to build a conservatory leading off the larger sitting room. He wanted the small room in the front made into a study. He wanted to landscape the garden.

'Leave that to me,' pleaded Philippa at the time. 'I enjoy gardening. I'd love to redesign the garden.'

'You'll be busy with the baby.'

'Not all the time, surely.'

Watching him now she thought he looked a man with a mission. He had always had a single-mindedness of purpose which she had envied. Nothing diverted him from a set course once he had made up his mind on it. His course at the moment was to get his diploma in anaesthetics, then to get his house in order. Lately, she had noticed there had been more contentment or, perhaps more accurately, resignation in his attitude, as if something he could not put right he had at last accepted. As he bent over to kiss Nicky good night, she had a sudden painful awareness of his oneness with his son. She had had that place in his heart once, but now no longer.

She had too much pride to let him see now how that affected her and instead said flippantly, 'You've got cobwebs in your hair. Have you been mooching around in the cellar?'

'No, in the attics. Do you know, there's enough room up there to build two more bedrooms.'

'But we've got enough bedrooms.'

'You can never have enough bedrooms. With one as a nursery and another I'd like to convert to a second bathroom, that only leaves three including ours.'

She wondered if he had in mind the thought of them reverting to a bedroom each. She had got used to sharing a bed with him and liked feeling the warmth of his body close to hers and waking and listening to his rhythmic breathing in the night. After sleeping on her own all her life she liked sleeping now with someone else in the bed.

He took from his pocket a small package. 'It's about time I gave you your Christmas present.'

'We were going to forgo them this year.'

'This one is long overdue.' He took a small leather box out of a jeweller's envelope, and gave it to her to open and felt quite surprised at the effect on her when she saw what was within. 'Do you like it?' he said.

It was an eternity ring set with sapphires and diamonds and fitted her perfectly. 'I was determined not to make the same mistake twice, and get one too big,' he said. Then again, 'Do you like it?'

She was still struggling with tears. 'I don't really deserve it.'

He didn't answer to that. 'I never did buy you a proper engagement ring. I hope this will redress the balance.'

Does he have to address me as if I were a member of the Hospital Management Committee, she wondered disconsolately. An important milestone had come and gone, and neither of them had had the courage to make the most of it. The urge to pull his face down to hers and kiss him full on the lips was overwhelming, but she felt to do so would cause them both acute embarrassment.

She put the ring back in the box and the box in its wrapping. 'Do you mind looking after it at home?' she said. 'I don't want it to get mislaid or damaged.'

It was an unfortunate choice of words. It recalled to both that other ring that *did* get damaged, irrevocably. He pocketed the ring without a word. He went across to the cot and touched Nicky tenderly on his cheek, then chuckled. 'He's trying to eat his fist,' he said. Everything Nicky did was a delight to him. He wished her good night but without a kiss, even on her cheek, perhaps because Nurse Wentworth came in just then to take Nicholas to the nursery. An omission that Nurse Wentworth noted and reported on to Sister later.

'Are all doctors like that in their private lives?' she wondered. 'You know what I mean – short on the loving side.'

'I wouldn't know,' Sister answered. 'I have never had a private life with a doctor.'

Of all the visitors Philippa had during her two weeks at the nursing home, the most bizarre was her neighbour in the room next door. With her own door open she had watched as parcels and bouquets of flowers were delivered to the next-door room day after day. Her curiosity was eased by Nurse Wentworth.

'She's stunning. She looks just like a film star and her husband is just as handsome. He comes every day to see her and brings her flowers every time. They must have pots of money – you should see his car. But he gives her lilies. Lilies! It's beginning to look like a funeral parlour in there.'

Philippa had the opportunity to see her glamorous neighbour that same afternoon. She was feeding Nicholas and managing to read *Housewife* at the same time, the only magazine she could hold with comfort in one hand because of its small size, when she became suddenly aware of a visitor on the threshold. Philippa gaped as this gold and white vision came into the room. From her ash-blond hair to the elegantly varnished toe-nails peeping out of her white satin mules, she shimmered.

'Oh, aren't you lucky,' she crooned. 'You have such perfectly wonderful nipples.'

Philippa had been complimented many times on her eyes, but never before on her nipples. A desperate urge to laugh came over her. She was glad Nurse Wentworth was not in the room just then for not to laugh then would have been an impossibility.

'I've got no nipples at all,' the other went on abjectly. 'Not so you'd notice. They are retracted or inverted or whatever they call it.' Tears welled in her lovely eyes. 'They're no use to my baby at all so I have to give her a bottle. You wouldn't know how I miss not being able to feed her.'

Nicky's eyes were melting with sleep. Philippa laid him carefully on the bed by her side. 'You have a little girl?'

'Would you like to see her?'

'Very much.'

She was tiny, and as Nellie had said when describing that other – just like a little doll; fair-skinned and blue-eyed with long silky lashes the same colour as her hair. She was a week older than Nicky and half his size.

'She really is a little darling,' said Philippa wistfully, allowing herself to dream. When it was time to give her back she felt quite a tug at her heart. Oh, Nicholas, why couldn't you have been a girl, she wept silently, and then gave thanks that he was not, for a granddaughter of Samuel Brooke was quite likely to grow up to take size nine in shoes and ride a motor bike.

When, during her second week, she was allowed to get up and sit out in her dressing-gown she had the most surprising visitor of all. Her stepmother!

She had never known Ursula's age but had put her, when she first knew her, to be in her early forties which would make her forty-seven or eight now. She looked considerably older. Her pale eyes had faded to an oyster colour and there was a nervousness about her that was quite alien to her character. Yet she was as svelte as always, and the jaunty little velvet hat she wore certainly didn't carry a utility mark.

'This is quite a surprise,' said Philippa, feeling that she had just made the most inane utterance of her life.

'I thought if I announced my arrival, you might put me off.'

'Why should I do that?'

Ursula gave a thin-lipped smile. 'We have never exactly hit it off, have we?' She walked over to the cot and surveyed the sleeping occupant. 'Your father would have been so proud,' she said softly. 'He always wanted a son.'

Philippa gathered her wandering thoughts. 'How did you know I had a son?' Ursula was the only one who had not been notified. She had thought about it and decided not to.

'I read about it in *The Times*.'

How odd. She knew Leo had intended to put an announcement in the *British Medical Journal*, but he had said nothing about *The Times*. It was not a paper they normally read, but it had universal appeal for the insertion of Births and Deaths and Marriages. Perhaps he was hoping the announcement would be seen by ex-college friends or army colleagues. He was so overjoyed at having a son she wouldn't have been surprised if he had yelled the event from the housetop.

Ursula had unbuttoned her coat and seated herself by the end of the bed. Philippa felt increasingly uncomfortable for small talk did not come naturally to her. 'Have you had any lunch?' she ventured finally.

'I ate on the train.'

'A cup of tea then?'

'I'd appreciate that.'

Tea was rung for and a tray was brought to them. They drank in silence, Philippa feeling Ursula's eyes upon her every time she looked away. At last good manners obliged her to ask after Charlie and immediately she wished she hadn't for the effect of that simple question on Ursula was shattering. She went to pieces.

'The bastard has left me,' she sobbed.

Ursula was not the sort of person to weep easily, but now she did so quite unselfconsciously, and Philippa looked on with a feeling of helplessness, not knowing how to comfort her.

At last the storm of tears blew itself out. It was too fierce to last long. Ursula dried her eyes and took out her makeup mirror.

'My God, what a hag I look.' She powdered her nose and reddened her lips afresh. Such a red slash in an otherwise colourless face gave her the look of a clown. A pitiful clown, Philippa thought. Ursula caught her eye, and gave her a fleeting and enigmatic smile. 'I'm sorry about that. It was the last thing I intended.'

'Perhaps you needed to get it out of your system.'

'Perhaps.' Ursula snapped shut her compact and replaced it in her handbag. 'I thought I could get through this with my dignity intact, but it's obvious that I can't, so I'll tell you straight out. I've come to ask you a favour – an extremely large favour.'

Though somewhat taken aback, Philippa said without hesitation; 'If I can help in any way . . .'

'I believe you really mean that, which is making it harder for me to go on. Now, if you had only gloated. . . . Oh dear, I am making this difficult for myself. I'll get the worst over first. Charlie has left me for someone younger and better-endowed, in the financial sense, I mean. He's left me penniless.'

'But the business.'

'There never was a business, not in the true sense of the word. Charlie's business was making money without actually having to work for it. The war gave him wonderful opportunities. All that talk of building up an engineering works on that old Stratford site – that was all my eye and Betty Martin. We've been living on the money we raised on the sale of that for the past eighteen months, and now it's all gone, and Charlie's gone too, and I'm left to cope as well as I can, which isn't too well at the present.' She looked down at her spread-eagled fingers. 'I sold the ring your father gave me to pay for this outfit. I couldn't bring myself to come to you in sackcloth and ashes. If I'm going down I'll go down with my colours flying, I thought, then I spoilt everything by crying like a boob.'

There was still much Philippa didn't understand.

'But the works in Slough – the government contract...'

'Yes, there was an engineering works in Slough and they did land a very effective government contract, but Charlie was only a sort of glorified office-boy and he didn't keep that for very long. He was sacked for selling the firm's petrol on the black market. It was only my intervention that stopped him from going to prison.'

'But you were hand in glove. You must have known what he was like.'

'I loved him.'

Again Philippa felt a surge of pity for this woman who had no pity on herself. She fought it down. 'You passed him off as your brother,' she said accusingly. 'In some ways you are as bad as he is.'

Ursula raised impassive eyes. 'He *is* my brother,' she said.

In the silence that followed Philippa heard the ticking of the clock pounding like the beat of a frightened heart. She stared at Ursula with incredulous eyes, wanting so much not to believe what she had just heard, knowing too well that it was true. Poor Daddy, she thought, thank God he is dead.

'Your *brother*!' she repeated stupidly.

'Half-brother to be exact. We only shared the same mother.' Ursula had adopted a conversational tone. 'I was six when he was born. It was a day I shall never forget. I had never liked dolls, stupid inanimate objects I thought them, but here was a living doll, warm and cuddly and full of life. I had never loved anyone before.

My step-father didn't like me, and my mother had no time for me, busy as she was running the shop. She didn't have a lot of time for Charlie either, so most of the caring was left to me. There was never anyone else who mattered to me as much as he did.'

'But you married. You were a Mrs Warwick when you first came to work for my father.'

'Yes, I married. I would have married Charlie if the law had allowed it, but as it was I had to find someone to look after us both, and in any case it was a good cover-up. Oh, don't look at me in that fashion. It was no great sin loving my brother. In some ancient cultures brothers and sisters were expected to marry, and I believe Lord Byron had an affair with his half-sister. It doesn't make his poetry any the less acceptable, does it?'

'Was your marriage to my father also a cover-up?' For that to Philippa seemed the worst betrayal of all.

'No!' Ursula's retort was immediate and sharp. 'I cared for your father, I would have been true to him, but after his illness . . .' A slight shrug, a ghost of an apologetic smile. 'I could never say no to Charlie. Nobody could say no to Charlie. Even Jonathan called him a likeable rogue.'

Philippa flinched to hear her father's name spoken in such a context. The whole idea of Ursula and Charlie carrying on their sordid affair with him lying ill in the next room, suddenly filled her with a sickening rage. She wanted Ursula out of her sight. 'If you've finished what you came to say will you please go now.'

'But I haven't finished.'

'I've heard enough.'

'Not what I came to ask you.' Ursula leant forward in her chair, her pale eyes fixed on Philippa with an urgency

Philippa found disconcerting. 'Charlie married his wealthy widow, and they set sail for America last week. Oh, I shall see him again one day, no doubt, when he's got through her money and has no one else to turn to, and like a fool I'll take him in. But that's not what I came about. I was wondering . . . no, I'm begging you to consider selling Byrd's House. I can no longer afford to live there but it's the only home I've got. All I want is enough money to buy myself a cheap little flat. There's so much needs doing to your father's house—' She corrected herself, 'I mean your house. As you know it hasn't been redecorated since before the war, and there are repairs that badly need doing. What it would cost to do it up would buy me a home of my own, and I would repay you. I'm not too old to find myself a job, not in these days of full employment. If you sell the house and make me a loan I'll swear on your father's grave that I'll repay every penny.'

It was a long speech for someone like Ursula who normally communicated, at least with her, in short and sometimes cryptic sentences. Philippa's first reaction had been to give a decided refusal, then she had second thoughts. What was the point of hanging on to the Woodside house, it was almost in as bad a state of disrepair as Aunt Dot's. If Ursula left she would have to find a reliable tenant, and twice in one year going through all that involved was twice too many. There was no denying the money would come in handy to pay off some of the bank loan on Rodings and any left over would go towards the cost of the alterations and improvements that Leo had set his heart on.

'I can't give you an answer right now,' she said. 'It's something I would have to talk over with my husband.'

Ursula nodded. She buttoned her coat, and drew on her gloves. 'I can't ask more of you than that.' Surprisingly, she kissed Philippa before she left, just a brushing of cold lips across her face. All the suppressed passion Philippa suspected her of was kept in store for her brother.

One last look out from those milk-coloured eyes, one last cynical smile. Ursula could not leave without her customary touch of malice.

'Don't judge too harshly,' she said, 'remember, few of us are without sin. Few of us have nothing on our conscience,' leaving Philippa with the heart-sinking thought that her father might have betrayed her.

Nicky was seven months old and in the process of being weaned before the sale of the Woodside house finally went through. It was bought by a local builder and the whole of that private road was due for redevelopment which made Philippa feel something of a traitor.

'There haven't been any houses built for over six years,' Leo reminded her. 'People are crying out for houses. You can't hold back the tide of progress. That new estate would have been built whether you sold your old house or not, so stop fretting.'

Fretting was something she did quite a bit of these days. Little things got on her nerves and she cried a lot. She wanted very much to give up feeding Nicky as she blamed this as the cause of her lowering health but Leo urged her to carry on for a little while longer. She began to see there were disadvantages in being married to a doctor for she couldn't pretend an illness she hadn't got. After a few searching questions, Leo knew better.

The only time that they came anywhere near quarrelling was over the sore question of Nicky's feeds. About a week after Nicky's homecoming Leo had come in from the surgery for a quick cup of tea before going on his rounds. And in the morning room he found Philippa on the point of tears, trying to pacify a crimson-faced and howling infant.

'What's up? What's the matter with him? You haven't left a pin sticking in him?'

Already at the end of her tether, Philippa now lost her temper. 'Oh yes, I make quite a habit of using Nicky as a pin-cushion, didn't you know! There's *nothing* wrong with him except temper. Now he's started crying he can't stop.'

'He is crying because he's either in pain or he's hungry,' said Leo coldly. 'An infant of that age doesn't cry like that without reason. When was he last fed?'

'Two o'clock. His next feed isn't due until six.'

'And you intend to let him scream like that for the next twenty minutes?'

'I sometimes give him a little warm water, unsweetened of course. That quietens him for a bit. . . .'

'If I were starving and some idiot offered me a glass of warm water, sweetened or not, I'd throw it at him. Have you ever experienced hunger pains – pains that gnaw at your belly? That's what Nicky is feeling now. Sit down there, woman, and feed him. That's what breasts are for, or did you think they were put there solely to hold up your bra.'

One look at Leo's face and Philippa did as she was told. A moment later peace reigned. Leo began pacing up and down the floor his face like a thunder cloud. There was a time when he had viewed her breasts in quite a different light but she didn't think this the moment to remind him.

'Where were you taught this tomfool idea of feeding at set hours?' he said, stopping before her.

'From Dr Truby King's book. It's the modern mother's handbook on how to rear a child. All mothers I know practise giving feeds at four-hourly intervals. It's just a question of having patience; the baby soon falls into a routine.'

The look he gave her made her feel about two inches tall. 'So all over the country mothers are feeding their babies at 6 a.m., 10 a.m., 2 p.m., 6 p.m. and 10 p.m, and so on. What happens if you don't happen to have a clock?'

She refused to be drawn. 'In time, babies find their own rhythm.'

'You mean the mother's time. This is what it's all about, isn't it – the mother's convenience? Hard luck if it's not convenient for the infant, he'll just have to go hungry. Well, there will be no more feeding by the clock in this house. You'll feed Nicholas when he's hungry, and if you're lucky he might fall in with your four-hourly routine, but I can't guarantee it will be precisely at the time Dr Truby King advocates.'

His tone, when he spoke again, had softened a little. 'Don't you realise all babies are not the same? Their requirements differ just the same as in other young animals. Take a lesson from mother animals, Philippa. They can't tell the time, but their young don't go hungry.'

He had long sinced stopped addressing her by his old pet names. She rarely heard the terms 'sweetie-pie' or 'pussyfoot' or 'dearest girl', now. She had to go back to his letters for that. Once, just to hear the name Philippa from his lips would have thrilled her. Now, contrary-wise, she longed for the old endearments instead. There are more ways of going hungry than starving, she thought. She wouldn't have minded some regular attention every four hours.

By the time Nicky was seven months old he could sit unaided and had grown two teeth. Philippa knew that to her cost at feeding times. She didn't begrudge Nicky the time it took to feed him, but she did find it becoming increasingly tedious because he took so long about it. He had, too, an uncanny way of staring at her while he suckled as if weighing her in the balance, and she couldn't be sure whether he found her wanting or not. His eyes, though widely spaced like his father's and grey like hers, were in shape and expression entirely his own. He was a handsome child. Her early fears that he would take after his grandfather had faded before she left the nursing home.

Her in-laws came up from Cornwall to visit her during her time there. Neither could see any likeness to Leo. 'He looks more like Churchill to me,' said Mr Brooke with a grunt.

Her mother-in-law murmured mournfully, 'I was hoping it would be a girl. I've got five grandsons already. Philippa, do you think you could produce a girl for me, next time.'

Sister who was in the room, spoke up. 'I rejoice when another boy is born. Think of all those little girls needing husbands. There were never enough to go round in my time.'

The day Leo caught her reading a novel while feeding Nicky was one she would not easily forget. She looked up to see him watching her. 'You even begrudge him the short time it takes to feed him,' he said.

'What a beastly thing to say. I don't begrudge him anything.'

'Oh no? What about your time, your attention, your love? When did you last kiss him?'

When you are nowhere near, she could have retorted. She was too embarrassed to kiss or cuddle Nicky in front of Leo, in case he too weighed her in the balance and found her wanting.

Now he took the offending book from her and threw it on the table. 'There will be no more of this. God knows what damage you've done to his psyche already.'

That was it! Philippa got to her feet and put Nicky into his father's arms. 'Let's see you practise what you preach,' she said. 'You obviously think I'm a rotten mother – let's see what sort of a mother *you* make.'

She ran up the stairs and into the guest room, bolting the door after her. Leo did not follow. She sat on the bed and strained her ears. He had obviously scored a goal for motherhood for she heard no angry or hungry cries. She had been supplementing Nicky's feed for some weeks, giving him diluted cow's milk sweetened with lactose which he took greedily. Leo was probably doing the same. Later that evening the telephone rang and shortly afterwards the car started up. An emergency most likely. Philippa crept into the nursery. Nicky was still awake and became excited at the sight of her, eager to be picked up. She took him on to her lap and undid the front of her dress.

'Of course I love you, my pet,' she said as her lips brushed the top of his head. 'My trouble is that I'm scared of loving you too much.'

*

It seemed to her that from then on Nicholas became the innocent cause of most of the disagreements in the house. None of them really serious until the question of schooling came up. There was a choice of the village school where all three of the Timms boys attended or a small private school at Beckton Market which had the reputation of getting all their pupils through the eleven-plus. Alternatively, there were many good schools in Norwich, but that was too far for a five-year-old to travel.

Leo was all in favour of the village school whose headmistress was a patient of his and for whom he had a lot of respect. Philippa wanted Nicky to go to the private school in Beckton because that could lead to the grammar school which had a history going back to the sixteenth century.

'What are your objections to the village school?' Leo asked. Nicholas wouldn't be five until Christmas but both schools were willing to take him at the beginning of the Michaelmas term.

'I want him to pass his eleven-plus.'

'For heaven's sake – we don't have to start thinking about that for another six years.'

'We have to start thinking about it *now*. It takes years to drill them for the eleven-plus. It's more of an intelligence test than a straightforward exam, and I've been told they slip in a few trick questions. Miss Adams at Beverley House keeps old exam papers and uses them for coaching her pupils. She even sets mock eleven-plus type tests for them. There isn't time for that at the village school, not with such large classes.'

'Thank the Lord for that – it smacks of conveyor-belt education to me. I'd rather he wasn't worried about exams, not at his age, or some years to come, and for that reason I'd like him to go to the village school.'

'I'd much prefer him to go to Beverley House,' said Philippa obstinately.

Nicholas who had been listening to this conversation with interest now piped up.

'And I'd much perfer to go and stay with Aunty Evelyn. She's got tons of ponies where she lives.'

Leo laughed. 'Out of the mouths of babes and sucklings, etc. It's a jolly good idea. Why don't you take Nicky and go off and stay with the Smiths for a few days. You look as if you could do with a break.'

'What about you?'

'Don't worry about me. I can find plenty to occupy myself with.'

And no doubt he could, thought Philippa, as on the journey to Brockenhurst, with Nicky sleeping at her side, she pondered the variables of that remark. She was dismayed to find that she had been experiencing an unpleasant sensation not unlike jealousy when he was out late at nights, or attending a social at those hospitals where he sometimes locumed as an anaesthetist. She was always invited on those occasions and sometimes accepted, but it reminded her too much of the time when Leo was in the army and she had spent the weekend at Coopen; that evening in the mess when she had sat outside the circle of young officers and their wives envying Leo his easy manner. He hadn't changed. When it came to banter he could hold his own with the best of them. But she had changed. Her old shyness had deepened into reserve. Such evenings, sipping wine and endeavouring to make small talk, became an ordeal for her.

He attracted women; he always had. His charm lay in his smile, she thought, for it was his smile that had first sent her weak at the knees. She had expected some of the ladies of the village to fall for him, and so they did. Female parishioners had for years been cherishing sentimental fantasies about the parish priest whose dark good looks and Welsh accent coloured their day-dreams. Now, with a few exceptions, the same ladies turned their sights on Leo. This was all harmless and Philippa knew that Leo would give them as much time and attention as if they were genuine patients, for, as he was fond of reminding her, hypochondriacs were just as likely to fall genuinely ill as anyone else.

'The only thing that bothers me about hypochondriacs,' he said one day in a tone of voice that showed his tongue was firmly in his cheek, 'is that they will swop symptoms in the waiting room. I find it very confusing.'

Since 1948, when the National Health Service came into effect, Leo's work had doubled, and this past year he had taken on an assistant. This assistant, a Dr Masters, had taken over Mrs Morley's flat which had fallen vacant at her death. Soon the house would come on the open market. Leo knew he would either have to buy the property or find premises to rent elsewhere. He was reluctant to take out another mortgage.

'There's the money from the sale of the Woodside House. I haven't touched it, take that,' said Philippa.

He had demurred at first. He had wanted her to keep that as a nest egg. 'I'll have it as a loan,' he agreed finally. 'And I promise I won't do an Ursula on you.'

Philippa knew he would keep his word. Ursula had not done so. She had sent off the first monthly repayment but nothing since. When Philippa had made enquiries through her solicitor she discovered her stepmother had left the country. Later, much later, she received an air-mail letter from America. She guessed who it was from before she opened it.

'Dear Philippa,
Sorry I reneged on my promise. Charlie phoned, he was in trouble over some money he owed a client – a client not to fall foul of. I can't say more. I came over to help him out, not intending to stay, but when I saw what a pitiful state he was in I couldn't leave him. I found him in a seedy hotel in a seedy part of New York, a mere shadow of his former self. His wife had left him and he was penniless. I've found myself a job as a shop assistant and we're living now in what they call a cold-water apartment. It will have to do until we can afford something better. I've paid off Charlie's debts and his doctor's bills, and when he's completely fit I'm sure he'll be able to find work of some kind. I've had a fairly easy life of it up until now, so I'm not grumbling if things begin to get difficult. All that matters is that we're together, but if at any time you could spare me a little cash, I'd be very grateful. I'll pay you back, I promise you.'

'Of all the bally cheek,' said Leo when she gave him the letter to read. 'Asking for more money – and that after she's cheated you out of two thousand quid.'

'She didn't cheat me out of anything. She was my father's wife and she made him happy. I should have gone halves with her when I sold that property. That's what Dad would have wished me to do. I often feel mean about it.'

'I shouldn't lose any sleep over that woman, she's had her pound of flesh and is likely to come back for more. If you're not careful, Philippa, she'll bleed you dry.'

'All the more reason then that you should have it.'

The train rumbled through a tunnel and came out into sunshine the other end. Nicky's head had fallen on her lap. Absent-mindedly she stroked his thatch of yellow hair. He was worn out from sheer excitement for a train ride to him was an unusual novelty, and even more so a ride on the Underground, 'the trains that open the doors by themselves,' as he described the tube. It didn't take much to make a small child happy, she thought. A car was no novelty. Nicky was out in his father's car nearly every day.

The first thing Leo did when they moved to Norfolk was to buy a car. A pre-war Standard, which should, in Philippa's opinion, have been sent to the scrapyard years ago. At the same time he had put his name down for a new car for which there was a three-year waiting list, and had taken possession of that in 1949. It had the new grill-shaped radiator and caused a lot of comment in the village.

'T'old doctor, do he be satisfied with a bike. Only hitched up his 'oss when it were urgent,' said one old whitebeard whose memory reached back before the Boer War. New cars were not so much of a novelty in the market town, and when Nicky, riding in the front with his father, spotted one his excitement was intense. 'Like Daddy's car. Look – look. Like Daddy's car.'

The train was slowing down. Only two more stops and they would be at Brockenhurst where Eve and Clive would be waiting for them. They had bought an eighteenth-century cottage on the fringe of the New Forest, with a garden that extended into the forest itself and which the ponies raided from time to time, especially in the autumn when windfalls lay thick on the ground.

But now it was still only August, and Nicky's 'tons of ponies' might not materialise. He wouldn't be disappointed. Uncle Clive would drive along one of the forest roads and park in some likely spot and before long the ponies would come thrusting their heads through the open windows to be fed with carrots and sugar lumps. It wouldn't be the old Rolls Nicky would be driven in, for that had gone to a private car museum when Clive retired.

'I couldn't afford it any more,' he said. 'It used to cost me thirty bob in petrol just to drive it out of the garage.' Now he drove a modest Hillman Minx.

Philippa had heard of the departure of the Rolls with mixed feelings. Though her grief for Joe had lessened to the point where she could remember him with tranquillity, every fresh sight of the Rolls brought a quickening of the heart. Unlike poppies which brought her nothing but pain. Now in August they were prolific, in the fields, in the hedgerows, along the railway embankments, in gardens from seeds borne on the wind or dropped by birds.

At Rodings some had infiltrated her herbaceous borders. Furiously she pulled them up. Leo said, 'They are not weeds, you know.'

'They are to me.'

'They're looked upon as a symbol of remembrance.'

'Not by me.'

Twelve

Philippa's last full day at Broom Cottage was spent in having a long and in depth heart-to-heart with Evelyn. Not all the time, for the morning was spent shopping at Bournemouth, but in the afternoon when both took chairs and papers to laze in the garden.

Bambi was showing in Lymington and Clive had taken Nicky off to see it as a farewell treat. Both women had been invited but refused.

'I saw it during the war in Norwich,' said Philippa, remembering the occasion only too well. It was one of the films she did not see except for occasional glimpses over Joe's shoulder. She didn't think she could sit through it again, not with such a memory lurking, and Evelyn preferred something featuring Bette Davis.

'All right, we'll leave you two to your confabulation. We've got more sense haven't we, Nick old boy?' He took Nicky's hand. 'We're better off without them, anyway, they'd only natter all through the film.'

Evelyn produced a packet of cigarettes. 'Can I tempt you? But of course, you don't smoke.'

'I do occasionally. But not in front of Leo, it wouldn't seem fair now that he's given up.'

'Given up smoking! But from what I remember you were always sending him cigarettes when he was overseas.'

'He gave up when Nicky was a few weeks old. Smoking gave him a hacking cough and every time he coughed he either woke Nicky up or made the child cry. Nicky was allergic to noise. Once when he was sound asleep and Leo had a particularly raucous coughing attack, he didn't exactly wake but his bottom lip dropped and we saw all the colour drain out of his face. Subconsciously, he must have been terrified. That was the day Leo gave up smoking.'

'And never lapsed?'

'Never.'

Evelyn gave Philippa a speculative glance. 'Leo worships that boy, doesn't he?'

'That's putting it mildly.'

'And you're jealous.'

Philippa rounded on her. 'What a horrible thing to say. . . . No, you're right. I am jealous, but not the green-eyed sort of jealousy – more envy, I suppose. I just wish Leo had as much time for me.'

'What prevents you telling Leo? Pride? Fear of being rejected? Tell me Philippa, do you still sleep together?'

'Occasionally.'

'And you'd like it to be more often.' Philippa didn't have to answer that for the answer was plain to see in the wistfulness of her expression.

'Well, for goodness' sake,' said Evelyn impatiently, 'you're a woman aren't you, and an extremely attractive one at that. You know how to get round him, surely. If you don't I can give you a few hints.'

Philippa blushed. 'I – I couldn't.'

'Why not for goodness' sake?'

'I just couldn't.'

Clive and Nicholas's unexpected return spared Evelyn the effort of thinking up a suitable answer. She looked at them over her sun glasses. 'Don't tell me there was a queue.'

'Oh no, nothing like that, actually we had very good seats. But we both got rather upset when Bambi's mother was shot so we decided to come home and feed the ducks instead. Down at the pool, coming?'

'We're comfortable as we are thank you. . . . Don't be late for tea.'

They watched as man and boy walked hand in hand into the forest. Eve turned to Philippa.

'That's a very sensitive little boy you have there. I hope you know how to handle him.'

'I don't,' said Philippa. 'I'm an indifferent mother. Leo said so – not in so many words, but that's what he meant. The trouble is I feel I shall be punished if I love him too much, and I couldn't risk losing Nicky too.'

Evelyn stared at her in disbelief. 'Are you trying to tell me that you actually believe you will be punished for loving your child too much?'

'You know what it says in the Bible about a jealous God.'

' "Thou shalt have no other gods before me," ' quoted Evelyn ponderously. 'You don't intend to set Nicholas up as a god, do you?' Her tone was sceptical.

'No, but so far everyone I've loved I've lost. Joe. Jennifer Anne. My father. Leo, in a way. I can't afford to take any risks with Nicky.'

'What a relief it is to know you don't love me,' said Evelyn drily, determined to mock Philippa out of her depression. 'I knew, when I caught you curtseying to the new moon, that I had a nut case on my hands, but this is going beyond reason. For goodness' sake, Philippa, grow up. You've got a darling little boy who loves you deeply. Don't for the sake of some foolish obsession deny him your love in return, for that is a sure way of losing him.'

Philippa digested this in silence, then said in a small voice. 'I only curtsey to a new moon in January,' which made Evelyn laugh so much she nearly tipped up her chair.

'There's hope for you yet,' she said, wiping her eyes.

And all might have been well had not a chaffinch then settled in a nearby tree. A flash of crimson, a glimpse of white wing bars, and then it took off again flying in graceful undulating sweeps across the adjoining heathland. Philippa clutched at her side as a sudden vivid image of Joe in that last fatal spin appeared before her and she cried out aloud. Evelyn was at her side immediately.

'What is it, dear? Are you in pain?'

Philippa hid her face in her hands. Between her sobs, her words came indistinct and haltingly. 'You know those nightmares I used to have after Joe was killed? I just had one now, sitting here watching that bird. I saw Joe and his plane spinning down into the sea as clearly as if it were really happening. Oh, Eve, it's not an omen, is it?'

'You and your omens – what are we going to do with you?' Evelyn hugged her close. 'There's a logical reason for everything. We've just been talking about Joe, you happen to have a very vivid imagination plus you're the most superstitious person I know. Philippa, you must try to put Joe out of your mind. That sounds cruel, I know, but it's the only way if you want to have a happy life with Leo.'

Philippa dried her eyes. 'I haven't known true happiness since Joe died. Something in me died at the same time, otherwise I think I wouldn't have been so desperate as to give his child away. I thought when I married Leo it would help me to forget; I thought when Nicky came he would bring Leo and me close again; I thought he'd be a common bond between us – but nothing has worked out the way I thought it would. Leo was always protective towards me, always treated me as if I were something precious – now that consideration and care is all for Nicky. If Leo thinks of me at all it is only as Nicky's mother, and as I said before, he doesn't think much of me as a mother, anyway.'

Evelyn resumed her chair. Philippa was over her storm of tears, but she looked pale and despairing and Evelyn grieved for her, but hardened her heart. Some straight talking was what Philippa needed.

'What is preventing you from telling Leo what you have just told me. Be straight with him. Say to him, "Leo I've cheated and lied and betrayed you, but I've paid for it. Please can't we wipe out the past and start afresh? Can't we start again and try to get back to as it was between us before you went overseas? If we really wanted it to we could make it work, and I want very much to make it work. . . ." Could you bring yourself to say all that?'

'I've never spoken to Leo like that in my life. He'd know I had learnt it parrot fashion.'

Evelyn nearly lost patience. 'I didn't mean you to use those exact words. I was just giving you something to work on. Don't you want to get back to your old footing?'

'If it were at all possible – yes, of course I do. But I know just what Leo would say.'

'What?'

'He finds it impossible to answer with a plain yes or no. When he says, "I'll think about it", it means no. And when he says, "That might be a good idea", it usually means yes.'

'And what will his answer be this time?'

'More than likely, "I'll think about it".'

'Meaning no.'

'On this occasion meaning just what he says. He hates to commit himself.'

'You make your Leo sound rather a devious character.'

Philippa was quick to refute that. 'He's not at all devious. He just hates hurting people's feelings.'

'It seems to me that he avoids facing up to facts.'

'We're all like that only some of us are better at it than others,' said Philippa mournfully.

Evelyn pursed her lips. 'What happened to that bubbly and joyful young woman who used to visit us at Manor Farm?'

'She became one of the war's walking wounded.'

Clive and Evelyn travelled as far as London with Philippa and Nicky the following morning, partly to see them safely on to the Norwich train but also to take the opportunity to visit the 1951 Exhibition at Battersea Park. It was an exhibition to rival the Great Exhibition that took place at the Crystal Palace just a hundred years previously.

After six years of war and five more years of austerity the government thought the people deserved a reward and the exhibition was the result. It was opened by the King and Queen in May that year on a twenty-seven-acre bomb site near Battersea Gardens, and rapidly became one of the great sights of London. Some of those living on the north side of the river, crossing the Thames for the first time in their lives, felt they had wandered into foreign territory. The Festival Hall, part of the exhibition, was one of the big attractions, others flocked to the Dome of Discovery, the Skylon, the Guinness Clock, a railway designed by Rowland Emett the cartoonist, and a magnificent funfair. But nothing Nicky saw at Battersea could top the magic of the trains whose doors opened by themselves.

They had lunch in the restaurant on the bridge at Liverpool Street.

'You are sure you'll be all right from now on?' Clive clucked around Philippa like a mother hen.

'Of course she will,' said Evelyn. 'Think of the number of times she did this journey during the war – and that in the black-out and with bombs falling. Cut up Nicky's meat for him, there's a dear.' She turned her attention back to Philippa. 'Now don't forget what we discussed yesterday. I hope to hear some progress in that direction next time you ring me and do let me know Leo's reaction to your new hair-style.'

'He won't even notice it.'

Evelyn had, during Philippa's short stay with her, persuaded her to have her hair restyled. 'You've worn it in a page-boy bob as long as I can remember. Don't you ever feel like a change?'

'Is that a polite way of telling me I'm too old to wear my hair this way?'

'I meant nothing of the kind. Too old! With features like yours you could get away with murder – even those dreadful earphones I can remember in my youth. But don't you think it's time you were a little more adventurous? After all, longish hair went out when the New Look came in – and that was all of four years ago.'

She got her way and Philippa was driven off to Bournemouth the very next morning. Evelyn and the stylist discussed Philippa's hair as if its owner weren't there.

'A perm?' suggested Evelyn.

'I had a perm once and it was a disaster,' cried Philippa with alarm.

They both ignored her. 'A very soft perm, ends only. It would be a pity to spoil the line with curls.'

When Evelyn saw the result – a sleek honey-gold cap flicked up at the ends – she exclaimed, 'Oh Gustave, you're a genius,' which said all that was necessary.

Philippa stared at the new face staring back at her. She was thirty-two and already panicking at the thought of being forty. The short and stylish haircut certainly made her look younger – twenty-five perhaps? She knew her visit to Evelyn would turn out to be a tonic.

Evelyn and Clive stayed by the barrier until the Norwich-bound train had snaked out of sight. Clive took Evelyn's arm. 'Am I barking up the wrong tree or is something up with Philippa?'

'You're spot-on darling, as always, but please don't ask me any more just yet.'

Evelyn had fully intended to ring Thornmere as soon

as she got home to check that the two travellers had arrived safely, but she was hardly inside the cottage before the phone rang. 'That's Philippa now,' she called to Clive who was in the kitchen brewing coffee.

But it wasn't Philippa, it was the operator saying she had a greetings telegram for a Mrs Smith.

'Speaking.'

The girl read out, 'Mum, where are you? I've rung you several times and no answer, hope I'm luckier with a telegram. You're going to be a grandmother. Love to you both, Robin and Felicity.'

Evelyn's shriek of delight nearly drowned out the formal 'This message will be confirmed by post' from the operator.

'On a greetings telegram? It must be a greetings telegram!'

'The sender paid for a greetings form, madam.'

Philippa and her problems were momentarily forgotten. Evelyn flew off to find Clive.

Leo was waiting for them on Thorpe station. He swept Nicky up into his arms and hugged him. 'You look tired, old chap – like a lift to the car?' and then he was off taking long loping strides with Nicky riding on his shoulders. Philippa followed after.

'Well hello, my dear. You're looking very swish,' she said, talking to herself. No kiss or hug for her unless the peck on her cheek could be counted as a kiss. No glance at her hair, and she was purposely carrying her hat. No, nothing like that, he had eyes only for Nicky. But having deposited the boy in the car he did come back to retrieve the suitcase.

'You should have left it for me,' he said, taking it from

her. He did look at her then, but only as a doctor. 'You've got dark rings under your eyes. Have you and Eve been burning the midnight oil?'

'Enjoying ourselves mostly, and this morning we all went to the South Bank Exhibition. There is so much to see and we didn't want to miss any of it.'

'Oh,' he sounded disappointed. 'I was hoping to take you and Nick to that.'

'Then you left it a bit late.' She spoke more sharply than she intended. 'He'll be starting school soon.'

'Yes, talking about school, I've fixed up with Miss Marlowe. Nick can start there on 5 September.'

Philippa went cold with silent rage. The village school, and he had made all the arrangements when she was out of the way. The least he could have done was phone her at Eve's and tell her, or better still discuss it with her.

She sat in the front passenger seat with Nicky on her lap. They had hardly left Norwich behind them before he was asleep. It was a silent and, on her part, withdrawn journey home. Only as they drew away from Beckton Market did Leo break it.

'Well, what do you think?'

'About what?'

'About Nick starting at the village school.'

'You know what I think. I also think it was a very underhanded thing to do going behind my back to Miss Marlowe.'

'Nothing underhanded about it at all. I just happened to meet her in the library and she asked after Nicky. I told her we were still undecided, as you thought he wouldn't stand much chance getting through the eleven-plus at the village school and she invited me back to the school house for coffee to discuss the matter. I'm telling you this before you'll hear it from some other source, knowing how gossip proliferates in Thornmere. The next morning our milkman's wife asked me if there was anything seriously wrong with Miss Marlowe as she is the sick visitor with the Mothers' Union and didn't know whether to take flowers or not. I told her I had never seen Miss Marlowe in better fettle since I'd known her and I left her trying to work that one out. So if you hear any rumour of an affair between Miss Marlowe and myself, my visit was just to decide Nicky's future.'

'And what decision did you come to?'

'That he starts at her school on 5 September.'

Suddenly a whole new set of emotions beset Philippa. Here was Miss Marlowe, a handsome and clever woman in her late thirties, the sort of woman attracted to someone like Leo, and Leo, naturally gallant to any female and more than likely unsatisfied with the intimate side of his married life; a powder keg of a situation awaiting that essential spark. Did it worry her? It certainly did. She made up her mind to put no more obstacles in the way of Nicky starting at the village school. All the same she couldn't resist a little dig when Leo brought her name once more into their conversation.

'You would enjoy her company, once you get to know her. She's a bookworm like you. Name any book you like, she's read it.'

'*Gone with the Wind?*'

'She didn't name *Gone with the Wind* specifically, but no, I shouldn't think so. It hardly seems her cup of tea.'

'A very superior person, your Miss Marlowe.'

'She's not at all superior. She's had a very interesting life. She was born in India, did you know?'

'I know nothing about Miss Marlowe.'

'She's familiar with one or two of the places I visited. What do you say to us having her to dinner one evening?'

'I'll think about it.'

Evelyn phoned to tell her the good news the following morning. Philippa was delighted for her. 'I've still got Nicky's baby clothes, as good as new. He grew out of them so quickly that they're hardly worn. Do you think Felicity would like them?'

'Would she not! – with clothes still on coupons. But what about yourself? You might need them again.' There was a crafty, almost beguiling note in Evelyn's voice.

'I have no say in that department,' said Philippa unhappily, which comment abruptly terminated that particular subject. They continued chatting on uncontroversial matters until Leo came down from putting Nicholas to bed which he always did if he was home in time.

'Any news from Evelyn and Clive?'

'They are going to be grandparents.'

'Good for them.' Leo glanced at his watch. 'There's a talk at the Memorial Hospital tonight on the future trends of anaesthetics. I'd like to put in an appearance. Would you have any objection?'

'Why should I mind?'

'No reason at all,' he sounded slightly despondent. 'I might be late, so don't wait supper for me. There'll be sandwiches and drinks laid on.'

It was on lonely evenings like this that Philippa wished she had a television. The only television she had seen was that on sets in radio-shop windows before the war. It was usually just a talking head barely visible behind a flurry of snow. She would watch for a bit then would walk away unimpressed. She didn't think the cinema trade need worry too much about a possible rival.

But now the newspapers were constantly writing about this new phenomenon. Only the other day she had read a piece under the heading, 'Britain going down the Tube' and thought at first it was something to do with the people's disillusionment with the present government. The article went on to say that the number of British homes with television would double within two years.

Not in Thornmere, Philippa was sure of that; half the homes hadn't even got electricity. She was in a particularly blue mood that evening, missing the lively companionship of Evelyn and Clive. She flicked over the pages of the *Radio Times*, seeing if anything might appeal to her. Arthur Askey? He was always good for a laugh and she was sadly in need of a laugh.

On Nicky's first day at school – his first step towards an ordered world, as Leo expressed it – he was taken by his father. Philippa was unable to show her relief when Leo volunteered to do this service, for she knew if she were the one to deliver him both she and Nicky would have been in tears. She could trust him not to cry in front of his father.

'You won't forget what I look like?' he asked her anxiously.

'I won't forget what you look like.'

'You promise you won't run away?'

'I promise I won't run away.'

'An' you'll meet me after school, like you promised?'

'I'll be there at half past two. Miss Marlowe lets all the new children leave half an hour earlier on the first day.'

When she turned up at the school and joined the little knot of other 'new' mothers, they drew away like a group of sheep suddenly confronted by a sheep-dog, eyeing her out of the corners of their eyes. She distinctly heard one voice a little above the others: 'You'd think they could afford to send him to a private school, wouldn't you?' More sly looks in her direction, unsure smiles, then the doors opened and out rushed a small platoon of over-anxious children. Nicky was not among them.

The mothers and their offspring dispersed, and Philippa stood on in splendid isolation. Where was Nicky? Had he been taken ill? She was beset with anxieties, then Miss Marlowe appeared.

'Nicholas sends his apologies but do you mind waiting until the battle is over.' Miss Marlowe had soft, brown, humorous eyes that belied the sardonic tinge of her voice. She laughed. 'His class is enacting the Battle of Bosworth with men and horses they made themselves out of Plasticine. Your young son intends to change the course of history.'

'History! At their age?'

'It's a game with them, and becoming rather rough at times. Nicky insisted that King Richard should have a horse so he made him one and now he wants to bring it home. Is that all right with you?'

'Of course,' said Philippa, finding that much against her will she was falling a victim to the warmth of the other's personality.

'And do please recognise it as a horse. It would make Nicholas so proud. By the way,' and Miss Marlowe smiled her friendly smile, 'I must tell you how delighted I am you decided to send him to my school. He is a most outstanding child. You must have missed him today.'

The house had seemed deathly quiet and unusually tidy, for Nicky, like his father, never put anything away after him. Leo had picked up this untidy trait in India when he always had a batman, white or brown, to nursemaid him. Actually, she had found time hanging on her hands, for Nellie had found her an admirable help who came in three mornings a week.

Elsie Pearson was a sturdy and capable woman who had, she informed Philippa, worked for Mr Harker at the Hall when she was just a girl. She was now living with her sister and niece in one of the cottages in The Street, and jumped at the chance of working within walking distance. Philippa, used to London wages, was surprised at how little the woman asked per hour and immediately doubled it. Elsie flushed with pleasure.

'I'll be able to give my sister a little more for my keep. She won't like taking it, but I'll make her, 'cos all she gets is her widow's pension.'

The partnership worked like a dream. Neither intruded on the other's province. Philippa, giving up her home into the care of another person, saw it take on a new dimension. It sparkled from top to bottom with wax and elbow grease, leaving her free to attend to her beloved garden, for beloved it was more than any other garden she had tended. She missed the forest trees, she missed Epping Forest. There were no primeval forests left in Norfolk, but no lack of trees either, and she wasn't counting those in the impenetrable plantations of forestry trees grown for commercial reasons. She didn't see them as trees but as sprouting pit props or telegraph poles.

There were many beautiful trees in the garden at Rodings, too many in fact for as saplings they had been planted so close together that now, over half a century later, some of the trunks were touching.

'It's a question of survival of the fittest,' said Leo after a heated argument over the question of thinning out.

Philippa was against it, for all the trees were forest trees, holly and oaks, an ash and a sycamore, and two beautiful limes that filled the garden with their pleasing fragrance in early spring. The magnificent willow, planted as a feature and now so large it overshadowed one corner of the lawn and scarified the grass around it, was spared after much pleading on her part, but Leo had his way with the others, as he always did when it came to a question of common sense.

Philippa ran to her bedroom and stuffed her head under the pillow but even that did not completely muffle the sounds of the axe. It took nearly a week for Leo to fell two trees in his spare time, then he gave up and called in professionals. The day they started Philippa fled to Nellie for sympathy which Nellie gave unstintingly though secretly she was in like mind with Leo.

'I wish it was possible to transplant trees the way you can bushes and plants,' she said. 'I wouldn't mind a few of your trees in our garden.'

She and Don had moved into their long-awaited new house just three years earlier, and the garden was only just beginning to look like a garden and not a 'repository for builder's rubble' as Don rather cheerlessly described it at the time. It had two conventional flowerbeds, a shrubbery, a lawn which the boys and a dog had scuffed unmercifully, and, behind some trellis work on which two climbing roses were being trained, a small vegetable plot.

'It'll look all right in a few years' time, if we're still here, but at the moment it looks so bare. I like a garden where none of the earth shows.'

'What do you mean, "if we're still here"? You haven't long moved in.'

'Nearly three years – 1948. Don't you remember? The

year of the Olympic Games in London? They called them the austerity Olympics – they were too, and things haven't improved. I wonder sometimes if we'll ever see the end to rationing. When you see all the lovely consumer goods on display in the shop windows of Norwich – then the hateful notice, "For Export Only", it makes you wonder who actually won the war!'

Philippa ignored this slight outburst; Nellie was never out of humour for long. 'You haven't answered my question. Why are you thinking of moving? I think this is such a pretty little house.'

'You've put your finger on it – *little* house. And this so-called through-room. Oh, it looked lovely when it was empty but once the furniture was in we could hardly move. And have you any idea what it's like on a winter's evening when we're all crammed in here, and one wants the wireless on, and another wants to play with his train set, and another practise his scales and Don having a pile of homework to mark, and me, if I want to get out my sewing-machine, having to beat a retreat to the kitchen. . . . We're all on top of one another.'

'Couldn't you light a fire in the boys' bedrooms?'

'Yes dearie, if I had the fuel to keep it in with. When coal comes off the ration there'll be no problem. By the way, if there's any wood for logs going begging, tell Leo we'd willingly pay for a load.'

'Don't be silly – take as much as you want, you'll be doing us a favour.'

At the end of her visit Nellie walked to the end of School Lane with her. 'And in spite of your qualms, Nicky has settled down at the school quite happily?'

'From day one, but I doubt whether he'll ever pass the

eleven-plus. They seem to play at games more than they do lessons.'

'My Don always says that a bright child will get on anywhere. You need have no qualms about your Nicky.'

The next morning Philippa reluctantly drew her curtains for she had doggedly refused to look out of the windows the day before. Now she looked on to an unfamiliar and spacious garden stippled by the sun's rays that poured through the wide gaps between the remaining trees. The shrubs and what flowers still bloomed looked more full of colour in this new fresh brightness, and where the overcrowded trees had been a whole new vista was now in view, the newly ploughed barley fields and beyond them on rising land some old farm buildings.

'Let there be light,' quoted Leo behind her. 'It's an improvement, don't you think?'

She agreed. 'I was wrong and you were right, as usual.' He could tell by her tone that she meant that flippantly, but he let it pass. He couldn't afford to lose her altogether.

And so the years rolled by, each one drawing nearer and nearer towards the dreaded eleven-plus, dreaded more by Philippa than young Nick who took everything in his stride. The years for Philippa went by as slowly as mutes at a Victorian funeral, each one marked by some personal or national event. In 1954, after fourteen years, rationing was ended, meat being the final item to come off coupons. Housewives ceremoniously tore up their ration books at a rally in Trafalgar Square. Philippa carefully put hers away. One day, she thought, they might be of interest to her grandchildren.

Later that same year she had her final letter from Ursula. Charlie had had a fatal heart attack and she herself was marrying again and moving to California. No mention was made of the money still. She left no forwarding address, and so passed unlamented out of Philippa's life.

So many of her old wartime acquaintances had fallen by the wayside. Doreen, her aunt's one-time companion, had emigrated to Australia with her husband and family, Jean Dickson (née Shaw) had had two more children and was now living in Glasgow. They kept in touch but only at Christmas. Like many other wartime friendships, once peace came their lives had diverged.

She still saw Mrs Toser and Red, neither looking much different to when she first knew them except that there was now more grey than red in Red's hair. He was the only person she knew who missed the war. He had loved the excitement of listening to the news, of pinning up the tiny flags on the map of Europe hanging on the kitchen wall, more so after D Day. The atmosphere grew tense in May 1945 when he ran out of Russian flags and Mrs Toser was dragooned into making fresh ones out of bits of odd paper and colouring them in with crayons.

'I never thought the day would come when I'd be sitting in my own kitchen drawing a hammer and sickle,' she confided in Philippa. 'My poor old mother would have turned in her grave. She hated the Reds.'

It was Leo who persuaded Philippa to learn to drive. Her restlessness, her constant sighs, did not go unnoticed. 'How would you like a car for a birthday present?' he suggested. 'It would be useful for me to have a second driver in the family.'

'You always said I'd never pass the test.'

'Only because of your sight. With glasses you should

be able to read a number plate at twenty-five yards. I can recommend an optician at Beckton Market.'

For once she didn't object. She knew she was long overdue for glasses to correct her sight. Only recently, in Beckton Market, she had flagged down a gas lorry mistaking it for a bus. When she was finally fitted with a pair they were a revelation to her.

She looked out of the window in the optician's surgery and for the first time in her life saw every tree, every leaf, every roof outlined as if by Indian ink, and not as through a mist.

'It's marvellous,' she cried. 'It's a miracle. I can see each leaf separately. Do normal people, I mean those who are not short-sighted, see every leaf separately?'

'They do.'

'I should have come sooner, shouldn't I? I don't know why I didn't – vanity I suppose.' She paused. 'I don't think I'll wear them always. I'll just put them on when I need them, then it will come as a revelation to me every time.'

The optician was highly amused. 'They won't wear out, you know.'

'No, but think of the bliss each time I put them on.'

'I can hardly believe this,' said the optician to his receptionist when Philippa had left. 'I've seen children get excited when they see things clearly for the first time, but never a woman of that age.'

The receptionist watched Philippa's progress down the street. 'I wouldn't mind exchanging my sight for her figure,' she said.

Next on the agenda was to get her provisional driving licence, then enrol at the driving school. She didn't get on very well on her first lesson. Her instructor was a suave and pomarded young man who took great pains to show her the cigarette lighter his last satisfied client had given him. That put her off rather, and at the end of a frustrated hour she decided she wasn't cut out to be a driver.

Leo fixed her up with another instructor, a fatherly man who did not smoke, and she got on much better, sufficiently well, in fact, to pass the test first time. But what gave her the greatest pleasure, even more pleasure than when she became the recipient of a full licence in the shape of a little red booklet with hardback covers, was a cheque for a guinea from a woman's magazine, payment for a published letter entitled 'Going through L-Fire'.

In 1956 Nicky passed his eleven-plus – not only passed it, but did so well he was offered a place at a minor public school in Essex, his father's old school in fact.

'I thought you were against boarding schools,' said Philippa. 'I remember you telling me how glad you were you didn't have to board. You said you could always tell the homesick boys by the look in their eyes and it used to haunt you. You said no son of yours would ever go as a boarder. You've changed your mind pretty damn quick, now it's offered free.'

They were back to square one, at odds about Nicky's future and bitter and acrimonious were the accusations flung at each other. The one that hurt most was Leo's charge that she wasn't a natural mother.

'What do you mean I wasn't a natural mother. I did everything expected of a mother. I never hit him, or shouted at him, or lost my temper with him. . . .'

'That's right, you didn't. And you didn't rock him to sleep, or sing him lullabies, or read to him in bed, either.'

Angry tears flooded her eyes. 'Are you accusing me of neglecting him? That's so unfair. I've always been a good mother.'

'There is no such thing as a good mother. There are either natural mothers or unnatural mothers....'

'Are you accusing me of being an unnatural mother?' Her voice rose to a shriek.

'No, I am not. You *are* not. I'm sorry, I went too far....' He slumped at the table and put his head in his hands. 'I think we had better leave it for now – we're getting too emotional.'

'It's time there was a little emotion around here,' she said bitterly. 'There is too much that is left unsaid. Well, I'm going to say it now. You accuse me of not singing lullabies to Nicky, of not reading to him in bed. When do I get the chance? You're always in there first, not singing lullabies, but teaching him to sing and bathing him, reading to him in bed. I let you do it because it seemed to mean so much to you....'

'And I did it because I thought you didn't care enough.'

She turned away to hide her tears. 'We've got rather low opinions of each other, haven't we? Perhaps you're right about boarding school. It can't be much fun for Nicky living in this loveless house.'

She heard Leo get up and walk to the door, heard him close it carefully after him. Then she fled too, not to her room, but along The Street and into School Lane and on to Nellie's house, her sanctuary.

Nellie opened the door to her. One look at Philippa's swollen eyes told her everything. She had seen it all before. She took her into the living room and sat her down in the most comfortable chair.

'We're in luck,' she said. 'Don is at a parent and teachers' meeting and the three boys are at some Scout jamboree or other in Norwich so we've got the evening to ourselves. Now, just stay put, I know just what you need.'

She came back with a cup of warm milk well laced with brandy and stood over Philippa until she drank it.

'And what is it this time?' she said.

'The usual – bickering over Nicky.'

'Why can't you find something different to scrap over? At least there'd be a novelty to it.'

'There's nothing else we care enough about to quarrel over.'

Nellie smothered a sigh and brought her chair up close to Philippa. 'How two nice people like you and Leo can be so bloody to each other is beyond my understanding,' she said.

'I'm not all that nice,' said Philippa gloomily. 'Sometimes, I hate myself.'

'You haven't answered my question. I know it's about Nicky – it's never about anything else. What about Nicky this time?'

'Whether he should go to the Grange House School. Naturally, I don't want him to leave home so young. I don't see why he can't give up his place to some other boy and go to the Grammar School – he'll get just as good an education. Look how your two eldest have got on.'

'But it's understandable for a man to want his son to go to his old school. You'll have him for his holidays. Gosh, I'd give anything for young Kev to be able to have the chance. He needs civilising.'

'Your Bobby won a place at an Independent school, but you didn't take it up. I never knew why.'

'I'll tell you why in four words,' said Nellie. 'We couldn't afford it.'

'But he won a scholarship.'

'That only covered fees and board. We would have to have supplied the uniform and books, and it couldn't be done, not without depriving the other two of things they needed.'

'But you've had no regrets.'

'Of course I had regrets. I still do. I say to myself there but for the sake of thirty bob a week goes a future prime minister. Now, what about a small glass of my potato wine?'

'I'll be tiddly.'

'Good.'

Philippa walked home, not in a state of intoxication, but certainly in better spirits. A few minutes of Nellie's company was as good as a tonic. Her anger at Leo had evaporated. Of course every man wanted his son to go to his old school – that is, if he were sentimental about that school, and Leo had never struck her as being sentimental. But there were a lot of things she didn't know about Leo, and going by some of the accusations he had flung at her that evening, a lot of things he did not know about her.

She paused at the gate of the Queen Anne house. She was reluctant to go in. It was so pleasant out here in the scented twilight. The nicotiana she had sown beneath the front windows were at their best, trembling like white moths in the half light and filling the small enclosed garden with their heavy fragrance. She had never expected anything to bloom in such close proximity to the walnut tree but the tobacco plants had, and her mind was busy on further possibilities.

Her latchkey was in her pocket. She opened the door and came face to face with Leo in the hall. 'I'm just brewing up some coffee. Fancy a cup?' he said civilly.

Her expression thawed. 'That would be very nice,' she said.

It was, of course, no more than she had expected. It was back to square one, again.

Nicky went off to Grange House in September. She hadn't kissed him since he was seven when he had gravely asked her one day as a favour to please kiss him at home before they left rather than at the school gate for the bigger boys always laughed at him when she did. And from then it rather drifted into no kissing at all, and there was certainly no question of kissing him now, for he was nearly as tall as she was, and sometimes she felt absurdly shy with him. His hair had darkened to light brown but his eyes were still that luminous grey which was like looking at a reflection of her own.

He shook hands with her without a sign of emotion, raised his cap, then got in the car beside his father. The house seemed perilously quiet. She went into his room and its unnatural tidiness brought a lump to her throat. I'm making a fool of myself, she thought. For God's sake he's only a hundred and twenty miles away, there was nothing to prevent her nipping over in her car to visit, but she felt dubious about doing that too.

She was fitfully hoeing the front garden when Leo returned. She had been there for an hour going over the same small flowerbeds with one ear cocked for the sound of the car. She was rewarded at last. It wasn't until she stood up and eased her back that she was aware that she had just hoed up half of the snowdrops and aconites she had newly planted. When Leo got out of the car he saw at a glance that she had been crying but made no comment. He told her he had left Nicholas in the capable hands of the housemaster's wife. He said this while he was hastily drinking the tea she had made him. He was in a hurry to see a patient suffering with emphysema.

'She wheezes like a pair of old bagpipes. I'll have to get her into the chest clinic as soon as I can. It'll only be a temporary measure, there's no cure at this stage, but they may give her some relief with her breathing. This is what comes of being a heavy smoker, I told her. She knows it, she gave up smoking a long time ago, but she left it too late.'

'You didn't leave it too late.'

He looked grave. 'I was a fool for ever starting. I used to kid myself I couldn't do without it, that it helped me with my studying.'

'I hope Nicky won't feel he needs to smoke when he comes to serious studying.'

'He's far too sensible a chap.'

'Leo, do you mind if I go down to stay with Eve for a few days?'

He gave her a keen look under lowered brows. 'If it will help you to get over the loneliness, then go.'

It didn't help to get her over the aching void that Nicky's departure had caused, but it did somewhat ease her loneliness. Nobody could feel lonely in the presence of such an outgoing pair as Evelyn and Clive. Mitzi's place by the hearth was now empty. A tiny grave planted with a white heather marked the spot where she now lay. To wish her alive again would have been unkind for she had lived for eighteen years which was a good age for a Siamese, and in the end was both blind and deaf. Towards the end of her life, poor Mitzi had had to take a back seat when grandchildren arrived.

First the two boys, one following quickly on the heels of the other and then little Sally, just three years old now, with jet black hair and eyes like velvet. They came over to Broom Cottage for the day while Philippa was there. She noticed how Robin had broadened out and with a fuller face his disfigurement was hardly noticeable. Unless she had got so used to it that it was just part of him, like his nose or his ears. Felicity was a tiny little woman with dark hair and dark eyes, eyes that were ever alert, watching not her children for she was rather casual about them, but their father.

The boys spent most of their visit out of doors. They were both large and well-built for their ages, and were never still, unlike their sister who could stand unmoving for minutes, just looking.

'There's something about me that fascinates little Sally,' said Philippa. 'Do you think it's my glasses?'

'No. She's seen me in my glasses dozens of times. She's just naturally drawn to you.'

Nevertheless Philippa removed her glasses and drew Sally on to her knee, burying her face in the child's hair as she did so. It was the texture of silk and smelled of baby shampoo. The longing to smother her with kisses was almost more than she could bear. Jennifer Anne would be thirteen now and blossoming into womanhood. Was her hair black like her father's, were her eyes still bluer than blue? A longing for her other child came suddenly to the surface; she had felt it more since Nicky went away. She smothered a sigh that was almost a cry for help. Sally smiled up at her.

'Read me a story out of your mouth,' she said.

'What on earth does the child mean?'

'She means she wants you to tell her a story out of your head, not read from a book. Clive's good at it. I'm hopeless. It should be no problem for you after your great success with *Fashion and Home*.'

Philippa racked her brains. 'Once upon a time there was a beautiful little princess called Sally. She had an alabaster brow, and hair as black as night, eyes like stars and lips like ripe cherries. She lived in a castle whose walls were made of gold and the windows of silver....' Philippa stopped. 'She's gone to sleep!'

'I don't blame her.'

The seven and a half years between Nicholas starting at Grange House and passing his A-levels seemed to Philippa in retrospect as if they passed like milestones, each stage on his journey marked by some unusual or important event.

She had stopped sharing a bed with Leo during the Asian flu epidemic of 1957. He and Dr Masters took it in turns to be on call at night. When Dr Masters himself fell a victim to the virus, Leo rarely got a complete night's rest. Philippa was a light sleeper. The bedside phone always woke her and then it took her an hour or two to get back to sleep. It was Leo who suggested she would be better off sleeping on her own, and when the flu wore off the arrangement still stood. A stubborn pride prevented her going back to her old room of her own accord. She waited night after night for the summons that never came. Perhaps Leo too preferred sleeping on his own for the old hesitant rap-tap-tap on her door routine started all over again.

But contrary to his sexual needs, or rather lack of them, his kindness and consideration to her grew ever stronger. Whatever she was doing, or wherever she was, he would come and seek her out as soon as he came home as if her mere presence in the house was a reassurance for him. She guessed he was using her as a stand-in for Nicholas, for his loneliness for his son was painfully obvious. And his longing for Nicholas in some way triggered off a renewed longing for Jennifer Anne. We have that much in common, she thought, pity we can't talk about it.

She did most of her day-dreaming in the conservatory. For some reason it was conducive to nostalgia, sitting there amidst a forest of geraniums and fuchsia usually with a cup of tea near at hand. One particular afternoon she fell asleep and dreamt of Joe for the first time in many months, a hurt and wistful Joe demanding what she had done with his child. She awoke to find her cheeks wet with tears and Leo standing by her side.

'You're pining for Nicky?'

She brushed her tears away. 'Well, actually, no. I just had an unhappy dream.'

She had either not said enough or said too much. She overheard him sigh as he turned away. He hesitated, then returned and sat down beside her.

'You've obviously got too much time on your hands. You're becoming too introspective. Why don't you make some new friends – join a women's group, or something?'

'I feel more at home with men than I do with women,' she quipped, meaning himself and Nicky, but the joke misfired. Leo's face darkened with displeasure.

'No doubt you do.' He rose from his chair and left her.

But next day he came and dropped some car keys into her hand.

'A little cheering-up present,' he said. And 'little' in one sense it was, for the keys belonged to one of the new Minis which was now parked in the driveway. Philippa could hardly believe her eyes. Bright red, shiny, smelling of new upholstery. She walked all round it then stared enquiringly at Leo who, whenever he produced a surprise, grinned self-consciously as he was grinning now.

'You mean, you went into a garage and bought it? Just like that! I thought there was a waiting list.'

'There is, but I ordered this months ago. I got a call from the garage earlier this afternoon to say it was in, and I went straight off and collected it. It couldn't have come at a better time. I wanted something to make up for yesterday. I acted rather stupidly.'

'And I was tactless.'

They were like children calling *Pax*.

He said, 'Come along, let's try out her paces.'

The Mini was capable of a top speed of 70 mph. Leo crawled along at 20. On the rear window was a strip of paper saying 'RUNNING IN'. Some men coming off work at a boatyard cheered as they passed on their bikes. Philippa giggled.

'They're taking the mickey.'

'Let them. I'm not spoiling the engine by going like the knackers.'

Nevertheless, on her own the following day, Philippa tried it out for herself and got the needle up to fifty. That was more than she had ever got out of her little second-hand Morris Eight. She felt quite reckless. After that the little red Mini was seen often in the village street and earned itself the name of the Red Peril, and Philippa toyed with the idea of driving down to Essex and taking Nicky by surprise, but decided against it. When she did visit Grange House it was in formal attire and to attend either sport's day or prize-giving.

In 1960 Nicholas was fourteen and a head taller than she was and two inches taller than his father. That year too saw the inauguration of the youngest President of the United States, John F. Kennedy. Young, wealthy and handsome, with a beautiful wife. There was a new spirit abroad as if a new era had been ushered in, an era of youth and hope and freedom. The war years had gone, banished with all the other ills like shortages, restrictions and unemployment. The people were free to work, to make money and live as they pleased. No more instructions or restrictions or worries about the future for the state promised to look after them from the cradle to the grave, and poverty seemed to be a thing of the past.

Nellie and her husband Don could now, if they wished, have a choice of any of the new houses being built, of any size they required. But they were quite happy where they were. Their boys would be leaving soon, the house was more than big enough for two and the garden had matured. It would be madness to give it all up and start afresh somewhere else.

Nicky had done extremely well in his mock O-levels, getting ten passes with high grades. When they tried to pin him down as to whether he was going into medicine or not, he was evasive, saying it was either that or one of the sciences. He hadn't made up his mind; school or puberty had changed him. He had become quiet and rather introspective. When he was at home he spent a lot of time in his room listening to his records, which his father was pleased to hear were mostly of classical music. To encourage him Leo had the piano retuned, but Nicky preferred to strum out a tune on his guitar, which again Leo took comfort from by the fact that it was of the Spanish variety and not electric.

The year 1961 saw the first man in space, Yuri Gagarin of the Soviet Union. Nicky got quite excited about this, flushed and talkative as he hadn't been for some months. Even after he had gone back to school his letters continued in the same strain. Leo got quite concerned. He confided in Philippa.

'I was worrying that he was drifting with no clear idea about his future, now I'm worried that he'll become either a communist or an astronaut, or possibly both. He so enthuses about the Russians. I believe he's delighted they've beaten the Americans to it.'

'I quite enthuse about the Russians too. They're so awfully clever. Literature, music, ballet, now space travel. There's nothing they can't do.'

'I know nothing of literature or ballet,' answered Leo impatiently. 'I know very little more of music or space travel. Would you answer Nick's letter? Tell him I want him home this half-term, and then we're going to have a serious talk about his future.'

'If I put it like that he won't come.'

'Then wrap it up a bit, you women are supposed to know how.'

August 1963 brought the Great Train Robbery and Nicky enthused even more about that; it touched his boyish sense of adventure. 'It was only a lot of old money that was going to be destroyed, anyway. Except for the poor train driver, no one was hurt. Honestly, it's causing more of a flap than if somebody had been murdered.'

'He may be the best brain of his class,' said Leo grimly, 'but he still has a lot to learn.'

'He doesn't realise the implications,' said Philippa soothingly. 'To him it's like something out of a Wild West story. And in any case at his age most boys rebel against the Establishment.'

'There's going to be no rebellion against this Establishment!'

Leo, thought Philippa sadly, was becoming more and more like his father.

But there was a rebellion, of a sort, the following summer when Nicholas reported that he had no intention of going off to medical school or university. He was going to have a few years off first to hitch-hike his way round the world.

'I've read and heard too much about it,' he said. 'Guys leaving school and going straight into college, getting a job, getting married, getting stuck in a rut. I want to see something of life first. I want to see how other people live, I want to learn about other cultures, and I want to see other civilisations and I want to learn it from life, not from books.'

Leo was white-faced with fear rather than anger. 'You're under twenty-one,' he said. 'I could stop you.'

'You couldn't stop me, Dad, my mind's made up.'

Leo turned to Philippa. 'Say something to the boy. He won't listen to me.'

But all she could thick of to say was, 'Aren't you even going to wait for the results of your A-levels?'

He smiled at that, a smile very like his father's. 'No. I

fear that if the grades are high and I rather think they will be, you might be able to talk me out of it.'

They had lost him, Leo could see that. He managed to control his feelings. To break down, to blubber like a child in front of his son – he couldn't afford that luxury.

'I opened an account for you in the Halifax when you were born. I've been adding to it regularly since – there's quite a tidy sum there now. That will give you a start. . . .'

Nicky was not ashamed of his tears though he quickly blinked them back. He held out his hand, his father grasped it. Both had a powerful grip and the handshake lingered.

Philippa said, 'You will come back?'

'I promise.'

'And you will write?'

'Whenever I get the chance.'

They went to Dover to see him off, driving down in Leo's new Rover. Nicholas was travelling light. Just a haversack labelled with the Union Jack.

The worst moment of all was saying goodbye at the terminus. Leo threw all restraint aside and hugged his son. Philippa went forward and kissed Nicholas briefly on his cheek. She too wanted to throw aside all restraint, she too wanted to throw her arms around her son but shyness, or perhaps a fear of revealing how much she needed him, held her back.

He was gone. He was just a speck in the distance. They watched the ferry until it rounded the horizon, then walked slowly and miserably back to the car.

Leo broke the empty silence with an accusation. 'One word from you and he would have stayed.'

'What do you mean by that?'

'Didn't you see that last look he gave you? He was

hoping against hope that you would say something. But you stood there saying nothing – showing no emotion. You didn't care enough.'

She refused to let that get to her though she was hurt beyond reason. 'What could I have said?'

'That you would miss him unbearably.'

'That goes without saying.'

He gave her a look that sent the blood rushing to her face. She flared up. 'You don't understand – you never will. Yes, you've lost a child, but I've lost two.'

'By your own choice.'

'What do you mean by that?'

'Do I have to spell it out?'

He strode on and she ran after him, uncaring of the curious glances thrown in her direction. I must look like a mad woman, she thought. She caught up with him as he was unlocking the car.

'I gave my daughter up because I loved her, and I've given Nicholas up for the same reason. You can think what you like, but that's the truth.'

He made no answer and they drove in silence for the best part of the journey, then with a sudden change of mood he reached out his hand and placed it over hers.

'We're tearing the guts out of each other,' he said sadly. 'I didn't mean it to be like this. If I've said anything out of order, I'm sorry. We're both overwrought. Let's start afresh and try to make a go of it – for Nick's sake.'

She nodded, biting her lip, unable to speak.

When they reached home there were two letters awaiting them. One contained the results of Nicholas's A-levels. He had two As and a B and the offer of a place at Cambridge. The other was to say that Mr Cleveley, the piano tuner, would be calling at twelve o'clock on the morrow.

Philippa handed back the letter from the examining board. 'I wonder if this would have made any difference.'

'I doubt it. He is a single-minded young man.'

They were two tired and disillusioned people and though Leo came to her that night, and though both tried, he found no solace in her or she in him.

Mr Cleveley came on the dot the following day. He was a precise little man who wore his wig like a hat, sometimes by chance tilted slightly over one brow. He was perpetually cold. He said, because he was always tuning pianos in unused rooms, the cold had got to his marrow. Philippa always banked up the fire when she knew he was coming. He kept his coat on until he drank the hot tea she had ready, then reluctantly divested himself of it and hung that and his bowler on the hall stand. That was her cue to make herself scarce. She couldn't concentrate while someone else was in the house, and would go about her chores listening to the untuneful noises that emanated from the drawing room until the moment to which she always looked forward. The tuning completed Mr Cleveley allowed himself the luxury and her the pleasure of playing a piece of music straight through.

She was in Nicky's room ostensibly tidying up, putting away the things he might not see again for many years, looking through some of his earlier school reports, laughing or weeping over the masters' remarks, when she became aware that there had come a change in the sound of the music from downstairs. Mr Cleveley was now playing 'Liebestraum'.

She flew down and into the room and he looked up, startled.

'Oh don't stop, please go on, I love that piece.' And when he had finished. 'Please play it once more.'

Having done that he sat back and rested his hands on his knees. 'Liszt knew how to pluck at the heart-strings,' he said.

It surprised her that such rich sentiment should come from the lips of such an insignificant little man. 'I have another piece, based on "Liebestraum". Would you play it for me?'

He glanced at his watch. 'If it's not too long.'

She kept it in a carved ebony jewellery box Leo had sent her from Bombay. A faint smell of musk wafted up as she unfolded it. She had not touched it in years and saw now that there was a slight tear in one of the folds. All that jumble of notes, all those strange hieroglyphics quite unintelligible to her could with someone more knowledgeable send her into a transport of bitter-sweet joy.

She gave the sheet of music to Mr Cleveley who looked at it and then at her. 'Love Song for Philippa,' he said, somewhat quizzically. He hummed a little of it to himself. 'H'm, this sounds interesting.'

He played it well, not with the same feeling as Joe, of course, but with enough to stir up memories she thought she had long since buried.

When it was finished, neither spoke. It was only a slight sound that made Philippa look round and there was Leo standing in the doorway. She hadn't heard him come in. 'Please don't let me interrupt,' he said.

'Mr Cleveley is just going, aren't you Mr Cleveley?'

Mr Cleveley looked a little flustered. 'Why yes, of

course.' He rose, Leo came forward. 'As a favour, please just run through it again. I missed the beginning.'

So Mr Cleveley 'ran through it' again, in rather a hurry this time as if anxious to get out of a situation he couldn't quite fathom.

Philippa saw Mr Cleveley out. He paused on the threshold, his bowler in his hands. 'Is that your only copy of that piece?'

'It is.'

'Then my dear, if you value it at all, I suggest you have some copies made.'

He got as far as the gate and then returned. 'I hope I won't offend you if I ask you this. Are you Philippa by any chance?'

'I am.'

'My dear, you have been paid a very great compliment.' He replaced his hat, at the gate he raised it to her, then walked to where he had left his car.

They always had lunch in the kitchen on weekdays. Leo rarely took the full hour. Today she had decided on poached eggs on spinach and went down to the end of the garden to the vegetable plot.

The barley field beyond their boundary was ripe for harvesting. It rustled like paper in the gentle breeze. Edging the field like a river of blood was a wide band of scarlet poppies. It seemed, she thought, as if the past was closing in on her.

Back in the kitchen she cleaned the spinach and put it on the stove to simmer, then filled the base of a poacher and put it on to boil. From the drawing room came the tortured sounds of 'Love Song for Philippa', as Leo struggled with the unfamiliar notation. He would get it in time, she thought. Leo was nothing if not a stickler. She called out to him that lunch was ready.

He made only one mention of the single sheet of music and that was to ask if she had another copy. When she said she hadn't, he advised her, like Mr Cleveley, to have some copies made. For the rest of the meal he lapsed into a thoughtful silence. She had not expected him to rave and rant for that was not in his nature, but she had expected a stronger reaction. For some reason she felt slightly cheated.

He spoke once more to ask her if he had told her that a deputy matron had been newly appointed to the Memorial Hospital. She told him no. He said her name was Miss Biddy – did that mean anything to her.

'No – why should it?'

'No reason.' He cut short his lunch as he was giving an anaesthetic to a patient of a Beckton dentist. As he passed her on his way to the door, he gently squeezed her shoulder.

She looked up in surprise.

'Take care of that music,' he said. 'It's too valuable to lose.'

Oh, why did he always make her feel such a worm.

The name Biddy was not familiar, yet she felt she had heard it in the past. So many people had crossed her path during the course of the war that it was impossible to keep track of them all. She wondered why Leo had asked her, for he was not one to put such a question without a reason. Miss Biddy? she would query at different intervals, until suddenly it came back to her two weeks later when she was sitting in the garden reading Nicky's letter, for the umpteenth time since its arrival.

He had got himself a temporary job in a packing

station on the outskirts of Paris, packing hampers for Christmas. He was sharing a room with another English boy, who was studying French. The job might last for another two weeks, then he was making his way through Provence to Italy. His roommate was thinking of chucking French and joining him. He'd write as soon as he got another fixed address.

So why do we worry ourselves about him, she wondered, and then because her mind was receptive to memories, the name Biddy loomed large and with it the image of a buxom young woman with a hearty manner. Sister Biddy of Bardney Place! – The one who had taken them over the house the day she visited with Evelyn.

She had a sudden sensation as if all the blood was draining from her veins, which so frightened her she went indoors and looked at herself in a mirror. Except that she was pale and her eyes looked mildly frightened there was nothing unusual about her, so why then did she feel like her own ghost?

She paced the floor. Leo had a session at the Memorial Hospital at least twice a week, which meant he had ample opportunity to exchange pleasantries with the new deputy matron. Perhaps the exchange of words had grown from pleasantries to confidences, though Leo was not one to discuss his private life. Still, he had a way of wheedling information out of people. She could hardly wait now for his return, and paced the floor restlessly at intervals until she heard the crunch of wheels on gravel.

Leo was hardly inside the room before she accosted him.

'I have remembered Sister Biddy.'

'I thought you would sooner or later.'

'What does she know? What did she tell you?'

'Could we discuss this like two civilised people, over a cup of tea?'

Over a cup of tea! Could anything be more prosaic. Then she saw how drawn he looked. He was obviously under stress. He could be fretting for Nicky of course, but something told her it wasn't Nicky that kept him awake at night.

She made him a cup of tea and waited while he drank it. Hers, she left untouched.

'Did you tell her who I was?'

'No. She knows nothing of your connection with Bardney Place.'

'How did you get on to the subject, then?'

'By chance, just chatting one day over a cup of coffee. She asked me what I did during the war; I asked her what she did and then she told me about Bardney Place. I didn't say anything at the time, but later I drew her out about it....'

'You were spying on me!'

He gave her a long, sorrowing look. 'On the contrary, I was hoping to find out something to your benefit....'

'And did you?'

'I found out where your daughter is.'

Philippa sat down very suddenly. The room was spinning round and she clutched the chair for support.

'Are you all right?'

'I just felt faint for a moment.' She paused. 'Where is my daughter, Leo?'

'Would it be wise for you to know?'

'I don't know about wise, but if I could just see her once, satisfy some longing inside me, then I think I could live in peace at last.'

'I was thinking something on the same lines otherwise

I wouldn't have told you all this.' He went to the sideboard and poured her out a small dose of brandy. 'Drink this down all at once, it will steady your nerves.'

It did not steady her nerves, they were twanging like harp strings but it did, after a moment or two, steady her heartbeats. Then he told her, in quiet measured tones, all that had passed between himself and the deputy matron.

First, her child had been adopted by the daughter of Brigadier and Mrs Abbott. She was childless and desperate for a child. Her mother saw a grand opportunity when Philippa came on her first visit and told her story. The daughter was married to a local Member of Parliament who owned property in London and Norfolk, and a stud farm in Kenya where he stayed during parliamentary recesses. When the Labour Party came to power in 1945 after their landslide victory, the Member of Parliament lost his seat. He immediately up-anchored and moved himself, his wife and child to Kenya where he had lived ever since.

She should have guessed the adoptive parents were more than mere acquaintances of Mrs Abbott. She had been so thorough in her questioning at the time, going well into details of Philippa's lineage. I should have realised then she had a personal interest in the transaction, thought Philippa. She cleared her throat. 'What is my little girl's name, now?'

'Dudley-Trehorne.'

'Jennifer Anne Dudley-Trehorne,' said Philippa falteringly. 'Quite a mouthful.' Then she broke down.

When she recovered – and Leo saw to it that she did recover for he stood over her until she had drained to the last drop the strong, black coffee he made her – he told her the rest of the story.

Tragically, after surviving the war without a scratch, the Brigadier and his wife were killed in a car crash in 1946. The property went to their son who several years later sold it to the Norfolk County Council, who in turn used part of it for administrative purposes and the rest as an agricultural college. The son retained the lodge to use as a holiday cottage and that was where Philippa's daughter was now. Her parents' permanent home was still in Kenya. Jennifer was sent to school in England, but returned to Kenya when her school-days were over, only coming over to England for the occasional holiday.

'So she's here on holiday, now?' Philippa was sitting on the edge of her chair as if to fly the minute she got all the information necessary.

'On business, actually. She's in partnership with her father, and is over here to buy some livestock.'

'Your deputy matron seems to be well informed.'

'She's the sort of person who likes to acquaint herself as far as possible with the lives of others. Not out of voyeurism, far from it. She's just interested in people.'

Philippa had a faraway look in her eyes. 'It's strange how everything has worked out, isn't it? Sister Biddy coming to work at the Memorial. Jennifer Anne happening to be in Norfolk just when I find out about her.'

'Life does sometimes play strange tricks like that, but your daughter being in Norfolk is immaterial. You would have gone to her wherever she was, wouldn't you?'

'Of course.'

'Don't ruin her life, Philippa.'

'I only want to see her, just the once. I won't pester her.'

'She may reject you.'

'I'll risk that.' She raised earnest eyes to his. 'You won't stop me going?'

He gave a lukewarm smile. 'I would if I could. I only hope for your sake that good will come out of this.'

She left for Bardney early the next morning. Leo had been up before her, checking the Mini (the latest of a succession), filling the tank. He had even left a flask of coffee in the driver's door pocket. He was composed and well in control of his emotions, yet he had a dejected air about him. Did he really think she wouldn't return? Did he care that much? But that thought didn't stay long in her mind, for Jennifer Anne took over. Jennifer Anne Byrd. Jennifer Anne Dudley-Trehorne. Oh dear God, if only it could have been Jennifer Anne Brooke.

She did not head directly for north Norfolk, she stopped off at Norwich first and parked the Mini outside a jeweller's in London Street. When she came out she had a belated birthday present for Jennifer in her handbag – a gold charm bracelet, the latest trend. One could hear them jangling on all social occasions.

She took the same route as Evelyn had taken on that June morning in 1943, when wild roses where out in the hedgerows and the scent of strawberries from the strawberry fields lingered with the tang of the sea. It was late for poppies but one or two scarlet splodges in the verges marked their presence. They no longer caused Philippa anguish, in fact she looked out for them, for weren't poppies not only a symbol of remembrance but also of peace?

The village of Bardney was no more than a handful of flint cottages, a church and an inn, and the big house. She had hardly been aware of it on her first journey, and it was too dark to see on her second when Clive and Evelyn had brought her there late at night and already in labour.

She pulled up at the lodge. It was a charming little building with latticed windows and overhanging eaves, and all four walls smothered by a crimson-coloured creeper. She was icy cold, but calm. Leo had given her a tranquilliser, and another to take if she needed it. She hoped she wouldn't have to resort to it.

The door was opened by a woman in late middle age whom Philippa took to be the housekeeper. 'If you're the Avon lady . . .'

Philippa smiled to herself. Somehow the gaffe made her feel more at ease. 'I'm not selling anything, I'm afraid. I just want to see Miss Dudley-Trehorne on a private matter.'

'Oh, I do beg you pardon. . . . We get so many different callers, because we're near the road, I expect.' Philippa was ushered into a room at the right of the door, that looked out on to the drive and part of the big house. 'I'm expecting Miss Jennifer any minute – she's just up visiting the stables. Do sit down, Miss – er – Mrs . . .'

'Brooke.'

She seated herself near the window so that she could see anybody who used the drive, whether coming or going. She had not long to wait before a girl in jodhpurs with a golden cocker spaniel at her heels came into view. Philippa stood up, screening herself behind the curtain and feasted her eyes. 'Jennifer,' she murmured. 'Oh, my beautiful Jennifer.'

She was not dark as Philippa had expected. Fair hair tumbled on to her shoulders giving her the look of a lithe young woman barely out of her teens. The colour of her eyes Philippa could not see. Blue they must be. Blue, bluer than blue – like Joe's.

And blue they were, a very dark blue, with the charm that usually sits so easily on those born to a gracious lifestyle and made Philippa feel gratified that she had actually given birth to this most lovely of girls.

'You said you wanted to see me on a private matter. . . .' She had a light, rather distinctive voice.

Philippa suddenly felt the necessity to sit down. She had been rehearsing her opening speech all the way from Norwich; now every word of it went out of her mind.

'I knew your mo— I mean, your grandmother. . . .' The words seemed to be catching in her throat. She took out her handkerchief and coughed into it.

The girl had been smiling before, now she became animated. 'Oh, you knew Granny. Oh, how heavenly. Now you can tell me more about her. I never knew her. . . .'

'No, I only heard the sad news yesterday.'

'And you came straight to see me. How very kind. How well did you know my granny?'

'She was very kind to me during the war.'

'She was kind to everybody. You must go into the church and see her memorial. The people of this village looked upon her as a kind of saint. How did you come to know her? I mean, if you don't mind me saying so, you are so much younger.'

Philippa looked down at her fingers, nervously locking and unlocking the catch of her handbag. Inside the bag she could see a corner of the jeweller's envelope. Was this the moment? 'I have a present for you,' she said, and shyly passed the package over to the girl.

'A present for *me*!'

'A belated birthday present.'

The girl's astonishment grew. 'How could you possibly know my birthday?'

'Please open it.'

The girl did so and blanched. 'I couldn't possibly accept such a valuable gift from a stranger....'

'Oh, please don't think of me as a stranger. I'm far from a stranger....'

'You knew my grandmother, but you have never seen me before in your life.'

'I was there when you were born. Do you think I could ever forget that day?'

Now the girl looked alarmed. She rose and edged nearer to the door. I've bungled this thought Philippa, I should have told her straight out, not beaten about the bush. Yet still she could not bring herself to say the fateful words.

'Jennifer,' she said, her voice little more than a whisper. 'How could I forget the date of your birth. How is it I *know* the date of your birth: 17 July 1943. Am I not right?'

'I was born on 6 December 1945 in Nairobi.'

They stared at each other. Two bemused and slightly alarmed women. Philippa put her hand to her mouth. 'Perhaps that is what you were told,' she said hopefully.

But by now realisation had superseded Jennifer's fears and pity filled her vast blue eyes. 'I think you're confusing me with the other Jennifer Anne,' she said.

'The *other* Jennifer Anne? I don't understand.'

'My baby sister who died before I was born. So lovely, my mother always said, just like a little flower. They called me Jennifer Anne after her.'

Silent tears slipped down Philippa's cheeks, splashed

on the back of her hands. She lowered her head. 'Please, tell me about her.'

'She died of spotted fever, what we call meningitis, just after my people had settled in Africa. My mother always believed that she picked up the infection on the ship going over. My mother didn't know at the time of my sister's death that she was already pregnant with me. That is sometimes the way, isn't it, after waiting years for a baby of their own, then adopting, then the mother falling pregnant. I've heard of it happening many times.'

The girl had run out of things to say. She looked helplessly down at the shattered woman. 'Could I get you coffee, or tea, or something stronger . . .?'

'No thank you.' Philippa pulled herself together. She snapped the bag shut and rose to her feet.

'But won't you stay and have lunch with us?'

Philippa shook her head. 'It is kind of you but I must get back to my husband.'

'There are some photographs of my sister at home. There is one particular one taken on her second birthday. Would you like me to send it to you when I get back?'

She had difficulty saying she would like that very much. Her hand shook a little as she wrote down her address. Apart from that she was in control of her feelings.

'And this bracelet. You must take it back.'

'No, I wouldn't know what to do with it. Keep it yourself or save it for the daughter you might have one day. Tell her it was from a well-meaning but misguided woman. There is one more favour I would like to ask of you. May I kiss you goodbye?'

They embraced without embarrassment. Philippa held the other Jennifer Anne in her arms and for a few precious moments imagined she was holding her daughter, then went swiftly from the room without looking back.

She pulled in at a lay-by overlooking the little fishing village where she and Evelyn had had lunch on that June day when she confessed about the adoption. Ironic that, she thought, rending afresh her already wounded spirits, for in giving her daughter up to what she thought was a better future, she had given her up to death. She had cried intermittently all the way from Bardney Lodge and still couldn't stop. She laid her face on the steering-wheel and gave way to racking, hysterical sobs that left her drained but strangely calmer.

This is one morsel of human interest that slipped through your net, Sister Biddy, she thought, but without rancour. All her bitterness was directed inwards.

What a mess she had made of her life. What a mess she had made of Leo's life. He had given up his early dreams of becoming a consultant anaesthetist because of her. She had known all along that a short spell in Norwich had not been the sole reason for his sudden decision to buy into the Thornmere practice. For her, knowing how much Norfolk meant to her, he had made the sacrifice. Through her he had lost his beloved son. For her he had winkled out information that would lead her, so he thought, to her daughter. And she had kidded herself all these years that he didn't love her!

And what had she given him in return? Nothing that she could think of right now, unless money on loan could be counted. She thought not.

How could she make up for it now? By loving him? She had never stopped loving him, but there were so many aspects of love, and she had been incapable of telling one from another. Now, she could look back with hindsight and realise that the frenetic love that she and Joe had shared, though sweet at the time and always memorable, would not have outlived the war. By the nature of things it would have burnt itself out in time, and poor, sweet, little Jennifer Anne would have been the victim.

She had never reached such giddy heights with Leo, nor had she wanted to, theirs being a durable love that could survive on less. But why should it? Was it too late to hope for a resurgence of their old romantic love? Not the heady, youthful love they had experienced in Edinburgh, it was too late for that, but a more steady affection built on a foundation of mutual liking and respect.

Was it too much to hope for, she asked herself again, as she restarted the engine and drew out into the line of traffic. She could but try. She could try also to win Leo's son back for him, allowing the boy enough time first to get the need for adventure out of his system.

Leo was hoeing the flowerbeds in the front garden, his eye on the road, unwittingly following her example the day she had waited for his return after taking Nicky to Grange House School. Was he, too, suffering the same anxieties as she had then, wondering if their lives would ever be the same again?

In the giddy days of her youth, when she was madly in love with love, she had thought of Leo as her rock, something she could cling to when in trouble, something that was always there when she needed it. That same feeling returned to her now.

He opened the car door for her and took a long searching look at her face, then put his arms around her. 'She turned you down,' he said sadly.